LET
THEM
LIE

LET THEM LIE

FLORENCE GILLAN

POOLBEG
CRIMS●N

Published 2022 by Crimson
an imprint of Poolbeg Press Ltd.
123 Grange Hill, Baldoyle,
Dublin 13, Ireland
Email: poolbeg@poolbeg.com

A catalogue record for this book is available from the British Library.

ISBN 978178199-702-4

www.poolbeg.com

About the Author

Florence Gillan is a retired teacher who lives outside Newry in the rolling hills of County Down with her husband Eugene, two dogs Honey and Rua, and a cat with no name. She spends much of her time in her native Sligo in the foothills of Benbulben. She has had a life-long passion for writing since penning her first novel, *Trageties in France*, at age nine. This is all the more impressive, given both her lack of knowledge of France and her inability to spell the word *tragedies*.

Let Them Lie is her debut novel.

Acknowledgements

Paula Campbell of Poolbeg made my dream come true when I received her email telling me she wanted to publish my story. Throughout the entire publishing process, she has been a source of calm reassurance and guidance.

The refining and polishing business was undertaken by my wonderful editor Gaye Shortland. I've learned so much and continue to learn under her guidance. Thanks, Gaye, for being so patient with me and helping to make this book the best version it can be.

Thanks to Paul Maddern for his hospitality at the River Mill writers retreat in Co. Down. I went there for an opportunity to think and write but I gained so much more than that, not least the recipe for his delicious orange polenta cake. My children thank you, Paul.

At River Mill, I met some wonderful writers who offered me sterling advice and encouragement. Thanks to Fíona Scarlett, Olivia Fitzsimons and Tracy Weller.

To my first readers who were kind and tactful and encouraged me to keep at it. Thank you, Mo Gillan, Martina Hamilton, Madeleine Skoronski, and Fiona Ó Murchú for all your patience – and, Fiona, thanks for teaching me how to punctuate. Seriously, you've all been brilliant! I couldn't have done it without you.

Thank you to Colum Lynch for giving so generously of his time when dealing with a very camera-shy client who needed an author's photo. You made the process painless.

I'm grateful to my lovely extended family of brothers, sisters, in-laws, nieces, nephews, cousins and an amazing godmother, Annie. They have been fulsome in their encouragement and so delighted to learn that my book is to be published.

Thank you to my fantastic friends, and my former colleagues in Bush PPS, far too many to mention. They have been my cheerleaders in all my endeavours. I appreciate all the fun and laughter you have brought to my life.

My four children, Rachel, David, Mark and Sarah have read, critiqued, offered suggestions and improvements and have put up with my many IT meltdowns. The number of times I have managed to lose documents is legendary and my resulting hysterical panic was comic. Through it all, they have had my back and I am very grateful. As their mother, I'd like to take some of the credit for their awesomeness!

Finally, Eugene my long-suffering husband, you have been a constant source of encouragement and pushed me into sending this story out. You mean the world to me.

Dedication

To the memory of my lovely parents, Mark and Mary,
and my sister Helen and brother Frank

PROLOGUE

The box sat on his lap, and he stroked each item nestled within. He held them one by one to his face, inhaling the memories and images they evoked. Soon they worked their familiar magic, soothing him. He held the ring the longest, enjoying how it glinted in his dirt-engraved palm. It was small and delicate, too tiny for adult fingers and yet it had slipped off easily. He slid it on his little finger; it stopped fast at his knuckle, looking incongruous. He felt close to his little one, closer than anyone else could ever be, remembering how he drew her breath deep inside, renewing and making him whole.

'Ye belong to your father, the devil, and ye want to carry out your father's desires. He was a murderer from the beginning, not holding to the truth, for there is no truth in him. When he lies, he speaks his native language, for he is a liar and the father of lies.' **John 8:44**

CHAPTER 1

April 2015

Racing from the school at full tilt, trying to dodge the fat raindrops dribbling from the sky, Aoife prayed her boss wouldn't see her. He'd want to discuss the latest suspension and she just didn't have the time. She slid the car out of the car park and joined the snarl-up of traffic converging from all corners of Dublin. God, what a week! If only she could stay home curled up next to Connor, watching a movie and eating takeaway! Instead, she was heading home to Sligo for her dad's anniversary. If it didn't mean so much to her mam, she'd have made excuses. But to Mam, the loss of Dad still ached like a yanked-out tooth.

Despite the passage of twenty years, the day he died was etched like scar tissue on Aoife's consciousness. When he didn't turn up at supper time, her mother had grown alarmed. Dad was a creature of habit, rising early every morning to milk the cows and in bed by ten thirty, worn out from his day. He was never late for a meal, always ravenous from working outdoors. Mam rounded up everyone in the locality to look for him. Aoife recalled the commotion all this drama created – it didn't occur to her that something bad had happened; she was convinced he would return with an exciting tale to tell. Soon the yard had filled with neighbours holding flashlights and blankets, with women talking in hushed voices in the kitchen. He was found in the early hours of the morning. The memory of his still body being carried upstairs still caused her chest to tighten.

Overhearing the whispered words of neighbours, as she sat huddled in the kitchen, she learned he had cracked his head on a stone wall in the top field. Perhaps he might have survived if they had found him earlier. He was last seen at lunchtime, so they thought the accident probably happened in the afternoon. It hurt to think of Dad lying out in the fields, alone in the cold and dark. Between concussion and exposure, he had no chance. The child Aoife had shivered with terror. She had never seen a dead body but it was the behaviour of the adults, rather than the stiffening body upstairs, that upset her most. Mam, always so comforting, sat frozen, staring blankly. When Aoife ran into her arms seeking consolation, she was met with a stony stare. Later, as an adult, when watching the movie *Invasion of the Body Snatchers*, it reminded her of her mam that awful night. Of course, by that time she'd realised her mother was in a state of shock. The child Aoife, frightened and confused, sought her sister and brother, but Sam and Kate, each locked in silent misery, had no time for a bewildered ten-year-old.

Her memories of her dad were few but treasured. He was always busy with the farm but took time to play with her, chasing her and throwing her high in the air, setting her heart racing with excitement mingled with terror. As she grew older, he lost interest in horseplay, concerned perhaps that he would hurt her. But he took her on long nature rambles, encouraging her to look up the common and Latin names for the flowers, plants and trees they observed. When she succeeded in these naming games, he would wink at her and slip her

4

a bar of chocolate, warning her not to let her mam know or he'd be a dead man. To this day she still could name most wildflowers and identify trees by their leaves. One day after she fell into a cluster of nettles and her leg stung hard enough to make her cry, he rubbed the stings away with dock leaves and explained about the plants he called nature's medicine, so she learned about willow bark, feverfew, and meadowsweet. But she was enthralled when he dwelt on nature's deathly side and warned of the perils of *Digitalis purpurea* (foxglove) and *Atropa belladonna* (deadly nightshade). She much preferred the Latin names as they conjured up an intoxicating mash-up of wonder intertwined with fear, much as his horseplay had done when she was a small child.

After he died, her memories of him dwindled until all that remained was a recollection of a benign presence, shrouded in a thick cloud of cigarette smoke, hovering on the outskirts of her childhood. Sam took on the vacated role of father and protector. With Kate and her mother burdened by grief, she turned to Sam in those early days and his fierce protective kindness sheltered her.

A blaring horn jerked her back to the present. God, how she wished she could have got out of this family get-together. She'd have brought Connor, but practicality demanded that he stay in Dublin to get his thesis finished. Marking the anniversary meant everything to Mam. She loved having the family together and, in anticipation, spent hours baking and preparing the house for visitors. It was lovely to see how her quiet, almost timid mother blossomed. Making this pilgrimage was a small price to pay when it made Mam happy.

The lights of the oncoming cars scorched her eyes. Night driving was not her thing. Connor didn't seem to mind; he usually took it on, knowing how she hated it. Instantly she felt comforted, thinking about Connor. They had met three years ago at her birthday party, which

Connor had crashed. Aoife smiled at the memory. Passing her door and hearing music and laughter, he just rocked up, acting as if he belonged. By the time she realised no one knew him, he had charmed her. Odd, because he wasn't her type, the opposite of the sporty guys she usually dated. But, tipsy as he was, he impressed her with his subversive humour and easy-going vibe. He asked her to a concert, and she agreed. After all, she liked the band and had nothing to lose by attending.

Six months later they moved in together and she felt an instant sense of belonging. Connor was the opposite of her practical self. He loosened her up, shook the seriousness out of her, and encouraged her to try new things. They had travelled, done parachute jumps and treks in the jungle, all at his instigation. He pushed her outside her comfort zone and opened her up to the joy of spontaneous adventure. After three years of cohabitation, they were now ready to take the next step and get married. Strange that the moment Connor became her fiancée their relationship entered its rockiest phase. The attitude of Connor as a boyfriend, which inspired and widened her horizons, now frustrated her. Did every engaged couple go through this period of adjustment? Getting married was a serious business and her practical side came to the fore, whereas Connor acted as though getting married was just a chance to party and celebrate. No doubt they would have a meeting of minds before too long. Hopefully, tonight Connor would take her absence as an opportunity to begin completing his thesis. Hopefully! Then they would be free to plan the wedding.

It was in this lighter mood that she drew up outside her mother's house. The soft light glowing from the porch illuminated the old two-storied farmhouse. Her mother must have heard the crunch of the car on the driveway for she stood in a pool of light in the doorway, waving eagerly.

As Aoife got out of the car, she was pulled into a warm embrace.

6

'You've got thin!' Agnes accused her, squeezing Aoife's arms as if to check for wasting.

'Thanks, Mam, that's what I'm aiming to be.' Smiling, she hugged her mother back.

'But, Aoife, I think that you're getting a bit too thin. I'm sure Connor doesn't want to marry a stick because as sure as anything that's what you're becoming. At least I'll have a chance to fatten you up this weekend.'

Aoife groaned. 'Mam, please don't start! Where's Sam?'

'He's locking up the sheds – the Caseys had loads of stuff taken from their outhouses recently, so he locks up all the time now. It's sad to see how much things have changed. In your father's time, a person never had to bother with locks at all.'

'What about Kate, has she come, and did she bring the kids?' Aoife asked, her eyes bright with anticipation.

'She rang to say she won't get here until tomorrow but you'll be glad to hear she's bringing Sandy and Colm with her.'

'That's great!'

The two women walked into the house, Aoife weighed down with her case and a bag containing wine and cake.

In the kitchen, she handed the bag to her mother.

'You're not a visitor, Aoife – you don't have to be bringing stuff!'

Aoife looked around at the old familiar things. Impulsively, she hugged her mother.

'It's good to be home, Mam!'

Her mother beamed back at her. 'I'm cooking a dinner – I know you city people have dinner in the evening so I expect you're starving.' Agnes, like most farmers' wives, cooked the main meal in the middle of the day. Farming was hungry work, and the cold weather encouraged the desire for a hot meal. 'Sit down there and we'll eat as soon as Sam comes in.'

'I hope you didn't wait to eat with me! I told you I'd be late leaving Dublin and to go ahead without me.'

'I know, pet, but Sam said he'd rather wait for you, so we could all eat together.' Agnes smiled at her daughter and, whipping an apron around her expansive waist, set about producing the meal.

Aoife, luxuriating in the atmosphere that drew her back into childhood, carried her case upstairs.

The bedroom door was open, and a swathe of moonlight flooded the room. It gave a beautiful, austere feel to what was a very homely space. As soon as she hit the light switch the elusive beauty vanished. It had changed little since her childhood. Originally, she had shared it with Kate, but her memories of that time were dim. She was only thirteen when Kate went off to train for nursing in London. At first, the belongings of her elder sister had dominated the room but, as Kate removed more and more of her things, it became Aoife's kingdom. As sisters, the age difference of four years created a gulf, but Kate was a benevolent sister who patronised her in a kindly fashion.

Although the teenage Aoife had lived in this room, she had never fully displaced Aoife the child. Long-neglected teddy bears and small cuddly toys sat on the shelves, forgotten. The ageing wallpaper still acted as a busy canvas for the tattered remains of Nelly, Eminem and NSYNC posters. Every time she came home, she had meant to rip those dated posters down, but a nostalgic part of her refused to break the link with the girl she had been. So, she resisted attempts to redecorate and hung on to her time capsule. The bed was covered by the same brightly patterned quilt that she had wrapped around herself when studying for exams. Aoife felt glad that at least in this small corner of her life things remained the same.

Downstairs she could hear the clatter of dishes, the lovely domestic sounds of home. She threw her bag on the bed and swiftly unpacked, hanging her clothes in the small wardrobe and putting socks and underwear in a drawer. Remembering it was Sam's birthday, she took the card she had brought from her bag and slipped it into her back pocket.

Taking the stairs two at a time, she burst through the kitchen door just in time to hear Sam ask, 'Well! Is she here?'

Racing over to him, she was immediately engulfed in a fierce bear hug. As a child, she had worshipped Sam, devoted to him in a dumb, dog-like way. To her, he was a hero. How did you look at a hero? Certainly not in the eye, so she had always hung her head and peeped adoringly up at him. Of course, over time she outgrew some of the awe, but never completely. It was through rose-tinted glasses she saw him even now. But she took the time to look him over more objectively. Sam was a big man, easily over six foot three, no longer the gangly youth he had been. His shoulders had expanded to match his length until he was a tank of muscle and sinew. His hair, once a scalded red, was now subdued with more than a scattering of grey. But his eyes were still as blue and clear as ever. Aoife had always considered her brother to be handsome, and at thirty-seven those looks remained. They stared delightedly at each other.

Shyly, she pushed the card into his hand. 'Happy Birthday, bro – sorry I forgot to post this.'

He tore it open, scanned the brief message and grinned. 'Hey, go on with you! I'm too old for birthdays. I told Mam I'd leave the house if she dared make me a cake, so she knitted me a jumper instead.'

'Oh God, what's it like?' Aoife asked, knowing her mother had weird notions about colour combinations.

He lowered his voice so Agnes couldn't overhear. 'Yellow and brown. I looked like an angry wasp. But I wore it yesterday, so she'll be OK with me abandoning it for a while, I hope.'

'I'm going to ask her to get you to model it for me tonight,' Aoife threatened, laughing as he raised his fist in mock anger.

'OK, you two, dinner is ready so get eating!' Agnes came and pushed her son and daughter towards the table.

Sam winked at his sister as he sat down. 'I could eat a bit, I suppose,' he said, heaping his plate full of stew from the bowl on the table.

His mother smiled fondly at him as she sat beside Aoife. She doted on her son, although she fiercely denied that was the case when teased by her daughters.

'How's work going?' Sam asked. 'Are those kids still driving you to distraction?'

'Well, they keep me busy. I'm enjoying my first-year class. They're a mad bunch but great craic too. I've promised to take them on a trip to Tayto Park if they behave themselves for the remainder of the term. But I'm not holding my breath that they'll manage to keep out of mischief.'

Aoife loved her job as a secondary-school teacher – well, most of the time anyway. But there were days when the work of shovelling information down the throats of reluctant pupils took its toll. She enjoyed the kids; she just wished the system didn't require her to bulldoze them into cramming for exams. There wasn't enough time to stop and think and explore with them. She regaled Sam and her mother with tales of school life as they ate and made them laugh as she told them of some of the antics of her students.

It was with great difficulty that she prevented her mother from piling second helpings on her plate. Sated, she sat back in her chair and sighed contentedly.

Agnes immediately jumped to her feet and arrived back at the table with a freshly baked apple tart and a jug of piping hot custard. Aoife, her stomach bursting, agreed to take a small slice. She knew only too well that resistance wasn't an option as her mother had baked it in honour of her homecoming. Sam showed no such reluctance and she watched as he practically inhaled an enormous slice.

Eventually, Sam finished eating and wiped his mouth with a paper napkin, crumpled it into a ball, and turned to his mother. 'I'd love a cup of tea, Mam.'

Aoife frowned as her mother got to her feet. Why couldn't he get it himself instead of ordering her mother around? She felt traitorous for thinking critically of her brother, but her mam seemed to have missed the feminist movement of her generation and lived to serve others, especially the men in her family. All her life Agnes O'Driscoll had cared for her husband and children. It was second nature for her to put their needs first. Wryly, Aoife realised it was also second nature for her children to expect her to.

'I'll put the kettle on, Mam,' she said. 'Why don't you sit down for a bit?'

At first Agnes protested but relented and sat back down beside Sam.

While Aoife scalded the teapot and boiled the kettle, she listened to the soft murmur of her mother's voice enquiring about the progress of work on the farm. She took out the china teacups and carried them to the table; her mother hated mugs. As she waited for the tea to brew, she shook some biscuits onto a plate. Agnes had a weakness for Fig Rolls. She joined her mother and brother and the three of them sipped appreciatively. The tea tasted so much nicer in her mother's house. Perhaps because, when she was here, she took time to make it properly, to use loose tea leaves, and to give it time to brew – the resultant tea was always more refreshing, and comforting. Or maybe it was just the lovely feeling of home that added flavour.

'How is Connor?'

Sam's deep voice shook her from her reverie.

'He's fine. He's working hard to finish his thesis in time for the wedding.'

She knew the next question before her mam uttered it.

'When's he going to get a job, love?'

Aoife sighed, irritated. 'As soon as he finishes his Master's he is going to take a job with his brother. He isn't interested in being an estate agent long-term, but it will give him time to explore his options.'

Sam raised his eyebrows.

'What's the problem with that, Sam? Not everyone knows what they want to do with their life straight off.'

'No offence, but most people have some inkling of what they want to do by the time they're in their thirties. Your Connor is a perpetual student. How many times did he jump ship from one college course to another?'

'OK! I admit it has taken him a while to find what he wants to do, but this time he will finish what he started. He is going to hand in his thesis in the next few weeks.'

'But what exactly is he qualified to do? He has an arts degree, and he's doing a thesis on some obscure poet. What is his long-term plan?'

Aoife lifted her cup and saucer, and walked stiffly to the sink. She had no answer for her brother. Connor was drifting along, and she was growing impatient herself. In a few months, they would be married and, if they wanted to buy a house, it would depend on her earnings.

She kept hoping that Connor would find his niche, accepting that writing poetry wasn't an occupation but a creative outlet. But she couldn't fault him for his commitment to his craft. He got up before six and spent a couple of hours writing before heading into college or his part-time job in the local shop and then, in the evening, he sat in their bedroom working for another couple of hours. Some nights she woke to find him still at work polishing up a poem or piece of

12

prose. It was a pity that being a writer didn't reward all this dedication. She knew it was impossible to make a living from writing poetry unless you were Seamus Heaney.

The job offer from his brother was a godsend. The brothers didn't get on, but Connor's parents had applied pressure and he was starting work in September. If only he would find it tolerable enough to stick at it for a year or two, at least until they could get some savings together.

Sam must have registered her downhearted expression when she returned to the table because he changed the subject. Shortly after, at Agnes's prompting, they went into the living room where they spent the rest of the evening staring at the fire, cracking jokes and discussing the goings-on in the locality.

Their mam said little, contentedly listening and dozing beside the fire. It was after twelve when they shook their mother awake and headed to bed.

Sam hugged Aoife on the landing. 'It's good to have you home, love,' he whispered.

CHAPTER 2

The sound of a cock crowing, followed by the bellowing of cattle, and the hum of milking machines jolted Aoife awake. In the city, the noise was perpetual and lost its power to intrude. She slept through blaring car horns, the brutal insistence of pneumatic drills ripping through pavements, and even the cacophony of her alarm clock. Connor joked that she would sleep through Doomsday. Here in the country, the morning sound leached into her sleep and turned her from unconscious owl to reluctant lark in an instant.

Throwing her arms back against the headboard, she stretched until her body ached pleasurably. Then springing out of bed, she ran with rapidly cooling feet into the tiled bathroom. She shivered as lukewarm water trickled from the ancient shower-head. Getting out of the shower, she cursed, realising that she had left her towel in the bedroom. Grabbing a small hand-towel for modesty, she raced into her room to retrieve it.

It was just past nine when she descended the stairs to have her breakfast.

The smells emanating from the little kitchen were enticing. Freshly grilled bacon, and the sound of frying eggs made her mouth water in anticipation. Funny, but she hadn't felt the slightest bit hungry until now.

Her mam greeted her with a beaming smile as she buttered toast at the counter.

'Sam is due in from the milking shortly, so you are just in time to tuck into a nice fry-up. Fetch some cutlery and sit yourself down.'

Aoife got a place ready for herself as Sam came through the back door. He removed his boots in the scullery and washed his hands. He was wearing his farm clothes – a holey jumper and a battered blue windbreaker. His unshaven face made him look scruffy and younger somehow.

They sat down to eat.

Agnes was her usual lively, chatty self but Sam, even for him, was unusually quiet.

'Is there anything the matter, son?' Agnes asked.

'It's Nell – she seems to have gone missing.'

Nell was a fifteen-year-old sheepdog, an ever-present feature of the farm. She wasn't a house dog but dearly loved nonetheless.

'It's not like her to just disappear,' Sam said. 'I hope something hasn't happened to her.'

'When did you last see her?' Aoife asked.

Sam wrinkled his forehead. 'I fed her at bedtime, and she seemed OK. She's getting on a bit, but she wasn't ailing. I hope she didn't get knocked down by some idiot coming home from the pub last night.'

Soberly, they recalled what happened to Bradys' Labrador last winter. Hit by a car, the poor dog had dragged herself home to die.

Now Sam had lost his usual hearty appetite and picked at his food. Aoife hadn't realised how attached he was to Nell. Like most farmers, he was unsentimental about animals. Nell wasn't a pet, she was a working dog, but over time what had started as a respect for her

15

herding abilities had become tinged with genuine affection. Her disappearance had clearly hit him hard.

'Look here,' said Aoife, 'why don't I take a spin round the roads and see if I can find her? She may have gone off for a run and just went too far.'

Sam nodded. 'That would be great. I'd look myself, but I have a lot on this morning.'

He took a final slurp of tea, wiped his mouth with the back of his hand, and went out.

The two women mused over Nell's possible whereabouts as they washed up.

Aoife was glad of her jacket as she walked out into the chilly morning. The sun was high in the steely blue sky. As she drove slowly down the country roads, she realised she had little hope of finding Nell but wanted to try for Sam's sake. Every so often she stopped to call for the dog and asked a few people she encountered along the roads. No one had seen Nell.

She was on her way back home when, in the distance, she heard the rumble of a tractor approaching along the road and pulled over to let it pass. Her heart sank when she saw it was Jack Costello from the next farm. *Feck it!* Even in mucky farm clothes, he managed to look elegant. Jack and Aoife had attended the same primary school, and it was from Jack that she had received her first kiss and delivered her only slap. Vividly she recalled the sharp sting of her hand on his cheek after he had decided that a slow dance entitled him to more than just a stroll around the floor. Despite the lapse of time, the memory still had the power to embarrass. She cringed as he swung himself off the tractor.

'Hi, stranger,' he drawled, winking at her.

16

Prick, she thought.

On the few occasions that their paths crossed, Jack always seemed to be mock-flirting with her. He held out his hand and awkwardly she extended her own. Her hand looked puny and useless in his larger, sunburnt one. His back was to the sun, forcing her to squint up at him. 'Hello, Jack, it's good to see you,' she said crisply.

He smirked at her. 'Is it?'

'Sorry, what do you mean?'

Jack laughed. 'It doesn't matter. Hey, when's the big day? Sam tells me you're getting married soon.'

After launching into an account of her wedding plans she trailed off, realising she was oversharing for what was merely a polite enquiry.

'What about you, Jack? Do you have any plans to settle down?'

He reached over to pull a stray feather from her jacket, making her flinch.

'Who, me? Get married? No, I had my heart broken a long time ago. A little virago told me exactly what she thought of me and I'm still recovering from the dent in my self-esteem.'

Pink colour washed over her face, and she cursed his ability to embarrass her. Desperate to change the subject, she asked, 'Have you seen Nell around? She's gone missing, and Sam is worried she might have got run over.'

Jack's smile dissolved. 'That's a pity. She's a nice dog. I'll keep an eye open for her, Aoife.'

He jumped back up onto the tractor and switched on the engine.

'You take care! See you later!' he called as he drove away.

Shivering in the cool air, she got back into her car and drove home.

The farmyard was deserted. Sam was probably checking on cattle or repairing machinery. As she stood looking around, she noticed the changes. The yard, usually untidy, looked almost immaculate. Someone had washed it down, and there wasn't a weed poking through the concrete surface. Her father used to get her to pull the stray wisps of grass that pushed through the cracks in the cement. Over the years the grass had enveloped more and more of the yard, but now it was free of its invaders. Where did Sam get the time?

Aoife wandered over to her mother's herb patch. Here too all was in perfect order. Rosemary, thyme, sage, and bay leaves competed aggressively for space. But there was not a weed in sight.

She bent down to tie her shoelace then whirled around when she heard a cough. Glancing up, she saw a young man, perhaps in his mid-twenties, very pale and thin.

He stood beside her, appearing slightly anxious. His fair hair blown about by the wind was already thinning.

'Are you looking for Sam?' she asked.

'No, miss, I work for Sam. My name is Karol.'

She realised at once he was foreign – his voice was accented and his speech patterns too precise. He was probably East European.

She stretched out her hand. 'Hi, my name is Aoife. I'm Sam's sister. I didn't realise that Sam had taken someone on to work the farm.'

He hesitated and held his hands up for her to inspect. There were very dirty.

She didn't withdraw her hand and they shook hands firmly.

'I have been working here two months with your brother.'

'Where are you from?'

'I am from Poland. I was born in Poznan. It is good to meet with you.'

'I hope you are enjoying your stay in Ireland. Sam doesn't work you too hard, does he?'

He smiled and shrugged, then raised his hand in farewell as he turned away and headed back up the yard towards the cowshed.

Aoife wandered back to the house where Agnes was cooking the dinner. She switched on the kettle and made herself and her mother a coffee. She had hers in a mug, but her mother drank from her usual china cup. Aoife remembered how her dad used to tease her mother for being posh, refusing to use a mug.

'No luck finding Nell, then?' Agnes asked.

Aoife shook her head. 'Sam is going to be upset. I tried everywhere I could think of. I even asked Jack Costello to keep an eye open for her. It looks bad, doesn't it?'

Her mother had glanced up at the mention of Jack's name. 'Do you know Jack is planning to sell his farm? Now that the parents are dead, he's going to move to Dublin. I heard he bought a few houses years ago, so he won't be short of a few quid.'

Aoife felt a twinge of annoyance that Jack had the foresight to buy property at the right time. Why hadn't Connor had similar foresight? After all, his family was in the property business. But, then again, Connor never had the spare cash or the steady income to invest. She knew that his brother James had amassed a sizeable chunk of real estate. Connor was against property owners and landlords on principle. So was she too, in theory, but it would be nice to have the solid security of bricks and mortar. Still, now that they were getting married, she hoped Connor would be more interested in financial security. Guiltily, she wondered if she was becoming very grasping and materialistic herself.

'When did Sam take on that new guy?'

'Oh, you've met Karol. He's such a pleasant lad and a hard worker. He doesn't keep set hours. Sam is dreading the day he leaves. He's very reliable – turns up every day like clockwork. Not like some who will only appear if their hangover allows.' Her mother was referring to the parade of locals who had worked for Sam over the years. They had often let him down, especially on a Monday morning.

Aoife left her mam preparing dinner and went up to her room to read. Immersed in her book, she lost track of time, until her mother calling her for dinner jerked her back to reality.

As soon as she entered the kitchen, she could sense the gloom.

Her mam was dishing out the dinner and looked shrunken. Sam sat at the head of the table; his head bowed. Karol was carefully washing his hands at the sink. Eventually, he too sat down, looking uncomfortable.

Her mother turned to her.

'They found Nell. She was in the old hayshed. She must have crawled in to die.'

'I'm so sorry, Sam. What happened to her?'

Sam's eyes remained firmly fixed on his plate. 'Nothing happened, she just died. She was a fair old age. It's better really. She didn't seem to have suffered.'

Immediately he changed the subject by praising the dinner and outlining the work that he had been doing and the work he planned for the afternoon.

Then they relapsed into silence for the remainder of the meal.

When they finished eating Sam got up and turned to Karol.

'Will you bury her out in the back? I'll show you where. It may take you a while, but you can knock off when it's done.'

Karol nodded as he too stood up.

After the men left, Aoife helped her mother clear away the dinner things. Agnes was very quiet.

'You were very fond of Nell, weren't you, Mam?'

'It's foolish to get too attached to animals. It's just that it reminds me of your father bringing home Polly. He wanted to make a good working dog out of her. But, instead, he turned her into a real auld pet. Remember, Aoife, you used to follow her around the place when you were a wee one. She died shortly after your father passed.'

20

Agnes's eyes filled up and Aoife thought what a pity that Nell should have died the day of her dad's anniversary.

'Do you still miss him, Mam?'

She nodded. 'He missed out on so much. He never saw you grow up, or Kate get married, or any of his grandchildren. I feel angry about that. He was so young, love – we should have had more time together – and, of course, you missed out on having a dad.'

Seeing the pain flicker across her mother's face, Aoife wanted to do something practical to help.

'How about I tackle some weeding? I bet Sam doesn't spare Karol to weed your flower garden.'

'Indeed, he does not. Sam is just like your father – he just doesn't see the point of garden flowers, but Karol does keep my herb garden tidy for me. Yes, I'd love it if you would make a start on it. I find my knees aren't able for kneeling to weed these days.'

'By the way, Mam, when are Kate and the kids coming?'

'Oh, didn't I tell you? She rang when you were out to say she'd get here at about six.'

As Aoife mounted the steps to the back garden, she noticed the neglect. Her mother's arthritis must be troubling her because the flower garden was suffocating under a vicious onslaught of weeds. Chickweed – or *Stellaria media* – she was pleased to remember the Latin name – was leading the attack, strangling and entwining everything in its path. She spent a satisfying half-hour ripping it off the defenceless flowers. As she dumped the weeds in the hedge, she remembered her father telling her that chickweed could be eaten, but she didn't feel her mam would appreciate her whipping up a batch of pesto with it or sprinkling it into a salad. She smiled as she imagined the look on Sam's face if presented with it.

Surveying the amount of work yet to be done, Aoife sighed.

Resolutely, she mounted a rear-guard action on the weeds from the far wall. As a reward for her efforts, she would allow herself a break when she had cleared at least one bed from its odious colonisers. As she worked, she noticed Karol entering the garden. He was carrying a shovel and a pickaxe. She glanced at her watch. It was nearly three o'clock. She had been weeding for close to an hour and the flower bed was only half-finished. Deciding to redouble her efforts, she promised herself that she would get this bed finished within the next half-hour. Then she would make herself a nice cup of tea and have a sweet treat.

In the distance, she heard the slicing sounds of Karol digging. She worked rapidly if a little less accurately and soon, feeling pleased with her efforts, was ready to take a break. As she headed for the house, she passed Karol and offered to bring him a cup of tea. He had taken off his jumper while he worked. He looked tired. Aoife wondered what kind of work he did back in Poland. His skinny frame didn't seem fit for hard physical labour.

Her mam, busy ironing, declined the offer of a cuppa. Aoife filled two mugs with tea and cut generous slices of her mam's gingerbread. Heading back to the garden, she signalled Karol to join her on the weathered garden seat. He perched beside her awkwardly, giving an impression of being about to take flight at any moment. But he gulped the tea and ate the gingerbread with relish.

Struggling to make conversation, she asked, 'Do you get back to Poland often?'

'I went back at Christmas.'

'I suppose your family misses you terribly.'

He nodded but was silent.

She was wondering if he'd even understood her until he said, 'I have a wife in Poland, Karina, and our baby we call Maja. I miss them.

But it is good to have a job here. Sam is a good boss – very fair, so I am happy to be here.' A warm smile lit up his face as he pulled out his phone and showed her a picture of a pretty, dark-haired woman holding a baby of about nine months. They were sitting in a sunlit garden or park. Both baby and mother were smiling.

'They're lovely,' she said.

Nodding and smiling, Karol replaced the phone in his jacket. Then gulping down the last of the tea, he headed back to where he was digging.

She watched him go. Gracefully, he picked up his shovel and resumed his efforts. She watched for a while, appreciating the smooth rhythm of his body as he worked. Eventually, her conscience prodded her back to her weeding. Besides, although there was plenty of sunshine, she was getting cold.

Rolling up her sleeves, she started on the next bed. It was standing up better to the weeds. The shrubs here were better established. As she worked, she daydreamed. When her father was alive and he set her the task of weeding, she used to imagine the weeds were an enemy launching an assault on a village, and she was a mercenary who was going to liberate the poor villagers. She allowed herself to slip back into this childish fantasy until she noticed it wasn't only the weeds she was ripping out in her enthusiasm.

Her thoughts turned to her wedding. She still hadn't got a dress. All they had done was to book the church, the hotel, and of course a band. They would have to organise themselves or things would end up in a shambles. Would Kate be willing to help? The four-year age gap separating them seemed less now that they were adults, but it would be nice to spend more time together. It was hard to get Kate on her own; she was so busy with the kids and Kenny. Her sister had always been there to help her through the minor crises of adolescence. She handed over money when her rent was short in college and gave gentle advice if asked. But it struck her how little she knew about her sister. For example, was Kate happy in her marriage?

Married at twenty and a mother by twenty-one. What did Kate see in Kenny? He was pleasant enough, but he seemed such a nonentity. He mooched around, found a perch, and blended into the background. Trying to engage him in conversation was agonizingly tedious. The only memorable conversation they had was about music. Unlike her, he was a big Country music fan and was amazingly knowledgeable about it. She had been so startled by his enthusiasm and passion for the genre that she faked interest too. It was a revelation to hear him talk so much and with such enthusiasm. The downside of that conversation was his insistence on gifting her with country music CDs and albums for subsequent birthday and Christmas gifts. Connor had thought she was a fan after seeing her collection. She was astounded one day to hear Kate say how fond Kenny was of her. Maybe she should make more of an effort to get to know him better – after all, there must be more to him than his taste in music.

As she continued to work, her back ached. Standing up to stretch, she noticed Karol staring into the hole he was digging. Then he turned his head and beckoned to her energetically. Glad of an excuse to abandon the weeding, she ambled over.

'See what I have found,' he said, pointing down.

She looked and saw the skeletal remains of a dog and beside it a package wrapped in black polythene, half-covered in clay. It must have been where Polly, their dad's old dog, was buried. Excitement swept over her – what could the package be?

'Hurry, Karol, lift it out!'

He jumped down into the pit and, scrambling about, scraped the package free and passed it up. She grabbed it eagerly, dying to examine it, but offered him a hand up out of the deep pit. He shook his head and scrambled up, brushing mud from his clothes.

She carried the box over to the bench where she had just lately enjoyed her tea break. Eagerly she peeled off the tightly wrapped black-plastic covering. It revealed what appeared to be a battered yellow biscuit tin. Its colour was faded by long immersion in wet clay, but it kept a recognisable buttery tinge. The eroded lettering on the tin was long past recognition. Her excitement subsided. It was too much to expect it to be a treasure trove. Probably Kate or Sam had buried a time capsule as children, and it had been long forgotten. Still, it was buried too deeply surely, to be the work of children.

Her attempts to open it were defeated as it was rusted shut. She called out to Karol, who was watching from beside the grave.

'Do you have a knife?'

Karol patted down his pockets and produced a small penknife. She used the sharp blade to prise the lid open. It took a bit of an effort and she squealed as she slit her thumb. Bright blood dripped over the tin, but the lid loosened, and she felt it give.

CHAPTER 3

The lid wobbled, and Aoife pulled it off and threw it to one side. Karol fussed over her bleeding thumb. Sticking it in her mouth, she stared at the contents of the box. Inside was a small, discoloured, cloth flour-bag. Not wanting to get blood on it, she dug in her jeans pocket, found a paper tissue and wrapped it around her thumb. She fumbled with the bag, which was knotted with coarse twine and wouldn't open. This time she got Karol to use the knife. She watched with mounting excitement as he slit the twine and pulled the opening apart.

He moved aside to let her examine the contents. Although he said nothing, she sensed his curiosity.

She upended the bag and watched as its contents tumbled out – a little dolphin earring, a ring, a scarf, a lock of hair tied with a shoelace, a tube of lipstick, and a hardback notebook. Aoife sagged a little with disappointment. She had been hoping for treasure in old coins or jewels, perhaps. Still, this was intriguing.

Karol replaced his knife in his pocket. Sensing his disappointment, she thanked him for his help. He left the garden, presumably to fetch Nell's body.

She examined the notebook. It was about the size of a paperback. The cover was red leather. Carefully, she opened it. Although the tin was airtight, some dampness had caused the pages to stick together. She didn't want to damage it by forcing them apart, but from what she could see of the writing the script was small and neat. Once more she felt excitement course through her. As she held it, she struggled to see if there was a name on the flyleaf, but her finger started to bleed, and the paper soaked up her blood like a sponge.

Karol caught her attention as he reappeared carrying a sack containing the body of Nell. She walked over to him and watched as he dropped the stiff bundle into the open grave. Sickened, she watched the body bounce as it hit the ground. Then she stood back as Karol filled in the pit. In moments, the sack was covered with black soil.

Karol stamped on the grave. He picked up his spade and, nodding to her, left the garden.

Poor Nell. It seemed wrong not to have Sam and her mother present for the burial. Perhaps she should have called them before Karol filled in the grave. Well, it was too late now.

Glancing at her watch, she decided she had done enough gardening. Replacing the items in the box, she headed back to the house and left it on the hall table.

Her mother had nodded off with a newspaper on her lap, her lined face soft with the vulnerability of sleep. A protective, almost maternal tenderness swept over Aoife. Agnes had not had an easy life, widowed in her late forties with three children to bring up and a farm to run. Had there been any men in her mother's life since her dad's death? She had no recollection of her mother going out, never mind dating when she was growing up. It must have been very lonely for her. Aoife tried to imagine how she would feel if anything happened to Connor, and her heart lurched uncomfortably. Poor Mam, channelling all her love into her children, the only thing she had left of her husband. She tried to imagine what she must have gone through over the lonely years of her widowhood and made her mind up to be a more loving daughter.

The sound of her approach must have disturbed her mother as she gave a small gasp and opened her eyes. For a moment she stared blankly at her daughter and then smiled.

'What time is it, pet?'

'It's gone four. Would you like a cup of tea, Mam?'

Agnes shook her head. 'No tea for me. I'd best be thinking about getting something ready for Sam's supper. I thought I'd make a few sandwiches for Kate and the young ones when they arrive. To tide them over till after the Mass this evening.'

'You sit here and I'll get something ready, Mam,' said Aoife.

But, before she could move, her mother had launched herself to her feet.

'You've been slaving for hours in the garden, love. Why don't you put your feet up?'

'Ah no, I'm fine.'

Her mother headed for the kitchen, then paused to ask, 'By the way, did Karol get Nell buried?'

About to open her mouth to tell her about the box, Aoife hesitated.

Instead, she said, 'Yeah, we buried Nell in the back garden. You know what – I think I will lie down for a few minutes. I'll be upstairs if you need me.'

She retrieved the tin from the hall table and took it upstairs with her.

She needed a shower. The water was hot, and she lathered soap generously over her body. Her cut thumb throbbed, robbing her shower of pleasure. She turned the water off and, reaching for a towel, dried off briskly.

Searching the bathroom cabinet she found a plaster, and awkwardly applied it to her injured thumb.

She pulled on fresh underwear and a tracksuit top and leggings, fetched her hair dryer and dried her hair.

Sitting on the bed, her curiosity mounted as she opened the box once more. Examining the items, she wondered why someone would have buried them. They seemed odd things to place in a time capsule if that was what it was. The hair looked human and was almost black and slightly coarse, and the shoelace holding it together was also dark. Who would bury a lock of hair? Perhaps it belonged to a girl who had died, and her lover buried the jewellery with her hair. It was all very odd. The earring, a plastic pink dolphin, seemed an unremarkable item to bury in a time capsule, similarly the pink lipstick which looked well used, and the scarf although colourful and pretty was made of polyester. The most interesting item apart from the notebook was the little gold Claddagh ring. It was small, clearly meant for daintier fingers than hers and, as she inspected it, she noticed it had the initials PF engraved on the inside.

She turned her attention to the notebook. Its leather had dulled to a faded red colour and its pages clung together as though unwilling to give up their secrets. Aoife smiled at the fanciful nature of her thoughts, but felt renewed determination to unravel this mystery. Rummaging in her make-up bag, she found a nail file. Carefully she slid the file between the first and second pages, slowly working to release them from their damp embrace.

The pages were covered in cramped handwriting. The writing was in ink, a fountain pen most likely, the handwriting free-flowing but very tiny. It would be difficult to decipher. With mounting excitement, she began to read.

I've made so many attempts to write my account and each time I've started I couldn't get what was in my head to surrender to the page. I felt terrified that she would read it. Strange that the first accounting I made to paper, I also feared being read. But if that Harpy came across my scribbling, I know for sure she would make good her threat and consign me to the mental hospital or perhaps to jail. So, caution was my byword and after I had written I would burn the pages and for a time feel peace.

Aoife felt the hairs on her arms rise. Who or what was the Harpy?

Freedom came eventually but dull grey liberty it was, until the day my love came into my drab existence and transformed it into a Life. The joy, the light I delighted in made me whole again and I believed I could be the man she wanted me to be. For years I felt no need to soak my pain and my cure onto the page. That is, until now. Paradise had fissures, and in those dark times I had to return to old ways.

Aoife was puzzled. This had the atmosphere of a gothic novel. Was that what it was?

It was loneliness that once more broke me and made me unburden myself at least onto the blank page. I have kept my secret for a long time now. The burden has not lessened. The strain of preserving my known life with this darkness that I have within is causing me more trouble with each passing month. I need — I must speak, or at least in this journal find some outlet. I fear I will burst, explode, or implode with the vastness of my secret and the deceptions I carry out daily.

I want to relive those terrifying, momentous days when I was a giant upon the earth. I had the power of life or death over those lost souls. I am lonely with the weight of the secret, yet to share it would mean absolute ruin for me, but also for the others.

Aoife stirred uneasily. What the hell! This story was getting creepier by the minute. What exactly had the writer done?

The others are a burden I cannot leave down. Sometimes as I lie beside her, I long to reach over and reveal to her my true nature. But I know she would not

understand – that my words would first puzzle and then frighten her. Her mind
cannot comprehend how I am. My secret would not fill her with admiration but
with terror and she would turn her face from mine in horror. I feel the pain of this
separation, this gulf between my need to share and her incapacity to understand.

Aoife stopped reading, her initial curiosity and excitement now
tempered with a dose of trepidation. Who had written this? It was
sounding distinctly sinister. Was it a diary or was it an attempt at
writing a horror novel? She continued reading but with some
reluctance.

So, I have chosen a safer means of revisiting the past. I suppose, too, I need to
leave some record of my deeds. Why, I don't know. For now, I will begin at the
beginning, my beginning.

I was born in pain. My aunt said that I emerged screaming like a demon
arriving into the world, my mother's cries and mine conjoined. The birth was hard
and my mother, torn and battered, never had another child again, whether through
choice or birth injuries I will never know. My father died when I was three, so I
have little recollection of him. But he left my mother with a small farm and seven
children to rear on its meagre fields. Survival was what our life was all about.
White-knuckle survival, staggering from one mealtime to the next. Somehow, she
did it. She fed and clothed us and sent us to school. There was no famine of the
belly, only of the heart. We were love-starved because all of Mother's energy was
used on just surviving. Many would say that, of course, her valiant attempts to
rear us were a deep expression of her love, but I felt impoverished. Perhaps that's
why – no, I cannot blame what I have become on my mother like some sad excuse.

At least in those early days, I had the companionship of my brothers and
sisters. They were older than me and far too busy to bother with a small child,
except for C. She tried to look after me and give me the affection Mother never
offered. I once asked C. why Mother disliked me so much and she lied and said I
was imagining things. That of course Mother loved me, she loved us all, she just
found it hard to show it. But I knew that although Mother was harsh and

31

demanding of all her children, she didn't withhold her emotions from me and they were of dislike, even hatred. I vaguely knew it was something I had done, but whenever I came close to remembering, my mind would shrink away. So not even C. would answer my questions about why Mother hated me.

As for the rest, my brothers worked like slaves on the farm, were released only to attend school, at which they did well, and got scholarships to go to the secondary school in town. My other sisters E. and B. were an added irritation once they realised my existence might have some value for them. Then each day issued their commands and complaints, 'Fetch me this, do that'. Cries of 'You need to make sure you clean my shoes properly' – 'Make me some tea' – 'You're spilling it everywhere!'. And so on and on. But C. was good to me. When she wasn't too tired, she would read me stories from the Bible, one of the few books to make their way into the house.

Aoife stopped reading, her heart pounding, and questions skittered uncontrolled around her head. Those initials and other references were causing her disquiet. It was becoming apparent that this was written by someone in her father's family. Was it a confession to some horrible crime? What the hell did it mean? She was curious to read on, but paradoxically reluctant to do so. The walls of the room pressed in on her, and she felt an urgent need for fresh air.

She pulled on her jacket, slipped the notebook into its inside pocket and hid the box under her bed. Whatever the notebook held, she didn't want to be in her room when she read it.

Running downstairs, she shouted to her mother that she was going for a drive and would be back in an hour.

It was good to be out in the air, and she looked forward to her first glimpse of the expansive Atlantic Ocean.

CHAPTER 4

Aoife pulled up as close to the rocks as she could go, got out, drew her jacket around her and slammed the car door. Her eyes drank in the ocean's expanse. It didn't disappoint. Everything was too much: the booming waves, the flinty blueness of the sea, the explosion of white waves cascading over the solid black wall of rocks, and the cloying pungent odour of sea wrack. The wind pushed at her, clamouring like a satanic child demanding attention. Her senses were overwhelmed by gusts of sea-soaked wind which battered her nostrils so hard and fast that breathing was painful. It was beautiful and terrible, and she loved it. Then, taking a last gulp of the aggressive air, she sat down on the cold rocks.

Reaching into her pocket, she drew out the notebook. The cover was peeling slightly. As her fingers clenched it, she fought a compulsion to fling it from her. For a fanciful moment, it seemed an evil alien artefact. Maybe she should give in to her compulsion and rip its pages out unread and let the wind and sea take them. But she knew she had to read on like a tragic Pandora and release whatever was sealed within its pages.

Opening the notebook, she noticed a flower pressed between the pages. Age had discoloured it, but it was a foxglove. She held it between her fingers as she read.

Life on the farm was a relentless monotony of work, sleep, and work sleep. Mother wanted us to survive. She had ambitions for us – modest ones, to be sure. She wanted us educated, to grow up without having to depend on charity or patronage. Pride in family, and pride in self, was her code of honour. So, we worked and slept for eternity on that farm. She scrimped and saved so that we could go to school and learn the things that would move us forward in life, but never so far forward that we forgot who we were, and who got us to the place we arrived at.

Gratitude was bred – no, beat into our bones. We owed everything to her. Without her, we were nothing. Gratitude is a hard legacy to bear. Its interest rate is high and hard to meet. But we knew what she expected.

I watched them all leave, my brothers and sisters, each driven away by her harshness. Well brought up, polite, educated, but not too educated – a credit to her. But as each one departed, the more I felt the bleakness of my existence. They sent money home from the far-flung places they emigrated to – Canada and South Africa. The money came, but they never returned. Their dutiful letters detailing their work and living conditions revealed nothing of their triumphs, fear, and failures. But with each missive came the folded bank drafts. With every visit of the postman, she glowed with pride as she accepted the airmail letters. She took as her right the congratulations of neighbours on her achievement in rearing such fine upstanding children. This was the only pleasure she allowed herself.

I envied them their escape. I knew that the path she had mapped out for me was to be different. At first, she wanted me to become a priest, but she soon realised that I was poor material for the life of a man of God. Instead, I was to be her companion, to work the few miserable acres that Father had left us. I was to be her whipping boy, the scab she could pick over whenever she wished. It might have been different if she had liked me, or even approved of me, but I could see that I was a disappointment to her. I wasn't clever like the others, or handsome. Instead, I took after my father's people – small, dark, and poor-sighted. I felt she hated the very sight of me. But perhaps I confused impatience and contempt for hatred. To hate suggests some measure of respect.

So, I stayed on the farm, unfitted for anything else. I trudged through life. The locals thought me odd. No girl wanted to be alone with me – not because I was a danger, but because I was a poor specimen to be seen in the company of.

If she hadn't enforced the wall of silence, I might have survived it. Looking back, I struggle to recall when it started and why. I must have transgressed and, instead of the strap, she employed a much more powerful weapon. I think she realised beating me was not affecting me anymore. I was sullen and unresisting, and this infuriated her as my passivity defeated her physical strength. It was then she changed tack. What age was I? I think about twelve.

One day I forgot to do some household chores or perhaps did them poorly and, to my surprise, she didn't shout or strike me. Instead, she just ignored me. I asked her what was wrong, and she turned her back on me. She kept up her silence for days while I pleaded with her to speak. I begged forgiveness for my failings and asked her to punish me but to please talk to me. But she never relented. She put my meals on the table and every morning gave me my list of jobs, but never said a word. After a week, I was sick with despair. I started shouting at her and even threatened her unless she spoke. She just smiled and whispered that if ever I touched her or disobeyed her, she would have the authorities put me away in the mental hospital. Everyone thought I was odd anyway, so they would soon see how I was a danger to myself and others.

Of course, she relented for periods and spoke to me about everyday things, but anytime I displeased her the impenetrable walls of silence descended. These periods of silence became longer and longer and the periods of reprieve shorter, but I tried desperately to please her. She kept me from school during these times of punishment.

Although I had no friends at school, at least there I had some company, some human interaction. My only solace was Toby, my collie dog. I whispered in his ear, and he licked and nuzzled me. But that too she removed from me. I arrived home from the fields for my dinner, only to see him driven off in the back of a neighbour's estate car. 'He's old and useless,' she replied grimly when I asked her why she had given him away. I wished she would give me away too, as I knew she believed that I too was useless. That was when my heart crumbled. She killed me at that moment when she took away the one thing that comforted me.

I hoped perhaps I could move away from her, and head to America like my sisters and brothers, but she put a stop to those 'notions'. I daydreamed of going to New York to stay with C, but that weak shaft of hope ebbed away too. All my youth settled in a dark, clean house entombed in silence.

Sometimes I longed to strike her, imagined my fingers meeting in the scrawny folds of her neck and squeezing, but I feared her, God, damnation, and the fires of hell. Once when she goaded me with my uselessness, my lack of manliness, I raised my hand to strike her and she laughed, and instantly my rage quenched but resentment and hate simmered as a stew left too long on the cooker. From then on, I thought of her not as Mother but as 'The Harpy'. Somehow it made her less connected to me and therefore easier to hate.

It was then I did the first 'bad thing'. I was full of rage and choking hate that I needed to destroy. Afterwards, my skin crawled with the horror of it. It was too late then. I tried to block it out as if by refusing to think about it I might undo it. My mind still can't dwell on that first time, and yet it showed me a path to peace, release from the walls of my prison. It was ugly, brutish, and it took too long before the struggle ended, and the last breath was expelled. I carried it in my tractor and buried it in the top field. I dug deep, terrified they would find it. And I swore on my father's grave that it would never happen again. But it changed me, gave me peace, and I could survive the deafening silence now as I had the company of the dead. Over time, I got better at achieving peace, and miraculously at the right time a sacrificial lamb always appeared.

Her hands shaking, Aoife stopped heading. Was the writer describing killing an animal? And how could killing it bring peace? This was sounding sicker and sicker.

But as my hatred of her grew, I had to accept that the Harpy is the only one who truly sees me as I am. She sees the darkness beneath my skin, and that's why she loathes me and won't even look at me. But age and illness have weakened her, and she needs my help more and more. I am heartened by this new helplessness.

The Harpy died one summer night. I prepared her last supper, and she went to her bed and never woke again. My brothers and sisters came home. They looked prosperous and old. I was twenty-one. After the funeral, when the last neighbours had wrung our hands and muttered words of comfort, the brothers turned to me and asked what I wanted to do with the farm. It stunned me to be consulted. Nobody had ever asked my opinion before. M, the eldest, took me out to the back garden. He suggested I keep the farm going. He pointed out that the Clancys had land for sale as all the boys were set on emigrating and they needed some cash. Mother had been putting aside money they had sent her and had saved a sizable chunk, and he advised me to invest it in land now that it was cheap.

So, the following day I went through her papers. She had left me everything in her will, including her savings. I knew it wasn't a message of love or acceptance from beyond the grave, just her desire to keep the land together, to prevent the others from selling. Of course, B howled about the unfairness of being disinherited, as she called it. She muttered about undue influence. But for once E came to my defence. 'He worked the land – he's entitled to it. We got education and freedom and he got all this,' she said, gesturing to the house and fields. That shut B up except for her tortured sighs, and even that subsided when denied the oxygen of our attention.

My brothers and sisters left three days later. I took my brother's advice and bought the farm next door. I didn't know what else to do. Freedom grew slowly. I had to learn how to make decisions, and how to know what I wanted. Soon I realised I was tied to the farm as surely as if she were still alive. I didn't know how to live outside it. And so, I stayed.

CHAPTER 5

The cramped handwriting hurt Aoife's eyes. Rubbing them, she sat listening to the bluster and roar of the sea. Any lingering doubts she had about the author dissipated. It had to be someone who lived and worked on the farm, and the details implied it was someone with six siblings and that suggested her father. He inherited the farm from his mother, and the initials referred to in the text – C, E and B – could be her father's sisters, Emma, Clarisse, and Baby. If indeed the writer of this was her father, then he was a sad and tortured soul. But what else was he?

The book lay on her lap. Her eyes still ached from the strain of trying to decipher the handwriting. She flicked through the pages and estimated that there were about fifty. Maybe it was just an outlet for a lonely man, allowing him an escape from the bleakness of his life. But her thoughts returned to the disturbing words she had read on the first page. What did he mean by leaving a record of his deeds and why would his love turn from him in horror – presumably that meant his wife, Agnes, her mother? Her guts twisted as she tried to reconcile the father she remembered with this scarily damaged writer. What was the 'thing' he buried? And did she really want to know?

Aoife replaced the pressed flower and closed the book.

She'd had enough. Her body was stiff and cramped. As she stood up on aching legs, her bum was numb from sitting on the cold rocks. Returning to her car, it was a relief to be out of the wind.

On the drive home, she forced herself to put the notebook out of her mind. It must be a work of fiction loosely based on reality. Maybe after the anniversary Mass, she could talk it over with Kate. But not now when the house was in uproar getting ready for guests.

She smiled in relief when she saw Kate's little Golf parked beside the shed at the rear of the house.

She hurried inside. Her sister was washing lettuce at the sink. Aoife watched her from the doorway. With a shock, she noticed how thin Kate had got. She was thirty-four years old but looked older, her brown hair aggressively pushed aside by grey interlopers.

Turning from the sink, Kate smiled. She dried her hands on a tea towel and moved across the room to throw her arms around her sister's shoulders, drawing her into a firm embrace.

As she hugged Kate, Aoife inhaled the clean smell of soap and antiseptic – a scent she always associated with her sister, a by-product of her work as a hospital nurse. It was so good to see her.

'Aoife, you look gorge! Obviously, Connor is taking good care of you. I want to hear all your plans for the wedding. Is Sandy still going to be a flower girl? Have you decided on the dress?' Kate pulled away, laughing.

'Of course Sandy is my flower girl and, no, I still haven't picked the dress. Maybe you could come up to Dublin with me and help me shop for it – what do you say?'

'I say yes!' Kate gestured towards the kettle. 'Do you fancy a cuppa?'

'Sure.'

Aoife noticed her mother had left out sandwiches in case her children got peckish. She nabbed one and ate it hungrily.

The two sisters sat companionably with steaming mugs of coffee.

'Mam told me about poor old Nell. I'm sure Sam's very upset. I can remember the wee pet following him about. Even though she was too old to be of much use on the farm, Sam took her everywhere with him.'

'Yeah, it's very sad, especially this weekend. Oh well, at least she didn't suffer too long.'

'Where did Sam bury her?'

'In the back garden. The new lad, Karol, buried her. I didn't think of getting Mam and Sam out to see her put under, but then perhaps I'm being sentimental.'

'We were all fond of her.'

The sisters reminisced about Nell for a while, and then Aoife asked, 'Where is Sandy? Didn't she come down with you?' Sandy was Aoife's godchild, and she always felt a close bond with her.

'Oh, she's out in the front room with Mam, glued to her phone and moaning about the abysmal Wi-Fi. I swear she watches more TV than anyone I know and if she isn't staring at the TV she's attached to her iPod or tapping dementedly on her mobile phone to her legions of friends.'

Aoife laughed. 'In other words, she's a typical teenager. What about Colm? Is he here too?' Before Kate had time to answer, Aoife's chair was shoved from behind and she watched as her young nephew raced past her towards the door.

'Hold up, young man, and say hello to your aunt!'

He stopped and shuffled his feet.

'Sorry, Aoife, I didn't see you.' He gave her his peculiar side hug and stood staring awkwardly at her as he tried to think of something to say to the aunt he infrequently saw.

She grinned at him. 'I hear you're doing great things on the team. Nana told me she's exhausted counting all the goals and points that you score.'

Colm squirmed and stared at his feet.

'How about I come and see you play next time?' Aoife asked.

'I'm playing next Saturday. If you're here you could watch with Mammy.'

'I'll do my best to come and cheer you on, Colm. Tell me this, do your mammy and daddy embarrass you with their screaming and cheering and giving out to the referee when you're playing?'

Colm looked away and muttered, 'Daddy doesn't come, and Mammy can only come if she's not working.'

Kate grimaced at her son. 'You know that your dad tries to make the matches and perhaps he'll be there on Saturday.'

Colm dropped his head, grunted, 'Yeah, sure,' and raced to the door.

Kate avoided Aoife's eye and returned to the sink where she busied herself putting the lettuce leaves in the salad-spinner.

'How is Kenny?'

'Kenny is OK, but he's worried about work. They're laying off people at his firm and I think he's afraid that he may be next on the hit list.'

Aoife got up and squeezed her sister's arm. 'I'm sorry, Kate. If the worst happens, will you manage?'

'We'll manage. My job is secure, thank God, but we have our mortgage to pay. Of course, things will be tight but we'll get by. But I'm afraid that Kenny will find it hard to cope with unemployment.

He's forty-five, and I'm not sure if he will find it easy to get another job. What I'm really afraid of, I suppose, is that he'll get depressed.'

Kate avoided Aoife's gaze and looked away, her eyes tipping over with tears.

'What is it, Kate? Talk to me. I know there's something more upsetting you.'

Kate wiped her eyes and smiled weakly. 'Kenny had a bad bout of depression about ten years ago. He was like a lost soul, he couldn't function. For three weeks he just sat in his dressing gown and stared at the TV even when it wasn't on. I got help for him, but for a year he was so low, almost broken. I'm worried that the same thing will happen if he loses his job.'

'I'm so sorry, Kate. I never realised that he suffered from depression. I suppose I've been so wrapped up in my world that I never noticed when things were bad with you.'

'Why should you, love? It was a long time ago and Kenny didn't want people to know. I don't know if I ever told you, but Kenny had a tough upbringing. He was in care for most of his childhood, and I think it left a mark on him that no amount of reassurance from me can shift. So, we just have to tough things out and hope for the best. Now, enough about my troubles, I want to hear about you.'

'Kate, we can change the subject, but I want you to know that I am always there if you need to talk. Promise me you will let me know how things are with you and Kenny.'

Kate grinned at her as she tipped the freshly washed lettuce into the salad bowl. 'I promise, little sister. I'll ring you and talk whenever I need to. But not a word to Mam – she doesn't need to worry, especially not this weekend.'

'Ah yes, Kate, what's the story about the anniversary? Is Father Francis coming here to say Mass or are we going to the church?'

'Yeah, Mass is here at eight tonight. It'll be just us and the aunts and a few neighbours. Mum has a mountain of food cooked, so plenty of leftovers to take away with you tomorrow.'

The mention of the anniversary Mass for her father prompted Aoife to ask, 'Kate, I was only a kid when Dad died. I have memories of him, but I have no sense of what he was like as a person. To me, he seemed kindly but remote. I never really knew him. What was he like?'

'Hang on a minute while I make us some fresh coffee. Is instant OK for you?'

'Yeah.'

'Fetch some of those bikkies Mam keeps on the shelf.'

Aoife got the biscuits and sat at the table where Kate joined her with two mugs of coffee.

'Now what were we saying? Oh yeah, about Dad. Well, I was fourteen when he died. So, I just knew him when I was a child and a teenager. He was quiet, Aoife – a quiet man. He worked hard on the farm, came in, read the paper from front to back, watched the news, and went to bed. And he smoked like a train – it used to worry Mam a lot. She was always on at him to give the fags up. He wasn't overly demonstrative but then what fathers of that generation were? I never remember him shouting at us. Mam was the disciplinarian. Occasionally she threatened us with him but we knew she was the one in charge. Every Friday he would peel off a few notes out of a tatty old wallet and hand them to her and they would drive to town where she would do the weekly shopping while he sat in the car and read the paper. When he wasn't busy, he could be fun. He used to let me ride on his shoulders and tell me stories. As I got older and turned into a bratty teenager, he was less interested in me or me in him.' Kate smiled reminiscently. 'I know he cared about me though. One time I got sick – pneumonia, I think – anyway I was very ill, and I remember he sat beside my bed holding my hand. He never spoke, and I drifted off

43

to sleep. When I woke the next morning, he was still there. I felt so special and proud that he did that for me. I'm sure Mam sat up many nights with me, but when he did it I felt loved, you know. My memories of him as a teenager are more tenuous. I was interested in boys and discos. If I wanted to go out, I had to negotiate with Mam – she was the sole authority. Dad always said "Ask your mother" if I ever appealed to him to be allowed out. He was a good man, Aoife, an old-time traditional father. He was the breadwinner, but he deferred to Mam about us.'

'What about Sam? How did he get on with Dad?'

Kate furrowed her brow. 'I remember the two of them always being out and about on the farm. Sam adored Dad and sometimes I used to be jealous of how much time they spent together, although I was in no hurry to do the hard, mucky work on the farm either. The plan was that Sam would go to Agricultural College and take over the farm, although before Dad died I think Sam was more interested in becoming a vet than a farmer. It's strange how things work out. The moment Dad died, he just decided that the farm would be his life. I can remember them having a few rows about the usual teenage things, smoking, sneaking out to meet girls, but Sam had a lot of respect for Dad. Why don't you ask him? Apart from Mam, he knew Dad best of all.'

While Aoife was pondering on her sister's words, the door flew open, and a whirlwind entered. Sandy was small and beautiful, a fourteen-year-old Goth in a black miniskirt and leggings, scary black eye-makeup and pale foundation belied by the exuberance of how she greeted her aunt.

'*Aunt Aoife!* Mum, why didn't you tell me Aunt Aoife was here?' she demanded of Kate. Not waiting for a reply, she turned to hug her aunt. 'How's Connor, why didn't you bring him with you? Have you bought your dress yet? Can I go with you shopping for my dress? And please, please, don't make me wear something cheesy!'

Aoife returned her niece's hug enthusiastically and then held her at arm's length so that she could admire her.

'No, I haven't bought my dress yet, and yes, we can go shopping for your dress – and no, I wouldn't dream of making you wear anything you don't like. Connor is busy working on his dissertation, but he sends his love.'

Grinning happily, Sandy sat down beside her aunt and mother.

They spent a happy hour chatting and catching up, Aoife promising not to go all 'teachery' on her and ask her about school. Instead, Kate recounted her daughter's exploits on the football field as Sandy pretended annoyance, but by the smirk on her face Aoife could tell she was delighted.

Agnes came into the kitchen to remind them that in an hour and a half the priest would be there, so they took the hint implicit in her words and got up to assist her in putting the finishing touches to the feast laid out in the dining room. It was a salad to beat all salads. Their mother had prepared gallons of coleslaw, potato salad, pasta, and rice dishes. There were also copious amounts of salmon, thinly sliced beef, and ham to keep the men happy. She had the unshakable belief that men had to consume meat or fish twice daily or they would sicken. To keep the ladies happy, she had outdone herself with scones, cakes, and fresh bread. There wouldn't be room for everyone to eat at the table so everything was laid out buffet-style so guests could help themselves, but the girls were directed to set places at the table for the priest and the aunts.

Meanwhile, Sandy had transformed a table in the front room into an altar by covering it with a thick white tablecloth and placing two brass candles at each end. She then arranged two rows of chairs in a semicircle around the altar.

At eight, Kate, Sandy and Agnes went upstairs to change while Aoife hurried outside to call Sam in to get ready for Mass.

CHAPTER 6

Sam was at the back door, pulling off his Wellington boots. Aoife watched him for a few moments. He did everything with slow, deliberate movements. Suddenly she flashed back to a memory of her father. It was the sharp darting way he moved. He could be completely still and then be a frenzied blur of activity, rushing through his work, tearing from one thing to the next, and yet he never seemed to be done. One task followed another in a torrent of activity. She remembered him kicking off his boots and hanging up his wet jacket, simultaneously splattering mud and muck about her mother's immaculate scullery to the soundtrack of her scolding voice. Sam was a sharp contrast, moving slowly but thoroughly and completing each task with little fuss or flurry.

She called to him, and he turned and smiled.

'It's OK. You can tell Mam to calm down – I'll be ready on time.'

Smiling, she ran upstairs, changed into a skirt and blouse, and applied make-up.

The priest had arrived when she went downstairs. Agnes was urging him to have some tea, but he reminded her he was about to say Mass. Father Francis was seventy-five and still working. Shortages of priests meant that retirement wasn't an option if you were fit and well. Aoife shook hands with him. She had always liked him. He was a kind man, and she never forgot his gentleness the night her father died. Realising how confused she was, he took time to talk to her and try to explain what had happened to her dad. His hair was white, and the blue eyes were now filmed by age, but he was still quick-witted and had a sharp sense of humour. He must find the local parish priest a pain in the arse. Father Kestler was one of those people who think they are cleverer than they are and were always eager to give everyone the benefit of their opinion, however ill-informed. Father Francis never complained, but once or twice she had seen him shudder, pained by the idiocy of his fellow cleric.

'Hello, Aoife, it's well and grand you're looking,' he said, greeting her with a warm smile.. 'Young Connor is a lucky man. How is he, by the way?'

'He's in great form, and I remind him how lucky he is daily, Father,' she said, grinning back at him. 'We're both looking forward to you marrying us in August.'

The arrival of the aunts interrupted their conversation. Their pungent and conflicting perfumes dominated the room. They presented a vision of contrasts. Aunt Emma, the eldest at seventy-six, was the most glamorous. White hair beautifully cut flattered her small oval face which, although well creased by time, still held arresting hints of her past beauty. The untimely death of her husband in an accident at his workplace left her widowed at an early age but also, thanks to a generous insurance claim, financially secure. Aoife enjoyed Emma's capacity to be charming and bitchy in equal measure.

47

Standing next to her, Aunt Clarissa was as plain as Emma was beautiful and as sweet-natured as Emma was acerbic. Abandonment by her husband after only three years together had taken its toll on her appearance. The shame she felt about this marital failure gave her a sad, diminished air made worse when in the shade of her glamorous older sister. She wore her grey dress like a uniform. Did she own clothes in any other colour? Clarissa was always hard up for money, so she dressed out of charity shops and steadfastly refused to take any money from her well-to-do sister. Aoife thought her wise to remain financially independent. Emma would be a benign dictator, but a dictator nonetheless. Clarissa was smart to hold on to her poverty and her independence.

Baby was the youngest sister, her given name long forgotten by everyone including possibly Baby. She wasn't even the youngest in the family. Aoife's father, Manus, was the 'baby' of the O'Driscoll family. But somehow the name suited her. At seventy-two, she resembled a chubby, wizened baby, all round eyes and pouting lips. The impression of childishness was enhanced by her plaintive, whiney voice. The oversized dresses she decked herself out in looked quaint and girly, yet aged her more than she realised. Baby had never married. Aoife avoided spending too much time in her company as it made her teeth hurt.

Although Clarissa was her favourite aunt, she enjoyed the waspish wit and animation of Emma, so she made a beeline to her.

'Aunt Emma, you look wonderful – you get younger every time I see you. Connor reckons that you have a portrait in the attic and that's how you look so gorgeous.'

Aoife laid the compliments on with a spade, knowing how Emma would lap it up.

'Darling Aoife, you are a tease! How is that lovely man? I'm so excited to see you both walk down the aisle. But what a pity it is that your dear father won't be there to take your arm on the big day. I suppose Sam will do the honours but of course it's not the same as having one's father. It was the same for me on my special day. My father died when I was a little one. Ah well!' Emma sighed theatrically.

Father Francis appeared before them in his vestments and a hush crept over the room as everyone took their seats.

Clarissa stood up and in a quivery but oddly moving voice sang an old hymn that Aoife remembered from childhood. The priest listened with head bowed and then began the celebration of the anniversary Mass.

Aoife drifted off, lulled by the familiar drone of the responses. She came to with a start when she saw people receiving Communion and hurriedly joined them. The Mass ended with Clarissa and her sisters singing 'Nearer, My God, to Thee'. Glancing across at her mother, she saw how tired she looked, worn out with all her cleaning and baking. Guiltily, she realised it was nearly three months since she had last been home. She would visit more often and, when she and Connor married, they would have her mother up to stay regularly.

People filed out of the room and Aoife made her way to help her mother with the food.

Sam waylaid her. 'Can you get some sherry for the aunts? You know what they're like, mouths parched with all the yakking.'

Reaching into the cupboard, she got out three bottles of sherry and poured out a sweet sherry for Baby, a medium for Clarissa, and a dry one for Emma. It reminded her of 'Goldilocks and the Three Bears'.

The ladies, delighted with their refreshments, were soon happily sipping and talking to Father Francis and Sam. When her mother joined them talk soon turned to Manus and the aunts reminisced about the old days when he was alive.

Aoife felt a shiver travel down her spine. For a few hours, she had avoided thinking about the box but now a creeping unease settled over her and she desperately needed reassurance. Hearing Connor's voice would help or at the very least distract her from her troubling thoughts.

She slipped out to the hall and rang him, sitting on the stairs while she waited for him to answer. It went to voicemail, so she just left him a quick message. She longed to hear his voice, to tell him about the box and the notebook. Caution prevented her from saying anything to Kate or Sam or, God forbid, her mother.

'Aoife, there you are!' Emma stood before her, dangling her empty sherry glass. 'I was wondering where you got to. Come and talk to me. I'm fed up with listening to those old hens I'm related to. I need some stimulating conversation and another sherry if I'm to survive this evening.'

Aoife put her mobile away. 'OK, why don't we sit in the sunroom? You go on ahead and I'll fetch your drink.'

Aoife took her glass and Emma tottered off.

Aoife replenished the glass and made herself a generous G and T. Shoving the sherry bottle under her arm, she carried both glasses to the sunroom. Emma was perched elegantly on the couch. She still had a good pair of legs and wasn't afraid to display them. Her eyes lit up when she spied the sherry bottle and she patted the space beside her.

They chatted for a while and then, when there was a pause, Aoife asked, 'What was Dad like?'

Emma glanced at her questioningly.

'I mean, I never knew him properly, I was a kid when he died. I just wondered what he was like as a person.'

Emma gave one of her direct looks. 'Do you really want to know?'

'Of course I do!'

Emma reached into her handbag and took out a photograph. She handed it to Aoife.

It was black-and-white, battered and creased, but she could make out a boy of about nine or ten. He was tall and thin and was staring unsmilingly into the camera.

'That was your father the year I went to America. He was a young lad stuck at home on the farm with our mother. I took that photograph. You asked me what he was like. It was so long ago and yet, this evening, chatting with the girls and your mother the memories came flooding back – I was a lot older than him. He was the baby of the family. When the older boys left and showed no signs of coming back, I think that mother intended him to stay put and run the farm and look after her. He hadn't much of a life while she was alive. The best thing that ever happened to him was meeting your mother. He was a serious man, Aoife, slow to smile, and he always seemed older than his age. When I came back from America, I found him as difficult to know as ever. He always struck me as a sad person. But your mother made him happy. You keep the photo – it's only getting destroyed in my bag. You know Sam is a bit like your dad, serious and hard-working.'

Aoife stared at it wonderingly. 'What was Granny like, Aunt Emma? Why didn't Dad have much of a life with her?'

Emma looked at her empty glass and Aoife took the hint and filled it up.

'Mother was a powerful woman. She brought us up and educated us and gave us every opportunity on little or no money. She refused charity and was very independent. But she was a hard woman – there was no softness about her. It wasn't difficult for me or the others to leave home, but we felt bad for your dad. Every year he got quieter and quieter. He worked his guts off on that farm and she never gave him a crumb of praise. He never had time to have a life of his own. I never remember him having friends or going out. When Mother died, he met Agnes. She worked in the office of the funeral undertakers that buried her. They started going out together and before too long they were saving hard to get married. We were all delighted for him. Your mother was such a lively girl we hoped she would lighten him up.'

'Did she? Did she make him happy?'

Emma patted her hand. 'Yes, she did. I can truly say that no woman could have made him happier, but …' Emma hesitated.

Aoife demanded, *'But what?'*

Emma sighed. 'I don't think your father was ever really happy. He had a dark sadness about him that I don't think ever lifted. In fact, when I heard about the accident I wondered if perhaps it wasn't an accident.'

Aoife glanced at her sharply. 'Are you saying that you think he killed himself?'

Emma looked contrite. 'Of course he didn't kill himself. It was just a foolish notion I had. Of course it was an accident. He fell, and the cold finished him. It was just when I first heard he died, I wondered, that's all. Don't mind me, I've had too much sherry.'

Aunt and niece sat quietly, each uncertain about what else to say.

Aoife's mind was whirling. The details in the notebook were disturbing and now, according to Emma, her father was a deeply unhappy man. Some unhappy men internalised their pain, others took their pain out on others. Which was her father? Was the notebook a safety-valve or something far worse?

The entry of Kate broke the silence.

'There you are! Come on, there's a feast for you to help consume,' she said.

Aoife picked up the photograph and silently they followed Kate to the kitchen.

CHAPTER 7

It was after midnight when Kate, Colm and Sandy went home. Sam locked up and Aoife and her mother went to bed, but only after they cleaned up. Mam couldn't bear coming down in the morning to an untidy kitchen.

Sleep proved elusive as Aoife's head was dizzy with thoughts spiralling on an endless loop. She tried calling Connor again, but there was no answer. Glancing at the clock, she saw it was after one. Sighing, she got out of bed and fetched the box and the notebook. She opened the lid and spread the items out. What did they all have in common? Exhaling, she replaced them and, with dread, took the notebook and read.

The one bright shining light in my life is A. I met her when I was arranging my mother's funeral. Unbelievably she liked me, and we began our courtship. I was too shy to ask her out and took to waiting for her to leave on her lunch break so that I could bump into her. I don't think I would ever have worked up the courage to ask her out if she hadn't suggested we go to see a picture the following Saturday.

I couldn't wait for the day to come and was waiting far too early for her to arrive. As soon as I caught sight of her tidy little figure rounding the corner, I ran towards her. She looked startled, and I worried my eagerness might frighten her off, but she seemed pleased. We didn't know what any of the pictures were like, so we just went to the one that A had heard was good. It turned out to be Jaws. I recall little of the movie except for its menacing music, but I remember every clutch of my hand and every time she buried her head in terror on my chest. I have seen the movie several times since but, despite its terrifying tension and the gore, for me it holds only sweet memories. It was in that darkened cinema as I held her hand that I knew I had come home. She was my angel, the only one who could bring warmth into my broken life.

The more I got to know her, the more certain I became that I had to marry her. I sensed she was my salvation. With her by my side, the darkness, the ugliness would dissipate.

She was sweet-natured and lively. When I was with her, I felt a lightness and I knew that if I could be with her, then I would be whole — a proper man. I couldn't believe it when she agreed to marry me. I felt as though I had a chance at life. We were so happy, and we seemed to laugh our way through every blessed day.

Our first married year together was a taste of paradise. I couldn't believe my good fortune. That such a woman loved me, chose to be with me, lie in my bed and bind her life to mine seemed a wondrous thing. Foolishly I believed that my ugly, painful past could be put aside, and my new life begin. Even more foolishly I started to think I was the man A. believed me to be.

The years slipped by. We had the children. With each child I saw I was losing her. Her attention, her obsession was with the welfare of the youngsters. I suppose that's being a good mother. But she stopped being my wife and became the children's mother.

My descent began after the first one was born. A was quite listless. I felt she was punishing me with her muteness. Once more the walls of the house rang with deafening silence interspersed by the wails of the child. She shut me out — I was alone again. I escaped to the farm as often as I could because our home was no longer a sanctuary. At least out in the fields I could get some sense of order and distraction.

But there was no ease in my head. It was as though the old dark days had returned and the Harpy was my sole companion, filling my head with her disappointment and criticism, pounding and pounding at me wearing me away to the bone.

Then fate came to meet me. I was driving the tractor onto the main road so that I could access a field on the next side road when I saw her. She waved me down. The girl was wet and cold and had been trying for a lift, but no one had stopped. I could tell from her accent that she was a foreigner. Of course, I helped her. I gave her a hand up onto the tractor and offered to drive her to the nearest village where she could get something to eat and hopefully continue her journey.

She giggled at the idea of getting a lift on a tractor. I don't know why I gave in to this impulse, but it started the chain of events that dragged me back to the old ways. I persuaded her that I needed to pick up something in my shed and that afterwards I would drop her off in town. She showed no uncertainty, no lack of trust, just nodded her agreement. Even as we drove to the shed, I was still unsure about what I planned to do. She jumped down from the tractor and sat on a potato box. I pretended to be searching for something, but I was watching her. She wasn't pretty, but she had nice hair – it looked soft. Later I stroked it, but I didn't feel sorry. I don't know why I did it.

But afterwards, I felt alive, strong, as though the life draining out of her was surging towards me, transfusing into me.

Aoife dropped the notebook as though its pages had burned her skin. Jesus! Was this possible? Was her father calmly describing killing a young woman? Her heart beat unbearably fast and she felt sick and dizzy. Taking a deep breath, she forced herself to continue reading.

I can't remember planning it, but I must have done. Why else had I brought her to the shed? But I believed I was acting automatically, as though following a script written long ago. She was easy to kill. I just twisted her head and felt her neck snap. She didn't leave a mark on me, she had no time to react, no idea of what was happening until it was too late. It differed completely from the first time. I didn't panic. I could take my time and enjoy our special time together. Her skin was silky soft and stayed warm for a long time. Nobody disturbed us. She looked as though she was sleeping. Then I wrapped her up in a tarpaulin, lifted her onto the trailer and hitched it to the tractor. I dug a hole – good and deep. I didn't want her unearthed by dogs. Afterwards, I decided it would be a good place to have a silage pit. No one would ever find her then. Exhausted and hungry, I went home to A. Strangely, I didn't mind the noise or the chaos that was my home. I felt at peace.

Aoife lay stunned in her childhood bedroom, staring at the posters and peeling paint until a wave of panic swept over her. Then she rushed to the bathroom and was violently sick. As she slumped on the cold tiled floor, watching her sick swirl away when she flushed the toilet, her mind raced. Was it possible that her father had just confessed to killing a woman for no apparent reason? Her thoughts shied away from the unthinkable. She stared at the tiled walls and saw patterns that didn't exist. She counted each tile top to bottom and side to side – anything to shut out the insanity of what she had read.

Creeping back to her bedroom, she stared at the notebook lying innocently on her bed. It defiled the room. What other horrors did it contain? How was she going to bring herself to read any further? She picked it up and flicked through pages and pages of tightly written script. *Oh God, how am I going to continue to read this? Should she show it to Sam?* She hesitated. Best to wait. Perhaps after all it was a work of fantasy. No need to do anything rash. She hid it in her drawer and switched out the light, but lay wide-eyed, afraid to close her eyes.

At last, she fell into an uneasy sleep. It was a relief when the morning came and she could get up.

CHAPTER 8

Sunday was always about food. Agnes went to early Mass, so she could spend the morning cooking dinner. When she had the family at home, she went into overdrive with her preparations. She spoke the love language of food. First was a thick mushroom soup, followed by roast lamb with crispy roast potatoes, vegetables from the farm, and a sherry trifle to finish.

Aoife was ill at ease among her family, aware that she was hiding something hideous. Out of the corner of her eye, she watched them as they sat around the table, Sam teasing Sandy about boys and Kate and Mam indulging the aunts by listening to their childhood stories. Aoife knew that her silence had not gone unnoticed. Aware of her brother looking at her quizzically, she forced herself to focus on the conversation. The food was tasteless in her mouth but resolutely she chewed and swallowed to stop her mother from commenting on her poor appetite. She was so busy masticating that she missed a question directed at her. Several pairs of eyes were gazing at her expectantly.

'*Well?* said her mother.

'Sorry, Mam, I wasn't listening. What did you say?'

'Is Connor planning a trip here before the wedding?'

'*Eh,* I'm not sure what his plans are. I know he's eager to get his thesis completed before the wedding so maybe he won't make it down.'

'Perhaps he could bring his parents down. They've never been down to visit. I'd love to meet them again and you can show them the hotel where you're holding the reception.'

'I'm sure his mum and dad would love to come for a visit, but we will have to wait and see.'

Aunt Baby beamed at her. 'Tell me again, Aoife, what your young man does for a living. I'm sure that you've told me before, but my head is like a sieve.'

There was an awkward silence. In the O'Driscoll clan, the idea of a man not having a proper job by the age of thirty was anathema.

'He hasn't got a job at the moment, Baby, but he's hard at work completing his Master's so he can provide for Aoife,' said her mam hurriedly.

Baby, aware that she had made a faux pas but not sure how, smiled, and nodded dementedly.

Aoife snapped at her mother. 'For God's sake, I don't need providing for! It's not the 19th century, and Connor will get a job when the right one comes along.'

A strained silence followed which Clarissa broke by asking, 'Sam, I'm sure you're very busy with the farm? I'm so glad you have some help at last. Your mother tells me that you have a young man helping. I'm so pleased as farming is hard work. I well remember Manus always coming in exhausted from a day of toil in the fields.'

Agnes, relieved to have a change in conversation, said, 'Yes, Karol is a lovely young man. We're lucky to get him. He's over here from

Poland and he has the most beautiful manners, and his English is first-rate.'

Sam nodded his agreement.

'By the way, Agnes, where's Nell?' said Clarissa. 'I haven't seen her since I arrived. I must give her a wee treat.'

Aoife tensed as she waited for someone to answer.

'She's dead,' Sam said, rolling his napkin into a tight ball and dropping it on his plate. 'She went missing on Friday and I found her in the barn on Saturday morning. She crawled in to die.'

'Oh Sam, I'm so sorry! I know you were fond of her.' Clarissa squeezed Sam's hand.

Baby, afraid of being left out, burbled, '*Aww*, the lovely wee dog! She was such a gentle creature. Imagine her dying this weekend when we are gathered to remember poor Manus! I'm sure she'll be sorely missed.'

Emma raised her eyebrows heavenward. 'Oh, do shut up, Baby, you never even liked the creature.'

Baby subsided sulkily, muttering beneath her breath.

'Anyone for pudding?' asked Agnes, keen to lighten the atmosphere.

Kate hurried off to help her dish up the dessert, and the conversation stayed on harmless topics for the rest of the meal.

After lunch, Sam went out to finish some work on the farm, and the girls left Agnes and the aunts in the living room with the Sunday papers.

They worked in silence. Kate cleared and wiped the table, Aoife loaded the dishwasher and they each busied themselves until the kitchen was restored to order. Then Kate sat down at the kitchen table and patted the chair next to her.

Aoife joined her.

'Is there something troubling you, sis?' Kate asked. 'You're awfully quiet?'

Sorely tempted as she was to blurt out her discovery, Aoife was unwilling to relinquish control. She needed time and space to think, to work out what to do.

'No, there's nothing wrong, Kate. I'm just stressed out about the wedding. You know how it is. There are so many decisions to make, and I suppose I'm getting fed up with the not-so-subtle criticism of Connor. I know Mam finds it hard to accept that he hasn't a job, but he will get fixed up with something eventually.'

Kate patted her shoulder. 'Mam just doesn't believe that there is anyone good enough for you. But she's very fond of Connor – we all are, and I know things will sort themselves out.'

'Thanks, Kate, for listening to me moan. I know that you have troubles of your own. I hope Kenny will feel better soon.'

The sisters finished cleaning, and Kate joined her mother and aunts who were dozing in the living room.

Aoife called Connor, but once again all she got was voicemail. Frustrated, she headed outside, where she found Sandy and Colm throwing hoops in the yard. For a few minutes, she watched her niece and nephew, and then barged forward and snatched the ball from Sandy. She aimed for the hoop and missed amid cries of derision from her niece. They messed about for half an hour until Mam called them to say goodbye to the aunts.

The three sisters were heading back to town to the small holiday home owned by Emma where the three sisters stayed when they were visiting. Clarissa was driving, so Emma called seniority and ensconced herself in the front seat, much to Baby's annoyance, and they were waved off.

Aoife glanced at her watch. 'I'm going to have to head soon, Mam. It's a long drive back and I have some prep to do for classes on Monday.'

'I'm going to miss you when you go, love. But I would rather you leave while it's still bright. I worry about you driving in the dark.'

Aoife fetched her things from the bedroom. She held the box and for a moment debated leaving it behind. Maybe she needed a bit of space from it, a bit of perspective. It unnerved her, but despite this she wanted it with her. Besides, the thought of her mam finding it terrified her. Again, she wondered if she should tell Kate and Sam about it. Shaking her head, frustrated and indecisive, she stuffed it into her bag.

When she went downstairs, Sam was back. She hugged him, kissed her mother and sister, and drove off to a chorus of 'Safe home!'

The journey back to Dublin was uneventful. She blasted music out all the way to distract her and it worked. As she drove through the city, her longing to see Connor increased. She couldn't wait to talk things over with him.

It was dark when she pulled up outside the flat they shared in Rathmines, the interior lit up like a department store. She was tired of telling Connor to switch off the bloody lights. He had no regard for either the environment or the waste of money in leaving lights burning throughout the flat. It annoyed her when he made her feel like such a nag. But it was good to be back with him again, and they still had the rest of the evening together.

Connor lay stretched out on the sofa with headphones on, listening to music, eyes closed, oblivious to her arrival. His long skinny frame was relaxed. He hadn't shaved since she had left, and his stubble scratched her skin as she brushed his lips with hers. His eyes flew open, and she melted a little as he smiled up at her. He was a study in brown: eyes, hair, and skin were all shades from the rich chocolate-brown of his hair to the intense liquid toffee colour of his eyes to the light golden brown of his skin. God, she had it bad!

'Hello, pet, it's good to see you.' He pulled her down for a strong welcoming kiss.

'I may never go away again if that's the welcome home I get,' she said with a giggle as she came up for air.

'Good! As I plan to tie you up rather than let you head off to the sticks again,' he said, laughing. 'Are you hungry, love? I have nothing cooked, but we could ring for a pizza. What do you think?'

She nodded. 'I am peckish although Mam did one of her usual slap-up Sunday dinners. I think I could manage a slice of pepperoni or two. Mam sent up lots of leftovers from the weekend, so we're set for the week.'

While he was ordering the food, she put the leftovers in the fridge and dumped her bag in the bedroom. It was a mess. Usually, when she was here, she could by dint of nagging keep some check on Connor's untidiness, but in her absence he had free rein. Sighing, she lifted dirty clothes off the floor and remade the bed. She sorted out her bag and put the box under the bed. After a quick shower, she pulled on a nightshirt.

The pizza had arrived, and Connor opened a bottle of red wine. She turned on the gas fire and they sat on the sofa and ate their food from the box and sipped wine. Lying back on Connor's shoulder, she savoured the pleasure of being back in Dublin. Suddenly the events of the weekend seemed like some insane dream. The box and that appalling notebook were just a silly game someone started a long time ago. Perhaps her dad had needed an outlet to the pressures he was under, and certainly his mother seemed a complete bitch. She pitied him for the life he must have had alone with her on the farm. Work, duty, and fear of God were harsh nourishment for a child to endure. It was no wonder that he used words as an outlet for the loneliness he faced. Perhaps there were other tin boxes with violent accounts of killings he wrote as a child. It was just a way for him to deal with stuff – like the stress of being a father. For a few peaceful moments, she convinced herself that was what the notebook was – a release, pure fantasy. But nagging thoughts intruded. What did the trinkets represent? Who did they belong to? Why the need to describe killing a young girl? It was creepy, to say the least.

She must have sighed because Connor looked at her with concern, 'What's up, pet, why so sad?'

Should she tell him? She felt tempted but then hesitated. Once she spoke about this, it would be out of her control, and it also felt like a betrayal of her father. It would be awful if Connor read the diary and concluded that her father was some kind of monster. Mind you, what other conclusion could he reach? Perhaps he would insist she did something about it – report it or show it to her mother? The idea of showing it to her mam horrified her.

So instead she shook her head and told him about Nell. She felt abashed as Connor was so sympathetic. He was fond of the old dog too and said he'd ring Agnes tomorrow and offer his sympathy to her and Sam. Listening to his concern for her family, she reflected that kindness was one of his nicest qualities. If only he would sort himself out career-wise.

With this thought in mind, as soon as he finished on the phone, she asked, 'Have you sent off the draft dissertation to Burke yet?'

She wished her words didn't sound so accusatory. His guarded reply didn't surprise her.

'I just have a few things to iron out. It will be ready soon. He isn't hassling me for it.'

Even though she knew this would not end well, she couldn't stop herself.

'But you promised you would get it handed in and out of the way.

Look, the wedding is only a few months away and you promised to get the dissertation finished so that you could start earning. Bills are mounting up, as you know.'

As she said the words, she knew how things would go. It was by now an old script – what he would say, how she would reply, and how the evening would end. The play ran true to previous performances, with Connor accusing her of nagging, she accusing him of procrastinating, of just drifting along. He snarled at her that she was just like his family – only interested in money.

'Perhaps you should marry James – he's more your style, anything to make a fast buck!'

She shouted that he was being ridiculous. They finished by glaring at each other. The only change to the usual scenario was that he stormed off to bed, and she stayed in the living room and poured herself more wine. Usually, she felt sad and guilty after these rows, but tonight perversely she was glad of the distraction. She turned on the TV and watched a lion devouring an antelope. It brought up disturbing images in her mind of her father with the young woman in the shed. Sickened, she flicked channels and eventually settled on an old British war film.

After a couple of hours, she followed Connor to bed. As she snuggled up to him, his rigid back refused to soften even when she put her arms around him. She knew by his breathing that he wasn't asleep, but not in a mood to forgive and forget.

Despite her exhaustion, it took a long time to drop off.

CHAPTER 9

School dragged for Aoife. The day pressed down hard and her tongue, heavy in her mouth, seemed swollen and useless. Her eyelids drooped, and she feared she would fall asleep if she closed them for longer than a blink. She glanced at the clock in the classroom: would the hands never move to end this relentless day? When the bell finally rang, instead of the expected relief, she felt only further lassitude. Desperate for school to end, yet reluctant to go home. She was too tired to face Connor and his hurt, too sick at heart to read more of her father's terrifying outpourings.

Remaining here wasn't an option. Already the cleaning staff was moving toward the classrooms to start their work. She looked at the discarded papers dropped on the floor, the knocked-over chairs and desks scarred with graffiti. What was the point of it all? The endless round of cleaning, and restoration of order to be followed by more mess and the casual, contemptuous littering of juveniles?

She dragged herself out of the room and visited the staffroom to retrieve her belongings. It was quiet, the only sound the photocopier and the rustle of papers. She called goodbye to the teachers who had remained behind, too absorbed in marking copies to reply.

The drive home was uneventful, with the usual traffic jam. She was too listless to listen to the radio and all the music on her phone was too upbeat for her flattened mood. Most evenings the thought of seeing Connor consoled her for the tedium of the homeward journey, but not this evening. The curtains were closed when she got home. So, he wasn't in yet. She opened the fridge, made up a salad of her mam's leftovers and fished out the remnants of last night's pizza for their dinner.

As she was setting the table, she heard Connor's key in the latch. He didn't come into the kitchen but went straight to their bedroom. She put out the frugal meal and called him to come and eat.

In stilted tones, she asked about his day and he about hers. The silence made her ache.

'Connor, I'm sorry about the row last night. I didn't mean to upset you.'

'Didn't you?'

'OK, so I'm practical, I'm worried about money, about paying bills, about buying our own place. What's wrong with that?'

Connor threw his hands up in the air. 'You're with the wrong bloke if it's security and forward planning you're wanting. That's not who I am, love. I don't want to work in the business. I'm suffocated just thinking about it.'

'So, what is it you want?' she asked, holding her breath.

'I want to finish this thesis, but I want to concentrate on writing poetry.'

'What? How in hell's name are we to live, Connor, on my salary? How fair is that?'

Connor sighed. 'I know you and your family think I'm a loser,

Aoife, but I can't pretend to be someone I'm not. I tried to work in the family business and loathed it, and I was hopeless at it. They only tolerated me because I'm family. I'm not interested in having a career as an estate agent. I want to write, and I'll take bar work or anything casual that's going to finance our lives together.'

'*Then how the hell do we pay for this wedding?*'

'Aoife, I love you, I do, but this big wedding doesn't matter to me. I want to be with you, but why do we have to do things on such a big scale? Why not get married and just ask family and later we can have a party for everyone?'

'Because that's not what I want.'

They locked eyes.

'Connor, I want a nice wedding with all my family and friends present, and I want a husband with a proper job. I get how important poetry is to you, but you can find time for that. I'll help you make time.'

'You don't get me at all, do you? I don't want to fit writing into my life. It *is* my life.'

'Do you know how pretentious that sounds? And where do I fit into your life? Think about it, we will no longer be flatmates – we're getting married, for God's sake. We must plan for our future, buy a house, and maybe even start a family. It will take two of us working hard to make that happen. You can't just indulge in a pipe dream while I do all the heavy lifting.'

'I didn't think you thought my writing was a pipe dream. You always encouraged me – were you just pandering to my ego?'

'Connor, I love your poetry, really I do, but you must see that it's unrealistic to depend on it. Lots of people hold down jobs and still write. Why can't you?'

'Because I can't. I could do bar work or work part-time, but I need to concentrate on what's important to me.'

'I thought I was important to you.'

They stared at each other in silence.

'Do you want to call the wedding off?' she whispered.

He didn't answer.

As she turned away, Connor reached out for her hand.

'I love you. You have to believe me. There is no one else I care about. I want to be with you. But I can't be what you want me to be.'

She pulled away abruptly. 'Then I suppose we better end this now. I would like it if you could move out soon. There's no point in prolonging this. I'm sure your brother can find you somewhere to stay.'

Connor stared at her in shock.

'Are you serious – you want me to move out?'

Aoife hesitated, but words spilt out that were cold and certain.

'Yes, I do. There is no point in dragging this out. Neither of us will change, so let's stop wasting each other's time. We can't keep having the same argument over and over again.'

They stared wordlessly at each other.

Then Aoife went into the bedroom. She grabbed her toothbrush, her make-up bag, and a change of clothes.

Connor followed her, a look of helpless disbelief working its way across his face.

'Where are you going?' he asked.

'I'll stay with a friend tonight – and I mean it, I want you gone by tomorrow evening. We can decide how to cancel the wedding arrangements later.'

As she put things in a bag Connor walked over to her. He reached out to touch her, but she pushed him away. He followed her to the living room.

'Aoife, we can't just end like this. Why not just take a bit of time, cool down, and work something out?'

'I am calm, and I don't think sleeping on this is going to make any difference. Neither of us is going to change who we are. So, let's just call it quits and sort out the details next week of how to disentangle ourselves from the plans that we made.'

She picked up her car keys and left.

Outside, she took big gulping mouthfuls of air. *Keep breathing, just hold on for a few more minutes.* She got into her car and let out a shriek like an animal in pain. Dropping her head on the steering wheel, she howled. When she was calmer, she knew she would have to go, terrified that the neighbours would see her, that someone would tap on the window and ask if she was OK. She started the ignition. Where could she go to sit and process what had just happened? There was the finality of it all – Connor and her, finished – no wedding, no us. There was only one option. Right now, she needed a friend, preferably one who would just shut up and listen. She drove to Sorcha's.

Her friend lived a couple of streets away. As she drew up, she saw Sorcha's car parked across from her ground-floor apartment. Good, she was at home. Still, she hesitated about going inside. To tell Sorcha that the wedding was off made it real – too real. Her mobile rang. It was Connor. She didn't answer. Sorcha must have seen her pull up because she waved from the window. The door was flung open.

There was no need for words, Sorcha gripped her in a tight hug that felt warm and safe. She was all softness and comforting folds of fleshiness, her fair hair brushing featherlike across her face as they embraced.

'I knew something was wrong when you didn't come in straight away. Do you want to tell me about it, or do you just want time to howl?'

Aoife couldn't answer.

'Come on in. This calls for tea and toast.'

Aoife wiped at her tear-soaked face as Sorcha led the way into the kitchen. She sat and tried to calm herself as Sorcha made them tea and hot buttered toast.

After she had gulped down some of the tea, she blurted, 'Well, there'll be no need to shop for bridesmaids' dresses next week. The wedding is off.'

'*What? Aww*, God, that's awful! What happened?'

Through rivulets of tears and a runny nose, Aoife tried to explain.

'He's just not taking it seriously, Sorcha. He doesn't seem to realise that getting married is a big deal. I mean, he thinks he can just get any old part-time job. All he's worried about is finding time to write his precious bloody poetry!'

'Oh, Aoife, I'm so sorry. But are you sure that you can't work something out? I know writing is important to him – maybe you should postpone the wedding until he's more established.'

'More established! Are you mad? It's a poet he wants to be, not a bestselling novelist! He's much too bloody grand for that! He'll never make a decent living, and he expects me to be the main breadwinner. Come on, I'm a bloody teacher living in Dublin – we'd always be struggling.'

'But, Aoife, you've always known how he felt about his work. Surely this isn't news to you?'

Aoife sprang to her feet. 'Whose side are you on? It's like you're making me out to be the villain of the piece.'

'Hey, calm down – of course I'm on your side but, Aoife, it's better you have this out now and not after you're married.'

Aoife slumped back on the chair. 'I'm sorry. You're right. I think I just expected Connor to get it that marriage changed everything. I mean I hoped we'd start a family soon, but I think Connor wasn't thinking that far ahead.'

Sorcha clasped Aoife's clammy hand. 'To be honest, Aoife, I always felt that you were great together as a couple, but I felt less certain of you as a married pair. I knew that you both were mad about each other, but I felt that the differences between you that drew you together might also pull you apart. Face it – you always knew that being a poet was important to him and yet you were putting him in a position where he would have to choose between being a regular guy in a regular job and doing the thing in the world he loved the most.'

'Are you saying this is my fault for trying to frogmarch him into marriage? He asked me, you know. I didn't torture him to marry me!' She pulled her hand away.

'Hey, calm down, I'm not the enemy. Of course he wanted to marry you. I just don't think marriage meant the same thing to both of you. For you it was about responsibility, moving on, having kids; but I think Connor just saw it as a nice romantic way of showing his commitment to you and a good excuse for a party.'

'For God's sake, Sorcha, everyone knows what marriage means! Why can't you see he is a completely irresponsible jerk?'

'Honey, he wasn't being irresponsible. It would be irresponsible to marry someone without being true to who you are. Connor isn't a nine-to-five man. He would drive you mad with what you would see as his lack of ambition. He is ambitious, but not for the things that drive you. You want him to be someone he's not.'

'Well, that's just great. If you noticed all that, why didn't you say something to me before now?'

'Because I hoped I was wrong and mainly because I'm a coward.'

The friends sat in the kitchen sipping tea and watching the night close in. They got a bottle of wine out and killed it, and its twin. It didn't help.

CHAPTER 10

The next morning, after throwing up twice and suffering a cold shower, Aoife returned home. The house was empty and cold. Connor must have stayed out all night. The sight of his duffle bag waiting to be packed made her heart crumble. Don't cry, she ordered. She had to go to work. Perhaps she should ring in sick? No, anything was better than brooding. She had better get a bus. It was lucky she didn't get breathalysed on her way back from Sorcha's. Thinking about work, she realised she'd eventually have to tell her work colleagues about her break-up. Even the bloody kids knew she was getting married. *Shit, shit!*

Her day was a tough one, with no free classes. In the past, the non-stop nature of her Tuesdays made her heart sink, but today she welcomed the distraction. The pupils didn't have an opportunity to mess as she kept them working.

Forgoing her morning caffeine infusion was tough but, putting on a cheerful false face with her workmates was a far tougher prospect so she hid out in her classroom. At lunchtime, she walked to a nearby café and drank a black Americano and ate a stale bagel. It suited her mood. The rest of the day she endured.

Once again, the house was empty. But it felt different, and she realised Connor had been back and cleared much of his stuff. There were gaps in the shelves where his books had been – mainly poetry and the albums they had collected together. She wandered into the bedroom. Most of his clothes were missing, just a few forgotten shirts sitting in his closet. His guitar was no longer resting against the dresser and his laptop was also gone. It was surprising how little stuff Connor had accumulated. The only evidence remaining of his presence were a few items in the laundry basket. Did he expect her to wash them, or should she pick them out and bin them? But he had left the bloody rocking chair behind. They called it the cursing chair because she swore at it so often when she stubbed her toe against it. Connor loved it and every night before getting into bed he would sit strumming his guitar, often playing the same riff over and over. A searing ache twisted her insides as she looked at it, torn between wanting to take a hammer to it and longing to stroke its smooth surface. Just now she didn't care about the wedding, she just wanted him back. Should she ring him, suggesting they forget about getting married and just continue to live together? But she knew she couldn't. A relationship needed forward momentum and, besides, trying to restore the status quo would be futile.

It was disturbing to realise she was after all her mother's daughter – a conventional girl who wanted the usual things out of life – a man with a job, a house, and later a family. Although she loved Connor, she didn't love him enough to change her worldview, and he couldn't be someone that he wasn't. If only she could let go of those middle-class values and just take a leap of faith with Connor, but she knew that if he couldn't make a living out of his poetry, she would grow to resent and even despise him. Aoife felt smaller for this realisation but couldn't deny its truth.

With faint surprise, she realised she had not given a thought to the box and its contents for hours, and now she sought the distraction it would offer. She was just about to go fetch it when her mobile rang.

It was Sorcha.

'Well, love, how are you?'

'My head has stopped pounding, but other vital organs are seriously impaired, especially the heart,' she said.

'Do you regret ending it? I mean, is there any chance of making things right between you two? You know you were great together.'

Aoife noticed how it didn't take a death to change the tense of a relationship already with Sorcha. They were in the past – great together then but now terminal.

'Yeah, we were, but that was then, and this is now,' she said.

'Do you fancy meeting up tonight or are you going to sit home and brood?'

Aoife decided she didn't want to be alone to weigh up the equally unpleasant options of dissecting her relationship or facing up to the horrors that the box held.

'Let's meet up. But I can't face talking. What about going to a movie? Are you up for that?'

They met at half past six. The local multiplex offered the usual fare: frothy romantic comedies, a couple of violent thrillers, or animated kids' shows. Only a masochist would choose a romantic comedy, but perversely that's what they did. Sitting in the darkened theatre, gorging on popcorn and ice cream, she let the silliness of the movie plot wash over her. Occasionally, she caught Sorcha casting anxious glances at her and offered reassuring smiles in return.

Soon it was over, and Aoife declined the offer of drinks. She hugged her friend and headed for home.

The silent flat seemed to reproach her as though blaming her for its echoing loneliness. She turned on the TV, set it to a news channel, and turned the sound down to a comforting hum, creating the illusion of life and company.

In her bedroom, the box on her bureau mocked her with the evil nestling within its tin walls. Opening the lid, she ignored its other contents and took the notebook out. It was important to keep referring to it as a notebook, not a diary. It must be a work of fiction. The writer must have felt a need to have an outlet, an escape from what was a harsh, oppressive existence. The writer had to be her father. She remembered her mam telling her how all his sisters and brothers had emigrated leaving her dad to mind the farm and take care of his mother. It was easy to imagine that a sensitive young man trapped by a cold, harsh mother on a small farm would feel the need to escape, to have an outlet for frustration and dark thoughts. Perhaps it was easier for him to fantasise about murdering young women, objects of frustrated sexual desire when really he wanted to kill his nasty, controlling mother. But it made little sense. Why write it after his mother died when he finally achieved some happiness? The now-familiar revulsion crept over her as she opened the pages and regarded the cramped writing.

It was as though a cork was pulled from a bottle, allowing everything within to burst out in a liberating frenzy. The pressure, tension, and the noise in my head subsided. I could be the husband and the father that A. needed me to be. I felt light, so light that I sang. This easiness delighted A. I could see that I had worried her, that she was aware of my former discomfort. We were closer than ever. She soon recovered from the dark sadness that had arrived with the baby and, although she was no longer just my girl as I had to share her with little S., I felt it would be all right.

Strangely, I felt no heavy dragging burden of guilt – catharsis yes, guilt no. Occasionally, it worried at me – not what I had done, but my lack of regret or fear of the consequences, of being found out. But then, I came to see that the girl was a gift, a saviour or sacrificial lamb. She didn't exist outside of her role, her service to me. Everything that followed showed me I was on a path, a path that I must follow wherever it led.

Hungrily, I devoured news reports about her. I learned her name – Anika. At nights when I couldn't sleep, I whispered it to soothe myself. They described her last known movements. A shopkeeper who served her revealed she spoke of going to Donegal later in the week. Motorists reported seeing her on the road out of town, heading north. There was nothing to tie her to me. The locality was full of talk about her. In church, they offered prayers for her safe return. A. even insisted we say a decade of the rosary for her. It's strange but I could talk about her disappearance, pray for her, and not feel guilt or shame or even a sense of hypocrisy. Everything I said, everything I did, I meant. I truly prayed for her soul. One evening, on television, there was an interview with her mother. She was a Dutch lady. I listened as she appealed for information about her daughter, talked about what a lovely girl she was, and how she was a wonderful daughter. I felt nothing. What did that mean?

But a month later it was old news, rarely spoken of, and that disappointed me. I missed the excitement and camaraderie that my little hiker generated. I missed the opportunity to talk about it, to listen to all the theories and opinions people had about her whereabouts. But I was careful not to keep referring to it. I drew no attention to myself. All I had to console myself was the pretty little dolphin trinket. I stroked it and held it next to my skin and I felt close to her again and able to relive our special time together. It wasn't perfect, but it soothed me, calmed me.

Aoife shuddered and dropped the notebook. She looked into the box and saw the innocuous little trinket unmarked by time or trauma lying on the lock of hair. Her skin crawled and she slammed the lid closed as if that would contain its evil. Her gaze dropped once more to the little book.

Of course, I didn't know then that it was just the beginning. The adventure was just beginning.

She tore her eyes from the page. It was unbearable. Could this be really happening? If it was, then she was reading the diary of a murderer and it was now apparent that, whatever this was, it was the work of her father Manus O'Driscoll. She couldn't bear to read any more. Several times she tried but fear, sick corrosive fear, held her back. This was hellish. According to the diary, her father was a murderer, a fucking psychopath. Whatever this was, it had to be a sick joke. It had to be! Should she talk to someone about it? Maybe she needed to tell Sam and Kate, but grinding fear held her back. To reveal the contents of the box would be to release all the evils contained within, allowing it to desecrate and destroy her world and her family. Once she showed them the box, everything would move beyond her control. If only she could talk to Connor. In the past, he was the one she would have turned to – or Sorcha. Should she tell Sorcha? It felt disloyal to reveal something so potentially damaging to an outsider, to someone not in the family.

But there was one other option.

CHAPTER 11

She arranged a special treat for Clarissa. Afternoon tea appealed to her aunt's generation: it was posh, with its recreation of the grandeur of bygone days, and yet comforting. When she decided to pump one of her aunts for information, she chose carefully. Baby was out of the question because of, well, being Baby. Emma was too sharp, too suspicious, and would not hesitate to prevaricate to protect her family. Clarissa was open without a suspicious bone in her body. Her innocent belief in the intrinsic good of everyone meant she was unlikely to be guarded. Hopefully, she could give her some insights into her father, and help her to gauge if he were capable of the horrors described in the notebook.

It took a little persuasion for Clarissa to undertake the bus trip from Bray to Dublin. They agreed to meet on Thursday at three. Normally Aoife would be at school till at least four, but she had lost a class group to a school tour, so was free so long as she dodged any cover for other teachers. She slipped out of the school at two and headed to the Dart where she met her aunt. Aoife suggested getting a taxi but Clarissa insisted she would enjoy the short walk to the hotel.

Afternoon tea at the Merrion was expensive, but Aoife wanted an uninterrupted talk and they were less likely to run into anyone she knew in the environs of the upmarket hotel.

Clarissa was impressed by the hotel, and she gazed in delight at the paintings adorning its walls. She fussed about the expense and suggested they go somewhere less exclusive and costly. But Aoife knew Clarissa was secretly pleased when she insisted they stay for the hotel's substantial and scorchingly expensive afternoon tea.

A pleasant server escorted them to a plush couch and took their order of tea for two.

Clarissa, delighted by such a wide selection of brews, after much hesitation settled on Earl Grey.

'Such a lovely treat, Aoife, but, darling, shouldn't you be saving hard for your wedding and not wasting money on an old trout like me?'

Aoife avoided her aunt's eyes. She hated to deceive Clarissa but couldn't bear to tell her about her broken engagement, at least not until she spoke to her mam.

'It's my pleasure, Aunt Clarrie. It's rarely I can persuade you to visit me in Dublin, so I wanted to make an occasion of it.'

While they waited on their order, they chatted. Aoife was careful to keep things light, at least until the afternoon tea had arrived. Clarissa was in a reminiscent mood and talked about growing up on the farm. She was deep in an anecdote about collecting hens' eggs and selling them to the local shops when the waiter arrived with the tea and hot water in silver teapots and cakes, scones and sandwiches served on a three-tiered cake-stand. Clarissa beamed her pleasure, and Aoife felt a pang of remorse that her motives in bringing her aunt to tea had been anything but pure. Still, she reflected, Clarissa appeared to be having a good time. She exclaimed in delight at the art-themed selection, and was especially pleased when she noticed that the little fancies were inspired by the work of Jack B. Yeats.

'How clever! I've never seen the like! Oh, Aoife, these sandwiches are delicious. I love smoked salmon.'

'My favourites are the watercress, I don't know why. Perhaps it's just the idea that a bit of green stuff could be so delicious.'

'That's because it's fresh. All this food tastes fresh, none of that processed rubbish you find in restaurants everywhere now. Mind you, it's far from watercress and salmon sandwiches I was raised!'

Seizing her opportunity, Aoife asked, 'What was it like for all of you growing up in Granny's house? I've often meant to ask you.'

'Well, it wasn't easy, you know. Times were hard, and they got even harder after Dada died. It was very sudden, quite unexpected. He was only in his forties, a bit like your father's passing, totally unexpected. Of course, in Manus's case, it was very unfortunate that no one was with him when he had his fall. Perhaps if they were he might have survived. The doctors say it was the exposure to the elements as much as the blow to his head that killed him. I know your brother felt terrible that he wasn't with him when he died. He felt bad that he didn't offer to help him on the farm that day.' Clarisse's eyes misted. 'I always think a sudden death like that is especially hard on a family. Like when your Uncle Milo died of a heart attack in South Africa. We never even got over for the funeral. It was very sad for Josie and his children, but at least he didn't suffer. Will I pour you a hot drop?'

'No, thanks, Aunt Clarrie, I'm still on this one.'

Clarissa poured for herself.

'But Grandad?' Aoife prompted.

'Your granddad, my father, died of pneumonia. He got a bad

wetting and, of course, he had a weak chest which didn't help him. He only lingered a few days. Mother was heartbroken. You know, Aoife, people often talk of a person being heartbroken after a loved one dies, but I could see it devastated our mother. She changed completely.'

'What do you mean? How did she change?'

'Well, before that, they were so happy together, always laughing, and I even saw them dancing occasionally around the kitchen. It was so lovely, especially as Mother wasn't the sunniest of people. She grew up poor and I think it made her very serious and a little dour, but our father brought out a spark in her. I think she adored him. All I know is that after he died, she didn't laugh or dance anymore. She became hard and bitter. I don't mean to criticise her, but it was like she took out her grief on us all, especially your father. At least we older children got to see a happier lighter side of family life – but your poor father never did. He was so young and scared and, when he went to her for comfort, she was impatient and cold. He couldn't understand what was happening and I'm afraid the rest of us were busy feeling sad and broken ourselves, so he grew up a very sad lonely boy.'

'Granny doesn't sound like a nice person, Aunt Clarissa,'

Clarissa shifted in her seat. 'I don't like to speak ill of the dead, but she was a hard woman. Mind you, she had to be tough to take care of seven children with very little money and a tiny farm, so I must forgive her. I owe her all my chances, my education, and my opportunity to go off and work. She was a hard taskmaster but I'm sure she loved us all. She just was poor at showing it, especially to Manus, and especially after Dada died.'

'But that makes no sense – it's so unfair.'

Clarissa squirmed, as if uncomfortable suddenly on the well-upholstered armchair.

Aoife was convinced her aunt was holding something back.

'What is it, Aunt Clarissa, what are you not saying?'

Clarissa shook her head firmly. 'It's nothing, really it isn't, and of course you're right, but mother wasn't reasonable about lots of things. We were all kept on a tight rein, and in all honesty we were all glad to get away from the farm. But we made sure we sent money to ease the financial burdens for both of them. I think she was very proud of us in her way.'

'But why didn't Dad leave too? Why did he stay on the farm?'

Clarissa flushed and looked guilty.

'What is it?' Aoife asked. 'What are you not telling me?'

Clarissa grimaced. 'I feel guilty about Manus, to tell the truth. We all escaped to far-flung parts – not that it was easy. It was hard to leave Ireland and go to a new country, but we felt we were gifted this opportunity to make a better life and, well, Manus staying at home made it easier for us to stay away. Sometimes I think we may have discouraged him from making a break with home because perhaps one of us would have to return in his place.'

Aoife hurriedly poured her aunt more tea to give her a moment to recover and wipe the tears that filmed those milky-blue eyes.

'I'm sure Dad didn't blame you – Mum always said that you were his favourite sister,' she said consolingly.

Clarissa smiled and patted her knee. 'Thank you, my dear, but what has made you bring this up suddenly? Is it that you're getting married and missing out on having your dad give you away?'

Aoife nodded, evading her aunt's eyes. 'I suppose so ... but can you tell me what he was like? Was he shy, or outgoing, did he have a temper? I was too young to remember him properly. Even the memories I have aren't too reliable. He never said a cross word to me, but I don't remember much about him except for him taking me on nature rambles. He never had much time for playing with me as he was always working on the farm, although I have a memory of him letting me ride on his shoulders.'

'Well, I suppose he was getting on in years by the time you came along. He must have been close to forty. He was a quiet person. I don't think I ever saw him get angry, at least not outwardly but then he didn't forgive easily either.' Clarissa paused uncertainly.

'Go on, don't stop now – who didn't he forgive and why?'

Clarissa looked even more uncomfortable. 'Well, he was upset with your Aunt Emma, but it's not my place to be discussing it. So please don't ask.'

Despite wheedling from Aoife, that was all that Clarissa would say on the subject, so they finished their afternoon tea and booked a taxi to return Clarissa to the DART station.

As they waited, Clarissa suddenly said, 'Aoife, dear, I've been thinking and, well, as you seem so interested in your father I wonder if you'd like the letters he sent me while I was in America?'

'Gosh, yes, that would be great, Clarissa, if you don't mind.'

'When I cleared out after our mother died, I found he had kept the letters we sent him too, well, not so much kept, as didn't throw away. I suppose I shouldn't have taken them, but they were mixed up in a box with other things which I took back to Dublin. I meant to return them to your father but I forgot all about it. I came across them again just before the anniversary when looking for old photographs to show Emma and Baby of us all as children. I didn't read them as they weren't mine. I suppose I should have burned them really but, in all honesty, I have a lot of difficulty in getting rid of things. Emma is always threatening to come over and have a bonfire. But if you would like them?'

Before her aunt could change her mind, Aoife insisted she would love the letters and Clarissa promised to send them by post when she had a chance.

It was beginning to spit rain so Aoife got the doorman to hail a taxi for Clarissa. When it arrived, they hugged goodbye, and Aoife waved her off.

The school was deserted when she arrived back to pick up her car. On the way back to the flat, she reflected on what she had learned about her father. He seemed more elusive than ever. The man Clarissa described was a sad loner living with a hard, tyrannical mother who seemed incapable of showing any affection to her children. It was nuts: Manus would have been a toddler when his father died. God, it must have been hard watching all your siblings escape, leaving you trapped with a woman who treated you like a slave. Could all that loneliness and darkness have soured him, have created a monster? And what happened between him and Emma? If she didn't have the diary poisoning her perceptions, she would feel very sorry for him and curious about his inability to forgive Emma. She would have to find an opportunity to talk to Emma and get her to own up to what happened all those years ago. Perhaps she could get her drunk. The silliness of the idea lightened her sombre mood and almost made her smile – almost.

CHAPTER 12

There was a theatre group visiting the school on Friday and, by a stroke of luck, most of her classes were scheduled to watch the performance. It was a restful day and the performance by the theatre company was watchable and quite amusing. The students certainly enjoyed it, judging by their rapt attention and uncontrollable giggles.

When the school day ended, she stayed back to catch up on some work in her classroom. The principal, Liam Deasy, stuck his head around the door.

'Still at it, Aoife? I thought all of you young ones had better things to do on a Friday evening than marking copies?'

'Well, I'm only staying so I can get all my work done and enjoy my weekend. But I'll probably head shortly.'

'By the way, I wanted to check that you applied for the post of responsibility that's coming up.'

'Oh yeah, I did, ages ago. When are the interviews?'

'Sorry, I have no idea, but the Board should be in touch soon with times and dates. Anyway, I'm glad you applied. Have an enjoyable weekend.'

'You too, Liam.'

Aoife had applied for a promotion shortly after she got engaged. So much had happened since then that she had forgotten all about it. She scanned through her application: it read well, and she had upskilled herself enough to impress the interview board. But her enthusiasm had waned. The very thought of having to spout educational jargon and aspirational gunk made her tired.

Recalling her afternoon with Clarissa, she was disappointed it hadn't revealed as much as she had hoped. Clarissa seemed fond of her brother. Surely she'd have noticed if he had psychopathic tendencies? The picture she painted of him was of a lonely figure, craving love and attention and getting neither. Why had his mother treated him so badly? Aoife was convinced that Clarissa wasn't telling her something – that she was being evasive. Also, the question remained: what did Manus have against Emma, and what did she do to upset him? She tried to recall any memories of Emma visiting when her father was still alive. But although she recalled the aunts arriving and being fussed over by her mam, she had no memory of her father and his sisters together. Looking back, it was almost as though he avoided them. Perhaps the letters Clarissa promised would give her some fresh perspective on her father's inner life.

The tin box and its contents remained undisturbed over the weekend. Aoife felt that if she read another piece of the diary, it would compel her to tell someone, so she avoided it and her empty flat. It was a relief to accept Sorcha's invitation to stay over with her on Saturday night. She planned to avoid Connor and his calls – which was easy as there were none.

It was infuriating to be ignored by someone that you are trying to avoid, she explained to Sorcha while sitting drunk and lopsided on the floor to where she had slipped for the third time.

'You see, Sorch, we're jush not combitable, I mean combatbabl,' she slurred as she tried to get up. 'Anyway, you know what I mean, don't ya?'

'Of course I know. Why don't you stay seated on the floor, pet – it's far comfier than the couch. Are you sure you wouldn't like something to eat?'

'I'm not hungry. I'm thirsty, very, very thirsty – give us over the old vino, Sorcha. You do know that you're my very, very, very bestest friend? I don't need Connor cos I've got you. Watz that song, come on, watz it called, you know the one?'

'I have no idea, but I do know you are going to feel horrible in the morning if you don't eat something, or at least drink some water.'

'*I got you, babe, I got you, babe* – that's the one. Hey, I got you, babe, and I don't need anyone else, especially not stinky Connor.' Aoife continued to warble the song with a total disregard for keeping in tune.

Eventually, at about three in the morning, Sorcha half dragged, half carried her onto the couch and removed her shoes, covered her with a blanket, and placed a basin next to her on the floor. This proved to be an excellent move as she was incapable of making it to the bathroom and was explosively sick when Sorcha shoved it under her face. She threw up twice more during the night with Sorcha holding her hair back as she retched in agony over the toilet bowl. Her friend walked her back to the couch and placed a cool face flannel on her forehead. Finally, in the wee hours, she attained the oblivion of sleep.

Dimly, as she drifted away, she heard Sorcha say. 'Man, you are going to wish you were dead when that head wakes you tomorrow.'

* * *

The screeching noise of birds, cars, footsteps, shouts and a cacophony of other painful auditory stimuli assaulted Aoife, just as a spear of sunlight escaping through a gap in the curtains blinded her.

'*Oh my God, I think I'm going to die, oh I want to die, please someone kill me, put me down,*' she whispered through parched lips as Sorcha leaned over her. '*Please, whatever you do, do not in the name of God open that curtain – there is a nuclear event outside and the flash may just incinerate me.*'

Sorcha giggled, 'I tried to warn you. I even hid the fourth bottle of wine but you wrestled me for it,' she said, smirking.

Aoife forced herself to swallow two paracetamol, promptly threw up and staggered back to the couch and stared at the ceiling, willing herself to die. Eventually she fell asleep.

The sound of her friend bustling about in the kitchen awakened her. Gingerly, opening one eye and glancing at her watch, she saw it was three in the afternoon.

Grunting, she got out of bed and stumbled to the shower. The tepid water did nothing to comfort her, but at least she felt clean and awake. In the kitchen, the smells and sounds of food cooking caused her stomach to lurch dangerously.

Sorcha, wrapped in an oversized chef's apron, greeted her cheerily and offered her a coffee from the pot on the table.

'God, no!' Aoife shuddered and poured a glass of water. 'Do you have any Lucozade?'

Sorcha shook her head. 'There might be some flat Coke in the fridge.'

Gratefully, Aoife drank the dark liquid Sorcha produced and promptly heaved it back up as soon as she made it to the bathroom toilet.

'OK, love, I think we write today off for you – back to bed with you. I'll draw the curtains and leave water for you. I think sleep is your only friend at the minute.'

Sorcha led her to her bedroom, opened the window and closed the curtains firmly so not even a chink of corrosive daylight entered the room. Then she crept away and shut the door quietly.

But sleep eluded Aoife. Her stomach churned, her head was one mass of pain. Even worse, this physical torment offered no protection against the onslaught of the twin agonies fermenting in her guts, Connor, and the bloody tin box. Her thoughts see-sawed between the two, making her relish the pain and vomiting which at least gave her respite from her thoughts. But eventually, mercifully, she drifted into a dreamless sleep.

Then it was Monday.

CHAPTER 13

Work was frantic. Someone pulled the fire alarm just after morning recess and, as teachers led students outside, it bucketed down with rain. The principal energetically signalled that it was a false alarm and by the time the wet, hyper students returned to class, Aoife was in a foul mood, her tolerance stretched to the limits by the reluctance of her students to return to work. They bitched about being cold and soaked to the skin and just when she finally got them settled, Tara O'Shaughnessy piped up.

'What happened to your ring, miss? Did ya lose it or something?'

Despite knowing she should just have ignored the comment, Aoife snapped, 'Why don't you mind your own business and get on with your work? You're always passing comments. Now be quiet and show me how you answered your homework, that's if you bothered to do it for a change.'

There was an astonished silence from the class and Tara coloured up and looked close to tears. Aoife realised she had gone too far, and this class was unused to being reprimanded so harshly. This overreaction would fuel endless speculation throughout the school. Aoife tried to make the rest of the class more pleasant and even made a point of being extra nice to Tara, praising her mediocre attempt at homework. But it was too late, and Tara wouldn't look at her except to sneak a scowl when she was passing. The bell for the end of class was rarely so welcome.

The rest of the day flew by because she kept busy, not even leaving her room for lunch. It annoyed her that she had forgotten to wear her ring. She should have realised a class full of teenage girls with romantic notions would notice her missing ring, but all she had to do was laugh and say she left it at home by mistake – instead she fuelled speculation by her over-reaction. She would have to wear it tomorrow.

Driving back to the flat, she wondered would Connor be there. Perversely, she hoped he was, but of course he wasn't. She felt a nagging sense of disappointment. Now that time had elapsed since their row and break-up, she had sobering time to regret and above all to realise how much she missed him. It was galling to realise how much a big wedding meant to her. Was she really so shallow? She had never thought of herself as being financially insecure, but she must be if she required a partner with a steady, well-paid job.

She fell in love with Connor because he was romantic and not interested in appearances, money, or living a structured life. He never pretended to be anything other than he was. It was she who changed the rules. In all honesty, she acknowledged that she never saw his poetry as something essential. She assumed it was a lovely hobby easily set aside while he got on with helping to secure a future for themselves and any children they might have. In retrospect, she knew he had never pretended that he wanted a regular job. He was always upfront about the things that were important to him. She realised she hadn't listened, or more accurately felt he would outgrow his romantic notions and buckle down to the reality of life just like his father and brother did. What a hypocrite she was to expect him to be a fraud, to just pay lip-service to his poetry, to treat it as a game, to be as materialistic and conventional as she! God, she missed him. Some of his things were still about the apartment like the leftovers of a brilliant party, reminders of funny tender moments, but like party detritus a sad reminder of the tidy-up ahead.

She had to be a grown-up – the tidy-up had to start. To begin with, she had to meet with him, preferably somewhere neutral, and discuss some way forward. Hesitantly, she called his mobile – of course, it went to voicemail. His cheery voice sliced through her heart.

'Hi, Connor, it's me ... I wonder can we meet up? There are things we need to discuss. Call me when you get a chance. OK! Bye!' She felt pleased that she left a brief coherent message. It was neutral and open-ended, so hopefully she'd hear from him soon.

Ten minutes later she called again. This time he answered.

'Hi there, I don't know if you got my message?'

'Yeah, I just heard it.'

'Well, do you want to meet me?'

There was a painfully long pause and then, 'Doyle's tomorrow at seven, OK?' He ended the call. He had sounded business-like, almost indifferent.

It was only five and there was a long evening to put in. She didn't want to call Sorcha again. With no better options available, she spent a couple of hours marking papers and doing prep for school in the morning. Then she made some dinner – an omelette that she overcooked, so it tasted rubbery in her mouth. Connor was a much better cook, but she would have to work on that skill if she ever wanted to enjoy food again. Sighing heavily, she switched on the TV, but all the soaps paled when matched against the melodrama that was her life. She watched a thriller she had heard was good but twenty minutes in she realised she didn't have a clue what was happening in it. Her head was in a vortex, and she felt herself slipping into a loop of regret and rage that made her feel desperate and ill. She switched off the TV and debated going online, but Facebook and Instagram and their faux-world community sickened her, and how would she respond to chat about her wedding? They had sent out Save the Date emails, and she knew her friends would want to hear about plans, dresses, and venue. There was only one way to deal with her head tonight, distract it with something even more horrific than a broken relationship and a wedding that needed cancelling.

She spent a few minutes staring at the box before opening it. She remembered as a child breaking her mother's favourite ornament – a pretty shepherdess – and how she put the broken pieces carefully into a shoebox and closed the lid. Earnestly, she whispered some prayers and a few magic words, hoping desperately for a miracle. Eagerly next morning she opened the shoebox, wishing hard that either the magic or prayers had worked. Of course, they hadn't. Her mother had been more sad than angry. She had wished her mam had punished her because it couldn't have hurt more than her sadness did. She felt the same way now. *Please let this be a joke, a piece of creative writing by my dad,* she prayed. But, as she reached into the box, she felt the same sense of sick disappointment as she viewed the contents.

It happened again: I've had two years of happiness with my girl, but then she got pregnant again. I worked hard this time, determined that things would be different. But with each passing month of the pregnancy, I felt her withdraw to some secret place where I couldn't find her. I was lost again in a cold, colourless world where my only function was to work and sleep. It was worse after the baby came. Just hold on, I told myself, she will come back to you. Once the baby is older and not so dependent on her, she'll be my girl again. But I feared that would never happen. A. seemed so listless, saving any pale animation for the new baby. The dreary days continued until I felt I was going mad. The silence scalded. Once more the Harpy rode on my back like a scold. I thought with death her hold would diminish. But the victory I felt when I saw her lying mouth agape on her bed was an illusion. For I now know, I carry her like a canker, rotting me from within.

Then it happened – release. I was driving the van, and I saw her. She was a pale, pretty little thing standing waiting for a bus. She beckoned me over and asked me if I had seen the bus she was waiting for pass by earlier, as she was worried she had missed it. I asked her where she wanted to go and offered her a lift, pretending it was on my way. I told her where I parked the car and that I would meet her after I bought a newspaper. I didn't want anyone to see me go off with her.

Aoife's stomach lurched with horror.

From the moment I saw her, I knew she would reach out to me, speak to me, and ask me for help. I wasn't the active agent, she was. Did I intend then to do what I did? I don't know. I hadn't planned it. It was all a happy accident meeting up with her, like a gift horse in truth. She chatted away in the van about her boyfriend and their plans to marry. It surprised me as she seemed so young. She had a tattoo of a red heart on her shoulder. It irritated me to see her spoiling her body with such childishness. I hoped none of my children would ever desecrate their bodies in such a manner.

After a while, I zoned her voice out as I worked out my options. I needed to get off the main road, so I turned off down a small country road. She caught my sleeve and asked why I was going off the main road. I muttered something about a shortcut, and it seemed to reassure her. She chattered on for a bit, but she must have noticed my silence because I sensed her mounting nervousness. She clutched the door handle, and I knew I needed to calm her. I told her I was nervous as I had noticed I was about to run out of petrol. Shortly after I stopped the car. I got out and asked her to get out too to help flag down another car to get us to a garage.

She looked relieved that my silence was so easily explained and, as soon as she stepped out of the car, I caught her to me and squeezed.

Oh God, no! This can't be true. Despite the warmth of the room, an icy chill ran through Aoife's body.

The skin of her bare arms felt soft, she struggled, I eased up and almost let her go but then when she thought she was getting away I squeezed again, catching her by her little bird throat. Releasing and squeezing slowly until eventually I had finished with her. I didn't rush. I wanted to savour it all. She drooped limply in my arms, and I sat in the hedge out of sight of the road and held her until her body began to lose its warmth. It was nice sitting screened by my car holding her close, enjoying her, caressing her. But I knew someone could come along any time, so I took the spade from the boot and hefted her on my shoulder. She was so slight it was not difficult to carry her into the bog and, with the soft earth, it was easy to bury her. I'm not sure I could find where I put her again.

Afterwards, I shuddered at the chance I took. Anyone could have passed by. But then again, it confirmed my belief in the fitness of my path. It was she who sought me out.

That night, lying beside A. drinking in the fresh clean smell of her, I felt restored. All would be well now, wouldn't it?

Aoife stared at the question mark in horror. She shut the diary and returned it to the box. She couldn't read any more, and the thought of having it in the room with her was repulsive. She locked it in the drawer of her work desk in the living room. Shaking out a sleeping tablet, she dragged herself to bed, put on her headphones, and listened to a podcast about fly-fishing. The monotony of the subject and the drone of the presenters eventually lulled her to sleep.

CHAPTER 14

The beeping of her alarm clock dragged Aoife into consciousness. Briefly, she debated calling in sick but feared adding petrol to the rumours of her broken engagement, no doubt fuelled by Tara and her ilk. This thought forced her to shower and scramble into her clothes. *Keep things in the present,* she counselled herself, *don't think any further than the present moment.* She took the precaution of putting on her engagement ring, to dampen down any speculation.

Her first meeting of the morning was with the IT teacher, a woman who had all the subtlety of a basking shark. She gave Aoife a once-over before her mean little eyes fastened hungrily on her left hand. She looked disappointed. Obviously, the gossip mill had spread from the student body to the staffroom. This copper-fastened Aoife's decision to avoid the staffroom and head straight for class. During the lesson, she used as many opportunities as possible to display her ring – so lots of whiteboard work – she never felt glad she was a leftie until today.

By the end of the day, Aoife had quelled curiosity and satisfied or disappointed the rumour mill, depending on their viewpoint. She decided not to bring any marking home with her but stay back to get on top of it. At five thirty she was ready to leave.

On the drive home, her stomach churned at the thought of meeting with Connor. She had just enough time to shower and grab something to eat before heading to Doyle's. As she dressed – jeans and jumper (she wanted to look relaxed and casual even if she wasn't feeling it) – she debated what to say to him, but her brain, stalled by her anxiety, refused to cooperate.

Doyle's was close to her flat, and she was there a little early. A quick scan revealed it was empty, not just of Connor but of any customers. *Shit!* She was hoping for a bit of noise and activity as a backdrop to their meeting. She ordered a G&T and found a seat at the back of the gloomy room. Usually, it seemed atmospheric not gloomy – was her mood affecting how she saw the interior? Or perhaps it was always this dispiriting and she just previously blocked it out in a haze of alcohol and happiness?

At the rear of the pub, she sat and waited.

Connor arrived at ten past seven, looking tired and crumpled but achingly familiar.

Her heart and stomach collided at the sight of him.

'Sorry, I got delayed. Can I get you a fresh drink?'

Aoife shook her head.

When he came back from the bar, he slipped into the seat beside her, not across from her as she was expecting. Sitting so close she could feel the warmth of his body. They both sat silently for an agonising while.

'You look tired – tough day at school?'

'Yeah, it was,' she mumbled.

Silence resumed and, feeling suffocated by its weight, in desperation she blurted, 'I suppose we should talk about what we're going to do.'

He didn't respond. He looked away and then down at her hand.

'I see you're still wearing the ring. I thought you'd have chucked that by now.'

Aoife flushed with annoyance. '*Here, take it!*' she snapped, dragging it off her finger, slamming it down on the table where it promptly bounced off. Their heads smacked as they both dived under the table to retrieve it.

They laughed, and the tension dissipated.

He handed her back the ring. 'What in the name of God would I do with that? I'm not planning to reuse it, ya know? I'd like you to keep it, really I would.'

'You could sell it and at least recover some of its value.'

'No, Aoife, I already got its value.'

Mutely she lifted the glimmering ring and dropped it in her bag.

'I suppose we'd better make some decisions,' she said.

'Why? What's the hurry? Why can't we just take a breather and work things out later?' he countered.

'Because we have to let people know – the hotel, the band, our folks and all the guests who may already have bought gifts. It's only a few months away. We can't leave people in ignorance.'

'I don't suppose you've changed your mind about us staying together and postponing the wedding? I love you, Aoife, that hasn't changed. I want to be with you always. There's been no one else I've ever felt this way about. Are you saying that you've stopped caring about me?'

He stared into her eyes and for a moment she melted, but only for a moment.

'Connor, what's the point of rehashing things? We have different ideas of what our lives should be. I wish I could say I was OK about you taking casual work so that you can work on your writing, but I know I'd resent you. Equally, I don't want you to resent me for having to let go of your dreams. It's only now I realise how different we are. I want a conventional secure life, a steady job, a house and a family. I guess I'm boringly conventional.'

'But I want a family too. We can make it work, I know we can. I'll still bring in money, we can still do the things you want, and I can still do what's important to me.'

'Connor, I know you mean that right now but, if you have to help support a family, it will be impossible to do that in part-time work where you can be let go at a moment's notice. I need security and, I'll be honest, I don't want to have to struggle to make ends meet. I wish I wasn't so boring and middle-class in my expectations, but I am.' Her eyes filled up and she stopped talking.

They sat in silence.

'So that's it then?' he said, his voice sharp with disappointment.

'Yes, I think it is.'

The silence between them once more grew oppressive and Aoife rushed to break through it by dealing with practicalities.

'Look, the first thing we have to do is tell our families. I'll contact mine tomorrow evening and, if you do it at the same time, we won't have anyone feeling offended about being the last to know.'

'Well, at least your ones will sigh with relief that you've got the "waster" off your hands. I bet there'll be rejoicing in the O'Driscoll family when they get the news.'

'That's not fair, Connor – you know they're very fond of you.'

'Sure, but they never thought I was good enough for you, whereas my family thought I was in clover when I met you. They finally thought I had become a sensible lad just like my brother.'

'Please, Connor, let's not do this. We have so many things to sort out. I've drawn up a list of what we need to do. Tell me what you're willing to do, and we can get things started.'

'Finished, you mean!' Connor stated bleakly. 'OK, I'll cancel the band and the hotel if that's what you want. You know we'll lose our deposit, don't you?'

'Yes, I do. I'll draw up a draft email to send to the guests and return any gifts and contact florists, car hire and cancel my dress appointment.'

'OK.'

'The last thing to sort is the flat.' she said. 'Neither of us can afford to keep it on alone. What do you think we should do?'

Connor smiled grimly. 'Well, you've already kicked me out, so I assumed you'd find one of your buddies to move in.'

'That's not fair, Connor! I was angry at the time, but I knew you could stay with family, or they'd fix something up for you – after all, they are estate agents and your brother has property. I figured they would help you out.'

'I'm not in the business of asking my family for favours. You keep the flat and I'll pay my share of the rent until you get someone to move in.'

'But where will you stay?'

'Don't worry, I have a few possibilities – just keep any belongings until I can move them, OK?'

'OK.'

'I'd better get on now,' he muttered.

Awkwardly they both stood, avoiding each other's eyes, and then simultaneously they reached for each other. It was a tight, silent embrace and Aoife felt her insides dissolve and her heart hammered so loud she thought the barman could hear it.

Connor buried his face in her hair. 'I love you, I love you,' he whispered, his breath hot against her ear.

Aoife felt her throat close over and could only gulp, 'Me, too.'

Then, abruptly, he released her and strode to the door without looking back. She slumped back on the seat and felt the scalding tears roll down her face. Stumbling through the mist in her eyes, she made her way to the Ladies', sat on a toilet seat, and howled as silently as she could into wadded-up toilet paper. Snot and tears covered her face. When the worst of the tsunami had subsided, she went to the sink to wash her ravaged face. Getting the mascara rivulets to disappear with only tissue and water wasn't easy as the soap-dispenser was empty. Eventually she decided that, although she didn't look presentable, her face was clean and that was the best she could ask for right now.

CHAPTER 15

The following morning, Aoife again considered taking the day off, but the thought of spending the day with nothing to distract her from thoughts of Connor but the diary drove her to abandon that idea.

Mercifully, the working day flew by, and she avoided the staff room, ducking the usual wedding chit-chat which was the hot topic of conversation as two other young teachers were planning their weddings too. The thought of all the excited chatter and comparing notes sickened her. Was it only last week that she had been the chief initiator of such conversations? It entered her head that everything in her life had imploded the day she opened the tin box and saw the diary. Its malign presence had enveloped her world, poisoning it.

Back at the flat, she checked her phone and saw five missed calls from Sorcha. She quickly texted to say she was fine and would be in touch. She had Cornflakes and chocolate for dinner and, opening a bottle of wine, decided she'd better get on with telling her mother about the cancelled wedding.

The phone in her mother's hallway barely had time to ring before being answered.

'It's lovely to hear from you so early in the week. How's work going, pet?'

Her mam's voice was warm with affection.

'Work is grand, Mam, same old same old. How are you? I bet you're exhausted after the weekend. Maybe next year we could have the meet-up in Kate's place and give you a bit of a break.'

'You must be joking! How old do you think I am? I'm not in my dotage yet and I'm more than able to organise a bit of food for the family.'

'OK, OK, I get it, you're a tough woman. I just worry about you, that's all!' Aoife paused and then continued, 'Mam, I've got a bit of news for you.'

Before she could elaborate, her mother burst out, 'Are you pregnant, love? Is that the news? I thought you looked peaky the last time I saw you.'

'No, Mam, I'm not pregnant. Look, Connor and I've been talking, and we've called the wedding off.' She heard her mother gasp. 'It's fine, really it is. We both felt for a while that we were making a mistake, that we weren't best suited for marriage. I'm mean, better to realise it now than after we got married.'

'But, Aoife, you seemed so well-matched, so happy in each other's company. Did he do something wrong – see someone on the side or something?'

'No, Mam, there's nobody else for either of us. We just didn't want the same things.'

'Oh, love, I'm so sorry, I truly am. Is there any chance that you'll change your minds at all?'

'No, Mam, we're cancelling things. In fact, will you give me Father Francis's number so that I can let him know?'

'Don't worry yourself about that. I'll let him know tomorrow when I'm at the parish council meeting.'

'Thanks, Mam, I'd appreciate that. I'd hate having to explain it all to him.'

They talked a little more before wishing each other goodnight. The call re-energised Aoife and she quickly drafted an email to send to all her wedding guests, informing them that regretfully the wedding of Connor and Aoife would not take place. After staring at it for ten minutes, she hit send. She visualised all the comments people would make on receiving the missive. Some would be tantalised and make up scenarios for what went wrong but most would be genuinely sorry and surprised.

Well, they'd done it. No going back now. She heard her mobile ping and saw a message from Connor. He had cancelled the hotel and band. As expected, they lost their deposit. She slumped on her couch and stared at his message on her mobile. It was strange, emailing guests and telling her mother had been difficult but seeing the words **'hotel cancelled'** set her stomach clenching and made hot tears pool in her eyes. She tapped out a reply, telling him she had told her mother and had emailed guests and that her mother would inform the priest. When she finished, she poured herself another drink and turned on the TV. Flicking from channel to channel and finding nothing to interest or distract, she switched off in defeat.

With dragging feet, she went to her work desk and fetched the box. She picked up each of its contents. What did they signify? She tried on the Claddagh ring, but it was too small for her ring finger. Who did it belong to? She returned it to the box, carried the notebook over to the couch and read.

Life continues to surprise me. People more than life, in truth. Take A., she's never been happier. She thinks I'm happy because her depression has lifted. She knows, of course, that I find the noise of babies, the demands, the smells difficult but she doesn't realise it's the loss of her that destroys me. If she were less of a devoted mother, it wouldn't matter. But once a baby arrives, no, even beforehand, I lose her.

When she is expecting, her anticipatory excitement makes me feel diminished, invisible even. She had been quieter this pregnancy. I think she was afraid of becoming flat and depressed again. When our little girl was born, she was worse, lower than I've ever seen her. The silence was roaring in my head again and I felt such anger towards the new interloper. I feel ashamed now when I see our wee angel.

I didn't feel invisible or diminished after 'that glorious day' — at least for a while. I felt calm, powerful, and truly able to be the man A. wants by her side.

Once they grow up a bit, I quite like the children. The lad's a great wee fellow. I can see a bit of myself in him — already he shows signs of being good with his hands, he's always making things with his marla, and you can see he's a born farmer. He follows me around the farm like a good one. A. gets so nervous when I take him up with me on the tractor but, at only six, he's already watching to see how to drive it. If it wasn't for him being too small to reach the pedals, I'd have to hide the keys.

As for my wee princess, I can see C. in her. She's so gentle and caring. I remember catching a wild baby rabbit once and taking it home for the young ones to see. Her brother grabbed it and would have squeezed the life out of it in his excitement, but she shouted at him to let it go free and she made me promise not to catch any more 'bunnies' as she calls them. She's a wee softie! She cried over that animal, terrified he'd not be able to find his mammy. I had to make up a story to comfort her about seeing the mother rabbit meeting up with him in the top field. It was the only way to get her to go to sleep. Her Auntie C was just like that, tender-hearted and innocent.

If A. knew how high the price was for me and the 'others', she would never have brought these little ones into the world, but then a life without her children would have been annihilation for her. She was made for motherhood. What could I do?

Aoife's mouth dried up and her flesh tightened against her bones. From her reading, it seemed her father killed someone whenever his wife was pregnant. The awful realisation hit her. Did he kill someone when her mother was carrying her? The thought made her stomach lurch. What should she do? The idea of reading any further, of finding out if the horrible book was going to reveal the death of some poor girl simply on account of her arrival into the world appalled her. Stumbling to her drinks cabinet, she poured herself another drink and went back to the couch.

With a rock in her stomach, she turned the page.

Life became wonderful again. There was a bit in the news about a missing girl but, because the body wasn't found, talk soon died out. I was both disappointed and relieved at its disappearance. I felt she hadn't got her due, and I missed the talk and speculation. I realised how lucky I was not to have been seen. There was a terrible moment when someone reported her getting into a van. But their description of the van was way off. They even got the colour wrong. But she had served her purpose, and I felt lighter, stronger, and better able to be a good husband and father. I kept back my keepsakes from each event, and I got great pleasure and peace from holding them, closing my eyes, and remembering every precious moment. They were holy relics that I kept hidden. Each time I felt the darkness and the doubts, I sat holding them until a calmness returned. My little travelling companion bequeathed to me her Claddagh ring. Its gold glinted in the sunlight on her little pale hand. I thought of her fondly whenever I held it. I wondered when I would need to renew myself again.

Shaking with revulsion, Aoife threw the diary on the desk and took two paracetamols, washing them down with brutally strong whiskey. Hoping for oblivion, she dragged herself to bed.

CHAPTER 16

She got little sleep that night. Staring at the ceiling, her stomach sick, her eyes scorching in her head, too terrified to close them, afraid of what images would burn the backs of her eyelids. It was a relief when it got light, and she could shower and get to work. Suddenly being the subject of gossip regarding her broken engagement was trivial and of no importance. If the contents of the diary got out, if the world knew that her father was a serial killer, then she would have something to worry about. On impulse, she rang in sick and decided that she would finish reading the diary and face up to whatever her father was, however grotesque.

She made herself some coffee, sat down at the desk and stared at the tin box as if contemplating hell. Steeling herself, she opened it and picked up the diary from where it lay looking so innocent and banal. So far it appeared as though a death followed each of her mother's pregnancies. Now she would have to find out if her entry into the world heralded the destruction of some poor girl. The diary appeared to have no time frame and, although it detailed two killings, it also hinted at something from the time before he married. As she glanced at the page, she noticed that the writing was less neat and cramped and more hurried and sprawling.

It's been a long time since I've visited my book of secrets. I've had no cause for a while to rid myself of the tension. But recently I've found a way of expanding my territory should I need to. My two little friends disappeared too close to home. I can't take risks now, not with everything going so well. But I know that when the Harpy rides on my shoulders and the world is too tight to bear, I have my means of healing. I feel excited by the prospects ahead.

A. has been busy for days, preparing for the visit of my sisters. They come as a pack, like a virus settling in. I don't mind C., but E. is a bossy, opinionated snob. I hate the way she lords it over my girl, acting as though A. is an intruder in our home. She constantly talks of the Harpy, but she calls her 'Mama' like she is some Edwardian miss. Bleating that Mama would do this, and Mama would do that. It makes my teeth grate and I have to leave the house to cool off. As for B., she was a whining spoiled brat as a child and now she's a whining, whinging pain as an adult. A. waits on them hand and foot. If I didn't stop her, she'd bring them breakfast in bed. They never ask A. about herself. It's like they think we have no life of our own, and it's their job to bring the light and colour of their world into ours. Each year they arrive, I dread it more. Even the children hate them coming. S. flinches as they slobber over him with their bright lipsticked mouths, ready to pounce and make their imprint on his pale little face. If he tries to avoid contact, they insist and force the boy to accept their vile slobbering. He can't wait to get away and scrub the sticky colour from his face. As for the poor wee princess, they are constantly lecturing her on how a young lady should behave as if either of those two eejits would know. Poor little pet, I offer her asylum in the henhouse by giving her jobs to do that will keep her as far away from them as possible. They're coming tomorrow afternoon. I have to pick them up from the train station, as if I haven't enough to do.

How will I tolerate this visit? E. is starting to look more and more like the Harpy. If she's not careful, maybe she'll end up the same way! She better not start issuing orders if she knows what's good for her. C. tries to act as though we're the best of friends but we both know this is a LIE. B. I tolerate like a foul stench in the knowledge that it will soon pass.

Noticing that the following pages of the notebook were stuck together, Aoife went to get a nail file to separate them. By dint of careful effort, she parted the pages. To her astonishment, everything between the stuck pages had been ripped out. She counted the torn fragments; fourteen pages were missing. The remainder of the notebook was blank. Tears of frustration stung her eyes. What had happened? What was in those missing pages and why had her father ripped them out? If indeed he had.

She reread the diary. Once more she tried frantically to convince herself that the diary was a work of fiction. But it contained too many references to actual people and events. The initials used were those of his sisters and his son and daughter. A. had to be Agnes. It was impossible to deny that her father had written it, but perhaps it was a coping mechanism, an outlet for her father whenever he felt overwhelmed. He suffered from the legacy of an abusive relationship with a very controlling mother, and the pressure of family life made him feel unable to cope, so he invented a means of releasing his pent-up emotions. He imagined killing these girls and that imagining allowed him to be a good family man.

It was like a man who turned to violent porn to cope with a sex life that wasn't fulfilling his needs. He would never act out the dark fantasies in the real world. No, he wouldn't, couldn't! Her father didn't live in the time of online fantasy sites, so he created his own weird but essentially harmless world. Possibly he injected realism by latching on to actual disappearances of girls and making himself the star of the drama.

Desperately, Aoife tried to cling on to this explanation. She didn't know her father well, but the idea of him killing people was ludicrous. It was unfortunate that she'd ever found the diary. This raised another question – who buried the diary? Why not simply destroy it? She had no answers. Still, her theory of her father imagining killing women to help him cope with his frustrations, although repellent, was something she could choose to live with as any other explanation was unbearable. But an insistent voice buried in the depths of her mind asked: 'What about the trinkets?' She knew the dolphin belonged to the girl called Anika and the other girl killed wore a Claddagh ring. These so-called keepsakes were in the box. Were these trinkets part of his sick fantasies? But did these girls actually exist? This was another question she couldn't answer.

And what did he mean about Emma ending up the same way as the Harpy? The diary said his mother died in the summer. Aoife leafed through the pages, her stomach clenched. She read over the passages about the mother's death. Was there a suggestion he had done away with his mother? He referred to her helplessness with pleasure. And the gloating way he described her lying dead on the bed after eating her last meal was sinister. Oh God, could he have murdered his mother? From what she knew of that woman she could hardly mourn her, but yet to kill your mother!

She poured herself a large glass of wine. This was crazy – rushing from one bizarre theory to another and without any real evidence.

She was spending too much time alone with this. It was time to bring in a fresh perspective. She decided to ring Kate to persuade her to meet up in the city. Her busy sister occasionally escaped family commitments and came to Dublin for some retail therapy. Kate was happy to hear from her and agreed to pop up on the train to meet her on Friday evening. Aoife even managed to persuade her to stay over until Saturday evening so there would be lots of time to talk. Kate probably thought her little sister wanted to talk about her broken engagement. She felt duplicitous letting Kate believe this, but she badly needed to talk to her – to sound her out about their father, perhaps even to reveal what she had learned about him. Sipping her now lukewarm coffee, Aoife debated over what she would reveal. Perhaps she would play things by ear – no point in upsetting her sister when she didn't need to.

She thought again about her explanation for her father's diary confession. If it was a fantasy, then what did the items in the box represent? She went back to her desk and looked at the innocuous biscuit tin again. It was old, and most of the lettering faded away. She couldn't tell the brand of biscuits. She removed its contents and examined them. The little dolphin earring was cheap and made of hard plastic. It was cute but unremarkable. The Claddagh ring was a little dull, but she could tell that it was gold. Reluctantly she tried it on her little finger. She shivered and wrenched it off. The scarf felt like silk but it was synthetic; the colour was bright, gay, against the cold metal of the box interior. She examined the tube of lipstick, a bright pink, but couldn't bring herself to rub it on her skin. The most sinister item was the lock of dark hair tied with a shoelace.

Aoife desperately wanted to believe her reassuring explanation for the events described in the notebook, but her head presented her with insistent nagging doubts. Unless she made some effort to find out who owned these items, she might never sleep again. She could at least find out if girls went missing around the time of Sam's birth. She had all day to fill in, so why not investigate? Her laptop took a while powering up and then she typed, '**missing women in Ireland**' on the search engine. She clicked on a Garda website and saw lists of men and women missing in Ireland over several decades. As she read through the various cases, she felt sickened at the possibility that her father could be responsible for some of them. In recent years, many of the missing men and women were foreign nationals. What human tragedy lay behind their disappearance?

She searched back through the years. 1978 was the year Sam was born so she checked out that list.

Her heart stopped when she saw the name Anika and looked at the smiling face of a young girl. That was the name her father mentioned in the diary. So, the name in the diary was related to a real girl who went missing. Did that mean her father was responsible for her death? It would be comforting to believe he just borrowed from reality but she could feel her hope ebbing. She stared at the beaming face and felt her stomach lurch as she noticed a dolphin earring dangling from one ear. Fighting the need to be physically sick, her unwilling eyes read over the details. The girl was Dutch; she went missing whilst backpacking in Ireland in April 1978. She scoured the internet for any more details. She came across accounts in local and national papers. It all fitted – her nationality, her name. God, even the dates fitted. Sam was born on the 3rd of April. Everything in the diary was true. Her mother was busy with her first child and had no time for her husband. He felt alienated and angry. Instead of showing his anger to Agnes or their child, he vented all his poison on an innocent stranger. This time she couldn't hold back as the contents of her stomach met her teeth.

CHAPTER 17

Garda Siochána
Missing Persons

Anika Bakker from Middleberg, Holland
Date: Missing since 26th April 1978
Born: 24/4/1955
Age: 23 years
Height: 5ft 7
Hair: brown
Eyes: brown
Build: slight
Nationality: Dutch

Anika was on a backpacking holiday around Ireland. She arrived on the 24th of April and spent two nights in Dublin in a city-centre hostel. On the 26th of April, she travelled by train to Sligo, intending to explore the northwest of the country. She had made plans to meet friends in Galway on Thursday the 4th of May. When she failed to turn up, her friends became concerned and contacted her family in Holland. The Garda were contacted, and Anika was reported as missing.

The last sighting of Anika was on Thursday the 26th of April, on the Sligo/Bundoran road. She was observed attempting to hitch a lift. Anika was wearing a bright-blue ski jacket and carrying a dark-coloured rucksack. If anyone has any information on the whereabouts of Anika, please contact the Garda station in Sligo or the Garda Confidential Line.

Aoife put the missing girl's name in the search engine and found newspaper reports that made her stomach twist.

Sligo Champion May 1978

Gardaí are appealing for the public's help in their search for a missing woman, Anika Bakker aged 23. She was last seen on the Sligo/Bundoran road on Thursday the 26th of April. Anika is a native of Middelburg, Holland. She is 5ft 7 tall, of slim build. She has brown eyes and long brown hair usually worn in plaits. When last seen, she was wearing blue jeans and a bright-blue ski jacket. Anika's family and friends are eager to hear news of her whereabouts. If you have any information, please contact the Garda Station in Sligo, or ring the Garda Confidential Line.

Sligo Champion July 1978

Vigil for Missing Backpacker

A candlelit vigil will be held on Thursday, 7th July at 7 pm in the Wine St car park in memory of Anika Bakker. Anika has been missing for over two months. The local community will be joined by the family and friends of the missing woman. Local priests and ministers will lead prayers for her safe return. Organisers of the vigil say they want to show their solidarity with her distraught family and friends. Anika was last seen on the 26th of April and despite an extensive Garda search has not been located.

Irish Times 1978

Anguish of Family of Missing Backpacker

Anika Bakker, a graduate of Groningen University in Holland, went missing while on holiday in Ireland. She arrived in Dublin on the 24th of April and contacted her parents to say she planned to stay for a few nights in a city-centre hostel. The hostel confirmed her arrival, and the staff and fellow hostellers remember her talking of plans to travel to the west of the country. On Thursday the 26th of April she took the morning train to Sligo. She had told friends that she wished to spend a few days travelling around the northwest of the country, arranging to meet up with them in Galway on May 4th. When she failed to arrive, they contacted the local Garda. Anika has not been located to date.

Irish Times 1987

Remembering Anika Bakker

Lotte Bakker, sister of missing backpacker Anika Bakker, speaks of the heartbreak endured by Anika's family since she went missing 10 years ago. Anika was just 22 when she planned to celebrate completing her degree in Economics at the University of Groningen by taking time off backpacking around Ireland. Ireland had a special place in her heart, and she had fond memories of holidaying with her parents in County Cork as a child. She arranged to spend a week on her own exploring the northwest of the country and planned to meet up after with old friends from university in Galway city. She rang her parents when she arrived in Ireland and told them she was staying in a Dublin city-centre hostel for two nights before catching the morning train to Sligo.

The hostel confirmed her arrival, and the staff and fellow hostellers remember her talking of her plans to travel to the west. She mentioned her desire to explore Donegal and Sligo and then travel on to Galway to meet friends. She was last seen wearing a bright-blue ski jacket on the Bundoran road at around midday. That is the last reported sighting of her.

Lotte says her family, particularly her mother, are heartbroken. Even though ten years have passed, her mother still cannot bring herself to give up hoping that her lovely girl will come home. Her father Pieter died two years ago and his wife, devastated by the loss of both husband and child, is desperate for any news about her eldest daughter. Lotte was a teenager when her sister went missing. She described Anika as a loving person, an animal lover and a keen athlete. She especially enjoyed swimming and surfing. Lotte said she looked up to her big sister and her loss has created a gaping hole in her life that is impossible to fill.

Anika had her entire life ahead of her. After completing her degree, she received many job offers before finally accepting a position in Amsterdam. She loved to travel and planned to save up for a trip to Southeast Asia.

Recently, her friends from school and college held a memorial to celebrate her life. It was a wonderful evening, a bittersweet experience for her family. She is gone, but not forgotten by her legions of friends.

Lotte believes that someone may have some information about her sister, and she begs them to come forward. 'What my family has endured is harrowing,' she said. 'My mother needs some peace, to know what has become of her beloved daughter. Her greatest fear is dying without knowing what happened to Anika.' Lotte asks anyone with any information to please come forward. 'Maybe you have noticed someone behaving oddly in the locality or even in your family. If you have any information at all, please bring it to the local Garda,' she implores.

She went on to say the Garda have been very supportive and the local community in Sligo and people throughout Ireland have shown great kindness to her family. She wanted to thank all those who wrote letters to comfort them.

Lotte consented to this interview, as anniversaries are opportunities to encourage members of the public to search their memories for any piece of information that might be useful.

Aoife couldn't bear to read any more. It was enough to know that the girl in the notebook was a real person with a life, a family and a future until she had the misfortune to meet Manus O'Driscoll. Her head began to spin, and the walls of the flat closed in on her until she was desperate to flee from it. But where to? Wherever she went, her thoughts and her dirty knowledge would follow her like a satanic shadow. Instead, she brought a bottle of wine to bed and drank straight from the bottle, staining the white sheets red as she gulped it down like medicine.

CHAPTER 18

After work the following day, Aoife prepared the guest room for Kate and made chilli for dinner. Her sister had got an afternoon train and hoped to be at her flat by seven at the latest. While cooking the rice, she contemplated what to say to Kate. Perhaps she should just get her talking about her childhood and how Dad had been as a parent. Referring to her father as 'Dad' now repulsed her. Her memories of him had been few but treasured and probably embellished with recalling.

It was like he was one of those creatures in video games her students played – Nephilim – half-demon half-angel. How did this monster square with the father she loved? She remembered helping him off with his wellies in the evening when he came in from the farm and him encouraging her to pull so hard that she fell over laughing. He had never spoken to her harshly and slipped her sweeties whenever she got a scolding from her mother. On reflection, he acted like a big brother, hiding her when she was in trouble and warning her when the annoying Baby was looking for her. These memories she had cherished, but she barely knew him. If she closed her eyes, the only other images that came were of his back as he headed out to the fields or him sitting watching the news as he smoked cigarette after cigarette. After her search online yesterday, she knew she should check out dates of girls missing around the time of her and Kate's birthdays, but she hadn't the stomach for it.

Her phone rang: it was Kate outside her flat. She raced downstairs to let her in.

After they hugged, Kate held her shoulders in her small capable hands and stared deep into her eyes as she asked, 'How are you coping, pet?'

For a terrifying moment Aoife thought that somehow Kate must have found out about the box, but then realised her sister was referring to her broken engagement.

'I'm fine, really I am. Come on in, I bet you're starving. How was it on the train?'

'Actually, the train was fine. I got a seat and even dozed off for an hour, so I feel great. What's for dinner? It certainly smells fantastic.'

Aoife cracked open the bottle of red that Kate had brought and got her sister to set the table while she dished up.

They chatted about their work and the family in Sligo until they finished eating.

'To tell the truth, I'm worried about Sam,' Kate confided as they brought their glasses of wine to the couch and sat, stretching their legs out.

'Why, is there something wrong with him?' Aoife asked sharply.

'Nothing I know about, but he hasn't been the same since Nell died. I suppose it was a reminder of when Polly died – you remember the collie Dad had. It died a few days after the funeral, and I remember how upset Sam was when he buried that dog. He showed more emotion about the dog than when he heard Dad died. I think the dog dying allowed him to express the pain of losing Dad.'

'Where was it buried, Kate?'

'I don't know – somewhere in the back garden. To be honest, everything was a bit of a blur back then. Can you remember Polly at all?'

Aoife had an image of an old dog stretched out in the sun beside her, as she lay on the grass reading a book about horses, one of her long-lost passions. Polly had been ancient and not like the playful puppy that she dreamed about. She had a vague memory of her father promising her a puppy whenever Polly passed away. He told her that poor Polly would be jealous if some young pup usurped her position in the family.

'Aye, I remember her, but she seemed so old and was always sleeping. I don't remember playing with her – she was just a presence in the yard.'

'Ah well, she was more of a working dog than a pet, but she was so attached to Daddy, always following him around the yard and greeting him every morning at the crack of day.'

'Did Sam and Dad get on well?'

Kate screwed up her face. 'It was a long time ago, Aoife. But, yeah, they got on well. They worked on the farm, and they went fishing sometimes.' She laughed wryly. 'To tell the truth, I was jealous cos they spent so much time together. I was a couple of years younger than Sam, and they always seemed to do stuff together. The year before Dad died, he used to take Sam on trips. I was a bit pissed off as I imagined Sam having adventures but, looking back, Sam wasn't in the best form after these outings, so they were probably a washout. I mean what a grown man finds interesting isn't necessarily going to appeal to a teenage boy, is it?' Aoife shook her head. 'I feel that I hardly knew

Dad. I was only ten when he died. I wish I knew what he was really like. You were about fifteen, so I expect you had a better sense of him.'

'Well, I have nice memories of him teaching me the names of trees and helping me collect flowers to press in my scrapbook. He encouraged me to look up their names. I think he bought me books about plants and flowers and birds. Remember, Aoife, he used to do the same with you. He was very interested in the natural world. Apart from the news, I think the only programmes he watched on TV were natural history ones. He was never into sports much. I think he used to watch with Sam, but I don't believe that he had any actual interest himself. Gosh, it's amazing what you remember when you get to talking!'

'Didn't you and Sam ever reminisce about Dad?'

Kate paused. 'Honestly, Sam never really wanted to talk about Dad. I think he felt guilty because Dad went off the day he died, and he never went after him. Perhaps he thought if he had been with Dad, then perhaps he could have saved him. I wonder sometimes whether they had words on the day he died because usually they were inseparable. It was rare for Dad to go off up the fields without Sam unless he was at school. In the last year of his life, he and Sam often went off together on what Dad called "adventures", but really I think they just went on trips to the marts or to buy machinery. Occasionally they stayed away till late and I got jealous, imagining they had wonderful escapades and I was excluded just because I was a girl. But after Dad died Sam wouldn't speak about him at all. He got angry whenever I talked about him. Nowadays, Sam would probably have been taken to a counsellor because he was so morose. It's a pity because before Dad died we were pretty close – at least we used to have a laugh and trade music magazines – but after the funeral he shut me out. Maybe he felt guilty for quarrelling with Dad – if they did.'

'What do you think they might have fought about?'

'Ah, it was probably nothing. Maybe Sam rebelled about helping Dad and acted like a typical teenager – I mean, he could be moody. I know he snapped at me often enough and made disparaging remarks about girls. But why all this sudden interest, kiddo?'

Aoife shrugged and changed the subject and they talked about a mutual friend who had been caught playing away by her fiancé when he returned early from a stag weekend. It was the talk of the locality. This gossip about broken romance brought to Kate's mind the romantic ruin of her sister, and the conversation took an annoying turn.

'Aoife, love, you must be so upset. Do you want to talk about Connor and the break-up?'

'It's OK. We both realised that we wanted different things in life. Seriously, there is no big story, no epic betrayal. We just realised that we had different expectations from married life.'

'Was it Connor's lack of a job, then?' Kate probed.

'That was part of it, but a lot more besides. I miss him, but better end things now than later when things got messy.'

'Kenny and I nearly broke up before our wedding.'

'I never knew that! What happened?'

'It was another girl. I mean, nothing happened between them. She was a blast from his past, a musician. I think he was in more love with the lifestyle she offered than her. Her career was flourishing, and she wanted him to be her manager. I knew if he took up her offer we'd be over. So, I gave him an ultimatum – me or her, and he chose me. I sometimes think he regrets it.'

'I'm sure that's not true, Kate. He's lucky to have you.'

'OK, OK, you don't have to defend me. I'm just saying I sometimes wonder if Kenny's bouts of depression have something to do with the feeling that he made the wrong choice and now he's trapped with me, and for Sandy and Colm's sake trying to make the best of things.'

The two sisters sat in silence together, and Aoife knew that there was no way she could talk about the contents of that innocent-looking biscuit tin sitting in her desk drawer.

CHAPTER 19

From the vantage point of her position on the couch, Aoife could see through a gap in the curtain that it was going to be a damp, dreary day. Kate had protested when she insisted that she sleep in her bedroom, but it made more sense to let Kate use it. She wasn't sleeping well, anyway. Aoife debated what to do with Kate for the day. Her train wasn't until six, and it wasn't often that she got time away from the family.

At nine she brought her sister tea and toast in bed.

Kate grinned and stretched out on the bed. 'This is a pleasant surprise. I can't remember the last time I've had breakfast brought to me. Be careful or I may never leave.'

'Enjoy, I'm going to hit the shower while you luxuriate. Do you have any ideas what you'd like to do today?

'Well, I'd fancy a trip to the National Art Gallery. I haven't been in years – the last time was to see the Turner watercolours about five years ago.'

'Sounds good – and we can mooch in the shops on Grafton Street and then we can search out somewhere nice for lunch.'

'That sounds great!'

At eleven o'clock, as they wandered through the galleries, Aoife felt a calm settle within her. The paintings performed their usual healing. The gallery was her favourite place to wander on a Saturday afternoon when the noise and mayhem of the shopping crowds got too much to bear. Today she stopped dead in front of the Louis Le Brocquy titled *A Family*. Something about that bleak, broken image pulled her up short. It seemed like devastation had visited the little nuclear unit portrayed. The parallels with her family were painfully reminiscent. If the cat with a red splash beneath its paw was replaced by her tin box leaking its awful secrets, the similarity would be complete.

Kate came to stand beside her. 'I never could bear that painting – it's so bleak and hopeless,' she said

'I think that's why I like it,' Aoife muttered as she moved away.

'Sandy would love this. Art is her favourite subject in school.'

'Well, why don't you come up again before the summer and I'll take Sandy for a cultural tour and you can indulge in the shops?'

'That would be great. I'm worried about Sandy, to tell the truth.'

'Why? Is she not well?' Aoife asked, furrowing her forehead.

'I think both she and Colm are finding their father's depression difficult. Colm is angry at him, and Sandy just looks worried about it all.'

'Look, Kate, let's go find somewhere to eat and talk. I know a pub not too far from here that does some nice fish and chips, and we can talk properly then.'

The pub was busy, but they were lucky enough to find a seat overlooking the street. They ordered their fish and chips with glasses of larger. They held off talking until they had finished eating and the waitress brought them a pot of tea.

'OK, Kate, tell me what has you so worried about Sandy. I thought she had a boyfriend and that all was good in her world?'

'Well, the boyfriend has gone. She won't tell me about it, but I think he was two-timing her and, to add insult to injury, he dumped her by text. Her self-esteem has taken a pounding.'

'*Aww*, that's rotten for the poor kid!' said Aoife.

'Well, to be honest, I'm kinda relieved they've broken up. She's only fourteen and he's a little shit. Colm told me he's always boasting to the older lads about his success with girls and he's a bit of a bully to the younger lads too. I think he's made a few cracks about Kenny being mental to Colm as well. So really she's better off without him. I just wish he hadn't bruised her ego so badly.'

'I'm sure Kenny is raging – he's crazy about Sandy.'

'Kenny doesn't know, and I don't think he'd care if he did. He's withdrawn so much. I have to drag him out of bed every day, or at least I did. The doctor started him on a new tablet and has told him he needs to spend more time in the fresh air, so now he's always mooching in the garden. He spends all his time in the shed until he hears me coming home, and then he's out weeding, clipping, and spraying. I picked up the weed-killer spray can the other day after he used it, and I swear to God, Aoife, it was empty. Maybe he used it all but I think he was just pretending to be spraying to keep me off his back.'

'That's awful, Kate. Perhaps he needs to see a counsellor or a psychiatrist?'

'Well, Dr Gibney has referred him to a psychiatrist, but you know how long the waiting lists are – it could be months.'

'But you were telling me about Sandy …'

'Yeah, well, I think both Colm and Sandy are being affected by

Kenny's illness. Colm is extremely angry – he has no trouble giving his dad backchat – but Sandy is getting withdrawn. Between that little toe-rag she was seeing and worrying about her daddy she's very down in herself.'

'Why don't you talk to the school and get her an appointment with the school counsellor? I've seen the counsellor in our school work absolute wonders, and it will give Sandy a safe place to vent. She probably doesn't want to worry you. I'm sure Colm could benefit from some help too – ask the principal if she can provide any support for him. Schools can be very discreet and none of his mates will ever find out.'

Kate wrinkled her forehead as she mulled over Aoife's suggestion. 'That's not a bad idea. I suppose I'm a bit reluctant to start telling people our business, but I've met the counsellor in the school and she seemed lovely. I'll think it over and maybe ask for an appointment to see her. And I've got a parent-teacher meeting coming up for Colm too, so, I might mention something to Mr Doran his teacher. Anyway, I'll think about it.'

'Well, any time you want to vent yourself, Kate, I'm here for you. You did enough listening to my woes when I was a young one.'

'Thanks, love, I will of course and any time you want to talk about Connor or, well, anything, I'm there for you too. Now how about we hit the shops for a little retail therapy?'

As the waitress came to their table Kate grabbed Aoife's arm. 'Put your wallet away – this is my treat.'

The sisters headed out to the shops and the rest of the day passed in pleasurable wandering through the shops, trying on clothes but buying nothing. They wrapped up their day by visiting Brown Thomas where they looked at all the insanely expensive shoes and designer clothes, but neither of them had the neck to try on anything.

Aoife walked her sister to the train and hugged her hard before waving her off.

As she trudged back into town, she mused on Kate's problems and was thankful she didn't burden her further with her discovery of the box. At least for the time being, the secret remained hers. She remembered Kate mentioning how Sam had buried Polly, and the only explanation for the box finding its way into the grave was that Sam buried it there. That meant he must know what the box and notebook held. Kate also said their father's death hit Sam hard, and he wouldn't talk about him. Perhaps discovering the box after their father died had devastated him, and he needed to hide it fast before their mother could find it. That would make sense, Sam would want to protect his mam and maybe in a panic he got rid of it by burying it with Polly. And yet, he had done a great deal to protect the box, wrapping it in heavy black plastic so that the wet soil wouldn't damage the contents. Did he plan to retrieve it? No, that made no sense: he buried it at least four feet down beside a decomposing dog. It was a puzzle, and only Sam could provide the answers.

She pulled up short, almost causing the pedestrian behind her to collide with her. Kate said that Manus and Sam went off on their trips. Did those trips to buy machinery or to go to marts include anything more sinister? Kate said Sam came back from them in bad form. Shit, could Manus have been trying to enrol Sam into some sick murder apprenticeship? Was he trying to make it into a warped kind of family business? Maybe Sam saw something or worse participated in some way and was horrified but Manus had somehow implicated him in his crimes. Maybe that was why they fell out. Aoife's throat constricted. No, there was no way her lovely gentle brother would do anything so horrific. But then who would believe that Manus O'Driscoll was a fucking serial killer either?

129

She was on the bus when with a racing heart she thought: Perhaps it was Mam, maybe she found the box and in shock and horror buried it with Polly. Her stomach lurched at the thought, but no way did that make sense. Mam adored Dad, she spoke about him like he was a saint. Could she be putting on an act? Her mind revolted at the thought. There was no way her mother could keep the charade of devotion going all these years, holding anniversaries to mark her love for Manus each year. Aoife felt reassured and her breathing calmed. In a panic, she realised she was at her bus stop and dashed to the door just as the driver was about to pull out. She gabbled apologies and stumbled onto the street.

Back in her flat, she made herself tea and watched TV for distraction. But it proved no use, and soon another possibility suggested itself. What if her mother discovered the box and its contents and was so traumatised that she went into a sort of fugue state and wiped it all from her mind? That would mean her image of her husband would remain intact. She would have put all the horrors of the box into the deepest recesses of her brain. For the rest of the night, her thoughts veered between believing Sam was the person who found the box, or it was her mother. At three in the morning, she gave up trying to sleep and scrubbed her shower instead.

CHAPTER 20

Work dragged, and she endured a rollicking from the principal because she had forgotten to cover a class and the wee 'feckers' had wrecked the classroom causing the next teacher to complain vociferously to him. There was no excuse for her forgetfulness, and she had to zip her lip and take the telling-off. He also inquired how she was coping, causing her to worry that the news of her broken engagement had somehow reached his ears. His concern was harder to stomach than his earlier annoyance with her.

There was a small parcel awaiting her when she arrived back at the flat. Clarissa had sent Manus's letters as promised. Before tackling them, she needed to eat. The choice was paltry – leftover pizza and a bottle of Chianti. She ate standing up, barely tasting the food, just gulping it down like a dog. Afterwards, she settled down with a glass of wine to open the package. There was a brief covering note from Clarissa, thanking her for her 'lovely afternoon tea' and asking her to pass on her love to dear Agnes. Clarissa was such a sweetheart. She arranged the letters by date. They were still in their envelopes, six blue airmail letters, four stamped from the USA, and three with Irish stamps. The handwriting on two of the letters matched the script in the notebook. Taking a deep breath, she opened them all and read them in order.

February 5th 1968

My Dear Manus,

Forgive the long delay in writing to you. But the sights and sounds of this amazing city have overwhelmed me. My three years living in London haven't prepared me for the sheer scale of this place. To say it differs from home is like comparing night with day. It surprises me how many languages I hear spoken in the streets. And the native New Yorkers have a way with the English language that even the movies don't convey. There are lots of different nationalities here, people from places I have never heard of. Emma is forever pulling me up on 'my gawping ways' as she calls them. But honestly, it's mesmerising to see all the sights of New York. Everything is vast. The buildings tower from every side making me feel tiny and unimportant like a little ant. But even more bewildering is the constant rushing everywhere. Nobody strolls or just danders along – it seems like everybody is on a mission that propels them like rockets from one destination to another. I know I must sound like the original country mouse, but that is exactly how I feel.

Oh, how I wish I was home with you! We could go fishing or play draughts in the hayshed. I think of you often. How has Mother been? Try not to let her get you down. She thinks the world of you, dear. Where would she be without you? But she can't admit it. As you well know, she has had a hard life. It is to her credit that we have all turned out so well. So, keep your head up. I have enclosed a few dollars for you. I have already written to Mother and sent her a bank draft, so this money is just for you. Why not buy some nice clothes for the next dance you go to? Perhaps there is some nice young one you have your eye on and you could take her out to the pictures.

Emma and Baby send their best wishes. They are well settled in NY. Emma is working in a fancy department store as you know and has got a big promotion. She is walking out with the store manager, and they all think well of her in Bloomingdales. Baby has settled in with the family that Emma recommended her to. They have a nice big house and only three children, so Baby can well manage her duties. She lives in and has her room and even a small stove for her personal use. She complains that she doesn't get too much time off. But then Baby is never content – God love her! I have got a job as a waitress in a small restaurant – called a 'Diner' here. The work is hard and I'm afraid I'm slow but, so far, the boss has been very patient with my mishaps. Mother always said I was a bit of a clot and, well, my customers would probably agree. That's all the news that I have for you. Keep well and write when you can. It's lovely to hear from home. But Mother's letters are brief, so I am depending on you for news.

Your loving sister,
Clarissa

26ᵗʰ April 1968

Dear Clarrie,

It was great to get your letter. I am glad to hear that you have a good job and are enjoying your new life Stateside. You never told me about your lodgings. I hope they are decent. New York sounds like another world – very different to our little bog-hole. It is so quiet here now that you have left. It's funny, I never minded the others leaving so much. The boys were all so much older than me and I was always just the lad to them, and Emma was a bossy boots who thought I was there to run messages for her, but she was OK, so I suppose I miss her too – but not Baby, whiney, tattle-tale spying Baby. Perhaps all those children will gang up on her and torment the living daylights out of her. I can imagine you shaking your head and tut-tutting, but you know what a dose she is.

Mother is keeping well. But she still has pain from her rheumatics and is very stiff in the mornings. I know you say that she means well, Clarrie, but sometimes I think she hates me. Maybe it's the pain but she is so harsh it's hard to bear. I keep busy as my day starts early and the usual routine of milking cows and tending to the crops keeps me well occupied.

Thanks for the enclosed money. I have opened a savings account in the Post Office. I haven't planned what to do with the money you sent, but perhaps I can use it to get away from here. Is there any job for me in the 'Big Apple'?' Seriously, I am not afraid to work at anything. Emma has always said it is the place to go if you aren't afraid to get stuck in, and you all know that I am no shirker. Let me know if you can think of anything. I am serious.

Everything here is as usual. The big story is the loss of two lambs by the Bradys. They claim dogs got at them and keep making accusations against any neighbours with dogs. I keep Toby locked up at night, but he wouldn't hurt a lamb or anything else.

I haven't been out to any dances. As for girls, you know me. I haven't much to say for myself and besides Mother would find some fault with the Blessed Virgin herself. Well, that's all my news.

Take good care of yourself.

Your loving brother,

Manus

May 12th, 1968

My Dear Manus,

Clarissa has just shown me your letter. I am most concerned that you should be even THINKING of coming over here. You are well aware of how much Mother NEEDS you. Who would run the farm and keep an eye on her health and wellbeing? I realise that a heavy burden of DUTY lies on your shoulders, Manus. But remember that duty is also a privilege. Remember all that our dear

134

Mother has done for you, for all of us. This is our opportunity to repay some of that great debt. Your older brothers and we girls are not in America for our amusement and benefit. We are here to help support Mother and give her some ease in her declining years. But your role is the greater. We DEPEND on you to keep the home fires burning; to be the man of the house so that we can do our part. Think! What would happen to Mother if you went off to America? To whom would Mother turn? Remember, we must all make sacrifices. We each have a part to play. You know your Duty. I trust you will put these selfish ideas out of your head and continue to be a comfort to Mother.

On a happier note, all are well here and working hard. I don't know what idea of the States Clarissa has given you, but it is Hard Work, with little time for idleness or gaiety. Your brothers Milo, Malachi and Patrick are well. They have good steady jobs. Milo is working as a clerk in a bank and Patrick and Malachi are working in construction. Because they are in Canada, we try to ring them regularly to make sure all is well with them.

I hope you're in good health, and I hope to see you at home in the next few years. How I miss all the comforts and consolations of home! But we all must make our sacrifices.

Your loving sister,

Emma

Aoife could hardly believe that this harsh moralistic letter was from Emma. Was she really such a prig? Feeling disappointed in her aunt, she continued to read.

25th June 1968

Clarrie,

Why did you show Emma my letter? I thought I could trust you. But you are just like Baby. You don't know what it's like for me here. Sometimes I think I might go mad. It's grand for all ye ones – you all got to escape from 'Her'! Emma is a sanctimonious bitch. I hate her! I hate all of you. Don't write again. I want no more of your money either.

Manus

5ᵗʰ July 1968

Dear Manus,

I'm so sorry you received such a harsh letter from Emma. She told me what she wrote. Truly, I didn't show your letter to her. She found it among my things and read it. It was wrong of her to be so hard on you. I know how difficult things are for you. But maybe Emma is right. Mother needs you now. But perhaps later, when things improve, one of us could come home and you could have your opportunity. Please don't be angry! I will try to get home next summer, and we can work out a plan for you to come over. Don't give up hope. Try and keep your head up. I will keep you in my nightly prayers.

Please keep writing to me. I miss you!

Your loving sister,

Clarissa

10ᵗʰ October 1969

Dear Manus,

Please reply to my letters. I haven't heard from you in months. I worry about you and remember you in my prayers every night. New York is a lonely place. Baby has left her job and is looking for a new family. She said the Smyths were awful people, and she hopes her next employers will appreciate her properly. But I worry she may find it difficult to find another position without a reference. Emma is still dating her colleague. I wouldn't be surprised if they marry. He had a big promotion at work and Emma thinks he will soon be in a very high up position in the firm. Mother writes regularly. She says she has had a lot of pain in her joints recently and has been taking comfrey for the pain. Perhaps she needs another visit to Dr Clarke. I know she doesn't like the expense, but she needs to be seen.

I hardly hear from the boys, but at least they contact their mother regularly. They landed good jobs in construction but I think they had the offer of further training so they should do well, and Milo has got a transfer to South Africa – it comes with a promotion, so he's delighted. I'm getting along fine but I get lonely at times.

Please don't give up hope of coming out here. I've been taking a secretarial course at night here and although I'm slow I am making progress. I've been thinking that as soon as my training is complete, I could come home and then you could take over my apartment. With your abilities, you would get a job in no time at all. You just need to have a little patience. Try not to let things get you down! Please write soon, I worry about you.

Love,

Clarissa

5th June 1970

My dear Manus,

It's been so long since you've been in touch. I can't believe that you would hold a grudge for so long. I know that you are angry with me and Emma. But please let me know how things are with you. Mother writes but rarely mentions you and I worry. Please don't keep punishing me this way. I'm doing everything I can to work out a plan for you to come over. In another year I'll have saved up enough money to come home and, with my secretarial training almost complete, I can find work at home, and I'll be able to look after Mother. Then you can come over here. Patrick has said there are lots of jobs in construction and you would do well. But please, let me know how you are. How is Mother doing? Is there any improvement in her pain and did she go to the doctor to have a full check-up?

Emma has got engaged to her beau and Baby is working with a new family.

She seems happier with them, but her contentment rarely lasts.

Your loving sister,

Clarissa

15th August 1970

My dear Manus,

I hope you are keeping well and that the farm work isn't taking too much of a toll on you. We all realise how difficult things are for you and that Mother can be difficult at times. Clarissa says you have stopped writing to her. I'm sorry if my last letter to you was harsh, but I felt I was only stating facts. Clarissa was most cross with me, but I was only doing what I saw was my duty as your older sister. Please do write to us as we are concerned for your welfare and of course Mother's.

I received a letter recently from Anne Casey. She mentioned that Mother has missed Mass for two Sundays in a row. Is she ill? In her last letter, she mentioned having stomach pains. Take her to Dr Clarke for a good examination. If money is an issue, please let me know and we can help with that.

Your sisters and I are busy with our jobs or at least Clarissa and I are. As for Baby, she is as usual between jobs. But, hopefully, the next one will be the charm and she'll manage to hold on to it for longer than a month. We don't hear much from your brother in South Africa but that's boys for you.

I'm sure Clarissa has told you of my exciting news. Thomas and I are engaged and plan to get married next spring. He has advanced well in the firm, and they appreciate how lucky they are to have him.

Your loving sister,

Emma

PS: Please keep in touch and let me know how Mother is doing. It's not like her to miss Mass.

5ᵗʰ October 1970

Dear Clarissa,

I received Emma's letter and, no, Mother hasn't been well. She had a bad stomach upset but the medicine the doctor put her on seems to have done the trick. Recently, she complained of chest pains, and I mentioned them to Dr Clarke. He wants me to bring her in again, but she is very stubborn and claims it's just indigestion and refuses to go to see him. I can't force her, so hopefully she's right and makes a full recovery.

I have no more news. Work on the farm progresses but prices for produce are low. I'm thinking of going into dairy and meat production as I can't keep up with the work of tillage farming on my own.

I hope you are keeping well.

Manus

Aoife was folding the letters back in their envelopes when a battered slip of paper fell to the ground. It was a telegram dated 25ᵗʰ of July 1971 addressed to Clarissa O'Driscoll.

MOTHER DIED SUDDENLY THIS MORNING STOP MANUS STOP

Aoife put the letters down. So that's what happened to the mother. Manus had noted her death in the diary and referred to her eating her last meal. A dreadful thought caused her to shiver. She remembered him writing of Emma ending up like the Harpy – dead. It added to her suspicions that he killed his mother. *Shit!* What about the foxglove pressed between the pages of the diary? What was the Latin name for foxglove – digitalis? She grabbed her phone and checked the Internet. According to one site, digitalis was used as a heart medicine, but it was also a poison that could prove fatal to humans and animals. Its leaves could be confused with comfrey. Wait, she read something in the letters about comfrey – yes, Clarissa said her mother was taking it for joint pains. Could foxgloves have got mixed up with comfrey and poisoned her? She googled comfrey as a medicine. It seemed people made tea from the leaves as it was believed to alleviate joint pain. Oh God, Manus knew about plants, he'd know about poisons. He wrote to Clarissa to describe his mother having stomach pains and chest pains. Perhaps he was setting the scene for killing her. Could he have been slowly poisoning her? Aoife's heart thudded. Was matricide to be added to the list of his crimes?

She reread the letters and was disappointed anew in Emma, and her harsh letter hammering words of duty and guilt, nailing shut all possibility of escape. If he had gone to America, would he have lived a different life? Been a good person? Or were the seeds of evil so deeply rooted as to be impossible to remove? Was he born evil, or did he learn it at his mother's knee? People survived worse childhoods than his and didn't turn into psychopaths or serial killers. But then she knew very little about his childhood. The notebook touched on the abuse he suffered – beatings, psychological terror tactics, and God knows what else. Could the seeds of evil be buried deep within her too? Was she also capable of perpetrating horrors with the right stimulus? The thought terrified her.

Unable to face going to bed, she brought a blanket from her room and wrapped herself up in it. But she still felt chilled to her bones. Opening another bottle of wine eased the chill a little.

CHAPTER 21

The day of the interview came. It had slipped her mind. It wasn't until overhearing a colleague talking about it during morning break that she remembered. Her emails confirmed that her interview was for late afternoon. Should she bother going? It all seemed pointless somehow. Still, it might distract her for a while at least. She reread her application and thought what the hell. The Assistant Principal post would be good to get. There were two posts available with eight people applying. She reckoned two of her colleagues were just interviewing to show interest and gain experience, two were 'chancers' and only did interviews to piss off management and the remaining four, which included herself, were in with a chance.

Sorcha texted and, when she heard about the interview, promised to keep her fingers crossed and persuaded Aoife to meet up later that night. Aoife was too tired to resist her friend even though she felt deathly tired.

In the meantime, she had back-to-back classes and teaching didn't allow time to focus on anything but dealing with the task at hand. The principal had her class covered half an hour before her interview slot. There was just time to grab a quick coffee.

In the staffroom, John Malloy, the German teacher, grinned and beckoned.

'How did you get on?' she asked.

'Total hames, Aoife – they asked me about some teaching and learning initiative I'd never even heard of but, instead of admitting it, I waffled on and realised by the blank look on their faces that I was talking pure shite so then I froze and after that I wasn't even sure they were speaking English I was that confused.'

'I'm sure you're exaggerating,' she said, smiling.

'Listen, whatever you do, Aoife,' Susan Brennan, the business teacher, remarked in droll tones, 'tell them that the new literacy and numeracy initiatives are a powerful tool for educators – at least that's what the guy on the interview board told me. I swear to God, Aoife, if he said 'tool' one more time, I'd have pissed myself laughing. I thought the interview would never end. The principal from the college is a total dose, and he rambles on and on. Even the lads on his side of the table found him a trial. Anyway, it's over now and please remind me never to put myself through this crap again.'

At five to two she was waiting outside the interview room, aware something was wrong. Usually, her palms were sweaty by this stage when waiting to be interviewed and her stomach was in a knot, but she instead felt bored. *Fuck*. She'd want to up her game if she wanted to get this promotion. But it seemed futile. What the hell was she doing applying for a promotion? If the news about Manus ever came out, she'd be lucky to hang on to the job, never mind delusions of climbing from the chalk pit to the higher echelons of management. The thought of appearing before the interview board and having to fake giving a damn about school policy made her want to hurl the meagre contents of her stomach.

She heard movement from the interview room and impulsively bolted, fleeing straight to the car.

For a time, she stared blankly at the trees across the road. Then, realising the students would get out soon and buses would impede her progress, she headed for home. Passing the corner shop, she stopped and ran in. The packet of Marlboro Lights she bought made her feel like a criminal with contraband as she stuffed them in her pocket.

There was nothing to eat in the house but pasta, so she boiled it up and melted parmesan cheese on top. She sat eating while watching a quiz show. What possessed her to buy cigarettes? The last time she smoked was three years ago. Connor had persuaded her to give them up, and she was never a regular smoker even then. Her phone buzzed. The principal's number appeared. Shit! Perhaps it would be as well to get the rollicking over with. It would have pissed him off that she ditched the interview.

Liam Casey's voice, leaking concern, asked, 'Aoife, I was wondering why you didn't show up at the interview today. Were you ill?'

Gritting her teeth, Aoife considered taking the way out he was offering and pretending she had a tummy bug that caused a hurried exit but instead blurted, 'No, I just decided not to attend. I didn't think I had a chance of getting the promotion anyway.'

'Well, you could have at least had the courtesy to let the interview board know. They waited for you, and we sent students all over the building in search of you.'

'I'm sorry about that. I guess I just wasn't thinking things through.'

'What has happened to you, Aoife? This isn't like you. You were such a dedicated teacher and a reliable member of the team. Lately, you've been turning in late to school and forgetting to show up to cover classes or for supervision, and well, to be honest, the Deputy and I are getting concerned about you.'

He waited for her to say something, make some excuse for the inexcusable. But she couldn't work up the energy to bother.

When she said nothing, he lost his patience. 'Aoife, I think you need to sort your head out. Perhaps spend the weekend deciding what your priorities are and we will talk on Monday morning. I'm very disappointed in you and I had to apologise on your behalf to the interview team. It was very unprofessional of you to just not turn up.'

Once again, she met his words with silence, and he hung up without saying goodbye. He was raging with her, and she couldn't argue with anything that he had said. She was letting things slide. Some days just showing up for work felt like an achievement.

She sat at her desk and stared at the copies she had yet to correct, and the notes she had barely started for her classes for Monday and with deliberation swept them to the floor. She retrieved the cigarettes from her coat pocket and ripped the cellophane off. Shaking loose a cigarette, she lit it from the flame on the gas cooker and inhaled deeply. It tasted foul, making her want to gag, which she reflected was a fitting metaphor for her life.

Time to find out about people of her father's ilk, she decided. After googling 'serial killer', the amount of information astounded her. For a crime that was described as extremely rare, the Internet seemed fascinated by it, and especially by its perpetrators. Did Manus fit the profile of serial killers? Did he share the same childhood and characteristics? It was true he had a lousy childhood, lousier than anyone knew, perhaps. It appeared that most serial killers started out killing or torturing animals before they moved on to killing people. She fetched the notebook and found a passage that she had half-remembered.

It was then I did the first 'bad thing'. I was so full of rage and choking hate that I needed to destroy. Afterwards, my skin crawled with the horror of it. It was too late then. I tried to block it out as if by refusing to think about it I might undo it. My mind still can't dwell on that first time and yet it showed me a path to peace, a release from the walls of my prison. It was ugly, brutish, and it took too long before the struggle ended, and the last breath was expelled. I carried it in my tractor and buried it in the top field. I dug deep, terrified they would find it. And I swore on my father's grave that it would never happen again. But it changed me, gave me peace, and I could survive the deafening silence now as I had the company of the dead. Over time, I got better at achieving peace, and miraculously at the right time a sacrificial lamb always appeared.

Was this a description of him killing an animal? He referred to it as a *thing* rather than a person. So, did Manus practise on animals and graduate to girls later? His reference to getting better at achieving peace and sacrificial lambs appearing when needed suggested he persevered with killing. She didn't know enough about him to see if he had the so-called effortless charm of a psychopath. She thought not, as he had no close friends. His family was his life. She typed, '**Are psychopaths capable of love?**' The findings were inconclusive, and her head ached. She rooted in her drinks cupboard and found a bottle of vodka, a leftover from a party – not a drink she normally loved, but she was glad of it tonight. She sat staring at the laptop screen, scrolling through endless accounts of gruesome murders, and interviews with smirking serial killers conducted by psychologists and journalists. Sickened, she realised they were all fetishising their subjects. These killers were horrible human beings whatever their childhood traumas, compulsions, and personality disorders. There was nothing to justify the endless fascination directed at them by the media, journalists, and moviemakers. Their victims were the forgotten ones. Nobody prepared documentaries on the lives of victims, mainly women who suffered for the nauseating pleasure and power trip of these sick individuals. There were few movies of how families survived after the wreckage these killers wrought in their lives and even those tended to focus on the perpetrators more than the victims. Disgusted at the idea that her father was like the people depicted, she slammed her laptop shut.

She wondered if she or her siblings carried within them the capacity to be evil. Was there some genetic stain dwelling dormant in their DNA? That she was part of the bloodline of such evil terrified her. She analysed every thought, impulse, and destructive act in her life. Were their latent signs of ruthlessness, cruelty, or lack of empathy in her nature? What about Sam – did Manus initiate him, and train him up as an apprentice killer? Jesus, was Sam continuing where her father left off? Could her lovely gentle brother be capable of doing such sick perverted things? Was serial killing a learned behaviour? Kate had described Sam and Manus setting off on their 'adventures' together. What did that mean? Manus in the diary referred to the 'adventure' beginning.

Gulping the raw vodka, she sat staring into space until she slumped into a drunken stupor and awoke to the banging on her door.

An irate Sorcha confronted her on the doorstep.

'Where the fuck were you?' Sorcha snarled, shoving her aside.

'What are you talking about, Sorcha?'

'We were to meet in McGovern's. Remember, you were to let me know how you got on at the fucking interview. I've been there for over an hour waiting like a dope and getting hit on by fuckers who think my body is their mood-board. Where were you and why haven't you responded to any of my messages?'

Aoife picked up her phone and saw that she had four missed calls and ten texts from her friend.

'*Aww shit!* I forgot all about it. I'm sorry, Sorcha.'

'Yeah, well, you bloody better be. I waited for ages in the pub. I thought we were going to have a proper night out and hit a club later on. In the end I gave up and got a taxi here and the bloody driver ripped me off.'

'Here, I said I'm sorry and I'll pay for the bloody taxi if that's what you're bothered about.'

'What? What's got into you, Aoife? You know it's not the money, I was looking forward to our night out.'

'I know, I'm sorry. I've just had a crappy day, and it put all our plans out of my mind.'

'OK, come on, tell me all about it,' said Sorcha with a sigh. 'Was the interview a disaster?'

'Actually, I didn't go in the end.'

Sorcha's eyes widened. 'Why? I thought you wanted this promotion. You're always banging on about how few opportunities for promotion come up. Why did you bail?'

'Look, Sorcha, would you mind if we talked about this some other time? I'm wrecked.'

'OK then, if that's how you feel, but as I'm here and you have clearly been hitting the bottle, how about offering me some?'

Aoife fetched her friend a glass, poured in a large tot of vodka and handed it to her.

Sorcha raised her eyebrows. 'I thought you hated this stuff? You must have had a really bad day.'

'Yeah, well, it's all there is – do you want it or not?' Aoife asked sharply.

Sorcha slammed the drink down, 'Never mind. I think I'll head home.'

Aoife watched her go and winced as she banged the door shut behind her.

CHAPTER 22

The last term passed in a blur of frantic energy. The school was a pressure-valve of tension, with assignments due, and the looming deadline of the state examinations. Even the slackers among Aoife's students delivered their essays and practice exam questions on time. And the classes she held in the evening had almost 100% attendance.

She waited until near the end of the term to let her colleagues know about her broken engagement but most of them seemed to have known the wedding was off. She obviously wasn't that good at hiding her emotional state. Susan, whom she was probably closest to on the staff, said people noticed she was in bad form for weeks and guessed there was trouble in paradise. The girls who were still engaged gave her a wide berth, as though fearing broken engagements were contagious. It was a relief to avoid the staffroom and spend time in her classroom reassuring her anxious, stressed-out students.

At night she slept badly, her dreams invaded by monsters and decomposing bodies jerking her to terrifying consciousness. Once awake, she spent those nights crying for Connor, bereft and heart-scalded by his absence from her bed. She missed him with a sharp sexual hunger, a longing that was overwhelming with its intensity. But most of all she missed his warmth against her body, a warmth that had made her feel secure and safe in an uncertain world. Some nights she grasped her phone and contemplated calling him, but sanity counselled against it. What right had she to disturb him? She had ended the relationship because he didn't fit her middle-class aspirations of living the perfect life. Now those aspirations seemed vapid. But she couldn't land her family dysfunction on him. Those nights, and they were many, caused her extreme tiredness coupled with a manic energy that she put to good use by cleaning the flat, sorting out cupboards, scrubbing her oven and inventing jobs to tire her body out.

She avoided the end-of-year 'piss up', unable to face the slobbering offers of sympathy about her broken engagement and the probing questions that the flow of alcohol would undoubtedly unleash. Instead, she stayed home, got dangerously drunk and passed out on the couch.

A week later, when the exams started, she went to the school to encourage her students and to look over the exam papers. There were no major surprises, and the students were happy with their efforts.

Now that the exams were over, she could no longer avoid the radioactive material emanating from the box lurking in her desk drawer. Perhaps she should go home. Her mam rang daily, and she kept promising to come home soon. So, taking a deep breath, she texted her mam that she would be down at the weekend, probably Friday evening. Now she'd better decide what to do about the notebook.

She hadn't been on the missing person website since May and still couldn't face it. Instead, she typed Anika Bakker on her laptop and came across a link to an old RTÉ interview with Anika's sister Lotte. It was unnerving listening to Lotte Bakker, then only in her early twenties, describing her sister and her hopes and dreams, all the adventures planned, but now aborted. Staring straight into the camera, Lotte begged for information about her sister's whereabouts. Several times during the interview she wiped away tears. Aoife felt sick with guilt. What was Lotte's life like now, 37 years since Anika's disappearance? She typed in the **Lotte Bakker Middleberg Holland** and found her Facebook page. Lotte was fifty-five and taught Archaeology at University College Roosevelt. Her hobbies were gardening and art. She had called her only child Anika. Aoife bit her lip until it bled and turned off her laptop, unable to deal with any more disturbing reality. God, she didn't fancy the long night ahead and feared sleep would be a forlorn hope.

Her mobile rang. It was Sorcha. Thankfully, Sorcha was not the type to hold grudges.

'Well, stranger, how are you?' she said.

'Grand, Sorcha, just chilling. Do you fancy going out tomorrow? How about us going to the cinema and grabbing a bite to eat?'

'*Aww*, sorry, I'm meeting someone tomorrow.'

'Sorcha McHugh, are you on a second date with your man from Tinder? Please spill!'

'Nothing to tell yet, but I do have my hopes. Listen, I can put him off, and we can have a girl's night. Say the word now!'

Aoife felt like agreeing, but that wasn't fair. Sorcha hadn't dated much since her last break-up with a guy she discovered had a fiancée. Therefore, she was understandably cautious about new relationships and this fella must be special if she was prepared to give him a chance.

"No, it's grand – tell me all about it when I get back from Sligo. I'm off on Friday for a while. Have fun and we'll talk later."

She ended the call with a promise to meet up as soon as she got back from the country.

The silence in the flat was an avalanche of white noise that made her ears ache. Desperate for the distraction, she turned on the TV but channel-hopping offered nothing of interest, and she switched it off in annoyance.

Later, in bed, she put on earphones and listened to a podcast. The sonorous voices lulled her to sleep, and she was elated to awaken and find the sun streaming in the window. It was a long time since she'd slept through the night with or without the aid of alcohol.

Getting up, she felt directionless. The day stretched ahead, long and empty. Why wait until Friday to head to Sligo? She would leave after breakfast and surprise her mother. Throwing a few clothes into a bag, she gritted her teeth as she took the box from her desk, double-wrapped it in plastic bags, shuddering at the thought of it touching her clothes, and placed it in her case. She breakfasted on dry Cornflakes and toast with hot black coffee as she was out of milk. She was on the road by nine.

She drove on autopilot, her body controlling the car but her mind flitting restlessly from thought to thought. She turned on the radio and blasted out music as loud as she could bear, resulting in painful eardrums but driving all disturbing thoughts and images from her mind. A good trade-off. At a filling station she bought coffee and doughnuts and had a picnic in the car, the sickly sweetness of the confectionary offering comfort.

When she arrived in Sligo, she stopped at a supermarket to pick up a few groceries for her mother. On impulse, she bought a pretty bouquet of summer flowers – she thought her mam would enjoy their bright sunny colours.

"Hi, Aoife, it's a nice surprise seeing you here. Are you down for long?'

Startled, she looked up to see Jack Costello grinning at her.

'Oh, hi Jack, yes, I'm down for a few days. I haven't been home yet.' Aoife paused, not sure what to say next.

Jack, looking sheepish, muttered, 'Sorry to hear about the engagement ending – that must have been tough.'

Aoife coloured. 'Yeah, well, these things happen and better now than later, eh?' Every clichéd piece of crap spilling out of her mouth sickened her and, mortifyingly, suddenly tears flowed down her face. The more she tried to stem the flow, the worse the deluge.

Jack squirmed and moved from foot to foot as though he wanted the pavement to suck him down. He desperately patted his pockets, presumably for a tissue. Aoife had a disconcerting memory of Manus handing her a brilliant white handkerchief to dab on a cut knee when she was a little child.

Jack gave up his futile search, and she pulled herself together and grabbed her basket and ran for the till. She delayed as long as she could, but at the shop door Jack stood waiting, a concerned look etched on his face.

Aoife forced a smile. 'Sorry about that, Jack. I'm fine now, but I have to run.' She hurried over to her car before he could say a word.

Struggling to keep her focus, she navigated her way out of town, but she drove far too fast, narrowly missing a dog that had ambled across the road. Slamming on the brakes she sat, her heart thumping furiously, pulled up on the roadside. A car beeped, and she was about to pull out when she saw it was Jack. He hurried over to her car.

'Are you alright?'

Once again, the sympathetic tone reduced her backbone to a wobbly gelatine and her eyes filled up.

'Look, you're in no fit state to arrive at your mother's. Why not call over to my place and I can make you tea and show you around? I don't think you've ever seen it, have you? Is your mother expecting you at a particular time?'

Aoife shook her head. 'She's not expecting me until tomorrow.'

'Okay then, follow me and I'll give you the grand tour.'

He didn't give her a chance to reply. He got in his car and drove off. In a trance, she followed him. He drove with exaggerated care and at a low speed that she was certain his car rarely experienced. For a second, she felt patronised and debated overtaking him and heading for home but, then again, she was curious to see his house. Her mam had raved about it, and the local community could talk of little else.

Driving along twisty roads, they eventually pulled up at a modern, glass-encased cube. As she drove around the side, she noticed the line of the building meandered around a sloping hill. The site was all about the views – which were breath-taking. Towards the south, there were panoramic views of the sea and to the west rolling hills and woodland. There wasn't another house in sight. How did he get planning permission? The planners in Sligo were pretty strict and it was in an area of natural beauty where they didn't like houses cropping up to spoil the vista for the tourists. There must have been another dwelling here, or the planners would never have permitted the building. The house, belying its first impression, wasn't one glass box but a series of interlinking rectangles around an enclosed courtyard. Aoife felt serious house-envy. It was a stunning example of what an architect achieved when given free rein.

Jack unlocked the front door, punched some digits on the alarm and beckoned her inside.

The hallway was swimming in a lustrous blanket of black polished concrete with tiny sparkles glowing like jewels amidst its depths. Aoife followed him down a passageway where he slid over a wooden panelling to reveal a vista that made her gasp. Beautifully furnished though the room was, all that her eyes sought was the sea beyond which lay spread

153

out like a magnificent living painting, sparkling and undulating.

'*Wow!*' she gasped, aware of how inadequate a word it was. 'You're very lucky, Jack. This place is stunning. I'm going to hold you to your promise of a tour.'

Jack grinned. 'Of course, but first – how about that tea or would you prefer coffee?'

'Tea would be great, thanks.'

As a teenager, like most of her friends she had fancied Jack Costello and time hadn't been unkind by removing his hair or giving him a paunch like a lot of the boys she knew from school. He was big but with little fat – not exactly handsome but with an expressive face that appealed the more time was spent with him.

'Sorry, what did you say?' she said, realising she had missed something he said.

'Take a seat over by the windows and I'll bring it over.'

She sat down on a giant purple couch smothered in soft oversized cushions.

In minutes Jack was back, bearing a tray with two mugs of tea, milk and sugar which he placed on a small coffee table in front of her. Then he sat down beside her.

Conscious of being swallowed up by the couch, she sat primly on the edge and tended to her tea.

'Why did your engagement end?' he asked, then seeing her guarded face apologised. 'Sorry, not my business.'

'It's OK. I suppose because we realised that we wanted different things from life. Attraction doesn't ensure compatibility.'

'Earlier, you seemed upset. I suppose that means that maybe you regret things ending. Perhaps you should try again. Maybe it's not too late.'

Aoife smiled wryly. 'It is too late,' she said firmly. 'But if you're asking if I miss him then yes, I do. I'm sad that things are over between us.' She took a gulp of tea. To change the subject, she began to talk about the house again.

Their tea drunk, he asked, 'How about that tour then?'

The house was spectacular. The interiors were so stylish that Jack admitted he had employed an interior designer. There was no expense spared. Upstairs the bedrooms, all four, were tastefully furnished. But the master suite was luxury incarnate, with windows capturing vistas of the sea and nearby islands.

Feeling emboldened, she asked him, 'Are you seeing anyone? This is a lot of house for one person.'

He shook his head and smiled. 'I haven't met anyone I want to share it with.' He winked and smirking added, 'Yet.'

Irritated, Aoife suddenly had enough of him, and went downstairs.

He followed. She faced him in the hall.

'It's time I was going. Thank you for the tea and sympathy, Jack. You have a lovely home. Thank you for showing it to me.'

She hurried to the door and drove away without looking back.

CHAPTER 23

Her mam's face lit up with delight when she saw Aoife, but wailed that she hadn't anything in for supper and that the sheets hadn't been changed since her last visit.

'Hey, Mam, it's fine! I brought something for supper and the sheets are grand. Now sit, and leave the cooking to me for a change. I'm going to do a cottage pie. I know you like that, and no, you can't help. Now go into the sitting room and watch TV.'

'What kind of person do you think I am – watching television in the middle of the day?' Agnes exclaimed in mock horror.

They laughed because she loved to watch quiz programmes and was addicted to her afternoon fix. She headed off and left Aoife to get on with the meal.

While cooking, Aoife's mind wandered. Her mam seemed in good form, but she could see the concern lurking behind her eyes. The antenna hardwired into mothers must work at full throttle, Aoife thought as Agnes always seemed to sense when there was something wrong. Thank God, the broken engagement offered an excuse to deflect from what really worried her daughter. *Christ!* If her mam knew about the box it would kill her. The horror of Manus's depraved life would blow her world to smithereens.

Aoife was just taking the cottage pie from the oven when Sam walked into the scullery. She popped her head around the door to say hello as he kicked off his boots.

He grinned and walked over in stocking feet to hug her.

'Pleasant surprise, thought you weren't coming till tomorrow.'

Aoife grinned back at him. 'Well, here I am.'

Sam shifted from foot to foot and muttered, 'Here, Aoife, sorry about you and Connor, I wish ...' his voice trailed away.

'It's OK, Sam. It was for the best but, to be honest, I don't want to talk about it if you don't mind. Now I hope you're hungry, I've made cottage pie.'

Sam's face pantomimed a look of stricken terror. 'Oh God, I better get the ambulance on speed-dial then!'

'Hilarious,' she said, aiming a tea towel at his head.

Catching it, he used it to dry his hands.

Soon they were sitting down to eat. They chatted about the farm and all the news from the locality. Aoife regaled them with an account of her visit to Jack Costello's new house. She didn't tell them about how she had made a show of herself in the supermarket. Agnes wanted a full description of the furnishings, especially what the kitchen was like. Hearing that he had a double oven, a microwave, and a hob, she wondered aloud what a single man needed with all that equipment, not to mention four bedrooms.

After dinner, they moved into the TV room where Agnes watched her soaps and the nine o'clock news. Soon she was snoring softly, and Aoife shook her gently awake.

'Mam, why don't you head up to bed? I'll bring you up a warm drink once you're settled.'

Tucked up in bed, she looked frail. She was still several years off seventy, but she looked older, or perhaps it was tiredness.

Feeling a surge of protective love wash over her, Aoife kissed her soft cheek lightly. 'Sleep well, Mam! See you in the morning.'

Her mother smiled back. 'It's good to have you home, love.'

Downstairs, Sam lay stretched out on the couch with his eyes closed. He seemed tired too. Farming was hard work, and Sam only had Karol to help. When was the last time he had a proper break away from the farm? Come to think of it, she never remembered him going away, even for a weekend. That was unusual, wasn't it? Did he ever have a girlfriend? She was certainly never aware of one. But then the age gap between the two had prevented shared confidences. Could her brother be gay? She had never seen him with a girl but then, as far as she knew, there wasn't much gay nightlife in town. But, then again, what did she know? Perhaps he went to Galway or Dublin? No, he never left the farm. Cows don't milk themselves. How much did she know about Sam? Hell, it was only a few days ago that she thought he was Manus's murderous apprentice. How sick was that? Sam was a good person – there was no way he ever hurt anyone. He didn't have it in him. Or did he, a traitorous voice in her head asked.

Aoife considered how best to approach him about Manus. What to reveal and what to withhold about her devastating discoveries.

Sam was staring. 'You look very serious, is something wrong?'

'Nothing wrong. I've just been thinking about Dad a lot lately.'

Sam continued to watch the flickering screen of the silent TV.

'Oh yeah! What about him?' His tone sounded disinterested.

Undaunted, Aoife continued. 'It's just I was so young when he died, and I suppose when I planned on getting married I felt sad he

158

wouldn't be walking me down the aisle. I feel like I don't know him, what he was really like.'

'My God, Aoife, Mam talks about him often enough! To hear her you'd never believe he was dead this past twenty years!' And he turned the sound up on the TV.

'I know that, but she paints him as a saint, a wonderful father and a devoted husband. He doesn't seem real somehow, and I really would like to know what he was like. You were about seventeen when he died. What was he like from the perspective of a teenage boy?' She leaned forward.

Sam was silent for so long that she was afraid he would never respond.

Finally, he said, 'Dad was a good provider, hardworking, but I'm not sure if he enjoyed farming. I think it was something that paid the bills and took care of us all. I used to enjoy working outside with him. It felt peaceful. But a teenager is far too caught up in their world to notice much about their parents. Ask Kate – she was probably closer to him.'

'That's not what she says – according to her, you were great pals, always off doing things together and she said that you hero-worshipped him.'

'Then she's wrong. Sure, we worked on the farm but we weren't particularly close. Look, I'm tired. I'm up early tomorrow and have a busy day.'

As he got to his feet, she caught his arm, 'Sam, what was he like? I need to know.'

He shook her arm off with a laugh. 'Why so serious, Aoife? It was so long ago I hardly remember him. Talk to Mam if you want to learn what he was like. I'm too busy for all that introspective shite.' He smiled tightly. 'See you in the morning, kiddo. Sleep well.'

She listened to the stairs creak as he went up to bed. Sitting back down, her stomach clenched. He was hiding something. What did he know about her father? It was true, Sam wasn't particularly introspective, but he was reluctant to talk about her father at all. Which possibly meant he either knew about the contents of the box, or he felt actual guilt about something he'd done – or maybe he was full of remorse for not being with their father when he died. Which was it?

An hour later, after cleaning up the kitchen, she too went to bed. The chilly bedroom mocked her with its childish detritus, and she longed to rip all the silly posters off her walls. Instead, she undressed, got into bed, and pulled the duvet tight over her head. She slept poorly but so did Sam. She could hear him moving about his room throughout the night. He left the house at six, which was early even for him. At eight she dragged herself out of bed, showered and put on jeans and a lightweight jumper because, even though it was the middle of June, the West of Ireland hadn't got that message yet.

Her mother was pottering around the kitchen and they both sat down to eat tea and toast.

She was washing up the breakfast things when she saw Karol and Sam talking in the yard. Sam looked intense and Karol was gesticulating. Sam strode off, his body rigid, and Karol stared after him with a puzzled expression on his face.

Aoife was out the back door before Karol could move off.

'Good morning, Karol – is everything OK? You look worried.'

Karol spoke slowly. 'Oh, hello, Aoife, everything is OK, but Sam is angry with me.'

'That can't be true, Karol – he's always saying how hardworking and reliable you are. Why do you think he is angry?'

'He's angry about where I buried Nell. He says I did it wrong, that it's not exactly where he told me to do it. But I didn't think that mattered – I didn't know I was digging up the other dog's grave.'

Aoife, struck with horror, could hardly answer. 'It's OK, Karol – he's just upset about Nell – and the other dog too, I suppose,' she forced herself to say.

Sam knew what was buried with Polly. Sam must have buried the box.

'Did you tell him about the box we found?' she asked Karol, barely managing to keep her voice from shaking.

'No, I never thought to. Should I say it to him now?'

'No, don't worry, I'll tell him later. It's a kind of surprise so don't bother mentioning it unless he asks.'

'OK, I will not speak of it if that is what you wish.' Karol looked uneasy.

Aoife hastened to reassure him. 'It's just some secret treasure trove he must have buried when he was a kid. I'm planning on giving it to him for his next birthday as a surprise.'

Karol's face brightened, and she offered him some breakfast which, as the diligent worker that he was, he declined – just as she knew he would.

Back in the kitchen, her mam was getting out her ironing board.

Aoife snatched the iron from her hand. As her mother protested, she said, 'Leave that! We are going into town for lunch and a whizz around the shops. No arguments, please, just get your coat.'

The day out was a great idea. She persuaded Agnes to try on a new dress and, despite initial protests, Agnes allowed her to pay for it. They had lunch in the local hotel and the two of them chatted away, her mother oblivious to the devastation that her daughter carried around with her like a virus.

CHAPTER 24

Agnes was also oblivious to the strained atmosphere in her kitchen on Friday evening. Sam arrived late for dinner and was uncommunicative, but Agnes was so busy talking about her lovely day out that the meal passed successfully.

Aoife insisted on doing the dishes before joining Sam and her mother in the living room where they watched one of Agnes's soaps.

At half eight Agnes decided to ring her brother Gerard and afterwards have an early night.

After she left, Aoife went and sat down on the couch beside Sam. He switched over to a football match and feigned interest, avoiding eye contact. When she asked him about his day, he was noncommittal, and when she asked if he was feeling OK, he snapped at her. So she flounced out of the room and sat reading one of Agnes's magazines in the kitchen.

Soon she heard him heading off to bed. She felt tired too, but the thought of going to bed with only the company of her thoughts and the ticking time-bomb in her suitcase was unendurable.

On impulse, she grabbed her car keys and headed for the pub. McCoy's was one of those country pubs where the generations still mingled. She might run into some old school friends and at least pass an hour or two. There was always someone from whom she could cadge a lift home. She herself had obliged often enough in the past.

The pub was buzzing; after all, it was a Friday night. She recognised a few familiar faces. But after half an hour she knew she had made a mistake. Many friends from primary and post-primary school sidled up to her, asking her about the wedding. News of the cancellation hadn't hit the locality. Mam must have kept a very low profile for people to have remained in ignorance. After telling multiple people she and Connor had broken up and assuring them that while she was sad, she wasn't heartbroken, and Connor did not 'do the dirt on her', her patience ebbed. As the evening wore on and some of her school friends got drunker, they started confiding that they had never liked Connor. When she knocked back her fourth whiskey of the evening, she decided to call it a night. Spotting old Mr Shea reaching for his hat, she figured he'd be good for a lift as the farm was just past his place. On her way to intercept him, she saw Jack Costello coming out of the Gents'. He waved her over and she agreed to have another drink when he offered her a lift. They chatted about mutual school friends, and he asked after Sam.

It was near to closing when they left the pub. She was pretty sure the locals observed their exit, and it would be the subject of gossip and speculation, but she didn't care.

When the cold air outside hit, she staggered, and Jack steadied her. Leaning against his body, she was acutely aware of how fanciable he was. He was a bit of a dick for sure, but feckin' cute.

'OK, where to, Aoife?' he asked.

'You know where I live.'

'You can't blame me for trying, can you?' Jack laughed and started the car.

'Wait! I have an idea! Why don't you take me to the sheds?'

He looked at her warily. 'Why do you want to go to the sheds? We can go back to my place if you like. I've got more whiskey.'

She smirked at him knowingly. 'I don't want whiskey.'

'What do you want?' he asked quietly.

And all of a sudden, Aoife knew exactly what she wanted. 'I want a no-questions-asked-nothing-made-of-it fucking ride! Do you think you can oblige? If yes, drive me to your sheds.'

'Look, Aoife, are you sure? I don't want to be taking advantage of you. Maybe we should wait until you're sober?' he said doubtfully.

'No, you look, Jack. I get it that you're trying to be sound. I appreciate that. But we're not kids anymore. All I'm looking for is something uncomplicated and, if you're not up for that, well, you can just drop me home and no hard feelings on either side.' As she spoke she felt that despite the occasional slurred word, she had put forward a compelling argument that no red-blooded man could resist.

Jack held up his hands. 'OK! But seriously, why the friggin' sheds?'

'Maybe if you take me there, I'll explain,' she said, batting her eyelids.

The sheds lay down a narrow track just off the main road. The security lights flooded the yard as they pulled up. She waited while Jack unlocked the door.

'We've lost machinery in the past, so I lock it every night now,' he explained in answer to her quizzical look.

He switched on the light, revealing rows of muddy farm machinery, and she turned to him in disgust.

'Where is all the hay?'

He burst out laughing at her dismayed face. 'We haven't kept hay here in years.'

Aoife sat on an upturned crate. '*Aww*, it's just that I have memories as a kid of hearing about how all the local teenagers came here for, you know ... a roll in the hay.'

Jack laughed. 'I can't vouch for that story but, if you've seen enough, maybe we can go to my place now?'

He caught her hand and pulled her out of the shed with its silent machines and the raw smell of oil.

When they got to the car, she stared at him defiantly. 'I don't want to go to your house – it's too like a show home.'

'Thanks very much!' Jack said, looking pissed off. 'I'll drop you home then.'

Aoife laughed at his aggrieved face. 'I want to go home but not just yet. This is a nice roomy car you've got. Let's hop in the back.'

Jack stared at her, incredulous. 'What? Right here and now?'

'Yes,' she giggled. 'No time like the present.'

She climbed into the back seat and Jack shrugged his shoulders and joined her.

'You are some girl, Aoife O'Driscoll! What about your reputation if someone sees us?'

'Let me worry about my reputation. Are we going to talk all night or what?'

'Definitely not talking,' he whispered as he pulled her face close to his.

Although the car was roomy, it wasn't designed for vigorous activity, but somehow they managed with Aoife straddling Jack and with the removal of a minimum of clothing. The sex was satisfying and intense and for the first time in ages she wasn't thinking, she was just enjoying the sheer physicality of their bodies, the rhythm, the build-up, and the release. Afterwards, she longed for a cigarette, although she hadn't smoked since the day of her interview.

Jack grinned, as though reading her mind. He got into the driver's seat and pulled a packet of fags from the glove compartment.

'I didn't know you smoked,' she said, inhaling the first dizzying hit of nicotine.

'I don't usually, but someone left them here ages ago and, well, the moment seemed to require a smoke.'

'That was great, Jack! Thanks,' she murmured. She sucked in another blast of smoke and announced, 'Oh man, that's foul! Open the window so I can ditch it.'

Jack switched on the engine and lowered the back window. She tossed the fag in the puddle just outside the car.

'*Shit!*' Jack exclaimed. '*Quick, get down! Someone is coming!*'

Heart thumping, Aoife slid down on the seat and Jack threw his jacket across her. He lowered his window.

'Hi, Pete, what are you up to?'

'Ah, it's you, Jacky boy. I saw the car, and I thought someone was robbing your sheds. I know you have some valuable stuff in there and there are so many bad ones touring the countryside, robbing as they go.'

'You're very good to be looking out for me, Pete. But I just was checking I had locked up. Do ya want a lift up the road?'

Pete agreed with alacrity and hopped into the passenger seat before Jack could change his mind.

Barely breathing, Aoife lay still in the back seat.

'Did ya mind that O'Driscoll lassie in the pub tonight? I heard her wedding is off. I wonder did her lad do the dirt on her? She's not a bad looking wan, is she?'

'She's alright,' said Jack, smothering a laugh. 'Well, here you are! I'll leave you here at the top of the lane.'

Pete and his alcohol-fumed breath departed from the car and, under cover of darkness, Aoife clambered into the front seat, still warm from Pete's arse.

'You're a shit, Costello,' she growled in his ear. 'So I'm just alright, am I?'

Jack laughed and kissed her lightly on the lips.

They drove the rest of the way in silence. At the house, Jack asked if she would like to meet up again.

She grinned. 'No, Jack, but you were just what I needed tonight.'

'I think I feel used,' he said, pulling a mock hurt face as she waved goodbye and blew him a kiss.

Later, after showering and brushing the taste of tobacco from her mouth, she was conscious of how relaxed she felt. She felt no trace of guilt. Why didn't she? After all, she had only just broken up with Connor and here she was having it off with a local lothario. Who was she? She slid under the duvet and slept for ten hours solid.

CHAPTER 25

Aoife woke energised and optimistic. Convinced she could cope with anything life threw at her. There was nothing like a good ride to lift the spirits. God, she was bad! Why no guilt, no feeling she had betrayed Connor? What had happened to her? Anyway, whatever it was, she would row with it. Time enough for regrets later. In this mood of invincibility, she showered and dressed at superhuman speed.

As she headed downstairs, she was aware that for the first time in ages the ache in her stomach could be attributed to hunger and not the usual dull misery. She hoped her mother was preparing one of her infamous coronary-on-a-plate fry-ups. She felt woman enough to devour it in minutes.

Aoife pulled up short when she heard raised voices coming from the kitchen. She listened in disbelief. Sam was shouting at Agnes. What the hell! Sam never shouted at anyone, let alone his mam.

'You had no right to sell them the land! I can't believe you've done this to me. They're down there with a digger. *A digger, Mam!* They're planning to carve up the field. What the hell were you thinking?'

Sam stood, fists clenched, towering over Agnes. His face was grey with a sheen of sweat. A glob of spittle perched on the corner of his mouth.

'What do you mean by "what right"? You may manage the farm, Sam, but as long as it's in my name I'll do what I please with it.' Agnes stood her ground, two bright flames of colour raised against the whiteness of her skin like a brand. 'How dare you speak to me that way? I'll do as I please with my land. I don't have to get permission from you.'

'Do what you want then, I don't give a fuck! But I promise you you'll live to regret it.'

Aoife held her breath, terrified that Sam was going to strike Agnes. She watched, fascinated, as his arm rose. Her mother, too angry to flinch, glared at him. They stood frozen by fury until Sam turned on his heel and left, yanking open the door and hitting his arm so violently on the door frame it was bound to leave a bruise.

Aoife hurried over to her mother who looked like her legs were about to give way and helped her into a chair.

'Mam, are you OK?'

Her mother's face was now the colour of chalk. 'Water,' she croaked.

Aoife hurriedly filled a glass from the tap.

Agnes had several sips and her breathing became less laboured.

'Take it easy, Mam, catch your breath.'

Agnes nodded and drank some more. 'I'm OK now, Aoife.'

But she wasn't OK. Her face had a greyish hue and Aoife worried that she might have a heart attack.

Seeing the concern on her face, Agnes squeezed her hand. 'I'm better now. I just can't credit what happened.'

'Mam, what was that all about? I can't believe Sam was shouting at *you* of all people. Are you able to tell me what happened?'

'I'll try, Aoife, but in truth I can't understand it. I was just about to bake some bread when he burst through the door like a wild thing. For a minute I thought someone had died. Then he started roaring at me and shouting over and over that I had no right! I thought he'd gone mad. I begged him to calm down and he caught me by the shoulders and shouted that I had no right to sell land to the O'Briens. Seemingly, he met them on the road with a digger all set to clear a plot of land I said I'd sell them for sites. But first they wanted to check it for granite, to see whether it was too rocky to build on.'

'But, Mam, I didn't know you planned to sell land. How come?'

'Because I wanted to get together a bit of money for you girls. Before it all went wrong for you and Connor, I thought the two of you might want to buy a house and I wanted to help with a deposit. And Kate is struggling with her mortgage now that Kenny isn't working so I wanted to be able to help her too. Anyway, it was only a piece of useless land down the lane. Your father never used it, nor did Sam, and I suppose I didn't think of it as part of the farm. Anyway, Kieran O'Brien came to me looking for sites for his lads. He offered me the going rate. I'm not a gom – I checked. Anyway, it went clean out of my mind what with your wedding being cancelled and I forgot to mention it to Sam. But why he was in such a state I don't know. Aoife, he frightened me. What got into him? It's like he turned into a different person completely, someone I didn't recognise. Oh God, Aoife, do you think he'll cause trouble and attack the men? He went haring out of here so fast and his mouth was practically frothing. I'm scared about what he'll do.'

At her mother's urging, they drove to the land she had promised to sell to Kieran O'Brien. The land was down a winding lane just off the main secondary road. She could see why Kieran wanted it for his sons. It was in a private spot sheltered by a copse of trees on one side and gently rolling hills on the other.

In contrast to the prevailing mood, the weather was beautiful, and the air was filled with birdsong and the whisper of soft breezes. But the bucolic idyll was shattered by male voices shouting and cursing.

Sam was standing in front of a digger and refusing to move as a group of men moved menacingly towards him, shouting foul words at him.

Kieran O'Brien, a short stocky man, rushed over to Aoife and her mother, barely waiting for them to step out of the car before he launched into frantic speech.

'Mrs O'Driscoll, Agnes, thank God you've come. Your young fellow has gone mad in the head. He's refusing to get out of the way of the digger. I told him you had agreed to a sale subject to my clearing the land to see if there is granite. But he won't listen. It's all I can do to hold my lads off him. In the name of God, will you talk sense into him?'

The two O'Brien sons were standing on either side of Sam, trying to get him to move from in front of the digger. They were small men but muscular. Sam towered over them but Aoife felt they wouldn't be past fighting dirty.

She hurried over to the men.

'Lads, why don't you back off for a while so that I can speak to my brother?'

The men looked uncomfortable and one of them muttered, 'I always knew he was a nutter' as he spat a gob of phlegm onto the ground, just missing Sam's boot.

For a moment Aoife thought Sam would hit him so she reached out and grasped his arm. His body was drenched with sweat and there was an animal smell rising from him that stung her nostrils.

'Sam, you have to calm down and tell me what's wrong.'

Sam looked confused, almost as though he didn't recognise her. Eventually, his face cleared.

'Aoife, please, you have to stop them!'

Agnes joined them. 'Son, what's happened to you? I can't believe you're making such a show of yourself. I'm only selling this bit of land for your sisters. They could do with a few bob. You know Kate is struggling to pay her mortgage. I just wanted to help out. This is only three-quarters of an acre. It's not even decent farmland. Your father never grew anything here or grazed an animal on it. He said it was useful for nothing.'

Sam's face paled even more and through gritted teeth he snarled, *'I don't want to sell any of it ever!'*

Agnes, shocked by his vehemence, stepped back.

Looking at her mother's stricken face, Aoife said, 'Mam, will you leave it to me? I'll sort something out.'

She walked over to Kieran O'Brien. 'Mr. O'Brien, will you take my mother home? We'll sort this out later. I need to talk to my brother. Just leave it for today and we'll sort everything out tomorrow.'

'See here, young Aoife, I have no beef with you or your mother but, well, a deal is a deal, and your brother has threatened my sons. I could have the Guards on him.'

'I know this is a terrible inconvenience for you, Mr. O'Brien, but my brother has a strong attachment to this land. He took it over from our father after his death. It was a big responsibility for him to take on as a teenager. I think he feels a responsibility to our father to mind it and keep it together. Look, let's sleep on it and we'll get it sorted tomorrow.'

Grudgingly Kieran O'Brien agreed, muttering about his time being wasted. Reluctantly he and his sons departed, taking Agnes with them.

Sam leaned against the abandoned digger. His body sagged as though all the air had left his body. Aoife wished she had a hip flask because the moment surely called for a nip of whiskey.

She squeezed his arm gently and was relieved when he didn't flinch away.

'Sam, are you OK?' It was a silly question because he clearly wasn't OK, but it did as an opener. 'Can you tell me what's going on? Why are you so upset?'

He straightened up and walked a short distance away. She gave him the time to recover. When he turned towards her, he looked more like his old self.

'Sorry, Aoife, Mam blindsided me. I saw the diggers and just lost it. She should have talked to me. She had no right to just agree to sell land like that. I know it's hers but I'm the one managing it, looking after everything. I can't believe she would do that.' His voice shook with emotion.

'She just wanted to help us out with some money, Sam. I don't need it, but Kate is struggling a bit. You can't blame her for wanting to help, can you?' She watched Sam closely. His breathing was more even but he still had a frantic look in his eyes.

He nodded at her words. 'I didn't realise she was worried about Kate. She should have told me.'

'Well, maybe she didn't want to worry you, Sam. But still, this seems an overreaction. Why is selling a small plot like this such a big deal? It's not even good land. Is there something else? Something you want to tell me?' She watched his face carefully.

Sam pulled away. 'I don't know what you're talking about. I just wanted to keep the land together,' he swallowed, 'for Dad. It's what he would have wanted. He always said he never wanted to sell land. I'm only doing as he wanted.'

Aoife felt the air vibrate. Sam was lying; he was hiding something. Perhaps he was scared of what the men would find if they dug up the land. And so was she. Sam had made her an accessory to their father's evil deeds, a reluctant ally. She knew that she would have to find a way to stop her mam from selling the land.

CHAPTER 26

Aoife offered Sam a lift back to the house. He refused and she watched as he strode stiffly off in the direction of his tractor. She sat in the car, trying to work out what to do. One thing was certain. She needed to stop her mam from selling to Kieran O'Brien, but it had to be handled carefully. She longed for a smoke, gritting her teeth she drove back to the house.

When she walked into the kitchen, her mother was ironing shirts with a fierce vigour. Aoife could feel the anger and confusion emanating from her. It was nearly lunchtime and she wondered were Sam and Karol going to join them. It wasn't like her mother not to be preparing something fresh to eat. Perhaps they were going to have leftovers.

'Hi, Mam,' she said, trying to gauge the atmosphere.

'Well, did you get any sense out of that fellow?' She laid her iron down with a thump on the board.

Aoife winced. 'Mam, can you sit down for a minute so we can talk?'

'I don't have time for talk. I have the dinner to get ready after I finish ironing his lordship's shirts.'

'Come on, Mam – I bet you have the dinner already sorted. However mad you are, you'd not take it out on Karol. Where is he, by the way?'

'Well, I did take a lasagne out of the freezer last night and I can heat it up. And you're right – however badly Sam has behaved I don't want Karol to miss out on his dinner. I'm sure he's famished. Luckily, before all this blew up Sam sent him off to the Kellys to help with the baling. He'll be here at one sharp.'

'So, you do have time for a chat. Come on, Mam, you know you hate fighting.'

'Well, I didn't start it!' Then realising how childish that sounded, she smiled. 'OK, Aoife, let's sit down and talk. But first, I need a strong cup of coffee.'

While her mam put away the ironing board, Aoife made two strong cups of coffee and placed them on the worn surface of the kitchen table. She waited until Agnes was sipping before she began to speak.

'I know Sam has behaved dreadfully,' she said.

Agnes nodded. 'No question about that,' she said.

'But I've talked with him and he's extremely sorry and ashamed of himself,' Aoife said mendaciously. But at least she'd got her mother to listen.

'As well he should be, Aoife. I was mortified in front of the O'Briens. I'm sure they think we're mad in the head with all that carry-on.'

'Yes, well, I don't think you realise how important the land is to Sam. He feels it's like a sacred trust he took on from Dad – to care for the land and keep it together. I think he feels it would be letting Dad down if we sold any of it.'

Aoife felt her cheeks burn with shame as her words caused her mother's eyes to fill with tears.

'Oh God, Aoife, I never knew he felt that way. I've taken him for granted, haven't I? The poor boy. Sure, he was only a youngster when he took the farm on and the care of you girls too. He made the farm pay and it took care of us all.'

Aoife could see her mother had made a 360 turn in her attitude. Before she was outraged and furious with Sam but now she was filled with compassion and remorse. Aoife felt guilty for manipulating her, but it was a necessary evil. *Evil* described it well.

'But why didn't he tell me how he felt and why did he get so angry?'

'You know men, Mam, they bottle up their feelings and then they explode.'

'But what will I do, love? I just wanted to see you girls looked after, especially poor Kate.'

'Mam, you don't have to worry about me. I'm not planning to buy a house any time soon. Once Connor and I broke up I realised it wasn't going to happen, not for a few years anyway. As for Kate, perhaps Sam could find some money for her, sell cattle or something. You know he'd like to help.'

'But what about the deal? Kieran O'Brien is going to be furious because I changed my mind.' 'Nothing was signed – he was only going to buy if the land suited him, hence the digger today. Just tell him you've changed your mind. I'll do it if you like.'

'No, Aoife, I started this business, so I'll finish it.' With that Agnes got to her feet and picked up the landline.

Aoife left her to it.

She went outside to look for Sam and found him in one of the sheds, tinkering with some kind of farm implement that she once would have been able to name.

'What do you want?' he said, jumping to his feet.

'Hey, dial the attitude back! I've talked to Mam and she's calling the deal with O'Brien off.' She watched the relief sweep over his face, wiping years away.

'How did you manage that?'

'Never mind the details but you need to apologise for being a dick. You really scared her, *and* you have to come up with some money to help Kate out. You need to build bridges with Kieran O'Brien too.'

'Screw Kieran O'Brien but thanks, Aoife. I'll make things right with Mam and I'll help with Kate. I didn't realise she was struggling.'

Aoife moved closer to Sam, lightly touching his shoulder. 'Sam, I need to know why you're so adamant about not selling any land? There's something you're not telling me, I know there is. Please, you have to trust me!'

Sam turned to her, his face so hard and full of loathing that she dropped her hand and backed away. He shoved her hard against the shed's damp walls. His breath felt warm against her skin and was interspersed with spittle as he roared in her face.

'Why don't you ever fuck off, Aoife! You're full of shit! I have no special reason for not selling the land except loyalty, something you know nothing about with the way you creep off after Jack Costello whenever you feel the need. How long has that been going on? You're acting like a horny slut! No wonder Connor dumped you. So why don't you do us both a favour and mind your own fucking business!'

Aoife stood gasping as he strode from the shed. Her shaking legs gave way and she slid slowly down the wall until she reached the filthy floor. She lay there panting until gradually her breathing returned to normal. But her heart still thudded violently. How did Sam know about her and Jack? Fuck, he must have followed her.

* * *

Just before dinner, from the vantage point of her bedroom window, Aoife saw Sam walk across the yard towards the kitchen. She crept downstairs and hovered at the kitchen door. She pushed the door open a crack.

Sam was standing uncertainly, watching his mother.

Then he called her. 'Mam!'

They stood looking at each other in silence and then she opened her arms and Sam walked into them.

He whispered '*Sorry*' over and over and Agnes hugged him tightly.

'You've carried some load for us, Sam. I know the sacrifices you've made for me and your sisters. I just didn't realise how much keeping the farm together meant to you. Aoife made me see that you want to protect Dad's legacy. I'm ashamed that I didn't understand. But, Sam, you need to talk to me in future and not let things get to such a head.'

Sam pulled away from the embrace and looked at her. 'Are we OK now?'

'We're OK,' she said, smiling 'Now get those mucky hands washed and call Karol for lunch.'

Aoife crept away.

Mealtime was strained. Aoife could see that Sam and her mam were still uncomfortable with each other but the fallout from the confrontation would gradually ease. As for her relationship with Sam, she doubted it would ever recover. He had frightened her and, worse, the ugly way he spoke about her seeing Jack had made her flesh creep. What she had witnessed today revealed a terrifying rage and hate in Sam. The way he behaved towards his mam was frightening and she was sure that if she hadn't arrived in time there would have been blows struck with the O'Brien brothers. She could hardly believe the man she saw today was the same brother who had acted as protector and father figure for so much of her life. Father figure – perhaps that's who Sam had become, a man remade in the image of his father – twisted and evil. Thinking about her actions today, she felt defiled. She was working with Sam to cover up for their father's crimes and perhaps even covering up for Sam too. He must know something. He buried the box so he must know what was in it. And, more importantly, what else had he done? Her stomach clenched as she thought about what he might be capable of.

A night spent tossing and turning left her feeling stiff and cold. It was two o'clock and she knew sleep would be an impossibility. How could she even look at Sam after their encounter in the shed? Her arm still bore the imprint of his fingers. Sam was just like his father – a monster cloaked by a false smile and a warm manner. It was all a facade. What should she do? What could she do? She was scared of her brother and of what he was capable of.

Just then she heard Sam's door opening and listened as she heard the creaks on the stairs as he moved downwards. She heard the back door open and then a few moments later the sound of a car starting. Where was he going to at this hour of the night? She went downstairs and made herself a hot whiskey and tiptoed back to her bedroom.

As she sipped her whiskey, her mind went to very dark places as she tried to imagine what Sam was up to. She dozed off, but was awakened by a step on the stair and then the soft tread of footsteps moving past her door. She sat bolt upright and checked the time. It was just after four. Should she confront him? But what was the point? He would only tell her to mind her own business.

She went onto the landing a while later and saw that there was no light under his door. She move closer and could just hear soft snores coming from within.

* * *

The next morning Sam looked shattered at breakfast.

'Sam, I heard you come in late last night,' said Agnes. 'It must have been after four. Was there something wrong?'

'Nothing wrong, Mam. I just went out to check I locked up the sheds last night.'

'Are you OK, Aoife? You look very peaky.'

'I'm fine, Mam, I didn't sleep well either.' She glared at Sam as she spoke.

CHAPTER 27

No more hiding or avoiding reality, Aoife decided. She had to gather together her courage and find out what exactly Sam was hiding. . In the kitchen the sun was streaming, rendering Agnes almost invisible as she bent over the contents of a frying pan.

'Morning, pet, you've slept late. How about some breakfast? I just cooked some bacon and sausage – Sam has eaten and gone – he's got a long day ahead. He's driving down to Mullingar to look at a second-hand tractor that's for sale.'

'Did he say what time he's coming back, Mam?'

'Oh, not till late. Now do you want this fry or not?' Agnes gestured towards the frying pan.

'No, I'll just make some toast.' How frustrating that Sam should choose this moment to go tearing off down the country! What was he really up to?

Wondering how she would put down her day, she decided to see if she could find out a bit about Manus's parents. Mam wouldn't know too much so where could she find out? She didn't even know what his parents looked like. Then she thought about all the accumulated detritus in the attic. She had a sudden recollection of a big case or trunk up there. That might contain some family history.

'Mam, you know that enormous trunk that's up in the attic? Is it OK if I have a look through it? One of my classes did a family history project, and I've just realised I know very little about the O'Driscoll side of the family. I know your side a lot better, but I'd love to do a bit of research on Dad's side. So, is it OK if I have a root through after breakfast?'

'Help yourself, love. I've been threatening to get rid of all the stuff in that trunk for years. Your dad's mother must have stored documents there from time immemorial. I wanted him to do a sort-out, but he kept putting it off. So, you're welcome. Now eat some breakfast and take just one wee slice of bacon with the nice brown bread.'

Aoife was surprised to find she ate it with relish. She gulped the hot tea, and chatted away with her mother.

After breakfast, she was swatted away when she attempted to wash up the breakfast things.

'Leave it, girl, I've little enough to do. Take a cloth with you to wipe that old trunk. I'd say it's thick with dust.'

Aoife unfolded the attic ladder and climbed up. The place was cold and dark. The harsh slash of illumination from the bare light bulb cast the darkness aside. Surveying the clutter, she sighed at the many boxes of Christmas decorations and baby clothes her mam had been too sentimental to dispose of. In the corner was a box containing old schoolbooks and copies. There was an exercise copy with *Sam O'Driscoll* emblazoned across the front. It was filled with short essays with titles such as – 'How I Spent My Summer Holidays', 'A Big Adventure', and 'A Day at the Beach'. She read the one entitled 'How

I Spent My Summer Holidays'. Eight-year-old Sam seemed to have spent the entire summer helping his daddy on the farm. He had even drawn a picture of himself and his dad on a tractor. For a moment Aoife felt she was spying on the young Sam – it seemed invasive to be reading his little essay. She closed the copybook and started looking for the trunk. Eventually, she discovered it right at the very back of the attic and had to shove boxes away to reach it.

It was one of those old-fashioned trunks from a bygone age when people travelled by mail coach and stopped at wayside taverns for rest. It was battered and worn. Where had it travelled over the decades, possibly centuries? It certainly looked aged. Examining the little silver snap-locks, she hoped she didn't need a key as there was also a keyhole. Unfortunately, the clasps were rusted shut. Frustrated, she glanced around for something to hammer on the locks to force them open, but then had a better idea. There was bound to be something in the kitchen to help deal with the rust.

Downstairs, a bit of searching paid off and back up in the attic she examined the locks again and this time, with an application of WD-40 and a little jiggling, she pried them open without too much effort. Luckily it was unlocked.

The case creaked as it opened to reveal its contents. These seemed to be mainly letters and legal documents. On top was a brown envelope with a photographer's stamp on the flap. Inside was a formal picture of a man and woman posing against a backdrop of heavy curtain-like material. The man was standing and the woman sitting with hands folded in her lap. His face was partially obscured by a huge moustache. He looked to be in his mid-thirties. The woman was a lot younger, only about twenty, but with a mournful expression in her eyes. Her lips were closed tightly, and her light-coloured dress looked as though it was made of heavy material – the sepia-tinted picture gave little away regarding the colour of the garments. Turning it over, she saw written in copperplate script: *Loretta Swan and James Patrick O'Driscoll on Their Wedding Day*. So, these were her father's parents, the father who died when Manus was a small child and the mother who was the harsh and unforgiving parent. The woman he referred to as the Harpy in the diary.

Aoife examined her closely – Loretta Swan. Following the fashion of the time, she wore her hair piled high on her head and, although she wasn't beautiful, she had a strong, handsome face. Aoife wondered what life experiences made her so hard, so respected, but unloved by her children. There were other envelopes with photographs of other family weddings. The group photos particularly struck her. All those people, long gone yet immortalised forever, sealed in time to this moment, this special occasion in their very best clothes, probably bought for the occasion. Nobody smiled in the photographs – they all tried to appear serious and sombre, but the camera couldn't freeze the liveliness in a person's eyes or a half-smile from a woman who seemed delighted with her new hat, decorated with artificial blooms, and there was even a knowing glint in a young buck's eyes as he perhaps contemplated meeting some pretty girl at the wedding breakfast later that day. All these people lived and breathed and had hopes and dreams, struggles and strife, but they were all now dust.

Aoife was soon immersed, poring over photographs of her aunts and uncles as young people. It was amusing to see a photo of Aunt Emma less than radiant in an old holey jumper, weeding a flower bed, and looking sulky. There were lots of old documents relating to land and wills. The only items of interest among them were letters with foreign stamps, the outpouring of duty and obligation for Loretta from her far-flung offspring. She scanned stiff letters from her sons, Milo, Patrick and Malachi who made lives for themselves in South

Africa and Canada, and once they buried their mother they never came home again. Well, except for their brother's funeral.

Their letters were short and polite, asking after Loretta and the farm and stressing how hard they worked. They made reference to their donations via bank drafts to their mother to help with the upkeep of herself, Manus, and the farm. None of them asked after their brother, and she could find no letters from them to Manus either. Letters from the aunts to their mother were longer and more plentiful. She recalled again Emma's response on hearing that Manus wanted to come to the US. Her weaponised use of guilt emphasised by capital letters and exclamation marks to keep him trapped at home showed her in an unpleasant light. This was not the aunt she thought she knew. He seemed to have a pleasant warmer relationship with his sister Clarissa. They all seemed to despise Baby. An assessment that defeated argument, based on her experience of that annoying child-woman.

As Aoife read old letters and pored over old photographs, she lost track of time. With a start, she realised it would be dinnertime soon. What had she been hoping to find? What was the point of continuing this trawl through her father's life? Would understanding him better change anything? Certainly not for all those young women who had the misfortune to encounter him.

She was just about to give up and return downstairs when she found them.

CHAPTER 28

The letters contained in pale-blue envelopes were tied up with a red ribbon and secreted at the bottom of an old suitcase. Some were addressed to her mother and sent to a Dublin address and the others to her father and addressed to the farm. Feeling like a snoop, which she was, didn't deter her from reading them.

10ᵗʰ August, 1972

Dear Agnes,

I hope you are well. I just want to say how much I enjoyed the visit to the pictures with you before you left for Dublin. I didn't think I'd like a musical but because you were beside me I enjoyed it. It's strange how things happen. When my mother passed, I thought nothing much would change. I would work away on the farm, same as before, and every day would be just like the last. But you changed all that, small perfect Miss Agnes O'Shea. You changed my life entirely. In that silly musical, people burst into song for no reason except that they were happy. For the first time in my life, I feel that way. Now, don't be worrying, I'm not about to start scaring the people and bursting into song when I go down Wine Street, but for the first time for me it seemed the world was in colour. You brought brightness and light into my life. You did that for me. I have one small request of you – please don't change, don't take away your light and colour. I couldn't bear to go back to the grimness again.

This is a strange love letter, I bet you're thinking. Perhaps I've gone a bit strange in the head. God knows enough people thought that of me before. But I like this strangeness, it feels warm and cosy and that is all down to you. I hate letter-writing but it's no chore to write to you. When you come back from the course in Dublin, I'll have a surprise for you. By the way, I had a job persuading your father to give me the address of your Dublin lodgings. I know he thinks I'm 'that odd O'Driscoll fellow' and he's not happy I'm doing a line with his lovely daughter. But although I'll never convince him that I'm good enough for you (an impossible feat for no one is good enough for you) perhaps he'll let me try to live up to you. It is my solemn ambition, lovely Agnes, to make you happy.

Life here goes on, the farm keeps me busy, what with milking cows, tending to crops and trying to fill in the time till you come home again. I'd give you local news if I had any, but as you well know I'm not too good at keeping up with the local gossip. I'll leave that to others to fill you in.

Keep safe in Dublin, don't be seduced by any flattery from jackeens, they are all mouth and no heart. Dearest Agnes, you have all my heart.

Love from your 'strange boy'

Manus

PS Never change, I couldn't bear it.

14th August 1972

My Dear Manus,

What a lovely letter! It's not strange at all, not that I'm an expert for yours is the only love letter I've received. Am I foolish to be telling you that? I'm glad that you enjoyed the musical. I hope you aren't working too hard on the farm. It's a lot for one person to manage alone. Are you eating enough? You're far too thin. I wish I had that problem, but I think I'm too fond of cakes to have a concern about that. That's all I seem to do up here, study and eat cream teas. I won't fit through the mortuary doors when I get back.

The course is going well, and I've met up with a few girls from Sligo who are up here doing secretarial courses. They are staying at my hostel, so it's nice to have people to go out and about with. I met your sister Clarissa while shopping in Easons. We were both so engrossed in choosing books that we backed into each other, so of course we had to go for tea and cake in Kylemore Café. She is such a friendly person and incidentally speaks highly of you. We plan to meet up and go to the pictures one of these evenings. So, I'll have no shortage of company.

The course is boring, to tell the truth, but Dad made me promise to do it. He's determined to give me what he calls the best start in life. I think he feels bad that I didn't get to go to college like my brother. Of course it was a disappointment, but I know how expensive university is and of course he needed my help in the business while Gerard was finishing his degree. They say every cloud has a silver lining and I think you must be mine. After all, if I went away to study, we would never have met, so all's well that ends well.

I have met none of those flashy jackeens you mentioned – at least not yet!!!! Seriously though, I miss you and can't wait for this course to be over. Only another week to go and then we can meet up again and soon you will be sick of the sight of me.

Affectionately yours,

Agnes

PS: What's the surprise???

20ᵗʰ August 1972

Dear Agnes,

It was so nice to hear from you. I'm glad that all is going well for you in Dublin.

I'm delighted you bumped into Clarissa. She settled in well after coming back from the States, and I think she's pleased to be home. She's got to know Dublin well, so should be able to show you around whenever you're free. It's funny that you mentioned your brother because I met him when I was delivering potatoes in town. He was with a girl, very flashy-looking she was too. He didn't introduce me, but they seemed much taken with each other. Perhaps there will be a wedding in your family to look forward to.

I have little news. The cows need milking, and the carrots need weeding as per usual. Before you came along all these jobs seemed mundane and pointless, but now I whistle while I work. Now don't laugh, but I even caught myself humming a tune from that musical 'Oklahoma' – you know the one – I think it's called 'Oh What a Beautiful Morning'. If anyone heard me, they'd think me cracked in the head. But they'd be right – I am cracked in the head over you.

I hope you don't think this letter is too foolish. I'm afraid to reread it in case I shrivel with embarrassment. Dear Agnes, please take good care of yourself. You are very dear to me!

Yours always,

Manus

PS: As for the surprise – wait and see!

These love letters between her parents showed how Manus was devoted to Agnes. He was unafraid to express his feelings for her and to please her. No wonder she held on to them. They confirmed what Aoife already knew: that the handwriting in the diary matched that in the letter written to her mother. It was disturbing to realise that the tenderness of those love letters to her mother were penned by the hand that was responsible for the evil ravings of the diary. All of the evidence mounted up. Anika had a dolphin earring. It stretched credulity to think that that was a coincidence. Her father was a killer. She just didn't know how many victims could be laid at his door.

She rooted in the box and found a small photo album containing a handful of pictures, including a small copy of Loretta and James on their wedding day, and a family snap of the seven children with their parents posed at the front door of the farmhouse. Manus the baby was held by one of his sisters, perhaps Clarissa. There were a couple of photos of the older O'Driscoll boys dressed in little suits, probably Confirmation suits.

She stared at a photograph of Manus aged six or seven. He was wearing short pants and a jumper, standing in a stream holding a paper boat. He stared at the camera, with no expression of either happiness or sadness, just a blank stare. He looked lost in thought. What had made him so damaged, so sick, that he'd commit such dreadful acts against defenceless girls?

She thought back to the letter he had written to her mam, begging her not to change. But she had changed, motherhood changed her. When Sam was born, Agnes became distant and cold towards him. Manus, feeling rejected, lashed out in rage. Anika had died when Sam was a baby, sacrificed to his sickness. What about the second killing mentioned in the diary? Kate was born two years later in March 1980. She needed to check the Missing Person site to see if there were missing girls in March or April of that year. The thought of checking her own birth date against those of the missing girls made her stomach clench. How horrifying it would be to discover her existence had snuffed out the life of a human being! Thinking about it made her skin crawl and shiver. But she couldn't procrastinate forever, and a fierce urgency to check the site for confirmation of her fears propelled her.

Once back in the privacy of her bedroom, she powered up her laptop and looked up the Garda website. Scanning through the list for a wonderful heart-soaring moment, she noted that there were no missing women for either March or April of 1980. Could it be a fantasy after all? She held her breath and rechecked the list. The only woman listed was in May, two months after the birth of Kate. She scanned the information.

Mary Bernadette Maher, a seventeen-year-old member of the travelling community, was reported missing in May. She had been on her way to visit her boyfriend and his family in Leitrim. Mary Bernadette's parents didn't approve of the relationship and thought she was going to stay with her aunt in Galway. Her aunt did not expect her, so the alarm wasn't raised for several weeks. Her boyfriend thought she had changed her mind. The last person who spoke to her was a woman who travelled with her on the bus from Longford. She told that woman she planned to catch a bus to Manorhamilton to meet her boyfriend. This sighting was on the 24th of April. But it was Wednesday, the 2nd of May, before they finally reported her missing.

That made her a possible match for the girl mentioned in the diary.

CHAPTER 29

An Garda Siochána
Missing Persons

Mary Bernadette Maher

Missing since Tuesday, 24th April, 1980

Born: 22/2/1962

Age: 17 years

Height: 5ft 3

Hair: brown

Eyes: blue

Build: slim

Details:

Mary Bernadette was last seen on the 24th of April at 4:30 pm. Several passengers watched her alighting from the Longford to Sligo bus. Her family believed she was going to stay with her aunt in Galway, but instead she planned to visit her boyfriend and his family in Manorhamilton, Co. Leitrim.

So, Mary Bernadette was more than likely a victim of Manus. Determined to find out everything she could about this young girl, Aoife searched online for local newspaper reports from that time. It took her a while to get access to the archived articles and pay the required fee to view them, but eventually she found a report on the missing girl and an interview with her boyfriend, Pádraig Flynn.

Longford Leader May 1980

Mary Bernadette Maher, 17, has been missing for several weeks. Concern for her safety is mounting. Her parents and extended family are heartbroken by her disappearance. Many rumours abound as to what has become of Mary Bernadette. The Garda have been questioning everyone who may know something about her disappearance.

According to her mother Bridget Maher, Mary B as she was known left her home to go to Galway and spend time with her aunt who had recently settled in Galway city. Mary B was to meet her aunt in Galway on Tuesday, 24th April. But her aunt, Mary Maguire, explained that she received a postcard from her niece saying that her plans had changed, and she wouldn't be staying with her after all. Mary Bernadette's parents were unaware of her change of plans and believed she was staying with her aunt. The aunt's account is backed up by information from her boyfriend Pádraig Flynn.

Mr Flynn told our reporter that he and Mary B were in love and planned to marry as soon as they were able. The romance

was not approved of by the Maher family. Pádraig Flynn arranged for Mary B to come to Manorhamilton to stay with his family until they got married. Mary B wrote to her aunt cancelling her visit so that no one would suspect their plans. The Flynn and Maher families had a falling-out several years ago, but Pádraig's parents were happy for the wedding to take place. They hoped that it would put an end to the feud. Mr Flynn said that Mary B hated deceiving her family but thought she could make her family realise how serious they were about each other. He hadn't bought her an engagement ring, but he had given her a gold Claddagh ring.

A hot wave surged over Aoife's body as she pictured the little gold Claddagh ring nestled in the box of horrors. Her father had mentioned how he was 'bequeathed' this by his 'little travelling companion'. *The sick bastard!*

The last sighting of Mary Bernadette was in Sligo town. It is not clear why she didn't take the Manorhamilton bus. According to CIE, she may have missed it as the Longford bus was late arriving. The Gardaí continued to look for Mary B and have carried out extensive searches. To date, they have been unable to find any sign of this young woman. An Garda has issued fresh appeals for information from the public.

Pádraig Flynn said that when his girlfriend didn't arrive, he believed that her parents had found out and prevented her from coming. They didn't have a phone in her caravan, so he wrote to her but received no letter back. Eventually, after over a week of no contact, he visited her parents, but they wouldn't give him information about Mary Bernadette. They still believed she was with her aunt in Galway. But his appearance caused them to contact the aunt and, of course, they then discovered that she had never been with her. By this time, Mary Bernadette had been missing for over a week. The family then notified the Guards. To date, there has been no sign of the missing girl. Her family prays constantly for her safe return. Pádraig Flynn swears that he won't ever give up searching for her.

Irish Independent May 1980

Boyfriend of Missing Girl Questioned by Garda

Last night Pádraig Flynn, 22, of Manorhamilton, Co. Leitrim, was questioned in connection with the disappearance of Mary Bernadette Maher, 17. The family of Miss Maher insist she would never have gone to visit him and believe that he had a hand in her disappearance. Her aunt claims that she received a postcard from Mary Bernadette saying she wouldn't be visiting with her after all but was instead taking up a job in Donegal town. Therefore, she didn't worry when she didn't arrive in Galway. Both parents and aunt claim the postcard is a forgery. Early this morning, the Garda released Mr Flynn from custody without charge.

Transcript of RTÉ Radio interview with P. Flynn April 1981, on the *Seán Collins Show*

Seán Collins: It's been exactly a year since the disappearance of teenager Mary Bernadette Maher. Mary Bernadette was last seen getting off a bus from Longford at Sligo Bus Depot on the 24th April 1979. Today I have in studio Pádraig Flynn, boyfriend of Mary Bernadette. Good morning, Pádraig.

PF: Good morning, Seán.

SC: Pádraig, it's been a year and still no word of Mary Bernadette. I know it's been a rough year for you. Perhaps you should begin by telling us a little about her?

PF: Mary B, that's what we all called her, was a lovely person. I met her through my parents. They were friendly with Mary B's folks and we knew each other for years. Her brother and I used to box together – we were all good friends.

SC: When did you and Mary B become an item?

PF: She had just turned sixteen, and we were at a local disco in town, and I asked her out to dance. She was always Mikey's little sister but that night I saw a different side to her. I know it sounds daft, but I fell for her big time. We started meeting up on the QT because her parents were very strict.

SC: Did they disapprove of you, Pádraig?

PF: It wasn't so much that they didn't like me, but it was that there was a bit of falling-out between my parents and hers. It was some bit of business and it got ugly and soon even Mikey and me couldn't hang out. But Mary B and I continued to meet up. We were meeting in secret for nearly a year and then her old fellow found out and he went mental.

SC: That must have been hard.

PF: Aye, it was.

SC: Did you keep seeing each other?

PF: We tried, and that's why they were sending her off to her aunty – to get her away from me.

SC: So, what did you do?

PF: We made a plan. I spoke to my parents, and they agreed to let Mary B stay with them. We planned to get married as soon as she turned 18. She was only a few weeks off it, and we hoped that if we got married her parents would come round because they loved the bones of her. We all did . . .

SC: Take a minute there, Pádraig. I can see that you're very upset.

PF: I'm grand, it just catches me hard sometimes. Anyway, I arranged for Mary B to come to stay and my parents were OK with it. They worried about how her family would take things. I think they were afraid it would make things worse. But they knew how I felt about her, and I suppose I wore them down. Mary B rang me from a call box to the garage where I worked to let me know what time to expect her. We planned that once she arrived in Sligo, she was to get a connecting bus to Manorhamilton and I was to meet her off the bus, except she never showed up. At first, I thought she changed her mind and went to her aunt's as her parents wanted. But it made no sense because she rang me the night before she left and told me she had sent a postcard to her aunt saying she had got a job in Donegal. She seemed so happy and was looking forward to staying with my parents.

SC: What did you do next?

PF: I had no number for her aunt, but my parents knew her next-door neighbours and we rang them and asked them to see if she was there. They said that the aunt had told them she had a postcard and Mary B wouldn't be staying with her. Then I wrote to her at her parents' place as they didn't have a phone. I waited and waited, and I heard nothing. At that stage, I wasn't sure whether to worry or be angry.

SC: So, what did you do next?

PF: I went down to see her parents. They didn't believe me

at first but when they got in touch with the aunt they were seriously alarmed and that's when they reported her missing.

SC: But by this time Mary B had been missing for well over a week.

PF: Yes, it was horrible. No one could remember exactly what she was wearing. But we think she had on a blue denim jacket as it was one of her favourite things.

SC: But there was something else she was wearing, wasn't there?

PF: Yeah. I asked Mary B to marry me, but I couldn't afford a proper engagement ring, so I bought her a gold Claddagh ring. I got it engraved with my initials. She loved it and said she didn't need another engagement ring. She told me she wanted to get a ring for me too, with her initials on it like a proper wedding band.

SC: Unfortunately, there was very little information about what had happened to Mary B after she got off the bus in Sligo. An eyewitness said they saw a young girl wearing a blue denim jacket talking to a man in a dark-blue van at the bus depot. We think that her bus from Longford was late getting in, and she missed her connection to Manorhamilton. The Garda appealed for the driver to come forward, but to date no one has come forward. That was the last sighting of her. Mary B disappeared without a trace. But, for you, the nightmare was to get much worse.

PF: Yes, it did. I was out of my mind with worry, but the Mahers believed that I had something to do with Mary B's disappearance. They started making accusations. Now look, I don't hold it against them. They were out of their minds with worry too, but Mr Maher went to the Guards and accused me of making away with her.

SC: What happened then?

PF: Well, they had me in for questioning. They were putting

199

together a case, saying that I fought with her because she wouldn't agree to come away with me. It was hard for them to prove anything, but I knew if I couldn't prove I was innocent of harming her, I'd be marked for life.

SC: So, what happened?

PB: Well, I got lucky. The day that Mary B came to Sligo I was working with a local farmer, and he was able to convince the guards that I wasn't anywhere near Sligo when she disappeared. Some locals saw me waiting for her at the bus stop in Manorhamilton, and I was working in the garage over the next few days. So, the guards let me go as they realised I had nothing to do with her disappearance. Eventually, the Mahers came to see that I was an innocent man, but it was a waste of time when the Guards could have been hunting down the person responsible.

SC: What do you think happened to her, Pádraig?

PF: I'd love to believe that she's still alive, but I don't think that's likely. There's no way she'd leave me and her family suffering like this. I think someone took her and killed her. Listen, she's not the first young one who's disappeared over the years. I think there is a maniac at work and my poor girl was unfortunate enough to meet him.

SC: Pádraig, thanks for coming in to talk to us about this very tragic time for you and the Maher family.

Sick at heart, Aoife returned to the Missing Persons site. She scanned for information about girls missing on or around her birth date, 16th February 1985. Two men were missing but no women were listed until late August and that woman was middle-aged. Aoife's relief was tempered by a nervous sense of unease. It would almost have been better to find a girl and know the worst. Tiredly, she switched off the computer.

CHAPTER 30

Sam still hadn't arrived home by supper time, so Aoife popped a pizza in the oven, and they ate in front of the TV. Sam texted to say that he was grabbing a bite at a hotel and wouldn't be home until after ten. They watched *Fair City*, Agnes's favourite soap, and then the *RTÉ News* at nine. It featured the usual depressing round-up of political shenanigans, scenes of ongoing violence in Syria and the tearful pleas of a Donegal woman for information about the whereabouts of her daughter who failed to come home after a night out with friends.

Aoife's body jerked to attention. A girl missing in Donegal. Sam had gone out last night. *No!* She couldn't let her mind contemplate that her brother had something to do with the disappearance of this young woman. '*Like father, like son*' – the phrase beat an incessant refrain in her head. No, this was wild imaginings. Sam might have had any number of innocent reasons for going out. He said that he needed to check the sheds were locked. But he was away for at least an hour and a half. What else was he up to? Aoife shook her head. She had to stop this crazy suspicious thinking or she'd drive herself mad.

Agnes took out some knitting and worked on Colm's birthday jumper. She found it very difficult to sit and just watch TV. Guilty at any perceived idleness, the knitting made her feel purposeful whilst indulging her passion for soap-watching. The news was the only programme where she felt it was appropriate to rest the knitting on her lap. She often dozed as she sat in her chair. Tonight was no exception and sleep had softened her face, making her look younger than her years. Framed by a cloud of fluffy hair, lips thinned with age were parted and little snore gasps passed from them at random intermissions. Her large capable hands, spotted with age and shiny with years of housework, rested on the sprawl of red wool on her lap. Over the years, she had gained weight but was neither fat nor thin, just well covered. Aoife felt a wash of pure love sweep over her, and tears pricked her eyes. Finding the room claustrophobic and overheated, she got up to leave.

The rustle of her clothing awakened Agnes.

'Ah, pet, did I fall asleep? You should have woken me. Oh dear, I bet I was snoring. Sandy slept over one night and teased me that I snored so loudly the cat leapt off her bed in fright, not that the cat should have been on her bed.'

'You're grand, Mam – you didn't make a sound. I was just about to make a drop of tea. Would you like a cup?'

When her mother nodded in agreement, she wandered into the kitchen and prepared a tray with tea, milk and some gingernut biscuits on a plate.

Agnes switched off the TV and brought over a little table so they could drink their tea in comfort.

'Did you find anything of interest in the attic, love?'

Aoife paused, then seizing the opportunity said, 'There were some photographs of Dad's parents and a few with his mother and brothers and sisters. What was she like? His mother, I mean?'

'We never met. Loretta was a very private person. No one in the village knew her well. I think when her husband died she found things difficult but wouldn't ask for help from anyone. Pride can be a terrible isolating thing.'

'What about the children, Dad and his siblings, surely they mixed in the local school? Did you play with his sisters?'

Agnes laughed. 'All his ones were teenagers when I was at school – some had even emigrated. I didn't meet them until we got married, apart from Clarissa that is.'

'But what about Dad? Didn't you know him at school? I know he was older, but surely you would have known him as a boy?'

Agnes shifted in her seat and said sadly, 'Your dad was what people today would call a loner. His mother dressed him in old-fashioned clothes and often kept him away from school to work on the farm. I think he was mistreated. She beat him, treated him like a slave and was constantly putting him down. At least that's what I gathered, though Dad never liked talking about her. You know, of course, that my father was the local undertaker and that's how your dad and I met. I helped him pick out the coffin for his mother and to organise the service. He was so lost. It's a terrible thing to say, but I think her death was the best thing for him. He could finally breathe.' Agnes stopped in consternation at her own candour. 'I don't know why I'm telling you all this. These things are best left in the past.'

'No, Mam, I want to know. Look, I know I shouldn't have read them but I found a couple of letters between you and Dad when you were away doing some course in Dublin. He sounded lost without you.'

For a moment Agnes looked puzzled and then smiled. 'That must have been when I went to Dublin to do a secretarial course. It was the first time we were apart since we started going out together. I'd forgotten I kept those letters – maybe it was because those were the only letters we ever wrote to each other. We were never really apart except for the very odd night – so my heading off to the big city was difficult for him. It's funny, but your dad seemed to think I was a real catch and that every fellow was after me. As if! I think he was afraid I'd get to like Dublin and stay. The truth was, I couldn't wait to get back home to see him.'

'What was the surprise mentioned in the letter?'

Agnes laughed in happy remembrance. 'He picked me up from the train station with a bunch of flowers and brought me out to the strand at Mullaghmore. It was really lovely. He had prepared a picnic. The food was awful, plastic-tasting ham sandwiches and tea out of a flask that was as black as muck and had so much tannin you could trot a mouse across it. But he went to all that trouble for me. No boy had ever prepared a picnic for me, and I was touched. Then he proposed. I said yes, and neither of us ever regretted it. Mind you, my father wasn't too keen, but he soon came round and although they were never close Dad could see how happy Manus made me.' She smiled at Aoife. 'I don't mind you reading those letters at all. I'm just sorry that you and Connor didn't have what we had. A good marriage is a wonderful thing. Mind, we didn't have it all rosy – in every life there are difficulties.'

This was the opening Aoife had been hoping for. 'What do you mean, Mam? I thought it was all roses with you two. Don't tell me you had any drama because I won't believe it!' She laughed, raising her eyes heavenward.

Agnes took a deep breath and paused, as if uncertain whether to continue. 'I never talked about it before but, although our marriage was good and we didn't argue, sometimes I found your father to be distant, moody. He found it hard to talk and whenever I mentioned his mother, he was very curt. I think she did him a lot of damage. One time when we had a small falling-out I gave him the silent treatment, and he got low, so quiet and withdrawn that it scared me. I made it up with him and asked him why he was so upset, and he confided that when he was only a young fellow his mother stopped beating him but, instead, if he did something wrong, she wouldn't speak to him for days, weeks even months – not a word. You can imagine how that must have affected him. So, I could nag, shout and roar at him but for me to go silent was like torture for him. So, of course, when I realised, I did my best to be cheerful around him.'

'There must have been times when you were down,' Aoife said. 'You couldn't pretend to be happy all the time.'

'Ah love, it wasn't hard. Your dad was a wonderful husband and a brilliant father to all you youngsters. But I have to admit there were a few occasions when I tried his patience, especially after Sam was born. I wasn't myself – the baby blues we used to call it, but it lasted months and I think it was a very hard time for your father. He had to put up with me being irritable and out of sorts.'

'Mam, you must have had post-natal depression – that was hardly your fault.'

'Yes, I know that now, but it was a tough time for us both and I think maybe harder for your father because it brought back unhappy memories.'

'Did you have it again after Kate and me?'

'After Kate, yes, but not as bad, thank God!'

'But after me, Mam, did you have it after me?' Aoife asked, her heart pounding so violently it hurt her ribs.

'*What are you two girls up to?*' Sam called from the doorway as he pulled his jacket off. 'I don't suppose there's any chance of a mug of tea and a sandwich, eh?'

Agnes got to her feet. 'Ah son, you're very late. I suppose you're exhausted. Did you buy the tractor?'

'No, Mam, it was a complete waste of time. He wanted too much for it and it needed a lot of work, so I left it and went to see a couple of other contacts. They may have something for me later in the year. In the meantime, I'll manage with the yoke I have.'

Aoife followed them to the kitchen and Sam washed his hands while Agnes made a sandwich with leftover meat. In a short time, he was sitting at the kitchen table tucking into his food.

Aoife was angry and frustrated at the interruption. She had been making progress and much of what her mother told her confirmed the accounts in the diary. Her mother had withdrawn emotionally from their father at the times when those girls went missing. Her depressed state was a trigger for her father, causing him to take out his frustration on those girls. If only Sam hadn't interrupted, she would know for certain whether her mother had been well and happy after she was born and, therefore, no one had died because of her arrival into the world. That she could have, however unwittingly, brought about the annihilation of another human being made her insides shiver. The moment had now passed. God knows when there would be an opportunity to talk to her mam in private again.

Sam interrupted her thoughts. 'I heard you were in McCoy's the other night in the company of Jack Costello. You'd want to watch that fellow. He has a reputation as a bit of a lad. I wouldn't want you rebounding in that direction so soon after Connor.'

'Why don't you mind your own effing business, Sam? I never heard you say as much as a positive word about Connor when we were engaged, so don't go pretending you give a crap!'

Aoife was furious that Sam was using his knowledge about her and Jack to embarrass her in front of her mother. When he smirked at her she longed to slap him.

Agnes looked uneasily at her two children. 'Ah now, Sam, I think Aoife is entitled to go out and mix with her friends without you making assumptions like that.'

'Yeah, Mam, it's none of his business what I do and who I hang around with.' Aoife's voice quivered with anger.

'I'm only watching out for you, Aoife. No offence meant!'

'Well, I do take offence. God, I forgot the way you can't sneeze around here without the whole place announcing you've got the plague and are about to die. But I didn't expect my brother to be joining the chorus. Look, I'm away to bed. See you in the morning, Mam!'

And she left, banging the door behind her.

She lay in bed wanting to confront Sam about where he had disappeared the night before and yet was terrified to do so. Another sleepless night awaited her.

CHAPTER 31

The following day was wet and cold, feeling less like June and more like dismal autumn. The rain misted down, and the clouds seemed to skim the earth. Aoife felt damp, depressed, and as irritable as a boil about to burst. The idea of the long soggy day stretching ahead filled her with dread. She went down to the kitchen, relieved to find it empty. A note was propped up against a milk jug on the table.

Morning, Aoife, I'm just off to the shops with Sam. If there is anything special you'd like for dinner, text me and I'll pick it up. Love, Mam

Aoife wrinkled her brow in annoyance. She wanted an opportunity to finish her conversation with her mother.

How was she going to put the day in? On impulse, she decided to go for a run. There was an old pair of trainers in her room, a bit ratty but they would do the job. In ten minutes, she had changed into trackies and shoes and selected some Van Morrison on her phone. She didn't bother locking up. The air was cool rather than cold and a wet mist seeped through her clothes. She sped up and ran at a fast pace along the empty country road. She decided on a 5 km route, which she and her mother called the Round because it did just that – brought you back towards where you started. As she ran, she turned the music as high as her ears could bear. She didn't want to leave any space for thoughts to push through. What she needed was just mindless running.

By the time she finished her route and jogged back up the avenue to the house, it was almost midday. Racing upstairs, she indulged in a long hot shower. Fleetingly she felt guilty about how much water she wasted but, given the myriad of environmental sins she had committed throughout her life, this barely registered. Her mobile ringing interrupted her musings. It was Kate, inviting her round for lunch. Sandy was dying to see her and hoped they might arrange a shopping trip at the weekend. Aoife agreed to meet up.

It was after one when she pulled up outside Kate's house on the outskirts of Sligo town. The house was part of a small development, a detached two-storey, looking ridiculously small nestled up against the backdrop of Ben Bulben. As she pulled up, Kate and Sandy were standing at the doorway.

'*Hey!*' called Sandy.

'*Hey, you!*' said Aoife as they hugged.

Kate smiled. 'Come on in out of the damp old day. Lunch is ready.'

Inside, there was no sign of Kenny, but then he was probably avoiding visitors. Colm was likely away at football practice.

Kate added to the array of serving dishes on the table. 'I know it's not exactly salad weather, but I couldn't let all this go to waste,' she said. 'Sit down, Aoife, and help yourself. Sandy, fetch some bread!'

'This looks great,' Aoife said as she sat down.

The others joined her and they all tucked in.

'Did ya hear the news last night about that young one missing in Donegal?' Kate said towards the end of the meal. 'It said on the midday news that there's still no word of her. God, it must be awful for her family!'

'Yeah, it must be such a worry for them,' Aoife said. 'Hopefully, she'll turn up safe and sound.' Her mouth felt dry and she desperately wanted to think about anything but a missing girl.

They fell silent.

Then, out of the blue, Sandy asked, 'Why did you and Connor break up? I thought you guys loved each other.'

'Sandy!' said Kate. 'Really! Don't be so rude.'

'It's OK, don't be cross with her,' Aoife said. 'Sandy is only asking what everyone else wants to know but is too afraid to ask. It's complicated. I can say we wanted different things out of life, but really I don't know. We loved each other. It's difficult to switch those feelings off. It's not as if one of us was unfaithful, but perhaps we didn't love each other enough so as not to let the differences matter. Anyway, I'm sorry not to have contacted you about the wedding being cancelled. I know you were looking forward to it.'

'I'm sorry, I didn't mean to be nosy,' said Sandy. 'It's just that I liked Connor. He was cool and talked to me like a regular person and not a child. And the two of you seemed so right together somehow. Anyway, I'm sorry if I've upset you.'

'Nothing you could say would upset me. After all, you are my favourite niece,' Aoife joked lamely.

Then Colm burst in from football practice like a muddy mini tornado.

Kate shrieked, '*Take every stitch off in the utility room and then march upstairs for a shower!*'

Colm grinned and hugged his aunt but dodged a kiss and two

minutes later they saw him racing upstairs in his boxers.

'*Don't forget to use soap and shampoo!*' Kate roared as he reached the top of the stairs. 'I swear to God he came out of the shower one day with wet hair in a suspiciously short time and I leaned in to sniff and I declare he had just stood under the shower using no soap at all. He seemed shocked that I expected him to at least use soap. He was under the impression that the water on its own did the job and girly things like soap and shampoo were an optional extra.'

Twenty minutes later Colm bounded downstairs and submitted to his mother's sniff test before urgently demanding food. He looked suitably horrified at being offered salad leftovers. 'I'm a man!' he declared. 'Feed me meat!'

So, his mother produced a frying pan and fried up two sausages, two rashers and an egg and deposited them in a long baguette.

The women watched in fascination as he annihilated the filled roll in double-quick time.

'You're a pig!' declared his sister in mock horror.

Colm then regaled them with stories of his training and of how the coach wanted him to play forward in the next game as he believed he was a great goal-scorer.

'Will Daddy be able to come and see me play next Saturday? It's a crucial game in the league?'

Kate hesitated, but she didn't need to say a word as disappointment and anger flared in Colm's eyes.

'He promised, he said he'd make the next game – so what's his excuse now?' he demanded belligerently.

'Now cool down, I didn't say he wouldn't make it, but you know he hasn't been feeling well lately. I'm sure he'll do his best to make it to your game – and I'll be there and Sandy too.' She ignored the eye-roll her daughter gave her.

'Yeah, whatever,' he grunted and headed upstairs. *'I'm just going to play games, OK?'* he called over his shoulder.

As they cleared away the remains of lunch, Aoife took her sister aside.

'So Kenny is still feeling low?'

Sighing, Kate nodded. 'I know he can't help it. His doctor put him on a new medication, but it will take weeks to kick in and, in the meantime, he has no energy, he just sits and stares at the ceiling. That's where he is now, lying in our bedroom staring at nothing,'

Kate's voice cracked, and she turned away, her eyes glassy with tears.

'What about his job, is it still under threat?'

'They're giving him redundancy. If he was in a different state of mind, he might have been able to fight for his job, but he's too worn down and listless. I think the firm is glad to get rid of him. He's been struggling for a while and this way they can let him go without a fuss. I thought at first it was the thought of losing his job that was getting him down but he's been sinking for months.'

'What's troubling him, Kate?'

'Kenny has stuff going on in his head that I have no idea about. He won't talk to me and we're still waiting on a referral to a psychiatrist. I want to pay for private counselling, but he won't hear of it. He can be very stubborn in his quiet way.'

Aoife reached for her sister and Kate clung to her, but then pulled away.

'I'm grand, really, I am. We'll get through this, I know we will.'

She loaded the dishwasher and the sisters worked away in silence.

They spent the rest of the afternoon watching an old Katharine Hepburn and Cary Grant movie called *Bringing Up Baby*. Sandy had originally wrinkled her nose when Kate suggested watching it. But soon was laughing at the witty dialogue and comic timing of the actors.

At five Aoife noticed several texts from her mam – she wanted to know where she was. She texted back that she was on her way, then hugged her sister and niece goodbye and left the house.

She was getting into the car when Sandy ran over and whispered, 'Is there any chance of you and Connor getting back together?'

Aoife avoided her niece's eyes and shrugged.

CHAPTER 32

Back at home, Agnes was bustling about the kitchen preparing the evening meal. As they chatted about their respective days, Aoife set the table. She had little appetite but knew her mother would be hurt if she didn't eat something. Better to shovel food into her mouth than deal with a litany of concerned questions.

Conversation between them was patchy and Sam was moody and preoccupied, barely speaking except to grunt at the end that he had to finish some work outside.

'What's wrong with him?' Aoife asked. 'He's very moody this evening.'

'I don't know, he was quiet all day. I think he's still annoyed about his wasted trip to Mullingar to see that useless tractor.'

They washed up the dishes and swept and tidied the kitchen together. The rest of the evening was spent watching the soaps followed by the nine o'clock news. At ten Agnes yawned and said she was going to bed.

Aoife felt frustrated. So much for her plan to continue her talk with her mother. She just couldn't wait another day.

As Agnes gathered her knitting, keeping her voice casual Aoife asked, 'By the way, remember what we were talking about yesterday? I was just wondering if you had a bad time after I was born or was it just with the other two?'

'No problem after you were born, Aoife love, I felt great!'

Aoife breathed a sigh of relief. 'It was probably because I was such a perfectly behaved baby!'

Agnes laughed. 'Perhaps you were, just don't let your sister or brother hear I said so, mind! Of course,' she paused, wrinkling up her forehead, 'I had my difficulties while I was expecting you. I think I was so worried about having the same bad experience I had with Sam and Kate that I worked myself up into a terrible state. The doctor wanted to put me on tablets, but I decided to ride things out, and I was right because the moment you were born I felt fantastic. Your dad and I were delighted with you. I thought he'd want another boy, but he couldn't have been happier when you arrived safely. I was so sorry to put him through all the stress and anxiety, waiting for you to be born. But, thank God, I felt so well after you arrived it was nothing like the others. All that worry and stress for nothing. But we got through it, and you were a bonny baby, sleeping and feeding like an angel. Well, I'm off to bed now. Don't forget to turn off the lights in here and the telly. God knows when Sam will arrive back in.'

Watching her mother's back disappear around the door, Aoife's stomach lurched. Her mother had been depressed during her pregnancy, not after it. So she had shut Manus out and he had been driven to God only knew what horrors.

Feeling sick, she got her laptop from the bedroom and checked

215

out the Missing Persons website. She searched for women reported missing in the months before her birth date. There were three people listed, one elderly man and two women. The women were last sighted in the west of the country. Neither had been seen since. One was a widow and mother of a ten-year-old child; the other was a student from Galway University. The women went missing two months apart. There was nothing in the report to link either with the remaining items in the biscuit tin, the hair, the scarf, and the lipstick. She needed to trawl through newspaper reports to get more information. But not tonight. She couldn't face it.

Reflecting on the fresh portal of hell opening before her, Aoife finally accepted she was going to have to talk to Sam and Kate. Avoidance was cowardly. She needed to face facts and the evidence that her father was a serial killer was mounting fast. Her heart smote her at the thought of her poor mother. Her world would crash into smithereens when she found out. Should she go find Sam and confront him? No, not tonight. What was holding her back was fear. She was afraid to ask Sam about the diary because deep down she was terrified he was a party to some of Manus's deviant behaviour. She was sick of the thought of what she might find out. Where on earth had he gone last night and was there any connection with the missing girl? Shuddering, she felt as though the walls of the house were closing in on her. She called upstairs to her mother that she was going to visit a friend and slammed the door before she could start quizzing her. There was only one person she wanted to see tonight. Someone who would help her forget for a little while at least.

Outside Jack Costello's house, she hesitated. Maybe this was a bad idea, but to hell with it. Aoife rapped hard on the door. There was a light burning in one of the enormous windows on the first floor. She picked up some gravel and chucked it at the window. After a few attempts, she managed to rouse Jack.

He opened the window and whistled softly when he saw her. '*Hang on while I put some clothes on!*' he called.

In a minute he stood at the door and Aoife admired the rumpled look of him. He smelled faintly of sweat and fading cologne.

'I knew you'd find me irresistible,' he said, licking his lips.

'Don't flatter yourself; it's more a case of any port in a storm. Are you up for a ride?'

'Jaysus, you're direct!' he said, ushering her inside. 'How do ya know I don't have a visitor?'

'Well, do you?'

'Nope, I'm home alone,' he smirked, 'but as to the riding, I'm not sure – I think you're too forward for my taste.'

'You weren't complaining the other night. Look, let's not waste each other's time – do you want to or not? Say the word and I'll go!'

'Hey, calm down, I'm only joking!' he said, raising his hands in surrender. 'Do you want a drink?'

'Maybe afterwards. Come on, where's this enormous bed of yours?'

He led the way, and they kissed as they stood in the bedroom.

Jack started talking romantic shite, and Aoife, afraid he would spoil her mood, pushed him onto the super-sized bed and straddled him. 'Less talk, more action, Jack!'

'Hold on, ya lunatic! Let me at least get my clothes off.'

Together, lying side by side, they pulled the clothes from each other, their nakedness making them grunt with harsh passion. The sex was fast and aggressive. Aoife didn't allow any foreplay, wanting only fierce unvarnished sex. She didn't want any faux tenderness or silly flirtatious talk, all she wanted was to be caught up in the sheer physicality of sex where she couldn't think or feel but just be.

Afterwards, their sweaty bodies stuck together. Then Jack rolled off and exhaled noisily.

'I'm feeling used, young woman,' he teased. 'Of course, maybe I'm just irresistible or perhaps it's the aftershave?' His teeth gleamed in the starlight.

'I told you, Jack, it was a case of any port in a storm.'

'Now I do feel used.' He looked a little crestfallen.

'You'll get over it,' she said, rummaging for her clothes and dressing swiftly in the dark.

'Are you leaving now? What about the drink I promised?'

'Some other time, Jack. Seriously, thanks for that, I needed it.'

He followed her buck-naked towards the stairs.

'Hey, by the way, tell that brother of yours to quit with the rally-driving. He nearly cleaved me the other night on the Donegal Road. He was hooring it, acting like a wee boy racer.'

Aoife pulled up short. 'What do you mean? Sam was in Mullingar yesterday not Donegal. You must have him mixed up with someone else.'

'Not a chance. If it's one thing I know it's cars and I'd recognise his old jalopy anywhere. Anyway, why don't you come back to bed? Ya never know, there may be a repeat performance in it for you.'

'Go back to bed, Jack, it's too cold for long goodbyes.'

Jack shook his head and then, shivering, trudged back upstairs.

Aoife pulled the front door closed behind her.

CHAPTER 33

Aoife, relieved to see the house entombed in darkness, crept upstairs. Once safely back in her room, her thoughts commenced their torment. Jack had said he had seen Sam on the Donegal Road. But Sam was supposed to be in Mullingar buying a tractor. How could he be anywhere near Donegal? Her heart skittered, remembering the news reports about the young girl missing in Donegal. Exhausted, she collapsed into a deep, dreamless sleep.

The sounds of hoovering intermixed with the soft lowing of cows and birdsong jerked her awake. Glancing at her phone, she saw it was after ten. She lay staring at the ceiling, thinking about her conversation with Kate and Sandy and her booty call with Jack. Sandy asked if she and Connor would get back together. Was that a possibility? Well, sleeping with Jack – a man she wasn't sure she even liked – wouldn't help bring them together. They had broken up because she believed they wouldn't work as a married couple. But now in the cold light of day, she could accept she had discarded Connor because he didn't fit into her ideal of a perfect marriage and of having a certain lifestyle. She wanted all the trappings of a so-called successful life. Her cheeks burned with shame at her materialistic attitude. OK, Connor would never make much money, but he had principles. And he would do his best for those he loved. Nice cars and big houses would never have been part of their life, but did that matter? Her father had provided well for his family. Manus worked hard and took care of Agnes and his children. The community respected him. But his feet were of shifting sand. He wore a mask and underneath the respectable exterior lurked a monster. With Connor, there was no pretence, no facade hiding an evil heart. A fierce longing for him swamped her. When she closed her eyes she could imagine them snuggled up in bed, his arms wrapped around her as they stared out at grey damp Dublin skies, plotting their adventures for the day.

Connor's special gift was his ability to draw magic and fun from the humdrum ordinariness of life. Aoife wept for what she had thrown away. Her stomach constricted when she thought about Jack. She knew she had mistreated him, but then she figured he was callous in his treatment of women too. Even when she was at school, he was the local 'bad boy', never staying long with one girl. Sex with Jack was a distraction from the nightmare her life had become. But what if Connor ever found out? OK, they had broken up, but sleeping with Jack was hardly honouring their relationship. Connor would feel betrayed if he found out. But then again, if he knew the truth about her father, he would be glad to be finished with the O'Driscoll family. Somehow, the thought of Connor turning away from her was too bleak to bear. Mam's words of the night before haunted her. The idea that her very existence had ended someone's life. And why? Because Manus demanded the undivided attention of his wife? The sick fuck!

Her thoughts returned to Sam. Was she seriously contemplating that he was a killer like Manus? The news reports said the missing girl went off to a club on Thursday at eleven and never returned home. Her mother reported her missing sometime the next day. If Sam was responsible for her disappearance why return to Donegal Friday night? It made no sense . . . unless he wanted to dispose of a body or remove something he lost or feared would implicate him.

Jesus! Was that why he was so frantic about the O'Briens digging up the land? Was it his own crimes he was covering up? She had never seen him so deranged by anger. Did she know him at all?

She could avoid it no longer – she must talk to Sam today. The walls of the room closed in, suffocating her. She needed to get out of the house. Pulling on clothes and runners, she shouted to her mother that she would be back in about an hour.

The path was through fields, slippery with dew. She enjoyed the exhilaration of pounding up hills and freewheeling down slopes. Deeply inhaling the fresh, intoxicating summer scents. The rhythm of her feet pounding and the whoosh of wind in the trees induced a feeling of peace and connection. For a time, she felt almost happy, her body floating in some peaceful place. She pulled up short at an oak tree. That was the tree she had climbed as a child. Could she climb it now? Finding the first foothold, her body remembered the rest and soon Aoife was sitting close to the top, surveying the countryside spread out below. Closing her eyes and resting her body against the body of the old tree, she inhaled all the verdant beauty. But brutal reality intruded. Where had Manus buried the bodies? Didn't he mention putting a silage pit over the place he put Anika? The thought of the farm being a graveyard twisted her guts.

Over the years Manus had increased his small holding of forty acres to nearly a hundred, comprising of grassland, woodland and bog, so the possibilities were endless. Abruptly, the beauty she had revelled in moments before lay tarnished, bloodied by what it hid. She half slid and scrambled to the earth below, skinning her knees.

Where was the silage pit? She had a vague memory that it was close to the sheds where Sam wintered his cattle. It wasn't far away, and her feet propelled her down the track leading to the sheds. Scanning the yard, she located the old silage pit. It was now a repository for rusting machinery and the discarded tires that were used to weigh down the fermenting silage.

Unbidden, a memory came to her of watching her father and Sam fork the heavy winter feed onto a waiting trailer. It hadn't been used since her father's time. Sam didn't use the pit anymore, instead he baled his silage, which he stored at the back of the sheds to make it easily accessible for feeding cattle. Had Sam stopped using the pit because of what he had read in the diary? She stared at the ground, sick at the thought of Anika's body decomposing underneath her feet. How many other bodies were there? Her thoughts returned to the missing girl in Donegal. Jack saw Sam driving recklessly on the Donegal Road. Why would he pretend to be going to Mullingar to buy a tractor and instead be going to Donegal? All her suspicions about Sam and Manus and their 'little adventures', as Mam and Kate called them, swarmed like angry bees in her head. Was she really contemplating that her brother not only knew about Manus's crimes but was implicated in them and was even carrying on the family tradition of serial murders?

Later, clean from her shower but feeling irredeemably soiled, Aoife listened as her mam exclaimed over the scratches on her hands and knees from her morning climb.

'I'm fine, Mam! Please stop fussing, I tripped and fell is all, but I think I've got a tummy bug, so I'll head back to bed for a while.'

'Sure, love – can I get you anything? Some Andrews Liver Salts perhaps?' She put her cool hand on Aoife's forehead. 'You might have a temperature. Your forehead is warm.'

'No, really, I'm fine, I just need a lie-down.' As she spoke Aoife backed out of the kitchen.

In her room, she lay on the bed staring at the ridiculous embers of her childhood, the tattered posters and the corkboard festooned with pictures of teenage friends pretending they were cool and 'friends forever'. She was in contact with two girls from convent days, but they met rarely and had nothing in common. Their lives had diverged too much. It was all an illusion: friendships that seemed perfect were held together by tenuous ties, like school, sport, or work. Without those posts to hold them together they drifted until all that was left was a faint trace like a rubbed-out drawing or a photograph faded by exposure to the sun. Would her friendship with Sorcha survive all the horror of her father's past? Would Sorcha avoid her eyes, let their friendship stale and die? Do we really love anyone or just the idea we have of them? Like poor deluded Mam locked in a fantasy, believing in a bloated caricature of her husband. And Sam, what was he hiding? How far did Manus involve him in his sickness? Aoife spent the morning in a semi-comatose state, the air scooped out of her body leaving her limp, unable to function.

Her phone vibrated. It was Connor. Her heart accelerated, making her gasp.

'Hi, I wasn't expecting to hear from you. How are you?' she said.

'Fine, well, not really, but what can I say? It's a crappy situation.'

'I wish things could be different,' she whispered.

Connor must have noticed the hesitancy and regret in her voice because he rushed to say, 'Aoife, can't we try again? We were so good together – there must be a way to fix things. Please don't say no – at least think about it. Please!'

Aoife's eyes smarted with brimming tears. 'I wish we could,

Connor, but I don't know how to fix things any more than you do.'

'Aoife, I'm lost without you, I can't write, I can't concentrate on anything. Why don't I come down and we could at least talk things over? Come on! We were together for four years, it must mean something.'

His voice soft in her ear.

'No! You can't come down. We'll talk when I'm back in Dublin, I promise. *Just don't come down. Please!*' Desperation and alarm made her shout. 'Look, I promise to ring you tonight and we can talk some more. OK?'

'OK, but I'm holding you to it, Aoife. I miss you so much.'

'Me too,' she whispered, ending the call.

In response to her mother shouting that dinner was ready, Aoife trudged downstairs. Both Sam and Karol were sitting at the kitchen table. Sam was quiet, avoiding her eyes, and Karol was extremely polite. He spoke with almost courtly politeness. If it wasn't for her mam chatting to him about his family and asking him about his little daughter, the silence during the meal would have been unendurable.

Aoife was acutely aware of Sam. He ate hurriedly, barely tasting his food. Getting up abruptly, he grunted that he had a lot on. Poor Karol, his dinner unfinished, started to his feet too.

Agnes glared at her son. 'What's the hurry? At least wait until Karol finishes his food!'

'I'm not stopping him.' Sam shoved his chair roughly against the table. 'Look, I'm away, you can come when you're ready,' he said curtly to Karol.

He left the kitchen, the door banging behind him.

Karol jumped up, but Agnes was having none of it.

'Sit you down, Karol. I don't know what's eating him, but *you* are finishing your meal. So sit back down.'

Karol returned to his seat and hurriedly ate a few more mouthfuls before getting up, thanking Agnes and darting out the door.

'What is wrong with your brother?' Agnes asked.

Aoife shrugged and silently cleared away the plates.

'Did you and Sam argue over something? There's been an atmosphere between you for a while now.'

'Mam, I don't know what you're talking about. Sam is just in a mood because he had a wasted trip to get the tractor and now he's behind with his work.'

'I suppose that's right, but I've never seen him so moody. He hasn't been the same since the business over the land. Well, there's nothing I can do about it. I just hope he doesn't take it out on the lad. He's been a godsend and we wouldn't want to lose him to the neighbours. Pat Casey is always wanting to borrow him to work on his farm.'

Aoife squeezed her mother's shoulder sympathetically and suggested they tackle some weeding in the garden.

They worked side by side for a couple of hours. Then Agnes, suddenly feeling tired, went off for a cup of tea and fell into a doze, her knitting in her lap.

Later, upstairs, Aoife, her chin rigid, grimly researched the two women missing between January and her birth date, the 15th August 1985.

Margaret Coyle, a 43-year-old widow, went missing in early February. Her husband had died six months earlier, and grief might have caused her to take her own life, but her body was never found.

Anna Haliburton was from Boyle and attended University in Galway. She disappeared on the 8th of March 1985. The photograph on the Missing Person website showed a dark-haired girl with a heavy fringe. She was 20 years of age, 5 foot 3, with red hair and brown eyes. At the time she disappeared, she was wearing jeans, a heavy brown jacket, and runners.

Aoife spent the next hour scouring the Internet for information on the missing young woman. She eventually came across a newspaper report from the *Irish Times*, written a year after Anna had gone missing. Holding her breath, she read.

Irish Times March 1986

It has been a year since Anna Halliburton, 20, disappeared while travelling to the family home in Boyle, Co. Roscommon. Anna and her twin sister, Susan, were studying law at UCG and made plans to return to their family home in Boyle. The sisters had plans to meet up with friends over the weekend. At the last minute, Susan decided not to go. An overdue essay necessitated that she stay and work over the weekend. Susan explained that Anna was the more organised and diligent twin. She had worked hard to finish her essay so she could get home for the weekend and catch up with old school friends. Susan bitterly regretted the decision to stay in Galway. 'If I had been with her, Anna would be here today,' she told our reporter. 'I'll never forgive myself.'

On the 8th of March 1985, Anna went missing. The Garda believe she missed her bus and tried to hitch a lift home. There were sightings of Anna on the outskirts of Galway town at 4:30 pm, dressed in jeans and a brown jacket. Susan described the anguish of being involved in the reconstruction of Anna's last movements. The Garda hadn't wanted her to take part, but Susan believed it was the right thing to do. The reconstruction resulted in the identification of Anna by a woman who was driving out the Sligo Road to get petrol. This lady offered Anna a lift as far as the petrol station, saying it might be easier to get a lift there, but Anna declined and said that she'd be sure to get a lift soon. There were lots of cars heading toward Sligo so she felt confident about getting a lift to Boyle. Anna's parents became concerned when she didn't arrive home and they reported her missing. They insist that Anna would never harm herself. They believe someone is responsible for her disappearance.

Anna enjoyed her studies and planned to train as a solicitor. She had everything to live for. Susan has since received her law degree from UCG and is currently applying to Blackhall Place to train as a solicitor. She said it was traumatic to receive her degree without Anna by her side. Her parents were too upset to attend the conferring ceremony. Susan described her sister as a bright, bubbly personality, a keen cross-country runner, with a desire to travel and see the world. The Halliburton family are heartbroken and continue to spend time and money trying to find leads to their daughter's whereabouts. They refuse to give up hope. A repeat of the reconstruction of Anna's last movements will feature on *Garda Patrol* this Wednesday evening.

Aoife searched for the reconstruction in the RTÉ archives and eventually found grainy footage from 1985. It began with the image of a young woman arriving at a bus depot and a voiceover declared Anna had missed her bus. The young woman was next seen hitching a lift on the Sligo to Galway Road. The reconstruction showed a middle-aged woman pulling over to speak to Anna/Susan. This woman offered her a ride to a filling station, suggesting she might have a better chance of getting a lift there. Anna/Susan refused the offer and is next seen standing by the side of the road thumbing a lift. The last sighting of Anna was at 4:45 pm, by a man on a motorbike. Aoife watched, fascinated by the slight figure of the girl.

At one point the face is visible: Susan, the mirror image of her sister, stands on the road, her thin face bravely hiding anguish.

Aoife's eyes swelled with tears, her throat ached and yet she was compelled to watch.

She bookmarked the page and searched for Susan Haliburton on Facebook. It didn't take long because either she never married or hadn't changed her name. Like a lot of older people, Susan wasn't too careful with privacy settings and had posted an upcoming event – her 50th birthday celebration in Dwyer's pub in Galway. Aoife's heart thudded. It was tomorrow night. This party looked like a sign, perhaps the universe was telling her to go and make living flesh of the words etched on the pages of the notebook. She was going to seek out this woman whose life was despoiled by Manus. It felt like penance or masochism, but either way she felt compelled to do what sanity counselled against. At least it would distract her from the missing girl and avoid a confrontation with Sam.

CHAPTER 34

On Saturday morning she worked out a plan. At breakfast, she mentioned a college friend had got in touch and wanted to meet up.

'We'll likely have a meal and go for drinks later so I'm going to stay over.'

Agnes looked pleased. 'Ah, that's great, love. I was thinking you were looking a bit peaky and meeting up with old pals is just what's needed to lift your spirits.'

So, Aoife packed an overnight bag and headed for Galway after supper. The roads were quiet, and she should make Galway around eight, giving her plenty of time to suss out the party venue. From her experiences in Dublin, she knew how to crash a party. Hungry students didn't embarrass easily, and she had blagged her way into many 21st parties for food and the prospect of meeting talent. It had mortified her law-abiding mother when she owned up to it in an unguarded moment. What she planned to do in Galway was stalking. It was crazy, but the impulse to see this woman overcame rationality.

Galway was quiet apart from a few revellers on the street. She passed a hen party: girls wearing wedding veils tottering down cobbled streets in impossibly high heels, maintaining their balance in a feat worthy of tightrope walkers. Once parked, she pinpointed the location of the pub using Google maps. Fortuitously, it was close by. The pub's bright, cheerful exterior contrasted with the dark atmospheric interior, which was already full of fun-loving locals and tourists. Music thumped dully in the background, unable to compete with the raucous cacophony of the happy punters. Hung across the stairs was a sign for the Halliburton party with an arrow pointing upwards. Should she book somewhere for the night? Aoife hesitated. Why stay over? She would only stay a short time. She could always tell her mam the craic wasn't great with her friend, to explain coming home.

Ordering a soft drink, she found an abandoned barstool and sat, and waited. It was too early to check the party out – she'd better wait – at least she had a seat. As Aoife sat her stomach knotted and twisted, forcing her to go to the loo. When she returned to the bar, her seat was gone. To hell with it, she thought, and ordered a gin and tonic and change for the cigarette machine. Going outside to a covered area full of smokers, she bummed a light. The drink was a good idea, it steadied her. The crowd outside were friendly and she chatted with the hen party she saw earlier. They had just arrived from Dublin and were keen to party hard. It felt good to be part of a normal cheery crowd, reminding her of carefree times.

At eight-thirty Aoife noticed a change in the calibre of people coming into the bar – definitely an older crowd, a steady stream heading upstairs to the party room. Shortly afterwards, a large group of glammed-up younger girls followed them, laughing and chatting. Well, at least she wouldn't stand out in a room full of oldies. Catching the barman's eye, she ordered another drink and followed them.

The party room was set up with tables arranged around two sides of the room. Seventies and eighties music blared from speakers, but most people were too busy greeting each other to dance. Aoife scanned the room for Susan Halliburton. Close to the door, she spotted a gaggle of people, shouting birthday greetings. Through a gap in the crowd she saw a middle-aged woman whom she thought must be Susan as she was the focus of all the attention. She was wearing black palazzo pants and a tight-fitting black silk top under a long dress-coat, multi-coloured and swirling. Blonde hair cut very short revealed a pale face washed out under the swirling lights that raced rapidly across the floor.

Uncertain whether to stay or go, Aoife finished her drink then went to the bar and ordered another. She moved closer to the ladies' toilets – in case she needed a quick getaway. Nervousness made her drink too quickly. She stood outside the circle of friends and acquaintances, feeling foolish and exposed.

People were lining up to partake of the food spread out on tables. Aoife was ravenously hungry but couldn't face joining the queue. She knocked back the gin, slipped into the toilets and locked the door of her cubicle. Sitting on the loo, she googled B&Bs to see if she could find somewhere nearby to make a booking. Everywhere was booked out, and she resorted to checking out nearby hotels for accommodation. The outer door to the toilets opened and her ears pricked when she heard some girls chatting.

'Your mother looks tired, Julie – this must be a tough night for her.'

'Yeah, it's a bit of an ordeal, to be honest. She insists on having these milestone birthday celebrations, as a way of honouring her twin – inviting all of her sister's friends from school and college.'

'It's a lovely thing to do but it must be so hard on her, remembering her dead sister.'

Aoife struggled to hear over the sound of a tap running but could just about make out what was being said.

'Mum never talks about Anna being dead, she always says she's disappeared.'

'But surely she can't really believe that, after nearly thirty years?'

'Of course she doesn't but she can't let go until they find a body, so she keeps on hoping for some news. It's eating her up inside. These birthday memorials help somehow, so I go along with them to support her, but I wish we could just celebrate *her* life and not have a ghost hovering in the background.'

'Shit, that's tough!'

'Yeah, well, it is what it is and anyway let's talk about something else. Are you in talks with Brian about getting back together, or are you still in unforgiving mode?'

'Ah, screw him! I don't want to talk about that eejit. Come on, let's go out and grab some food.'

Aoife sat in agonised silence as she listened to the girls leave. The conversation she overheard brought home to her with fierce clarity how damaged Susan Halliburton must be. Because her mother was pregnant with her, Manus made this girl, Anna, suffer and die. Thank God those pages were missing from the diary. To have read the description of Anna's death would have been unbearable.

Eaten up with guilt, she sat on the toilet, trying to stifle her tears. She didn't want to leave the safe enclosure of the cubicle but eventually forced her leaden legs to move. When she was sure the room was empty, she stepped out, washed her tear-ravished face, reapplied some lipstick and ran damp fingers through her hair – hoping to look less like a survivor from Day of the Dead. She really should go. Someone would notice she didn't belong here if she waited much longer. Bracing herself, she made her way through the throng towards the stairs and the safety of the pub below. She didn't get far as the music was turned off and the attention of the partygoers was directed towards the front of the room where Susan stood side by side with a younger woman. Unable to help herself, Aoife manoeuvred her way along the wall towards the front.

The two women stood hand in hand. The young woman, presumably the daughter Aoife eavesdropped on earlier, took the mic, wished her mother a happy birthday and thanked everyone for attending. Then she handed the mic to her mother.

The festive party atmosphere died down, and the silence in the room was respectful. Aoife could hardly breathe.

'Thank you all for coming here tonight, and thanks to Julie for helping to arrange this evening. Friends, you are all familiar with my marking of these milestone birthdays. Most fiftieth birthday parties are just about celebrating life and survival to date, but this party acknowledges absence too. My beloved sister Anna should be here, marking this half-century with me. I often wonder what her life might have been. Would we have worked together? Would she have travelled the world, married, had children? We will never know. But although Anna has disappeared from our lives, she has not been forgotten as your presence here testifies. It is heartening to see so many of her old friends here celebrating her short time among us. Anna's memory cannot be wiped away as easily as her physical presence. Her loss has left me feeling like an amputee. Without my beloved twin, I am incomplete. But please don't let my words here spoil your evening. Anna loved a good party, so please, my friends, have fun, reminisce, and drink the night away. I don't have a cake for my birthday anymore, but if you will all help yourselves to a glass of champagne being served now by the kind staff of Dwyer's, I'll propose a toast.'

She waited patiently until everyone had a drink in their hand and then raised her glass.

'*To Anna!*'

The party raised glasses and joined in the chorus of '*To Anna!*' then Julie stepped forward and led the singing of 'Happy Birthday' for Susan.

Aoife stood holding the glass of champagne in hands that trembled uncontrollably. She placed it on a table untasted. Slowly she moved through crowds of dancers towards the bar and ordered a double gin and tonic, drank swiftly, and stood staring with eyes blind with tears.

'Hi there, I was wondering if you are one of Julie's friends? I don't think we've met, have we?'

Horrified, Aoife realised that the woman standing beside her was Susan. She froze, unable to think of a coherent sentence, and just stared stupidly at her.

'Are you OK, love? You look faint. Should I get Julie for you?'

'I'm fine, please don't bother Julie. I just have stomach cramps – really, I'm grand – my boyfriend has rung for a taxi, he'll be here in a minute.'

'Look, Julie is just over there – I'll get her for you. What did you say your name was, pet?'

Aoife's mind raced in circles trying to invent a name while Susan, concern etching lines more deeply in her pale face, waited for her to speak.

'Joan, my name is Joan,' she mumbled.

Susan waved at her daughter and Aoife saw Julie moving towards them. Her stomach rolled. God, she was going to throw up. In desperation, she turned and made for the door. Pushing frantically through the crowd, she could see Julie and Susan scanning the floor. She raced downstairs to the pub below. It was packed to bursting and

Aoife shoved her way roughly outside. She moved around the corner to the smoking area, gulping in the fresh cold biting air. With shaking hands, she pulled a cigarette from the packet. She left the packet on a nearby table while she searched in her bag for a lighter. A beefy man obliged with a light but then he annoyed her with awkward chat-up lines. It was only when Aoife told him to fuck off that he abandoned his courtship attempt, leaving her if not in peace at least alone.

God, what the hell was she doing? Why hadn't she the sense to book in somewhere? It was too late now to find anywhere to stay; she'd have to sleep in the car. Were there laws against sleeping in cars? Aoife shuddered at the thought of some garda tapping on her window and hassling her. Feck it, she'd risk it and drive home. It was late, the roads would be empty, why not chance it? OK, she was over the limit, but in the light of all the shit in her life was drunk driving such a big deal? She'd be careful.

Walking briskly to her car, she was encouraged by the speed and accuracy of her footsteps. She was fine to drive. Reaching for her car keys she realised she has left her fags at the pub. Cursing, she debated going back to retrieve them, but there was no point as someone had probably whipped them by now.

In the car, Aoife decided that getting a coffee might be a good idea so she would stop for one when safely outside town. Starting the engine, she drove slowly and carefully. It was going to be OK. Just ahead was a filling station. Aoife pulled in and got a black coffee from the machine. She got in line to pay then her heart thudded in alarm. The man in front of her was wearing a Garda uniform. *Shit! Shit!* Her stomach lurched and her body broke out in a clammy sweat. He moved off and she paid for her coffee and bought a bag of crisps too. She didn't want them but at least they would remove the smell of drink from her breath.

She walked to the door. The garda was sitting in his car with a colleague. *Shit!* Better wait until they drove off. How stupid could she be? If she got done for drunk driving, she would be in serious trouble. *Shit! Shit!* Aoife moved back into the shop, her hand stinging from the hot coffee. But the pain sharpened her wits. Setting the coffee on a shelf, she pretended to be looking for a magazine. Quaking, she saw the garda re-enter the shop. He went up to the cashier and asked for the toilets. When he re-emerged and left the shop, Aoife took a magazine and went to the counter. The man at the cash desk stared at her and she figured she must look like a petrified fish. She also bought a packet of cigarettes. Out of the shop window, she saw the Garda car pull out and head back in the direction of Galway city.

Aoife hurried to her car and shoved coffee and crisps in her mouth, practically inhaling them. She needed to sober up fast. Gradually her heart returned to normal and, taking a few calming breaths, she began to feel more in control of her body. She struggled with the cellophane wrapper on her cigarettes but eventually liberated one. Why did they make the packets so bloody hard to open? Sucking in the nicotine, she moved off, leaving the window open to rid her car of smoke and hoping the cold would keep her alert.

She drove with great care yet was mindful not to drive too slowly either in case of attracting attention. Cold to the bone from the open car window but alert, she reached Sligo town and drove through without mishap.

She was less than a mile from home when she pulled in. The thought of her mother hearing her arrive and asking fifty questions about why she was back and maybe guessing that she wasn't sober unnerved her. Why not go to Jack's? It was late but maybe he would be OK about it. She turned the car and headed there.

CHAPTER 35

It was after two when she pulled up outside the glass cube. The security lights came on as she arrived. Coming here was madness. Jack didn't deserve to be awoken by a drunken madwoman. Better to face her mother's disapproval than drag Jack into her mess. Aoife had restarted the engine when she spotted Jack standing at the door in his boxers. He waved to her. It was too late to drive away. Reluctantly, she got out of the car.

'Sorry, Jack, I shouldn't have called, I didn't realise it was so late.' Jack stared, his face creased with concern, 'Are you alright?' 'Yes, of course, I am. Look, I'll be on my way.'

As she made to move away, Jack grasped her arm and manhandled her into the house.

'You look like shit, girl. Come inside and I'll make us some coffee – you seem like you need one.'

Aoife felt her body drain of adrenaline and all resistance fell away.

'Can I use your bathroom?'

Catching sight of her face whilst washing her hands, it was clear why Jack was concerned about her. Rivulets of mascara tracked down her face and her eyes were bloodshot and glassy. She must have cried all the way back. Using liquid soap, Aoife washed away all traces of make-up. She was clean but curiously featureless, as though her face had lost definition and was a putty-coloured mask.

Jack knocked on the door.

'Are you OK in there, Aoife?'

'I'm grand, Jack, I'll be out in a minute,' she said, slapping herself hard across the face. Pain shook the inertia away and had the added benefit of giving some colour to her cheeks.

Jack was making coffee and toast in the kitchen and motioned her to sit up at the kitchen island. He insisted she eat and allowed her time to do that without asking her anything. For this respite, she was grateful. Aoife didn't realise how hungry she was and, as if reading her mind, Jack produced another slice of brown toast and watched as she ate ravenously.

'OK, Miss Aoife, what gives? Something has upset you. Where did you come from in this state?'

'Jack, please, I can't talk about it, please don't ask, I'm such a mess.' Tears ran down her face again.

Jack offered tissues and looked away as she wiped her eyes and blew her nose.

'Are you sure it wouldn't help to talk about whatever has happened?'

Aoife shook her head. Jack was decent not to press her for an explanation. Perhaps, seeing she was at a breaking-point, he didn't relish having a drunken woman sob all over him. Whatever the reason, Aoife was grateful.

'How about staying over? You can kip in my guest room and tomorrow you can lie in as long as you need. If I'm gone in the morning, make yourself at home and raid my cupboards for food.'

'Thanks, Jack, this is very good of you. If I arrived home like this, Mam would be on my case with questions and most of all I'd worry her to death. Can I crash now? I'm shattered.'

In answer, he led the way upstairs and ushered her into a bedroom just across from his room.

'Oh – I must get my overnight bag – I left it in the car,' she said.

'I'll get it. You didn't lock the car, did you?'

'No.'

He left and returned a few minutes later with the bag.

'There are towels in the bathroom,' he said. 'I'll bring up some water and painkillers for the morning, OK?'

'Thanks, Jack, that would be great.'

Aoife pulled off her clothes, dropping them on the floor, dragged a nightshirt over her head and collapsed into bed. She was asleep in minutes.

The next morning, the low rumble of farm machinery roused her from sleep, and she stared at the ceiling disorientated. Where was she? Then memory came flooding in, flooring her: the party, meeting Susan, the drunken drive back and arrival here. Christ! Jack must think she was a lunatic. God, her head hurt, and her mouth tasted like a pub ashtray.

Tempting as it was to hide out here, she'd better get moving.

Jack had thoughtfully put a glass of water and some painkillers on the bedside locker. Taking two tablets she washed them down with water. The stench of crisps and cigarettes seemed to seep through her pores. Fuck, she needed a shower.

The shower delivered piping hot water and after drying off and putting on fresh underwear she felt somewhat restored. Opening her make-up bag she applied moisturiser, mascara, and lip gloss, and she felt capable of facing the world, or at least Jack.

Downstairs, the cavernous kitchen was intimidating in its emptiness – this didn't deter her from searching the cupboards until she found some Cornflakes. She was just swallowing the last spoonful when Jack walked in.

Aoife gritted her teeth. She had hoped to get away without meeting him.

'Good morning, gorgeous! How are you today? Feeling better?'

'Good, thanks, Jack. Sorry for busting in on you. I wish I had a good explanation, but I haven't. Look, I'll get out of your way and leave you in peace.'

She got to her feet and moved towards the door.

Jack placed a gentle hand on her shoulder. 'Wait, Aoife, don't rush off. Stay and have a coffee with me. It's nice to have company for breakfast. Come on!'

He led her back to the kitchen island with its steel and leather stools.

Aoife's resistance disappeared, and she sat and watched as Jack made the coffee, talking about different blends he had tried and asking her about restaurants she had frequented in Dublin. The desultory chatter soothed her, and he even made her smile with stories of old Pete and the tricks he played on him as a young lad.

'Why don't you chill out here and I'll cook you something nice this evening?'

'You cook?' she said, raising her eyebrows in mock surprise.

'My many talents would surprise you, young woman. Well, what about it?'

'No, Jack, I've taken up enough of your time and Mam will expect me home, but thanks all the same.'

'You are no imposition on me, Aoife. I've always enjoyed your visits – although some more than others,' he said, smirking.

His lame joke was all Aoife needed. She was starting to like Jack, but his silly innuendo restored her to sanity.

'No, Jack, Mam will expect me. But thanks for the hospitality,' she said stiffly.

'Hey, Aoife, I'm sorry. I'm a dope. I didn't mean to upset you. I know I can be crass, but you know I like you, don't you? I suppose that you're still dealing with your break-up, and I just want you to know you can call here anytime – day or night. OK?'

His words touched Aoife and she hugged him tightly when leaving. She knew she was being a complete hypocrite – using Jack whenever she felt like it and yet finding fault with him with little cause. He had been more than kind to her and she was acting like a complete cow!

He waved her off from the doorway and she felt a rush of gratitude towards him. She had a nasty habit of making snap decisions about people. To her, Jack was a shallow womaniser, but she could see there was more to him than she had assumed.

No more assumptions about Sam or her father. What she needed were hard facts. Tonight, she would tackle Sam and find out exactly what he knew about Manus and how involved he was in those 'adventures'.

CHAPTER 36

Aoife spent her day plotting how best to waylay Sam. He came in at six for his supper, ate in sullen silence, was short with Agnes and ignored Aoife. How would she get him alone, out of earshot of their mam?

At eight o'clock, when he went out to check the sheds were locked up, she followed him.

'We need to talk,' she said.

Sam started at her approach. 'What the fuck are you doing creeping around? I'm tired so in no mood for "talking",' he said, mimicking her voice.

'Sam, we must talk. It's about Dad.'

Sam pushed past her.

'If you won't talk here, I'll talk to you in the house. But we both want to avoid Mam hearing, don't we?'

Sam stopped and glared at Aoife. 'What's that supposed to mean? Why should I care what Mam hears?'

Aoife bit her lip hard. 'Come on, Sam, stop pretending. We both know about Dad, about what he did.'

'Jaysus, Aoife, you're mental! Connor dumping you has turned your head. Why don't you piss off and leave well enough alone?'

Aoife, heart thumping, stood her ground. 'Sam, listen to me. I think you know a lot more about Dad than you're telling. But if you don't want to talk, then I will.'

Sam walked away, taking big angry strides.

Aoife ran after him and grabbed his arm. 'I found the box.'

Sam stopped, and for a moment she thought his legs would buckle as he swayed. Placing his hand on the wall of the shed for support, he turned to face her.

'Take my advice, Aoife, and forget you ever found it. You'll be sorry if you don't.'

'Are you threatening me, Sam? Is it a case of like father like son?'

Without warning, Sam grabbed her shoulders and shook her so hard her teeth chattered. Aoife felt real terror as she looked into his blanched face. A face that no longer looked like Sam's but that of a desperate cornered animal.

She fell back against the wall as he released her and exhaled deeply.

'OK!' he said. 'We can talk. But not now, let's wait until Mam goes to bed. After she's asleep, we'll come out here. I don't want to talk in the house.'

Aoife nodded and rubbed her shoulders as Sam strode back towards the house.

She followed slowly. Now that the moment had come, she felt a dragging reluctance to continue. Thoughts of the missing girl in Donegal tortured her. Sam frightened her. He seemed as much a stranger as Manus. A familiar face masking an alien. If Sam confirmed what she believed, then there was no hiding out, no pretending this was all a big mistake. She would have to decide what to do. That's if she had any choice.

Back in the house, they joined Agnes who was watching her programmes, oblivious to the tension between brother and sister. Sam apologised for being grumpy earlier, explaining he hadn't slept well. Agnes seemed happy with that and suggested a game of 8, 5, 3. As was usual with that card game, it went on for ages. To her delight, Agnes won. Having replaced the cards in the pack, she yawned and took herself off to bed.

Sam whispered after she left. 'We'll wait for an hour or so until she's well asleep – OK?'

Aoife nodded.

They were heading outside when Aoife's mobile rang. Cursing, she answered quickly; worried the ringtone would wake her mother.

'Sorry, Sam, I have to take this, it's Connor. I'll make it short.'

Connor's voice sounded urgent. 'Hey, Aoife, listen, I know I should have waited for you to call back, but I decided we needed to talk in person.'

'Connor, now is not a good time. I'll call tomorrow, OK?'

'Too late, love. I'm almost at your mother's house now.'

As he finished speaking, car headlights shone in the driveway.

Aoife stared at Sam in consternation. 'Sam, he's here. I didn't know he was coming.'

'Well, I guess we have to postpone our little chat,' Sam said, walking away.

Aoife said a rapid prayer that her mam wouldn't wake up. Perhaps if she got to the car quickly, she could stop Connor from coming into the house. She urgently motioned to him to stay in the car and slipped into the passenger seat.

'Look, I'm sorry for landing in on you. Don't get mad. I've arranged with Kate to stay with her tonight, and we can talk tomorrow.'

'Shit, Connor, why didn't you warn me you planned to come tonight? This isn't a good time!'

'Yeah, I know I'm pushing things but, Aoife, you sounded so down on the phone and when you didn't call back, I got worried. I care about you – please don't shut me out!'

Listening to Connor's voice, her tense body relaxed. It was a relief to postpone her talk with Sam. But she had no idea what to do about Connor.

'Tell me again, why are you staying with Kate?'

'I called to Kate and Kenny first. I wanted to suss Kate out about whether there was any chance of us getting together again. I planned on booking a B&B, but Kate persuaded me to stay. Besides, I wasn't sure what sort of reception I would get here.'

'But why come tonight, why not wait until morning? It's after eleven, for God's sake!'

'I know, you're right, but I just felt I needed to see you. Do you want me to go away?'

'I don't know what I want, to be honest, Connor.'

'Listen, what's wrong? Aoife, you haven't been the same since your dad's anniversary.'

Aoife longed to confide in him, to rest her head on his shoulder and let all the torment spill out, but caution stilled her mouth. Who was Connor to her – an ex-fiancé? Could he be trusted to keep silent if she told him about Manus?

'I'm fine! I just have a few family issues to deal with. Go stay with Kate tonight. Tomorrow we can meet. How about I call to Kate's after ten?'

Reluctantly, Connor agreed to leave. What had possessed him to come down? Thinking back to the conversation she had with him earlier, she had sounded downcast and Connor hated to see her upset, so maybe it wasn't surprising that he did the knight-in-shining-armour thing. She set him up for it. It was good that she still mattered to him.

Sam had gone to bed when she returned to the house. She thought about going to talk to him but she felt tired, too tired to handle any more drama.

Back in her room, her mind spinning, she wondered was there any hope for her and Connor. Not to get married, that fantasy was an alternative universe away, but to live together. God knows she would need support when all the horror about her father came out. With Connor by her side, perhaps she could survive the shame and ugliness of it all. But then, once he knew the truth he would never want to be part of her toxic family. And what about Jack Costello? How would Connor feel about the fact that she had slept with another man so soon after their engagement ended? Aoife squirmed with guilt. Sleeping with Jack helped to distract her from the devastation in her life. He meant nothing to her, but Connor would feel betrayed, broken engagement or not. He would never understand, and she could never explain without betraying the secret. The only hope for her relationship was to keep silent about Jack. Nobody knew about their fling, and Jack would never tell. All she had to do was keep quiet. After all, she was becoming an expert at keeping secrets.

CHAPTER 37

Morning dawned, with its intrusive sun seeping through a break in the curtains and stabbing Aoife in the eyes. Last night was a cluster-fuck! Sam would be hard to pin down today. Aoife's intuition proved correct when she saw her mam making sandwiches and filling a flask with tea.

'I'm just getting a wee picnic together for Sam. He got a call about a tractor for sale in Roscommon – it sounds like a great deal. So, he's going up to take a gander. I thought I'd make sure he has something to eat on the journey.'

'Mam, you do realise Roscommon is only about 70 kilometres away and there are lots of filling stations with food bars and coffee and tea machines along the way?'

'Of course! But I know what they charge too. Sam will enjoy this much more, and he can stop wherever he likes. When Daddy used to go off on business up the country, I used to make him a picnic too.'

'Where did he go?' Aoife asked sharply. At her mother's startled glance, she moderated her voice. 'I never realised Dad travelled much. How did he manage the farm when he went away?'

'Usually, it was just a day's jaunt and one of the neighbours would milk the cows. He went to the marts to buy and sell cattle and, like Sam, he sometimes bought machinery second hand and of course, there was the greyhound racing. Jimmy Kelleher kept a few dogs and Manus liked to go to the tracks when Jimmy had a dog racing. Not too often, mind. Manus was a steady man, and he didn't bet much either, but sometimes he liked to go off on a little trip – his little adventures as he called them.'

Aoife felt her flesh crawl. She had assumed that any of Manus's attacks took place close to home, but he could have travelled anywhere. On her phone she searched for greyhound tracks, aghast to see them dotted all over the countryside. Manus could have attacked women anywhere on his so-called 'little adventures'.

Sam was crossing the yard when Aoife accosted him. He held up a hand, 'Don't start! I have to go to see this man. The tractor must be replaced. I promise to talk later.'

'*Tonight?*' she demanded.

'No, not tonight, but I promise we will talk about everything tomorrow. How about telling Mam that we want a night out in McCoy's and instead pull in somewhere and discuss everything?'

Aoife nodded.

'Why did Connor show up? I thought the wedding was off?'

'The wedding is off but he wants to talk over a few things.'

Sam strode away, muttering, 'Talking can be overrated.'

Checking the time, Aoife realised she'd better get going to see Connor. It was nearly ten o'clock. How would it look to Kate and Sandy? They probably thought that this was reconciliation and that the wedding was back on. Crap! What was she going to say to Connor?

Ah well, there would be time to think on the journey. Did her reaction when she saw him last night encourage him to think they might get back together?

The explosive contents of the box dwarfed all the difficulties she put in the way of getting married. All those concerns seemed pathetic now.

When she pulled up outside of Kate's, Kenny was mowing the lawn. He pretended not to see her, but she went over, forcing him out of politeness to turn off the mower.

'Hey,' he said listlessly.

'How's it going, Kenny? Kate tells me you aren't feeling great?' Aoife despised herself for avoiding calling Kenny's illness what it was – severe depression. He shrugged and Aoife was robbed of words as she looked into his large empty eyes. 'Kenny, I'm sorry that you feel so bad. I wish there was something I could do.'

Once again Kenny shrugged and turned back to the mower.

Aoife stood for a moment, watching him move slowly across the lawn.

The door of the house burst open, and Colm came bounding out. 'Hey, Auntie Aoife, Connor's here. We had a class game of football in the back. He's not bad for an ould fella. Are you getting back with him? I think you should. Connor's nice and can play the guitar – he promised to teach me when you get back together.'

'Colm Tynan, there is no way that Connor said any such thing. You are an absolute rascal. Where is everybody?'

Colm crooked a finger towards the garden. '*He's* over there and Ma and the others are in the house.'

Aoife noted the dismissive way he referred to Kenny and grabbed him. 'Now listen here, Colm. Your dad isn't well.'

'He looks OK,' Colm grunted, kicking at the ground with his foot.

'Not all illnesses are the same. Your dad may not be physically unwell but he's not feeling good inside where you can't see.'

'Yeah, I know – my mate's dad says he's mental.'

Aoife swore silently, wishing she could kick the mate's dad right in his ignorant head.

'He's not mental. He's depressed and can't help it. Do you think he wants to feel sad all the time or to miss his son's matches? He'd be there cheering you on, but he's just not able now. So, you must be patient, because he will get better; but it's going to take a while and you need to keep reminding yourself that he thinks the world of you, but right now he's not able to show it. So don't listen to eejits like your friend's dad. He knows nothing.'

Colm stopped squirming and looked at her sadly. 'I know, but it's hard when all the other dads are at everything and all I have is Mammy. The lads are always asking why he never comes anymore, and I don't know what to say. Last week I hit Martin Collins cos he slagged Dad off, and the coach told me I'd lose my place if I did it again.'

'OK, I understand, and we can help sort things out with your coach. But no more fighting and try to give your dad a break. Remember all the good times you spent together for starters, OK?'

'All right, Auntie Aoife, I will.' Colm's face lit with a tentative smile 'Thanks.' With that, he disappeared around the back of the house.

Before facing Connor, Aoife took her sister to one side, 'Kate, Colm and I had a wee chat. He tells me that he got into a fight with another lad who called Kenny names. Did you know? Colm thumped him and the coach gave him a warning.'

'Ah, no! I knew Colm was finding things tough, but not that he had been fighting. God, what should I do?'

'Well, for a start you need to put the coach straight about what's happening with Kenny and its impact on Colm.'

'Yeah, the coach is OK, I think he'd understand, but I wanted to keep things private. I suppose I felt ashamed of Kenny too. I know he can't help it, but sometimes I get so frustrated.'

'You know, Kate, Colm isn't the only one who could do with help – you can't be dealing with Kenny's depression on your own. There are lots of agencies out there that support relatives of people who are depressed. It's an illness, not a disgrace, Kate, so hold the head up.'

Kate smiled at Aoife. 'When did you get so wise, little sister?'

'*Aww*, I was born that way – it's only now that you're seeing it.'

The sisters laughed and walked inside.

CHAPTER 38

Connor was sitting cross-legged on the floor watching a documentary on migratory birds. He glanced up and sprang to his feet when he saw Aoife.

'I'll leave you alone,' Kate offered.

Conner raised a hand to stall her.

'No, stay put, Kate, I've imposed enough. Aoife and I can go for a drive.'

Aoife nodded agreement, and they headed out to the car.

'Where to?' Aoife asked.

'You choose.'

'Right, the beach then.'

Conversation was limited during the twenty-minute drive.

Eventually, Aoife asked, 'How did your ones take the news of the wedding cancellation, Connor?'

'As expected, they were disappointed and ripping that I fucked things up. The consensus was that I must have done something awful to scare you off. The parents wanted to ring you and persuade you to take me back. It was all I could do to stop them from pounding on your door and demanding to speak to you. I was getting the feeling my ones wanted to be rid of me at all costs.'

'Did you explain why we broke up?'

'What was the point? It would only confirm their belief that I'm a complete waster. What about your family?'

'It disappointed them, of course. They're very fond of you, and of course Sandy was raging she wouldn't get to be a bridesmaid. By the way, thanks for remembering to cancel the invitation order at the printer's. I completely forgot and only realised when I got their email confirming you had been in contact. It's mad how much we have to do. Anyway, I think we've cancelled everything and that's a relief, isn't it?'

Connor grunted assent, and the journey continued in silence.

The beach, a golden highway stretching for miles, lay ahead. They gulped in the fresh sea-scented air and clambered over the piled-up stones that led to the sandy beach below. The tide was a long way out. Keeping in step, they remained silent for what seemed to Aoife a torturous time. But, for all that, she couldn't bring herself to break the silence, and so it continued.

Then Connor said, 'How have you been?'

Aoife avoided his eyes, her tongue clogging up a dry mouth.

Connor came to a stop, waiting for a response, but she hurried onwards.

'Let's keep walking,' she said. 'I'm OK, what about you?'

'To tell the truth, love, I'm feeling fucked-up. I can't believe that we're not together anymore. On the phone the other night, I felt hopeful you regretted the break as much as I did – was I wrong?'

He stared straight ahead but Aoife was aware of the stiffening of his shoulders as he waited for an answer. Aoife stalled for time, unsure what words would come out of her mouth. She was a mess of jumbled, churning emotion. But cutting through it all was a desire to reach out and touch him.

'I don't know what to say, Connor. I really don't. Of course I regret we are no longer together, but then nothing has changed, has it? We want different things.'

Connor broke in. 'Listen, you asked about my parents and, well, I think my mother guessed that the lack of a steady job or career path was the main impediment, and she came up with a solution that might help. She offered to lend us a flat rent-free for a year so that we could save up for a deposit and I have a mate who works in publishing and he's offered me a job. I'd be mainly proofreading, the money isn't great, but I can supplement it by working part-time for the business, showing clients around houses at weekends and evenings. There would still be a lot of time to write so, really, it's a win-win and I've sent in my thesis on Friday morning, so I've freed up loads of time.'

'I don't know, Connor. It's nice of your mum, but do we want to be beholden to them? I thought you wanted nothing to do with the family business.'

'Look, I'm happy to do this. It's for us, so it's no sacrifice. I'm willing to try because I don't want to lose what we have. Come on, Aoife, we're great together, we find the same things hilarious, our politics are the same, we like the same TV shows and books – face it, we just fit, you know we do. When you're not around, I feel as those I've lost my best friend. Tell me you don't feel the same way?'

Aoife felt torn, desperate to somehow blow on the embers of their relationship and get another chance with him. But how could she build a life on lies and secrets? Stalling for time to think she said, 'I'm not sure that it's enough though. If it were, we would never have broken up. I think without knowing it we have grown apart in some ways and

I don't want you to have to compromise for me. I wouldn't be much of a best friend if I did.'

Connor gazed at her, his eyes intent, and she knew his brain was whirring with answers to reassure her qualms.

'OK, I get it that maybe we shouldn't bounce back into marriage, perhaps we need to wait and see, but I think we are worth fighting for, don't you?' He grasped Aoife's hands tightly.

Now more than ever she needed Connor, his kindness, goodness, and love, but never had she felt so undeserving of it. To share her life, he would have to live with the poisonous secret festering at its heart. How could she ask Connor to share in the ignominy and disgrace that her family would endure once all the details of Manus's perversion came to light?

Connor noticed her hesitation and squeezed her hands tighter. 'What's wrong, love? There's something else, isn't there? I know you so well and you've changed. There's something wrong. Please tell me what's wrong and I can help.'

Aoife shook off his hands. 'I can't explain right now but maybe in a while we can talk again, but for now we need to give each other breathing space.'

'Is there someone else?'

Connor's question caught her off guard, and when Aoife hesitated his face froze and then coalesced into an ugly rictus of disbelief and disgust.

'God, you work fast. Who is it, and how long has it been going on? What an idiot I am to believe our break-up was over financial bloody insecurity! What a joke!' He savagely smacked his forehead with a clenched fist, staring at her, his eyes wild.

Frightened by his outburst, Aoife grabbed his arm to stop him from hitting himself. The pain and hurt written across his face sent darts of shame through her.

'Connor, please, believe me, I was never unfaithful while we were together, but I admit I had a fling since then. It meant nothing! I wish I could make you understand! There is so much that I can't tell you right now.'

'Wow, you are one fast worker! Barely split up and you're screwing someone! I can't fucking believe it!'

Aoife shrank from his rage and disgust. 'OK, Connor, you have every right to be angry, but perhaps now you can see how impossible it is for us to be together. Let's turn back and I'll take you back to Kate's.'

'Don't bother; I'll make my own way back.'

'Connor, don't be ridiculous – you can't – this is miles from everywhere.'

Connor glared, his face contorted in misery. 'Just get away from me, leave me alone. Just piss off. I don't want to look at you.' He turned his back on her and walked away.

Sickened, Aoife turned back towards the car. As soon as she had a signal, she called Kate asking her to pick up Connor and begging her not to ask questions but just come and get him. She gave Kate Connor's number so that she could meet him at the beach. Then, resting her head on the steering wheel, she felt the tears stream, scalding her cheeks. It was too late for her and Connor. She didn't deserve him, probably never had. Manus had planted a fungus within her, and it continued to infect and destroy. All this fantasy of having a normal life was insanity. The reality was that her father was a serial killer. That was what she needed to concentrate on, instead of sleepwalking in an imaginary universe where she could have a normal happy life.

CHAPTER 39

The one blessing in this entire miserable fuck-up of a day was that her mam didn't know that Connor was there. The thought of trying to field questions from her mother made Aoife shudder. It was frustrating to have to wait another day until she and Sam could talk. She longed to get out of the house and get howling drunk but, recalling where that last led her, she opted instead to raid the drinks cabinet as soon as dinner was over. Grimly, she resolved to go online tonight and see if she could correlate areas where young women went missing with her father's movements. In effect, she should look for his stalking grounds. Shivering at the thought, she reminded herself it was time to grow up and stop avoiding reality, however gruesome.

Her mam was washing dishes at the sink and listening intently to the radio. Could her mother be blind to the dark side of her husband; or had she suspicions and chosen to turn the other way? Did she know her mother at all? Was she hiding things? Were there places she chose not to look? She had always taken her mother for granted and assumed she was what she appeared to be, an old-fashioned woman, not very interested in the wider world outside of her family, but always dependable, always reliable. But did one ever know one's parents? After all, parents had a vested interest in being responsible role models, a source of wisdom and stability in an otherwise scary world. But in reality it was all pretence. She had older friends from work, who married young and now had children approaching teen years, and she knew they presented an image to their children that belied their past lives as amateur coke-heads and major party animals. Now they acted as though butter wouldn't melt in their mouths and were horrified by the slightest infractions of their children. It was almost like their own past misdemeanours never happened. Perhaps all parents were frauds. But try as she might, Aoife couldn't imagine her mother hiding knowledge of Manus's depravity. Then again, she never figured her father to be a serial killer either.

Aoife had never considered her mother as a person outside of her role. Never seen her with her mother-guard down. Not once in all her life had she ever seen her even a little tipsy. Friends often related tales of their mothers getting pissed at weddings or parties and making a show of themselves. But her mam was invariably the same sensible woman. Was it peculiar that she didn't have close friends, just good neighbours? Not once did she recall her having a night out with the 'girls' like her friends' mothers did? Her life was insulated, contained, almost repressed. Was there a reason she never let herself get close with people? Was she hiding something? Looking over at that gentle face, Aoife felt shame for distrusting her mother and yet ...

She left the room quietly and went upstairs.

On her phone were three missed calls from Kate. She texted: **Can't talk, please don't ask!** She was unable to deal with her thoughts about the fiasco with Connor, never mind trying to explain them to Kate. It showed how disassociated from reality she was that she didn't think that her fling with Jack was important, that it was a major betrayal of all they had shared. She had been so busy looking for diversion and escape from the chaos looming in her life that it seemed justified. But in retrospect it allowed Connor to escape the sickness pervading her family. If he only realised what a lucky escape he'd had.

Agnes pulled her from her thoughts by shouting up the stairs that the dinner was ready. Aoife called out that she'd eat later – she was just going to have a shower.

After the shower she lay down on her bed and did some deep breathing to release some stress. Unbelievably, she drifted off to sleep and woke at three thirty feeling muggy and hungry. She found a banana and a packet of crisps and they helped fill the hole in her stomach. She could hear the TV blaring so her mam must be listening to one of her quiz shows.

Perhaps she could make herself useful and do some prepping for the supper to save her mam the bother. Downstairs, she checked out the fridge and spotted some sausages and rashers. If she could find a couple of tins of beans and boil up some spuds, she could provide herself and her mother with a nice simple nostalgic meal. It was too early to cook anything yet but she could at least wash the spuds and leave them ready for cooking.

Agnes came in as she was washing the potatoes and smiled when Aoife told her what was on the menu.

'Oh, that's a blast from the past! Leave it with me, pet, I'm feeling a bit restless. How about we eat at six? Why don't you go off and read a book or go for a nice walk?'

Aoife debated how to fill in the time until supper. It was just gone four. The laptop, or 'portal to hell' as she now thought of it, was waiting for her upstairs. But she couldn't face her research on Manus without a few stiff drinks. She'd go for a quick run. After changing into sweats, she sent Connor a text. She didn't know what to say but settled for: '**Hope you got home safe**.' It felt lame but, equally, she felt adding sorry would sound trite.

Getting out of the house was a good idea. The air was slightly humid but not too warm to run. Aoife set off at a fast pace – she needed to get tired out, to quell the thoughts swirling like angry wasps around her head. She turned up a track at the rear of her house and ran so hard a sharp pain in her side forced her to stop. A horn beeped as she was catching her breath.

It was Jack. He pulled up right beside her.

'Hey, are you alright?'

'I'm grand, just got a stitch!' she snapped.

Jack frowned at her. 'What's eating you? I was only asking because you look like death warmed over. Are you sure that you're OK?'

'Yeah, I'm fine! Really I am, Jack,' she said in a more measured tone.

'Can I give you a lift back or something?' Jack smirked suggestively.

Aoife felt a wave of revulsion. The revulsion was directed not at Jack but at herself. For this, she had put the last nail in the coffin of her relationship with Connor. She had felt entitled to use Jack because of the shithole her life had become. Not that it seemed to bother Jack.

'Look, I'm going to carry on with my run now so ...'

As she turned to go, he reached out and brushed his fingers against her arm.

'I heard Connor was down and I hope that ... I mean, I want you to know that I haven't said anything to anyone, OK?'

Aoife smiled. 'Thanks, Jack, but Connor knows and let's just say we are well and truly over now.'

'Ah Aoife, I'm sorry, that's tough. How are you holding up?'

Aoife clenched her jaw. 'I'll live.' She turned and raced up the track.

Faintly, she could hear Jack starting his engine.

Back at the house, she saw that she just had time for a quick shower before supper.

The Angelus bell was ringing on RTÉ as she sat down to eat with her mother.

Agnes told her that Sam had called to say he wouldn't be home until late. She looked worried.

'Sam is working far too hard. Even with Karol to lend a hand, he's taking too much on. He hardly gets a minute to himself. After your father died, I suggested he sell the farm or lease it, but he insisted he wanted to farm it just as Daddy had. I worry sometimes that he never gets a break. He hardly ever goes away, not even for a wee holiday. I'm afraid your brother is missing out on life. Do you know, I don't think he's ever had a long-term girlfriend? He must be so lonely sometimes. There was a girl he was dating around the time your father died – she was lovely, but he broke it off a week later and he never seems to have found anyone special since then. When he was younger, he would go off to Bundoran to the dances occasionally. In fact, at one time, I thought he might be seeing someone. But these last few years he never goes anywhere. Well, apart from his card nights on the first of the month.'

'What card nights?' Aoife asked, holding her breath.

'*Aww*, just a wee thing he does with old school pals. He goes off to different houses and plays a few games. He's never very late but he seems happier after he has these outings. But I'd love it if he met a nice girl. Someone to share his life with and not be stuck minding an old one like me. Do you think staying on the farm with me is cutting his chances of meeting someone?'

'Mam, I doubt it — not everyone wants to marry and have kids, you know.'

Agnes gave her shoulder a little squeeze. 'OK, love, I forgot for a minute about you and Connor. I'm sure you'll meet someone else soon.'

Aoife could feel her nerve-endings tingle and a surge of tears press against her eyelids. It took all her strength to smile brightly and nod.

They finished their meal in silence and Aoife sent her mother into the front room to watch TV while she cleaned up. She allowed herself the brief luxury of crying as she loaded the dishwasher and swept the kitchen floor. Then she turned out the lights in the kitchen and with grim determination resolved to shed no more tears from now on.

She joined her mother to watch the nine o'clock news and, when her mother settled down to watch a movie, she inspected the drinks cabinet, liberated a bottle of Irish whiskey and took it up to her room where she steeled herself to do further research.

CHAPTER 40

Anika Bakker 1978 – Sligo/Donegal border
Mary Bernadette Maher 1980 – Sligo
Anna Halliburton 1985 – Galway
Catherine Gillespie 1986 – Mullingar
Louise Kavanagh 1988 – Dublin
Susan O'Brien 1992 – Clonmel

There were greyhound stadiums in many of these areas but, equally, Manus could have been attending marts, or collecting machinery when he came across these women.

She stared at the first three names on the list, sickened. Those poor women died because her mother's depression had triggered something dark in her father. They had their futures stolen from them. Their lives with all their possibilities were wiped out because her father was a fucked-up monster. Her father the destroyer had taken away their lives, scarred their families and robbed the world of all the difference their presence might have made. They had lost their lives when they were at their most vital. No, not lost their lives as though they had been careless – no, they hadn't lost their lives, they had their lives ripped away from them. Now all that remained were names on a Missing Person site and the tormented memories of those who loved them. They had no future, and their loved ones had lost that future too. Mary Bernadette's mother would never get to be part of her daughter's life and all its possibilities. Pádraig would never get to marry his secret love. Lotte Bakker had lost her sister and confidante. Susan had lost her twin, and all the adventures they could have shared. God knows what other lives and private hells existed behind that simple list of names. She didn't want to know. She felt an obligation to honour their memories by at least finding out a little about the lives stolen, but she was too weak and cowardly. It was enough to know they existed, and there could be many more that she knew nothing about. Her father was in his mid-twenties when he married. He could have been venting his hate and rage for years. She recalled reading stories of 'the disappeared' in places like Columbia and Guatemala. How it tormented the families not having a body to bury. They spoke of their desperate need to find out what happened to their loved ones and to lay their bodies to rest. It wasn't a lot to ask, was it?

But it was a lot to ask for her family. They were innocent victims too. Their lives would be destroyed if she went public with what she had discovered. How could she do this to her mother, Kate, and Sam, not forgetting Sandy and Colm? Poor Colm was struggling with having a broken father – imagine piling all this horror on his young shoulders!

How long had Sam known and why hide the box? He must have buried it when Polly died, and that happened shortly after Manus had died. When had he discovered it? After the funeral? Or had he known before Manus died? But he might have his own secrets to hide. Her

264

mam had said that he used to disappear off to Donegal to dances. She thought he might be seeing someone. But perhaps he was continuing his father's work. She thought about the missing girl in Donegal. No! She couldn't believe that of Sam. Her Sam! Questions swarmed round and round her head, making it ache. How had Manus got away with it for so long and where did he bury all those girls? It was extraordinary that they had disappeared without a trace. Were their unmarked graves on the farm? From her vantage point on the tree the other day, she could see the diversity of the farmland. Her father had never been much of a tillage farmer – he kept dairy cows and animals to sell at the mart, but he wasn't interested in growing potatoes or vegetables, unlike most of the farmers in the area. He gave up growing things in the early 80s as it was labour intensive. Sam followed in his footsteps. The phrase made her shudder. Sam didn't follow in her father's footsteps, he just hid them. Perhaps he was afraid to plough the land because of what it might expose. How deep did a grave have to be? Karol had dug about four feet to bury poor Nell. She recalled Westerns that she watched with Sam as a child, and the bad guys all seemed to agree on six feet to bury a body. The outlaws often made their victims dig their graves – what a refinement of torture to be forced to prepare your final resting place.

Aoife's mind recoiled at the thought of how those young women had suffered. Did they feel terror or were they like Anika, taken by surprise with little time to react or feel fear? But perhaps some of them fought back, their sufferings prolonged like Mary Bernadette. Images of her father's face contorted with hate and rage imposed themselves on her retina and froze there until she rubbed her eyes harshly. Obviously there must have been a sexual element – presumably the killing itself provided release – but did it go further than that? In the diary, Manus spoke of spending time with the dead

265

women. Unable to contemplate these disturbing thoughts, she closed her laptop. Filling up her glass, she pulled the eiderdown from the bed around her shoulders. That her father was a monstrous killer was horrific enough, but the thought that he was a rapist too was a horror too deep to bear.

What about Sam and those mysterious monthly trips away from home? She never heard of him playing cards before. She didn't think he liked to gamble. And his secret trip to Donegal when he said he was in Mullingar. What did it mean? She looked at her phone. The news feed said the young girl from Donegal, Jane Cornell, was still missing. Could Sam have done something to her? Her skin crawled as though covered with tiny ants as she thought about it.

If only she had someone to talk to. Normally, Sorcha would have been the friend she shared all her worries, hopes and dreams with. But this was a category of horror that she couldn't unleash on a friend however close and, besides, how could she swear her to secrecy, to make her accessory to withholding information on a crime? It was impossible. A wall of loneliness settled over her. She poured more whiskey, hoping to numb herself, at least until morning.

At twelve she heard Sam come in. She listened to the indistinct murmur of voices as he spoke to Agnes and then a short time later heard her mother slowly climb up the stairs to bed. Sam followed soon after.

Two hours later she groggily climbed into bed. Despite the whiskey, she lay awake for a long time and when she did lose consciousness her sleep was fitful, beset with troubling dreams that disappeared from her memory like water trickling down a drain each time she awoke.

CHAPTER 41

Aoife pulled sleep-glued eyelashes apart, tormented by the light streaming through the partly closed curtains. She glanced at the clock. Unbelievably, it was half past twelve. Groaning, she dragged herself to the bathroom. She stood inert under tepid water until it ran cold. Shivering, she dried off and dressed, then went downstairs.

Agnes was in the kitchen washing lettuce at the sink.

She turned her head and smiled. 'Ah, there you are. I peeped in earlier but you were sound asleep.'

'Yes, I stupidly stayed on my laptop till the early hours.'

'Well, you'll have to fend for yourself now, pet. We've already eaten. We had a light lunch – we'll have the dinner in the evening.' She beckoned to Aoife to come closer and, putting a finger to her lips, whispered, 'Baby is here. I had to produce a quick meal for her. She caught the early train from Dublin. Sam had to pick her up. I don't know what possessed her as she rarely travels alone. I think she must be lonely.'

'Where is she?' Aoife asked. That was all her mother needed – a plump elderly toddler with an insatiable desire to be coddled and minded.

Agnes gestured towards the living room and continued to whisper. 'I'm taking a lift into the shops with Sam in a while – there are things I need. Lovey, would you ever mind keeping Baby entertained until we get back? I've defrosted a lasagne and if I'm not back you could pop it in the oven at around five and maybe prepare a salad. But I won't be that long.' As she spoke she gave her hands a quick rinse under the tap and dried them on a tea towel.

Aoife hadn't the heart to refuse, not that she actually could.

'Why has she come?'

'She mentioned coming for a visit a while back but I forgot all about it,' Agnes whispered. To be honest, I could do without her but she's your dad's sister so I couldn't refuse. You know how it is.'

'Is that you, Aoife, dear? I'm in the front room,' came Baby's querulous tones.

Sighing loudly and cursing under her breath, Aoife called, 'I'll be in with you in a minute, Baby! I'm just making a coffee!'

Sam and Agnes had left, leaving her to baby-sit Baby.

Gulping at the hot coffee, she joined Baby where she sat ensconced on the largest armchair, a tray of tea things on a low table in front of her.

Baby was a study in roundness. Her frame was slight but encased in so much flesh that she resembled a springy ball. Her eyes were round, and her mouth appeared to be making a perpetual *ooh* shape of shock or disapproval. She was wearing her usual grey dress and was wrapped in two layers of enveloping shawls in hues of lilac and pink, with her bulging feet encased in sturdy brogues.

'Aoife, it's so nice to get chance to talk to you alone. We hardly spoke at your dear father's anniversary. I was so sorry to hear about you and your young man. But it's better to find these things out sooner than later and have to rue your choice.'

'Sorry, what do you mean about finding out things?'

'Ah now, Aoife, I can read between the lines as well as anyone and I think we all felt that your young man had a straying eye. He was shiftless too, so really you had a lucky escape, my dear.'

'Baby, I don't know where you're getting your information, but it's all wrong. Connor is a wonderful person and our reasons for breaking up had nothing to do with his behaviour.'

Baby opened her eyes wide. 'Oh my dear, I just assumed when you suddenly broke up that perhaps he had been misbehaving.'

'Well, you are wrong. *Connor* wasn't the one misbehaving as you called it.' Aoife deliberately stressed Connor's name, knowing the construction Baby would put on it. She watched with satisfaction as colour washed over Baby's face.

'I see,' she said icily.

'Well, Baby, you're looking well. The Wicklow air must agree with you. I see that you're finished your cup of tea. Would you like a fresh drop?'

Baby looked a little mollified and assented to another cup of tea which Aoife poured.

The conversation was turgid until Aoife used this opportunity to see what her aunt's take was on life on the farm when she was a young girl. After all, she had quizzed everyone except Baby, and she was the closest in age to her father.

'Baby, I'm thinking of working on our family history and, although I have lots of information on Mam's family, I don't have a lot on the O'Driscoll side. Emma and Clarissa are always saying what a fantastic

269

memory you have. So would you mind helping me out?'

Aoife could see that flattery was paying dividends.

Baby flushed with pleasure. 'Well, my dear, I would love to help but I'm not too good on dates, you know.'

'That's OK, Baby, I can work out the dates, but I would love some background about your parents and where they came from. I mean, I don't even know if they were from this area originally. I really would appreciate your help.'

Baby was positively blushing with pleasure. 'Well, why don't you ask me some questions and I'll do my best to answer them for you.'

'How about you tell me all about your parents and I'll record you for posterity?'

Puffed up with self-importance, Baby waited eagerly while Aoife pressed record on her mobile. 'This is exciting,' she lisped.

'Perhaps you could start by telling me about where your parents came from, how they met and so on?'

'All right!' said Baby and screwed up her face, struggling to remember. 'Well, Dada was from Leitrim originally, but an elderly uncle left him the farm here and so they moved in the 1920s. Mother was originally from Dublin but was sent down the country where she met our dear dada. They had seven surviving children. I think Mother lost two children between me and Manus. I'm sure it made her very sad, but Mother wasn't one for feeling sorry for herself and, well, in those days you just got on with things. None of this crying and weeping and making much of everything, as is the fashion nowadays. Anyway, they were both devout Catholics and raised us to be regular in our religious duties. Mother was strict and she didn't believe in spoiling us, but Dada was great fun. I remember him giving me piggybacks when I was small. It was so exciting to be so high off the ground, and he loved to gallop away like a crazy horse.' Baby smiled reminiscently. 'But is this what you want, Aoife? I don't think I have too much more to tell.'

'No, this is exactly what I want – a first-hand account. You never know, I might write a family history and dedicate it to you.'

Baby beamed delightedly at the blatant flattery. 'Well, poor Dada didn't have long with us. I'm not sure exactly what happened, but he got pneumonia or pleurisy and died. It was so sudden. I was only seven and I was so upset but, as for Mother, I think it broke her heart. I can't ever remember her smiling or being happy again. Of course, it wasn't your father's fault, but I don't think mother saw it that way.'

'Hey, what do you mean, Baby? How could it have been my father's fault? He was only a child.'

'Oh dear, I'm always leaving things out. Let me see ... Ah yes, Manus was always an active wee fellow and one morning in late summer he escaped from the yard and wandered over to the neighbour's and, well, he fell in a river at the end of their garden. Luckily for him, Dada went after him and jumped in and rescued him. Well, what with taking care of the little lad and getting him warm and dry, Dada neglected himself. I don't know if I mentioned he had a weak chest, perhaps even asthma – well, anyway he took a dreadful chill and before too long it had spread to his lungs. Poor Dada was dead shortly afterwards. But mother was devastated. I'm not sure if I imagined it but she made this noise when the doctor told her he'd died – it sounded like what the old folk would call a Banshee.' Baby shuddered a little at the memory and went uncharacteristically silent.

'But surely Grandmother couldn't blame a small child for what happened. It was an accident.'

'Well, true, but Mother was furious that Manus had disobeyed her and left the house. I remember her saying "If you only did as you were told, your father would be alive today". She shook him so hard

271

that my older brothers had to rescue him. But I'm sure she forgave him, and we all kept her busy after Dada died. It was hard work on the farm, but she was a remarkable woman really ...' Baby's voice stalled as she saw Aoife's shocked face.

'My God, Baby, your mother sounds awful. Why would she land all that guilt on a small child?'

'Oh, I'm sure Manus got over it. Children don't really understand, do they, and it never stopped him from wandering. He was always outside playing. Sometimes he'd even forget to come in to eat. So, I'm sure he was having fun.' Baby looked a little uncomfortable.

'Was she hard on my father, Baby, did she take her anger about what happened out on him?'

'Well, I don't know, Aoife, those were different times and people didn't pay so much attention to children then. But Manus had a thick skin – he never seemed to care if Mother was harsh. But, really, I suffered the most. I was to make my Communion that year and Mother told me I could have a little party, but because Dada died I didn't even get a new dress – just a hand-me-down from Emma and she was much bigger than me – I'm not saying she was fat, but she definitely had big bones and because mother was so upset she took little care with the restyling. I was lost in it, and I had to wear Clarissa's shoes and her feet were huge, so I had to stuff the toes of my shoes with newspaper and I got blisters.' Noticing that Aoife was looking distracted, Baby paused and asked, 'Well, have you more questions for me? I have lots of information about our school days, you know.'

Aoife shook her head but then asked, 'No, wait, how did Dad get on at school? Did he have friends?'

'Well, I was five years ahead in school, so I didn't see too much of Manus at school and he was always missing days. He had to help on the farm, you know, we all did.'

'Yes, but he was the youngest – surely his older brothers would be more useful?'

'Well, of course they helped out, but Mother was determined that we all get a decent education and be able to get good jobs and, to be honest, poor Manus was a bit slow.'

Aoife felt a stirring of rage against that harsh woman and how she had robbed her dad's childhood and poisoned his future. She was conscious that for the first time in ages she had referred to Manus in her thoughts as 'Dad' rather than 'Manus'. Calling him 'father' or Manus gave her some disconnect, some distance from the intimacy calling him 'Dad' implied. For a moment she felt a stirring of compassion for the boy he once was – only for a moment.

Baby's querulous voice returned her to the present, 'Aoife dear, play it back – I want to hear how I sound.'

Aoife played the recording back but left Baby to listen alone.

CHAPTER 42

Exhausted from her trip down memory lane, Baby went for a lie-down. Aoife was relieved to get away from her phlebotomizing presence so she could think. Loretta Swann appeared to be a monstrous person incapable of loving anyone except perhaps her husband. Maybe before his death, she had normal maternal emotions before they became corroded by grief, but to blame an innocent child and then spend a lifetime torturing him was the act of a sadist. Did she create the monster her father became or were the seeds always there? Aoife thought back to the diary entries and how Manus spoke of his mother isolating him, punishing him physically and with her words, but most effectively with the violence of her silence.

What were her origins, this long-dead grandmother? Baby said they "sent" her from Dublin. Who sent her, her parents perhaps? What had made Loretta Swann such a cruel, unforgiving woman? From the snippets she had gleaned from her aunts, Loretta seemed to have been emotionally cold and inspired not love but respect and fear in her children. She vaguely remembered two of her uncles – Malachi and Patrick. They had come to her father's funeral and one or two of the earlier anniversaries but now, apart from the odd Christmas card, they remained lost in the wilds of Canada. They didn't seem to have any actual contact with their sisters. And what of her aunts? Wasn't it strange that none of them had children? Of course, Clarissa's husband deserted her shortly after their marriage. Baby had never married or had children and seemed too self-absorbed to care about anyone but herself. She didn't know if Emma was unable or unwilling to have children. Did any of her uncles have children? Did their experience of childhood put them off from becoming parents? What insights might they have into Loretta? What did it matter, anyway? It was too late now, too late for Manus and too late for his victims. No amount of understanding of what drove her father would bring his victims back.

On an impulse she rang Emma. Clarissa would be too kind and determined to mitigate Loretta's behaviour, to find reasons to explain or excuse, but Emma would be more honest … at least she hoped so.

She was about to give up when Emma finally answered.

'Hello, darling, I wouldn't answer until I saw it was my favourite niece. To what do I owe the pleasure?'

'Now why would I need a reason to call my favourite aunt?' Aoife parried.

Emma gave a deep throaty laugh. 'I know you've got that dose Baby staying so I'm guessing you need a bit of respite and sanity, and you know just whom to call to give you that.'

They laughed and exchanged a few barbs about Baby. Emma never felt loyalty to the family should impede her waspish tongue.

After a few minutes, Aoife got to the point.

'I was chatting to Baby, and she told me something weird, and I hoped you could supply the facts. I know that Baby sometimes gets the wrong end of the stick.'

Emma took a moment before responding, and when she did Aoife detected a note of caution in her voice.

'What's the silly goose been saying then?'

'Well, Baby was talking about your parents, and she told me the story of how as a small child Dad nearly drowned and had to be rescued by his father.'

'I suppose that's accurate enough. Manus escaped from the garden when he was a wee fellow and fell into Bradys' river.'

'Baby said that your father died shortly after that and that your mother blamed Manus for causing his death.'

There was a long silence, and Aoife was afraid Emma had hung up.

'Emma?'

'I'm here. I don't know why Baby is wittering on about that. It was aeons ago, for God's sake, Aoife!'

'Yes, but is it true? Did Grandfather die because of rescuing my father and did Grandmother blame him for causing his father's death?'

Emma cleared her throat and sighed. 'I haven't thought about this for a long time, Aoife, but it's typical of Baby to drag past tragedies into the present. I bet she found a way of making this tragedy about herself too.'

Aoife said nothing and waited, forcing her aunt to speak.

'When Manus escaped from the garden, we were all worried sick. Dada raced over the road to find him. I think the river was the first place he headed. We weren't worried about the road because there wasn't much traffic then except for the occasional tractor, not like nowadays. Anyway, Dada jumped into the river and rescued Manus. It wasn't deep, but for a three-year-old like Manus, it would be lethal.

Anyway, he brought him home. Mother was in a state and stripped Manus and wrapped him in a blanket. But Daddy was her chief concern.'

'What was wrong with him?'

'Dada had a weak chest because of childhood illnesses, and of course he had asthma. Treatments weren't great then, and poor Dada had a severe attack a few hours later. He died that evening. Mother was distraught. She adored him. His death did something terrible to her. Baby is right that she blamed Manus for what happened. I remember her pulling him out of bed, shaking him and shouting terrible things at him. She even said she wished he was dead. I know this sounds terrible, Aoife, but you must remember she was mad with grief. Eventually, my brothers calmed her down. Clarissa took Manus to stay with a neighbour until after the funeral.'

'Oh God, Emma, he must have been traumatised.'

'Perhaps you're right, Aoife, but in those days people thought children were very resilient and Manus seemed fine. Of course, he asked for his dada but the boys told him not to speak about him in front of Mother. Soon he was acting as usual. We didn't think it did Manus any lasting harm, and he never spoke about what happened. I think he was too young to understand.'

'But, Emma, did your mother continue to blame Dad for what happened?'

'Yes, I suppose she did. She said nothing more to Manus about it but she was harsh with him. That was why Clarissa made such a pet of him. She was trying to make up for Mother's coldness.'

'But that's child abuse, Emma, to lay all that on an innocent child. Did nobody reason with her, make her see it was cruel to treat a child that way?'

Emma sighed. 'Aoife, you must understand those were different times. Malachi had a word, but it only made things worse, so Manus just kept out of her way. Over the years I have realised that ours was not a happy family. Mother was a hard woman. But, Aoife, our mother had a tough upbringing. I learned later that she was in care for most of her early life. I think the only bit of happiness and normalcy she experienced was when she met Dada. When he was alive, she was happy or as happy as she could be. Even as children, we knew he came first. It was from Dada that we got all the fun and affection. I remember she used to watch him play with us and she looked so lost. I don't think she had ever experienced a normal childhood.'

Aoife listened in silence and Emma, perhaps stung by the perceived judgement it contained, rushed on.

'Aoife, there was so much that happened in the past that you can't ever understand. I know that Mother sounds hard but –'

'She sounds like a monster, Emma, a monster that you all enabled.'

'That's not fair to us or her. After she died, I did a bit of digging into my mother's past and I think her parents put her into care. I think they got rid of her because they thought she was bold, which back then meant that she was interested in boys. But it may have meant there was abuse happening in her family. It was a strange time. Inconvenient people ended up in mental asylums, Mother and Baby homes, Industrial schools and orphanages. She didn't have a good start in life, and the one person with whom she experienced a bond died. Look, I'm not saying what she did was right, but if she was a monster others created her. I know you think we let Manus down and you're right, we did, but we were in survival mode too. Try not to judge any of us too harshly. Besides, the sun came up for your dad. He met Agnes, and they doted on each other. So, in the end, it all worked out well, didn't it?'

Aoife's eyes stung with tears. 'Yes, Emma, things worked out just fine in the end,' she said as she ended the call.

CHAPTER 43

Aoife was lost in thought after the call with Emma. What a family history! Unable to feel compassion for Loretta and Manus, all she felt was disgust. Did knowing they both had shitty childhoods make any difference? Did their pain give them the right to inflict suffering on innocent others? She brought Baby up a cup of tea and a biscuit and watched a movie that she was sure she had seen before, but it put in some time.

Glancing at the kitchen clock, she realised she had better get the dinner in the oven or her mother would have a mickey fit.

She laid the table while waiting for the oven to heat and by the time she had got the salad ready and made up some garlic bread, the lasagna was ready to pop into the oven. She poured herself a glass of the cheap wine her mother used for cooking, wrinkling her nose up against its sharp acidic taste, and ate some cheese and crackers to rescue her taste buds.

Sam's car drew up outside as she took the lasagna out to rest and put the garlic bread in to cook. Agnes bustled into the house carrying shopping bags in each hand, rushing around unpacking, and detonating anxious enquires about the dinner, about Baby and worrying that she had forgotten something important in the shop.

'So long as you brought wine, we're good,' Aoife said. But she needn't have doubted her mother as Agnes, grinning widely, proffered a bottle of Chianti from her shopping bags.

Dinner had a festive air. Having a visitor meant everyone set out to be more entertaining or at least chatty. Agnes, despite an earlier lack of enthusiasm for Baby's visit, was delighted to have a visitor to fuss over. And perhaps she had noticed the cool atmosphere that existed between her children and was glad for a break from it. She asked Baby lots of questions and Baby obliged with long meandering tales of life in the city and how difficult it was to navigate around with all the traffic and road works. She moaned about her neighbours (very noisy and foreign), her sisters (most inattentive), her landlord (most unhelpful with repairs), her doctor (very abrupt and unsympathetic) and a myriad of other complaints. Sam and Aoife tried not to catch each other's eye in case they gave way to the laughter. Aoife, amused by the trivialities of her aunt's life, was struck by how rarely they shared laughter anymore.

Dinner over, Agnes insisted on doing the clear-up because her head was wrecked listening to Baby, but ostensibly to give her children "quality time" with their aunt.

Ensconced once again in her favourite chair, Baby beamed at them expectantly.

Sam whispered to Aoife, 'Ask Baby to tell us about the time the waiter in the Ritz tried to pick her up. I love the fact that she thinks it was her irresistible personality and dazzling looks that attracted him, completely unaware he was taking the piss.'

So they entertained Baby while amusing themselves, encouraging her to talk her usual silly nonsense. Baby, who was deficient in self-awareness, didn't know she was being trolled. The fun only ended when Agnes appeared with glasses of sweet sherry for Baby and herself. She cottoned on to the fun that was being had at the expense of a blissfully unaware Baby and hastily started talking local gossip.

Time passed and more sherry was drunk, until Sam nodded to Aoife and mouthed, 'McCoy's.'

Taking the hint, she announced they were going to the pub but wouldn't be late.

Agnes offered apologies to Baby for being deserted by her niece and nephew. Then, to their consternation, Baby said, 'I haven't put foot in McCoy's in years. I'd love to see all the changes. Am I alright to go as I am?'

Stumped for words, Aoife gaped at her. There was no way Baby was coming with them, but how to deter her?

Agnes came to the rescue. '*Aww*, Baby, you'll not be deserting me for that draughty old place! You won't recognise a soul there. Old Mrs McCoy is long gone and so is the brother. Stay at the fire with me and we'll see if there's an old movie on and I'll make us a hot whiskey. Off you go, you two, and don't be waking us when you're coming in half-cut tonight.'

Baby was placated by the prospect of a hot whiskey and Agnes winked at her children as Baby reluctantly agreed she would be better off staying put.

As she pulled on her jacket, Aoife reflected remorsefully that Mam and Baby would be disappointed in their anticipation of hot whiskey after her purloining it last night.

Sam was sitting waiting in the car. It smelled of the farm, cigarettes, and Sam – not unpleasant but a little overpowering. Aoife cracked open a window.

'Well,' he said, 'where do you want to go?'

'To the shop first – I want a cigarette – unless you've got some here?'

Sam rummaged in the glove compartment and unearthed a box containing a single cigarette.

'OK, the Spar will still be open. Do you have any preferences for smokes?'

Aoife shook her head.

They didn't speak on the way to the shop, and Sam went in and came back with a packet of Major.

'This OK?' he asked.

'Anything that contains nicotine that I can inhale is fine by me.'

'I didn't know you smoked anymore. I thought you gave it up years ago.'

'Well, I'm what they call a social smoker, but I think I could get my full-time commitment back.'

Sam started the engine again. 'How about we drive to the Head? There won't be many people about at ten o'clock. It's getting darker earlier, so we should have the place to ourselves.'

Aoife nodded. But the idea of being alone with her brother on a deserted headland made her shiver.

The silence was unbroken until they reached the Head.

CHAPTER 44

On the Head, the wind always blew, and waves crashed pounding onto the static rocks below, fitting scenery for an emotional tsunami.

Sam shuffled two cigarettes out of the packet and after they were lit and they had each taken a savage pull of nicotine he spoke. 'I've kept this thing locked away inside for so long that sometimes I can almost believe it never happened. I've guarded my tongue against anything slipping out so that it's hard to speak now.'

Aoife, her chest constricted, hardly dared to breathe. Keeping the box a secret for a few months had crippled her. How had Sam coped all these years? Reaching out, she touched his hand.

Sam shrugged it off. 'Don't look at me or touch me or I won't be able to tell you ... I've buried this so deep that I'm afraid I won't find the words. Just give me a minute to sort things. I need to order it in my mind, get it clear, OK?'

Aoife nodded and, sensing it would make it easier, she too stared out to sea. The silence stretched unendurably and yet Aoife was reluctant to hear the story interred within Sam.

'You don't remember Dad well, do you? He was a quiet man, but great for a young boy to be around. He loved wildlife and knew the names of every tree, plant, and flower – we'd go birdwatching and he was so knowledgeable about all aspects of nature. Being outdoors was his natural habitat. We went fishing, tracked deer and laid traps for rabbits. He wasn't sentimental about nature but was always quick and humane whenever he killed an animal. We regularly had rabbit for dinner and hare and of course lots of fish. Mam hated having to gut fish and he would laugh and do it for her. He was interested in everything to do with the outdoors. I couldn't spend enough time with him. I would have skived off school, but I knew he wanted me to get a decent education and I wanted to please him. We made plans for me to attend agricultural college and take over the farm one day. It was an idyllic childhood. I can honestly say Dad was never cross or rough. Of course, there was hard work too, and he expected me to do my share. But he was so interested in everything, and in my reactions to them, it was beguiling. People don't realise how amazing it is to have an adult listen, especially a parent. It makes you feel important and clever, as though what you think matters.' Sam paused to inhale deeply from his cigarette. 'Dad and I were inseparable, but he always had time for you and Katy. Sometimes I'd get jealous because he'd tell Katy long stories at bedtime, and I'd hear her laughter and resent her for taking him away. He stayed ages putting her to bed and sometimes I'd be sulky or try to make him stay longer with me, but he'd smile and say, "Sam, you're my special man and who knows what adventures tomorrow will bring". Then he'd wink, and I'd feel deliriously happy again. As for you, he was forever bouncing you up in the air and tickling you until you were a helpless mess of giggles. But when he looked at Mam, it was clear who came first. Dad adored her. He used to bring her little posies of spring flowers and gifts of sweets and perfume whenever he was away. The only time I ever remember him getting cross was if we upset or disrespected Mam. Then he'd say: "Your mother is the best and when you've got the best you make sure to treat her well."'

Sam ground his cigarette out and replaced it immediately. His voice was growing hoarse, so Aoife passed over a bottle of water from the well of the car. God knows how long it was there, but Sam drank thirstily and said, 'I need to step out and get a breath of air, OK?'

Aoife watched him pacing over and back on the sea road. He looked old, face hunched low over his chest and large hands thrust deep in his pockets. She felt a sharp pity for him, for all of them, perhaps even a little for Manus.

It was stuffy in the car, so she opened the window wider to allow the smoke out and the sea winds to replace it. Watching his slow tread back, she could see that Sam dreaded this unburdening because it provided not just release but a reckoning too. Aoife's mind shifted away from that reckoning.

He got in the car again. His voice shook a little when he spoke. 'I suppose it's natural for fathers and sons to draw apart when the teenage years come, but initially we became closer. We made plans for the farm. He gave me my first drink when I was fifteen. He told me I needed to learn to drink sensibly and not make a show of myself like the neighbour boys who headed out to the local discos and got lit from the drink their older brothers bought for them. I never wanted to join those lads, they seemed like idiots, but sometimes I got led astray too. Once I went to a field with some lads after school and milled into half a dozen cans of cider. Dad found me puking in a ditch. He didn't get mad, just snuck me upstairs and told Mam I had a bellyache from eating sour apples. Not too far from the truth really.

285

It saved me from a good telling-off as Mam was very much against me drinking, at least until I was eighteen. So, Dad was even more of a hero to me. Things changed when I turned sixteen. Like most teenagers, I questioned authority, and I noticed there were lots of things Dad didn't know. He was so old-fashioned in the way he looked at things. It was like he lived in the past. He was so definite that I was going to take over the farm, but I was going off the idea. In fact, I was much more interested in becoming a vet. When I tried to talk about my changing plans, it was the first time he got angry, and of course that justified me being an absolute dick. I started getting lazy about helping on the farm and didn't finish jobs on purpose just to annoy him. None of this happened all at once. It was a slow change in our relationship.' Sam paused and took another swig from the bottle. 'Then one day Dad started talking about girls … I was seeing a young one from the Mercy. We weren't up to much, just holding hands and long kisses, but I thought the world of her. Mam found out and started teasing me at the dinner table, mortifying me, and of course Kate joined the slagging. Dad was silent. He looked angry but he said nothing. The next day when we were checking fences he brought my girlfriend up in conversation, "You know, Sam," he said, "there are two kinds of girls: good women like your mother and sisters, and slags.' He paused and stared at me. "Make sure you choose the right kind." That's all he said but he knew my girlfriend – her brother was at my school and played on my football team. He seemed to be suggesting she was a slag. The way he said it repelled me. The look on his face was so ugly, he didn't seem like Dad any more. It shocked me. He didn't say another word, but it ended our uncomplicated relationship. I'd lost my way with him. Of course, life went back to normal, I continued to see my girl but somehow my feelings for her felt tarnished, spoiled. Dad and I continued to work together on the farm but, apart from that, I avoided spending time with him. I know it wounded him and Mam couldn't understand why I had suddenly become so difficult and moody. Perhaps she told herself that it was just a teenage thing. But, for me, it was the beginning of my disillusionment – my·discovery of what sort of man my father was.'

CHAPTER 45

Aoife's body tensed, she didn't look at Sam, yet was acutely aware of his presence, stiff and coiled, his voice growing lower to almost a whisper and his breathing punctuated by heavy sighs.

'Saturday, the 9th of April, was my seventeenth birthday. I wanted to go out with the lads and itched for the birthday tea to be over. I was ungracious, despite knowing all the trouble Mam went to, making a cake and cooking my favourite meal. Dad glared as I eyed the clock, and I knew he felt I was an ungrateful whelp. He didn't have to say a word – I could see it in his eyes. But it only made me double down on my rudeness. When Mam gave me my present, I barely thanked her. She had gone to great expense to get a Walkman. I had hinted about wanting one for weeks, but I refused to show my delight – just to piss Dad off. But, of course, it hurt Mam, who was dying to see my reaction to the gift. Anyway, I took off and met the lads. We met up at the Community Centre for the local disco and I had a court with my girl, Annie. Funny, I can still remember us dancing to Wet Wet

288

Wet. Their song "Love Is All Around" was Number 1 for weeks and it felt so good holding her. That was the last time I ever touched her, the last time I ever felt clean again.' Sam smiled wryly. 'I came home and slipped away to bed before anyone noticed I was the worse for wear. And I slept in the next day until around two o'clock. I could hear Dad and Mam talking in the kitchen. To avoid being seen, I dodged out the back door and hid in the shed that Dad used as a workshop. My head felt too delicate for an interrogation. I was mooching about in the shed, hoping he'd go away, when I noticed a slab in the wall out of alignment. Out of nosiness, I went to investigate and realised the stone covered a gap in the wall. I thought to myself, Dad's got a secret booze stash. I pulled the stone away and found a yellow biscuit tin inside. It looked too battered to be used for biscuits, but curiosity led me to open it. I found what you found inside.' He paused and glanced at Aoife.

'Go on,' she said.

'Well, of course, all the little trinkets in the box puzzled me. I wondered if it was a place Dad kept secret mementoes, maybe even love letters from old girlfriends. Thinking it might give me an edge over him, I opened the notebook and God knows I've wished ever since I never touched it. Well, you know what's in it. At first, it baffled me, but the handwriting looked like his. It was weird. The way he talked about life on the farm and his mother made my flesh creep. I wanted to stop but was hypnotised, like in those old tales about snake charmers. He described killing a girl and doing things to her. There were descriptions, each more graphic than the last. It was disgusting. The way he described the pleasure he got from choking those girls made my stomach sick. However much I wanted, I couldn't stop reading, discovering more and more depravity until, unable to bear it anymore, I dropped the notebook to the ground. I don't know how long I stood there – it was as though my legs had turned to stone. Then Dad came in. The minute I saw his face, I knew the diary was real. Shock, fear, rage and then pleading chased across his face in quick succession. It could have been comical if it wasn't so horrifying. First, he demanded to know what I was doing prying in his shed, then when I picked up the notebook, he grabbed it and claimed never to have seen it before, then he said it belonged to his brother Malachi. He lurched from one lie to the other and I couldn't stop staring. It was when he called me "son" that the walls closed in. Frantically he ripped pages from the diary. I couldn't bear being near him and bolted for the door. He grabbed at my shirt, but I kept going. I ran out to the fields and kept running until my chest burned and I gasped for breath. Eventually, I collapsed close to a stone wall. Over and over my mind raced about what I read, then bizarrely I wondered what there would be for dinner. My body brought me back to reality when I emptied my stomach on the grass. And I sat there, snot running down my face and crying like a child. Then I heard him climbing the hill. I'd have fled except my legs turned to jelly and I waited, unable to move.'

Sam rested his head on the steering wheel. Aoife, aching for him, waited patiently. His hand trembled as he lit another cigarette.

'God, I need a drink. I don't suppose you're one of those women who have everything in your bag to cover all emergencies, are you?'

'Keep going, Sam, you've done the worst part now. I know this must be brutal.'

Sam was incredulous. 'You think that's been the worst part? No, little sister, that was only the beginning. There is a lot you don't know, and I don't know if I want to tell you the rest!'

Watching his face, it seemed as if Sam, her kind, lovely brother was dissolving and for a horrifying moment Aoife was convinced that Manus had corrupted him. Had made him a party to his killings and that now Sam carried on his father's murderous work. Thoughts of the missing girl made her shiver. She pulled her hand, which had been resting on Sam's arm, away as if it was burnt.

Sam, perhaps reading her thoughts, smiled grotesquely. 'He even has you fearing me now, doesn't he?'

She replaced her hand tentatively on his sleeve. 'Sam, please go on. Whatever there is to tell, say it now. I promise I'm here for you,'

Sam laughed, a harsh sound. 'Shit, you're sounding like a terrible movie now.'

'Please say whatever you have to, I need to know,' she pleaded.

Sam lowered his head and, sucking deeply on his cigarette, said, 'You asked for it!'

Aoife's mobile shattered the silence, its upbeat ringtone mocking them.

'Jaysus, Aoife, why the fuck didn't you turn that yoke off?'

'Sorry, sorry – ah feck, it's Mam. Shit, why is she ringing? There must be something wrong. I'd better answer.'

Slipping out of the car, Aoife answered her mother who, it turned out, was just belatedly concerned about Sam drinking and driving. Aoife set about reassuring her and told her to go to bed and stop fretting.

She returned to the car to the disturbing sight of Sam staring savagely ahead. He appeared frightening and unapproachable. But nothing was going to prevent her from hearing the rest of his story.

'Mam's just worried about you drinking and driving. Now, please, continue. We need to end all the secrets now.' She could see that Sam's nerve had failed. She squeezed his hand. No longer afraid of him, she saw him transformed into a terrified seventeen-year-old boy facing up to the fact that the father he thought he knew and loved was a monster.

'Dad reached the top of the hill and somehow I got my legs to work and lurched to my feet. We just locked eyes, but then his slid away. *"Tell me the truth!"* I screamed at him. It was pathetic. He tried to make excuses, said it was all make-believe. Then I asked him about the things in the box, were they make-believe too? He couldn't look me in the eye, and I shouted I was going to tell Mam. It was then I saw the fury and hate in his eyes. He walked towards me and grabbed me by the throat and, I swear to God, Aoife, I thought he was going to kill me. I nearly pissed myself, but then I started punching his chest with my fists and kicking him. He held me back with one hand like I was a wee boy and the ugliness in his face died away and he was Dad again. That's when I killed him.'

CHAPTER 46

Darkness had crept in while they sat in the car, and an impressive array of stars twinkled in the sky, creating the illusion of isolation, as though they were displaced from humanity by their position on the headland.

Aoife sat transfixed, ears straining to hear his whispered words. Not daring to move, her heart thudded so fiercely she feared Sam must hear it too.

'When he eased the pressure on my neck, I shoved him as hard as I could. He swayed on his feet and then toppled over. As long as I live, I'll never forget the thud of his body hitting the ground and the smack of his head against the stone wall. For a moment I froze, then leant over him. I wasn't sure if he was still breathing and couldn't bring myself to touch him. The dog started barking, I hadn't even noticed Polly was there but now she began barking frantically and trying to lick Dad, to lick the blood running down his face. I grabbed her collar; and she whimpered and growled as I dragged her away. Dad didn't move. Aoife, I didn't know which I feared the most: that I had killed my father or worse that he'd survive, and I'd stare into those eyes and see the devil he was. Then a feeling of calmness came over me, survival instinct I suppose. I took off my belt and attached it to the dog's collar. Desperate to get away, I ran, dragging Polly away from Dad. As I neared the farm I decided to put the dog somewhere safe in case she would return to be with Dad. I was afraid that her barking would alert people. I locked Polly in the old stone henhouse in Dorans' field. No one would hear her as the Dorans had long since emigrated and leased the farm. To this day, I can still see Polly's frightened eyes staring up as I shoved her inside. I wedged a stone against the door. Her pathetic whines followed me as I ran back towards the house.' Sam wiped his eyes and nose.

'Take a breath,' Aoife said.

Sam lit another cigarette and sucked the nicotine deep into his lungs. Then he continued.

'I forced myself to go into the shed to retrieve the notebook. It was still lying where he dropped it. I put it back in the box and replaced it in the hiding place in the wall. The pages Dad had ripped out lay scattered on the ground. I ripped them into tiny shreds and stuffed the pieces in my pocket. Luckily, there was nobody about when I got on my bike. As I cycled, I scattered the torn fragments to the wind. I hid out at my friend John's place. We played Gameboy all afternoon. It was like escaping from a nightmare and stepping back into safety. John and I didn't talk much – teenage boys got engrossed in games, sports, and music, and those were my salvation. I doubt whether John noticed a thing and, if he did, he put it down to me having a hangover from the night before. We played endlessly and it was almost as if the fight with Dad hadn't happened. Around six, Mrs O'Connor drove me home and at first everything seemed normal. Mam was getting ready to serve supper, Kate was setting the table with bad grace and ordering you to lift your comic books. Mam was cross because I had disappeared for the entire day. Then she looked puzzled and said, 'I wonder where your father is. It's not like him to be this late.' She sent me to the yard to call him, and I did just that. Standing in the middle of the yard, I hollered "*Supper's ready!*" for all I was worth. But I couldn't bring myself to use his name. I don't know what I thought would happen. Dad could have come walking into the house as part of me wanted, and part of me dreaded. While eating, Mam got more and more worried. Dad didn't have a mobile phone, so she had no option but to wait. By eight, she was alarmed. She quizzed me about when and where I'd last seen Dad. I lied and said that earlier I thought he was heading to the bottom fields to check on cattle. She asked why I didn't go with him, and I said he didn't want me. The lies came easily. I almost made myself believe them. I was innocent, not a killer.' Sam's hand trembled as he reached for the water bottle and gulped. 'Another hour passed and then Mam got on the telephone and rang the neighbours. No one had seen him. By then it was dark and raining hard. The neighbours organised a search party and headed for the bottom fields. Of course, there was no sign of him, and with a hundred acres of land to comb and the light fading everyone was fearing the worst. Eventually, at about four in the morning, they found him. From the safety of my bedroom window, I watched them carry him into the house on a makeshift stretcher of coats. I don't know which I feared more at that point, finding him concussed and alive, or dead. It wasn't until I heard Mam's frantic cries I knew he was dead, and relief washed over me and so too did grief and most painful of all sick dragging guilt.'

Sam reached for another cigarette and Aoife hardly dared breathe.

'The ambulance came, the priest, every neighbour in the townland and further afield. Mam was in shock, her voice frozen and indistinct as though she had been to the dentist. Kate tried to comfort me, but I snapped at her, and she drew back, upset and puzzled. But I couldn't bear to be near anyone. A touch of a hand felt like a scalding burn. The next few days were a nightmare. I was terrified they would find out what I had done. There was a post-mortem, and we had him back two agonising days later. I never slept. They said that Dad had fallen and struck his head on a sharp stone, cracking his head and causing his brain to fill with blood. I couldn't bear to be around anyone at the wake and funeral. Two of Dad's brothers flew in from Canada and just made the funeral and I barely registered them. I know they tried to talk to me about the farm, but I blanked them and soon they left me alone. They flew back two days later. The aunts fussed around Mam so I could avoid them, but I couldn't avoid the questions that she kept asking over and over about where exactly Dad was heading to and how he ended up in the top field. I know she wasn't blaming me, but she was desperate to find out everything about his last hours. To stop her, I started crying and saying it was my fault and it was only then that she stopped asking. She told me what a wonderful son I was and how proud Dad was of me. It was then I remembered poor Polly. When I got to the henhouse, it was too late. She'd had no water for days. I carried her back to the house and poor Mam's face when she saw her! She blamed herself for not noticing the dog was missing. The next day I retrieved the biscuit tin from the hiding place, and I buried it with Polly.'

Sam stopped speaking. Aoife felt the weight of the silence weighing down.

'Oh, Sam,' was all she could say.

He looked at her grimly, 'So you see, I killed him.'

'Sam, it was an accident, you didn't intend to hurt him.'

'Sure, but I did everything to delay finding him. Perhaps if they got to him sooner, they might have saved him. Aoife, I wanted him to die.'

Aoife took his hand. Sam tried to pull away, but she wouldn't let him. 'Sam, you were only a young boy, who discovered your father had done horrific things. You were in a state of shock and panic. Stop torturing yourself! Why didn't you go away, become a vet as you planned, why stay on the farm?'

'Because Dad trapped me, I thought about what I had read about those girls. They never found the bodies and he must have put them somewhere and, being a farmer, he had an extensive burial ground, didn't he? How could I let out the land or sell it? If there was anything found, everything about him would come out. I couldn't do it to Mam and you girls. I knew that my punishment was to protect the land, to stop it from revealing its secrets, and I hated every minute. I dropped out of school and just surrendered to the farm, and it stole my life.'

'Is that why you never married, Sam?'

'How could I ask any woman to be my wife, to have children with this horrible stain deep inside me, corroding all that's good? I couldn't bring children into the world with his legacy polluting them.'

Once again, the car was toxic with cigarette smoke and the brother and sister sat squeezing hands, each one crying for lost innocence and the reckoning that was to come.

CHAPTER 47

Sam drove them home. They agreed to meet the next morning after Sam gave Karol his work for the day. Each was silent, depleted. The house was in darkness except for the soft glow of a porch light. They slipped quietly in the back door, grateful that their mother was asleep.

As Aoife watched Sam go into his room, she berated herself for not asking where he went in the early hours of Friday. But she couldn't face any more ugliness.

Later, lying in bed, Aoife realised they had both avoided deciding what to do next. As she drifted off, she knew they couldn't put it off much longer.

Morning brought a revisiting of the dull ache in her stomach. Downstairs, Agnes was full of cheerful chat, asking about who they met in the pub. It was hard to come up with lies when she felt so exhausted, but she satisfied her mother's curiosity. Unable to face food, Aoife drank black coffee. Sam was in the yard, according to

Agnes, and Baby was still in bed, so at least Aoife was spared dealing with her whining complaints.

It was an overcast day, oppressive with swollen dark clouds. Feeling claustrophobic, Aoife needed to go out and breathe in air, however muggy and still. Outside offered little relief, as she felt the dark sky pressing down. Sam was walking across the yard, his shoulders hunched and head down.

'You OK?' she asked.

He shrugged. 'I thought I'd get some relief from telling someone about it all, but I just feel like I've had my insides scooped out and put through a mangle.'

'This bloody weather doesn't help, does it? Look, we have to decide what to do about –'

Sam gripped her elbow and propelled her forward. 'I don't want to talk here, Karol is somewhere about.'

'OK, where then?'

'Let's walk up to the scene of the crime, will we?'

Without waiting to see if she was following, he strode out of the yard, keeping up a gruelling pace through two fields until at the top of the second field he stopped dead in front of a low stone wall.

He stared at it. 'I don't know which stone he hit when I pushed him. The next day, the rain had washed the blood away.' He laughed harshly. 'If it could only wash away our sins so easily.'

'Sam, please don't.'

He glared at her. 'OK so what do you want to do about Dad the psychopathic serial killer? Any plans? I'm dying to hear about them.'

'Look, I want justice for those girls. I read about the families, and what they suffered. Decades on, they still don't know what happened to their loved ones. We could bring them some measure of closure.'

'But we don't even know who his victims were.'

'Well, we know the name of one – Anika – and I've read news reports and interviews given by her sister. I think I know the names of two others; I'm pretty sure Mary Bernadette Maher was killed after Kate was born and the girl he murdered when Mam was expecting me was Anna Halliburton. I've seen her twin sister. Sam, he killed these women after each of us was born. Our births were some kind of trigger. Mam suffered from depression during and after her pregnancies and he couldn't cope. Her silence must have reminded him of the way things were with his horrible mother. God knows how many other girls he killed. There may even have been some before he met Mam. There needs to be an investigation. The families of those girls need to find out what happened to them. If we go public, they can find the bodies.'

Sam was staring at her incredulously. 'Go public? That sounds very noble, but what about our family? What about our mother? This would destroy her. Mam remembers her husband as a saint, and you want to show her a monster? It would kill her. Could you live with that, Aoife?'

'You haven't studied the fucking diary or spent hours researching his victims. If we do nothing, then it makes us accessories. We can't pretend anymore. The diary is real, and we must take it to the Guards. Why didn't you destroy it, Sam? Was it because, even as a young boy, you knew his secrets couldn't remain hidden? Is that why you buried it instead of burning it?'

Sam lunged and grasped her arms, roaring, '*I haven't pored over his fucking diary, but I've lived with the consequences of his fucking life, haven't I? I've paid a fucking price – tied to this farm like it's an open prison. I've had no life! Afraid to have relationships because how could I burden any girl with all my fucking baggage? So don't lecture me on fucking responsibility! You've lived this hell for a few months, I lived it for twenty years. A life sentence, with no possibility of parole, just more of the same shitty existence!*'

Abruptly, he released her and turned his back. Aoife rubbed her arms and calmed her breathing.

'I'm sorry, Sam. I can't imagine the hell you've been living. But it's never going to end unless we do something. Do you want to spend the rest of your life tied to this place, a protector of that evil bastard's secrets and crimes? This could be your chance to come out from under the yoke of guarding his depravity.'

'What about Mam, Kate, Kenny, Sandy, and Colm? Can you imagine what it would do to them? If the Guards get involved, they will tear the place apart and all hell will break out. There will be press, TV reports. Imagine fucking reporters swarming all over our lives interviewing neighbours and friends of our family. How would Mam survive that? Or Colm and Sandy? They're just kids, it would destroy their lives. We couldn't do that to them. People might even say Mam knew about what he did and covered it up! You know what the internet is like! Some would even say she helped him kill those women. Her life would become an unimaginable hell.'

'OK, Sam, I'm not suggesting we rush into anything. We have to talk to Kate, and of course eventually to Mam. I know everything that you're saying is true, but I don't think we can use our pain and distress as an excuse for continuing to hide this. I'm telling you, Sam, I've looked up stuff about these girls and their families. Those families are living in limbo, desperate to get answers. I think they have all accepted their missing relative has died but they want a body to bury – we can give them that.'

'Aoife, would you be able to live with how this would rip our family apart?'

'I don't know, Sam, but we can't pretend any more. Whether we remain silent or reveal what we know, it's going to impact us. But at least we might help those families.'

'What about you, Aoife? Have you thought about how this is going to derail your career? You've talked about wanting to be principal in a school someday – who's going to employ the daughter of a notorious serial killer? Hell, even your school is going to struggle with the notoriety. What if parents don't want you teaching their kids? What about Connor? I know you've broken up, but this would be the last nail in the coffin, wouldn't it? *And in any future relationship!*

Aoife nodded as the truth of his words hit home. 'Yes, you're right, it would be brutal but, Sam, I can't sleep knowing about those young women. The secret is burning me up. How did you manage all these years? God, you were only a kid of seventeen. How did you keep it buried within you?'

Sam stared at the stone wall, grimacing. 'At first, it was like carrying a rock on my shoulders, and the torment of keeping the secret was so bad I wanted to die. For months I barely slept and when I did it wasn't an escape but a journey to hell. The nightmares and waking terrors continued until I was terrified of going to bed. Kate, who was always my ally, I had to push away. How could I talk about Dad, about who he was? I knew I hurt her, but I couldn't bear her talking about how much she missed him. I was terrified I'd scream out the truth. So, I avoided her and took over the running of the farm. I worked so hard that eventually I even got a little peace. Work was my salvation.'

'What about your school pals, Sam?'

'For months I avoided them until Mam insisted I started going out. I remember the first time I let my guard down and got drunk. I got maudlin and hinted at my terrible secret. Then, when the lads challenged me, I got belligerent and started a fight. Soon, I earned a reputation as a mean drunk, and no one wanted to be in my company. It was a relief in a way. It was like I had the mark of Cain and soon they all left me alone.'

'You must have been lonely?'

'Well, I had you, didn't I?'

'What do you mean?'

'You looked to me after Dad died. You were such a lost little thing. So, I played with you, read stories, and took you for rides on my tractor. You saved my life. With you I could let down my guard. It was the only peace I got.'

'Oh Sam, I remember you being so good to me. Kate was too busy to have any time for me, and Mam was desperately sad, but you looked after me and taught me things. Yes, I remember those piggyback rides, picnics in the fields and excursions at the crack of dawn to see the rabbits and foxes as they woke up. I never thanked you, Sam, but you made my childhood magical.'

'Well, little sister, you made mine bearable.'

They stood in silence until Sam straightened his shoulders.

Impulsively she caught his arm. 'Why did you pretend that you went to Mullingar the other day? Jack Costello saw you coming from Donegal.'

'Aoife, that's my business but, since you ask, I was seeing a friend.'

'Sam, I have to know. Mam says that you disappear on the first of every month. She says you play cards, but that's not true, is it?'

'My, you have been busy playing detective! I suppose you had me down as a murdering psycho like dear old Dad. *Fuck it!* It's because of that wee girl who went missing in Donegal – did you think I killed her? Christ, Aoife! Is that what you think of me?'

Sam's eyes bored into her, and she saw such a gully of pain and bewilderment there that her flesh felt like it was dissolving.

'Oh my God, you really think I made that girl in Donegal disappear.' Sam slumped down on the stone wall.

Aoife's heart hammered painfully against her chest as she waited for him to speak again.

'OK, Aoife, I can see that I'll have to tell you everything as you obviously believe that I'm just like our father.'

Aoife wished she could say she didn't care, that she believed him to be nothing like Manus, but a faint doubt lingered. She nodded.

'Fine,' he said tiredly. 'If you must know, there is a very kind woman I see in Letterkenny. Her name's Carmel. She not looking for a conventional relationship, but we take care of each other. I'm not going into the details, Aoife. I'm allowed some private life, but I'll ask her to call you and confirm that that's where I go every month.'

'But, Sam, that time you were coming from Donegal it wasn't the first of the month.'

'No, Aoife, that's because I ended our arrangement. I had a feeling you knew about the box, and I thought I'd best keep her out of everything. Are you satisfied now?' Sam moved away from her and stared hard at the stone wall. Then he turned to her and said abruptly, 'How about we go over to Kate's tomorrow afternoon? Mam has one of her Active Age Group excursions and she'll be away most of the day. We'll tell her everything and we can discuss it, OK?'

Aoife nodded, and they walked in silence back to the farm. The relief she felt about Sam was tempered by the shame she felt for suspecting him of such evil in the first place. Manus's toxic legacy was continuing its evil.

Sam returned to his work and Aoife went to her room and checked the dresser drawer where she had hidden the biscuit tin. She planned to change its hiding place, not sure she trusted Sam not to search for it and destroy it even after they agreed to meet with Kate. At the base of her wardrobe was a broken slat. It was a perfect space to hide things as a teenager, things she didn't want her mother to find like cigarettes, booze, and birth-control pills. She used to drop her contraband in and then cover it with jumpers, so it was safe from inquisitive eyes. The tin would be safe there.

Her mobile beeped a text message and she opened it, hoping and yet dreading it would be from Connor. It was Sorcha suggesting they get together for a night out. Aoife ached for the days when the biggest decision was where to go for a night out. Was it only three months since the anniversary? In such a short span everything had changed and now their lives were on the cusp of being torn apart. The conversation with Sam rumbled around her mind, torturing her with doubt and indecision. Everything he said was true. It would alter forever their lives once they went to the Guards. Her job as a teacher would suffer. Sure, she had job security but the rumours and comments from students and colleagues, not to mention the circle of hell that is social media, would be unendurable. But the bulk of the devastating shit would land on her family here in Sligo. If she said nothing, she would be committing a crime. She would be knowingly withholding information from the Guards and, worse, letting all those families of the victims live in perpetual limbo. It was too cruel to let them continue to be tormented by dark imaginings or, worse, to live in deluded hope. As she left her room her insides twisted, conscious of the malign presence of the biscuit tin secreted in her wardrobe.

Today she would take some action and arrange the meeting with Kate. She would need time to read the diary and to listen to Sam tell his story. Her mam's rare day out was fortuitous, they could meet without her getting suspicious.

Kate answered after the first ring.

Aoife's mind went blank and for a moment she couldn't speak. Then she blurted, 'Kate, Sam and I need to talk to you in private tomorrow. Can you come over? Mam is going off for the day with the Active Age Group.'

'Aoife, what's wrong? Is it Mam? Is she sick?' Kate said, her voice rising.

'No, Kate, Mam's fine. She's in great form, looking forward to her day out. Sam and I just need to talk something over with you. So can you come over?'

'You're being very mysterious, but how about you two coming over here? Colm and a few pals are going to an Adventure Zipline park, and Sandy is spending the day at her friend's getting glammed up for a night out. Kenny will be about, mooching in the garden, but he won't bother us.'

'That sounds great. We can call over around two if that suits you. Don't be making us any lunch now.'

After the call, Aoife texted the information to Sam, and they spent the rest of the day avoiding each other.

CHAPTER 48

Agnes was in the best of spirits, excited about the trip. She had only recently been persuaded to join the Active Age group and this was the first of their jaunts she had signed up to go on. They had arranged an excursion to Ballina and then on to the seaweed baths at Enniscrone. All morning she fretted about whether her swimsuit still fitted and tried on several outfits before declaring herself ready. Aoife teased her about having a boyfriend as she fussed so much about her appearance. To Aoife's surprise, her mother blushed and transformed into a woman still eager for life's possibilities. Could her mother be interested in romance? After all these years? She refused to be drawn, but Aoife noticed it was an elderly man who arrived to collect her and take her to meet the tour bus. Agnes rushed out the door in her eagerness to prevent Aoife from meeting him. Before pulling the door behind her, she called out that there was food in the fridge and issued instructions on how to prepare it. A perpetual mammy!

Aoife turned on the radio to ease the silence that followed her mother's departure. She kept busy, doing little household chores to hurry the morning away. At lunchtime, Sam came in and they ate a simple meal of soup and bread. They spoke very little, just the usual politeness. Afterwards, Aoife collected the tin box from its hiding place and they left.

On the drive over, she was torn between an urgency to get there and finally make some decisions, and a stomach-churning reluctance to arrive. All the while she felt the presence of the box like an unexploded bomb on the back seat.

Kenny was outside, breaking up an old fence that had rotted. They waved to him but he barely acknowledged their presence.

Kate met them at the door and hurried them inside. 'Kenny is just making work for himself, digging up plants he thinks are old and useless, cutting trees, tearing down fences, burning rubbish, weeding, and mowing almost every other day. He does it to get away from me.'

She led them into the conservatory and went to bring in a tray of mugs of strong coffee. Her thin face was white and pinched, and her hands shook a little, spilling the coffee as she handed one to Aoife.

'Well, what's the big mystery? It doesn't sound good. Between worrying about Kenny and the kids I hardly slept.'

Aoife didn't know how to start.

Sam said, 'Give her the diary and then we can explain.'

Kate wrinkled her nose in puzzlement. 'Guys, what's going on?'

Aoife opened the biscuit tin and handed over the diary. 'I found it when we buried Nell. It was in a box in the grave with the remains of Polly, Dad's old dog. You need to read it. Sam and I will go to the kitchen and drink our coffees there.'

Kate looked alarmed. 'Aoife, what's this all about? You're scaring me?'

'I'm sorry, Kate. This will be a hard thing to read. It's Dad's diary and he's done some really terrible things. Take your time and when you're ready we can talk.'

They left Kate sitting on a wicker chair, diary in hand, as they went to the kitchen to drink their coffee. Sam stood at the back door and smoked incessantly while Aoife paced the floor, unable to settle. How do you prepare someone to read something so awful, so life changing? Should she have told her more? Then again, perhaps it was better to read it with a mind uncluttered by too much information. God, Kate was going to be devastated!

In a state of the greatest tension, they waited moment by moment to hear Kate's voice calling them or for her to appear in the kitchen distraught. Both resisted the urge to go back into the conservatory to see if she was alright.

But there was no sound or movement from the conservatory. After an hour, by unspoken agreement, they went back out.

Kate was peering into the garden, the diary abandoned on the table.

She turned towards them and what they saw on her face was anger.

'You're telling me this drivel was written by Dad?'

'Kate, it's his handwriting,' Aoife said, 'and it refers to his life here on the farm before and after he married Mam. I know it's hard to take in, but it's not fiction. The things he talked about happened. I have information about that girl Anika. She went missing at the time he describes.'

'How do you know he didn't just fantasise he was a killer just to create drama? I mean, come on, guys. this is our father! Daddy wasn't a sick, perverted killer. I can't believe you accept this rubbish as fact. Come on, Sam, surely you don't believe this nonsense, do you?'

He sighed. 'Sit down, Kate – you need to listen to what I have to say.'

Kate sank into the sofa, silenced by his reaction.

Sam and Aoife sat and Sam began to speak, staring at his clasped hands.

Kate's face registered horror as she listened to Sam's account of the day he found the box and confronted Manus. When he described his father's death, Kate shuddered, her face blanched.

Sam sat slumped, tears streaming down his face. 'I'm sorry, Kate, please don't hate me!'

Kate went and knelt at his feet and took his face in her trembling hands. 'Oh, poor Sam, how you must have suffered! To have kept this secret, it must have torn you up. God, you were only a boy – why didn't you *tell* me?'

'How could I ruin your life too? If I told anyone, our lives would have been hell. I was terrified of going to jail for what I did. And, if everything about Dad came out, our family would be pariahs. It was impossible, I couldn't do it. I just couldn't.'

'So that's why you wouldn't go to college and train as a vet.'

'Yes, Kate, I had to guard the farm in case a body turned up. I had to stay to protect us all. You understand, don't you?'

'Oh, Sam, of course I understand. God, you've been a hero. What a terrible price you paid for keeping Dad's secret for all these years. It must have been unbearable.'

'Whenever it got too much, I realised why I was doing it – for all of you and especially for Mam. Aoife was only a kid, and I had to be a father to her – to be strong. I thought that after you grew up, got jobs, and married, then I could come clean. Every year it got harder and harder. And then, Kate, you married Kenny, and Colm and Sandy came along. I couldn't bring everything crashing down on top of you all. The farm closed in on me and I knew there was no escape.'

Kate gripped his hand, knuckles white as bone. 'God, that explains why you were so distant after Dad died. It was like you had deserted me. When we were kids, we had such craic together and ganged up against the parents sometimes. Then, after Dad died, you didn't have time for me anymore. I felt I'd lost you as well as Dad.'

Aoife watched them. Sam and Kate had always been uncomfortable with each other. Now she understood why. They had each turned to her as a respite from loneliness. Kate was the big sister who offered her boyfriend advice, make-up and fashion tips, and her unconditional love. While Sam acted as a father, at times so strict that Mam had to remind him he was her brother, not her father. They turned to her because they had lost each other – Kate by the distance Sam put between them and Sam because he didn't trust himself with the secret around Kate, so to protect her he had shut her out.

Kate replaced the diary in the tin and closed the lid. 'If it's OK with you two, I want it out of my sight for a while at least. Let's go back to the kitchen. The box is perfectly safe here. The kids won't be home for hours, and Kenny has zero interest in anything.'

She made fresh coffee, and they sat at the kitchen table drinking it.

'Aoife, I suppose this is why you started asking me all those questions about Dad when I visited you in Dublin?'

'Yeah, I wanted to understand what he was like. My memories of him were vague. I knew he played board games with me and gave me rides on his shoulders, but I wasn't sure if those memories were real or just conflated from all the talk Mam had about him. I mean, he seemed so normal. How did we not see?'

Sam took a drink from his mug and said, 'It was odd he never seemed to have any friends – men he went to matches with or met in the pub. I remember sneaking into McCoy's once when I was about fifteen and he was sitting at the counter on his own, while across the way the neighbours were laughing and cracking jokes. I thought maybe he was just shy, but perhaps the locals suspected him or at least noticed some oddness in him. I dodged out of there before he saw me. I told you what he said about the girl I was seeing. It made my skin crawl. What about you, Kate? Did you notice anything?'

'This is mad! I can't believe this is our father we're talking about. He was such a kind man. He used to tease me about the music I liked and the pop stars I wrote fan letters to. Not for one moment did I feel uneasy about him. He was just Dad. To be honest, this still feels unreal, like I can't equate what I read in the diary with the father I grew up loving.' Kate's voice was breaking. 'Dad was just Dad. Sometimes he stopped me from going out to things but, apart from that, he was sound. OK, as a teenager I thought he was old-fashioned, but I felt safe around him. This is bizarre! I understand why you didn't tell me about him, Sam, but, Aoife, why for fuck's sake didn't you tell me what you found?'

'Like you, I couldn't believe it at first. I tried to convince myself that it was all made up, that Dad was writing a story, or possibly venting his frustrations about his fucked-up life. I couldn't believe it was real – that he did those terrible things he described. But then things started adding up, and the more I investigated it, the more it seemed true. I had to get to the truth. After I looked at the Garda Missing Person sites, I couldn't lie to myself any longer. Several women went missing at the time Mam had you and Sam and was expecting me, young women like Anika. I matched three missing women to those timelines, but I think there were more. I don't know how many bodies are out there.'

'You seriously think there is a connection between each of our births and a missing girl?' Kate asked.

'Didn't you notice? He says it in the diary. Whenever Mam had a baby she became depressed and withdrawn and he turned his anger on those poor women. We just don't know how many other victims there are because so many pages were torn from the diary.'

Kate dropped her head into her hands and then looked up, her eyes wide with horror. 'What about the things in the box? Are they some kind of trophies?'

'There are five items in the box, and I think I've figured out who some of them belonged to. I think the hair is from an earlier victim before he met Mam, the earring belonged to Anika and the Claddagh ring to a girl called Mary Bernadette Maher. The initials engraved on the inside are her boyfriend's. I don't know about the scarf or the lipstick.'

'God, this is such a nightmare. I don't want to know any more. I keep hoping if I splash my face with cold water, I will wake up and it will be over.' Kate covered her face with her hands again and rocked back and forth.

'I know this is a lot to take in, Kate,' said Aoife, 'but we have to deal with it. The question is, where do we go from here?'

'What do you mean? Where do we go? Where is there to go?'

'Kate, all these women, their bodies have to be found. Their families need to bury them. You see that, don't you?'

Kate stared at her sister, blank confusion replaced with horror. 'Are you planning to call the Guards? You can't mean that, Aoife – it would wreck all our lives. Mam would die of shame and shock. She believes her husband was the most perfect man in the world and you want to tell her he was a fucking monster, a serial killer? Are you mad? Do you want to kill her?'

'No, of course I don't but what other way is there?'

Kate leapt to her feet. '*Say fucking nothing and pretend this box never existed!*' She stepped up to her brother. 'Sam, you can't want this to go public! To have Guards swarming over the farm, neighbours talking about us and, oh God, my children! Can you imagine them trying to

313

live down the fact that their grandfather was a perverted evil killer? For fuck's sake, Sandy gets mortified when I wear a short skirt in public and poor Colm is just about coping with his dad being the way he is. This would destroy them! And, Sam, you could go to jail for hiding this, and if it came out that you caused Dad's death you'd be charged with manslaughter at the very least. Do you realise that?'

'I know, Kate, I know,' Sam said, shaking his head.

'Kate,' said Aoife, 'you must see that –'

'No, Aoife, you're mad! You can't do this!'

'Look, Kate, I felt the same way at first –'

'*No, you didn't.* You don't know what this will mean, safe in your bubble in Dublin. And you don't have kids. You can hide out, we can't.'

'But what about the victims and *their* families?' Aoife said, her voice rising.

'*I don't fucking care!* I don't know them, and those girls are dead, nothing will bring them back. I can't believe you would sacrifice Mam and your family just so you can feel you've done the right thing.'

Sam broke in, his calm voice a contrast to the shouting of his sisters. 'Look, we don't have to decide anything today. Why don't we sleep on it?'

'*Why didn't you burn that book and destroy the box when you had a chance all those years ago?*' shrieked Kate.

Sam flinched as though she had struck him. They stared at each other in horror.

Then Kenny walked in.

CHAPTER 49

Kenny stood staring, his hair standing on end and eyes blinking rapidly, 'Is something wrong?' He looked at his wife.

'It's OK, Ken – come on outside and I'll explain,' Kate said.

Kenny glared suspiciously at Sam and Kate but, when Kate tugged at his arm, he followed her to the hallway. Sam and Aoife listened to the murmur of voices. Aoife's body was shaking uncontrollably.

Then Kate returned.

'Did you tell him?' Aoife asked.

'What do you think? Even Kenny would react a bit if I told him about his psychopathic father-in-law. He may be in a depressed fugue but the news that his father-in-law's farm is spilling over with murdered women might dissipate even that.'

Aoife flinched at her tone. 'OK, Kate, I think we should go. There's no point in rehashing things now. We'll talk again tomorrow?'

'Wait just a minute. I know exactly what Aoife wants to do, but you haven't said much, Sam. Do you agree with her? Are you willing to bring all this horror down on your mother and niece and nephew? To say nothing of your poor aunts – they wouldn't survive it either.'

Sam sat staring at his stained farmer's hands.

The sisters waited, not daring to speak.

He sighed heavily. 'I've kept this secret for so long that talking is difficult. I lost friends because I was afraid to go on the piss in case of letting something slip. I couldn't get serious with a girl for the same reason, so to talk about this now seems alien. My mouth is stiff and when I try to speak the old creeping fear comes back. Kate, you asked what I think we should do. Well, listening to both of you, I can see what each of you says is true. As you say, Kate, it would destroy the lives and mental health of all of you – the people I've been trying to protect all these years. Including the children – *especially* the children. Their lives would be a living nightmare. Would they even survive it? As for myself, if we go Aoife's way, at worst I'll end up in jail for manslaughter, at best there is no more hiding, no more secrets, and I can speak and breathe and maybe even get away from here. The farm has been a millstone weighing me down, so escaping from it would be like breaking out of prison. But, like Kate, I fear the disgrace, and the chaos, losing control. I had control these last twenty years and if we go to the Guards, then I've lost that control.' He exhaled deeply.

Aoife was about to speak but was shushed by Kate.

Sam continued. 'If we keep this secret, then at least the secret is shared. I'm not alone any more, and I don't have to watch the people I've loved and protected for this lifetime destroyed. Then my silence will have meaning, but I'm still trapped by this place until I die. So, in answer to your question, I don't know. I feel like I'm twisting on a rope. I want to get away from here and be free of this guilt and shame. If you knew how often I wanted to end my life, but I held on because of what would happen to the farm if I'm not here to guard it. What would happen if they unearthed bodies? It would explode in your faces or, worse, people might think I did those horrible things. Sometimes I even thought I was the killer not Dad.'

Sam dropped his head to the table, and the girls watched in distress as his body shook with sobs. Kate held him, and for the first time in twenty years she was the protector.

He slowly regained control and Kate handed him some tissues to wipe his face.

'So, we are at an impasse then,' Aoife said.

'I don't think so,' said Kate. 'You're the only one who wants to go public with this. I don't, and Sam is conflicted. We should destroy the box and its contents and just go on as if nothing has happened.'

'*As if nothing has happened?* How can we act as if nothing has happened?' Aoife said. 'We can't pretend we don't know what Dad did. This isn't some minor misdemeanour, Kate. Dad was a bloody serial killer. I'm sorry but we must bring this out into the open – then at least we can get free of it.'

'*Get free of it – are you mad? We'll forever be known as the family of a serial killer! Don't you get that?* Is that what you want? How can we stay here among neighbours and friends with all the gossip? Think of the media attention alone! It would kill Mam, and what about Sam? Do you want him to go to jail for being an accessory? Maybe they will look again at Dad's death and charge him with manslaughter. Maybe they will conclude Sam committed the killings? He'll be able to "speak and breathe", he thinks – but do you think he'll stand up under questioning?' Kate pointed to Sam slumped over the kitchen table.

'See here, Kate, he can't take anymore. I'm going to take him home and we can talk tomorrow.' Aoife stood up and touched Sam on the shoulder. 'Come on, Sam, let's go home.'

'Aoife, please, I'm begging you, don't do this!' Kate pleaded.

'Kate, I'm sorry but if you read about those wretched girls and the giant hole that their absence has left in their families' lives – it is pitiful. They need to know where their loved ones are buried. Think of it, Kate – if Sandy ever disappeared, wouldn't you be desperate to get answers, and not condemned to years of silence, continually hoping for news, for some scrap of information to come out so the wondering and hoping could end and some peace and closure would be possible?'

For a moment Aoife thought her sister would strike her

Instead, Kate snarled, *'That's a low blow, bringing Sandy into this. But if we do what your precious conscience advises, her life and Colm's will be contaminated by this filth. But, of course, your conscience is more important than them, isn't it?'*

Aoife brushed past her sister and walked into the conservatory. She could see Kenny through the glass, moving slowly amidst the flower beds.

Kate stood at the doorway, her cheeks stained an angry red.

Aoife turned to face her. 'Kate, you need to take time for all this to sink in. We'll wait a few days and then meet up again. I promise not to do anything until we get a chance to discuss it again, but I don't think I'll change my mind.'

Kate nodded, too exhausted to argue further. She looked anxiously at the box. 'Are you taking it away now?'

In answer, Aoife stooped down and picked it up.

She carried it outside to the waiting car, Sam and Kate following. She put the box in the back as Sam got into the passenger seat. Thankfully, Kate hadn't tried to hold on to it. She didn't trust her sister not to get rid of it. In all honesty, she couldn't blame her for wanting to.

Kate caught Aoife in her arms and hugged her fiercely and silently.

318

She leaned in the window and stroked Sam's cheek. There were no words left to say.

The drive home was silent, despair lingering like a carcase rotting on the side of the road. Aoife checked her phone. It was gone six o'clock. They had been talking for hours. Mam would be home soon. Suddenly, she was ravenously hungry.

Back at the house, she stashed the box back in its hiding place and hurried down to the kitchen. She scoured the fridge for food. Without bothering to ask Sam if he felt hungry, she set to and prepared fried eggs, bacon and sausages and served it up.

They made sandwiches with eggs and bacon and slathered them with ketchup. Everything was washed down with hot, sweet tea.

They didn't talk, just ate and drank, avoiding each other's eyes.

CHAPTER 50

The next day, Agnes, full of chat about the wonderful outing, surprised them by announcing she was going to the pictures with a friend. She acted so mysteriously that Aoife had a shrewd idea that the friend was the man who accompanied her on the trip to Enniscrone.

That evening, Agnes spent ages getting ready and Aoife was startled to see her wearing make-up. Apart from a quick splash of perfume and a moderate dollop of lipstick, her mam usually never bothered with cosmetics. But she appeared downstairs wearing eye shadow and mascara. It was very discreet, and it enhanced her looks, making her eyes appear bigger and bluer. She was a fresher and younger version of herself. On being complimented, she grew bashful and threatened to wash all the make-up off. It took all Aoife's tact to dissuade her. She did however suggest she change the outfit, which was far too formal for a trip to the cinema.

'We may go for a drink afterwards,' Agnes confided, blushing a little.

By the time a car arrived, driven by a dapper elderly gentleman, she was wearing a pretty summer frock and had a pale blue cardigan slung jauntily around her shoulders. Aoife felt a wash of protectiveness as she watched her slip into the white Golf.

Sam was amazed when Aoife told him their shy mother was dating. 'I'm glad she's having a little fun. God knows she hasn't had much of a social life.'

'Will I see if Kate wants to come over, now that we can talk in peace?' Aoife said. 'Or maybe you need a break from all this?'

'Aoife, I haven't had a break from "all this" as you call it for twenty years – yeah, call her.'

Kate answered at once. 'Yes, Aoife, what is it?' She sounded wary.

'Mam is going out this evening, and Sam and I wondered if you'd like to come over.'

After a brief pause, Kate said, 'I'll be there in about a half an hour,' and ended the call without saying goodbye.

Sam went back outside to finish a few jobs. The house, uncharacteristically silent, made Aoife conscious of how rarely her mother left home. She had gone into purdah after the death of Manus. How heart-breaking that the few tentative steps she was taking into life again were about to be crushed by the juggernaut heading their way.

She tidied the kitchen to pass the time. On hearing Kate's car pulling up outside, she put the kettle on. Her sister greeted her coolly, glancing at her with wary eyes. Aoife busied herself making a pot of tea, and was pouring out when Sam walked in. They sat down, each careful to avoid touching each other. It was like they had a contagion they were desperate to avoid.

'Where's Mam gone?' Kate asked. 'It's not like her to be out two nights in a row.'

'We think she's on a date,' Aoife said.

'You're joking! Mam out on a date? I don't believe it!'

'Well, maybe a date is putting it strongly, but there is this guy from the Active Age Group who has been friendly and asked her out to see a movie.'

'*Wow!*' Kate exclaimed. 'Good for her.'

'She even put on make-up – I swear she was giddy as a teenager.' Aoife continued, happy to keep the light atmosphere going.

'Well, there will be an end to all that if you get your way, Aoife,' Kate said.

At that, silence settled over them and they sat avoiding each other's eyes.

At length, Sam spoke up abruptly. 'Well, we better get started, hadn't we? We must come to some decision.'

'Look, lads,' said Kate, 'I was thinking about it all – and you don't have any proof. All we know is that Dad had a crappy childhood, and his way of coping was writing about murdering people. He made it more real by using real-life disappearances to hang his fantasies on.'

'Well, how do you explain his reaction when Sam found the box?' Aoife demanded. 'Why did he attack him?'

'Because Dad was ashamed – he didn't want Sam to know about this dark side of his life. And he was afraid of Mam finding out. She had Dad on such a pedestal, and he couldn't bear her to know about these sick fantasies. That's all they were. Aoife, you and Sam have conflated all the stuff in the notebook to mean more than what it is – the delusional fantasies of a man tortured by an abusive childhood.'

'OK, so you're suggesting he made the whole thing up,' said Aoife. 'The diary was a complete fantasy inspired by real-life events. Then how do you explain the trinkets in the box? We know Mary Bernadette had a Claddagh ring – how do you explain that?'

Kate nodded. 'But don't you see, that's just it. Dad wanted to make it feel real, so he bought things that would make it more credible to him. It makes sense, you know it does.'

'And what about the initials PF engraved on the ring?'

'He could have heard about that on the news.'

'And had PF engraved on the ring? How could he risk asking any engraver to do that?'

'Well, he wasn't in a stable state of mind, was he?'

Sam looked at Kate bleakly. 'I wish what you're saying were true, but when I confronted him he throttled me, and for a minute I thought he was going to kill me. I had his finger marks on my neck for days, terrified that Mam would see them.'

'I know you don't want to believe all this, Kate, but we have to accept facts,' Aoife said. 'The Guards can investigate, see if the things in the box belonged to any of these missing women and then we can know the truth. There are too many coincidences. Maybe you have lingering doubts, but Sam and I don't. Do you think we want to believe Dad was this monstrous person? But he was and I think deep down you know that.'

Kate didn't respond but her eyes filled with trears.

'Kate, will I fetch the box?' Aoife asked. 'After all, you haven't had much time to examine it.'

'*I never want to see that bloody box again!* If I could send it to hell to join its author, I'd be delighted!'

'So you *do* accept Dad committed the murders?' Sam said.

'Let me see the box again, so I can convince myself it's real.'

As Aoife fetched the box, Sam asked, 'Did you get any sleep at all after we left, Kate?'

'No, not for a moment, but then I'd say you've been staring at the ceiling a lot over all these years, Sam. I'm truly sorry you didn't feel able to talk to me and share the load.'

'Ah, how could I do that? What would be the point of ruining your life too? Besides, I was afraid of going to prison for killing Dad.'

'Sam, that was an accident, self-defence.'

'You said it yourself yesterday – that I could be jailed for manslaughter. And how could I prove it was an accident? I left him alone to die. I didn't get help to save him.'

'Jesus, Sam, I can't imagine the hell your life has been.'

Sam nodded and relapsed into silence.

Aoife returned and placed the box carefully on the table. 'Do you want time to read the diary again, Kate?'

Kate reached for the box, stopped, shuddered, and shook her head.

Aoife sat down. 'OK, we have to decide what to do. As things stand, I believe we must put all this information in the hands of the Garda. It will be horrific, but we have no choice. I'm no lawyer but doesn't it make us accessories if we sit on this?'

Kate spoke, her voice shrill. *But Sam is already an accessory!* He could get into serious trouble because he kept all this information hidden, not to mention his fight with Dad. Aoife, how will going to the Guards help anyone? OK, it will give the families closure but it will inflict a new nightmare on them too. And it will create new victims. How can we do this to Mam? She deserves better. Aoife, your intentions are good but the price we will pay for your peace of mind is too high and I for one don't want to pay it.'

Aoife opened her mouth to argue. But she was stilled by Sam's raised hand.

'Wait a minute, both of you. I can see you can argue this out all night and every night and never agree. But, as I'm the one most affected by all this, I should get to make the final decision about what we do. Kate, I can see why you want to bury this but, with respect, I don't think you understand what keeping a secret like this does, how

324

it eats you up inside and squeezes everything else out, so you feel like a rotting husk. I haven't lived these past twenty years, just existed. I've paid a terrible price for my silence. And Aoife, I know you will feel tormented by your conscience if we keep our secret. It would drive a rift between us all, a rift that would hurt Mam and destroy our family.'

'*And Aoife's choice wouldn't destroy the family?*' Kate said with savage sarcasm.

'I know, Kate – you're right, it would. I am not arguing that going public is the least destructive course of action – but I want you and Aoife to recognise that keeping silent would not be an easy path to follow. It would be a burden we three would have to bear together. A heavy burden of guilt and pain. A cross to bear. I know. I have lived that.'

'OK, so what are you saying, Sam?' Aoife said.

'What I'm saying is that I get to decide what to do. I've earned that right, don't you think? And I am the person it would most immediately impact.' He stared grimly at his sisters and they each dropped their gaze. 'So are we agreed?'

The two girls nodded and wordlessly they got up and hugged each other tightly.

CHAPTER 51

April 2017

Aoife had been expecting the phone call. She had been expecting it from the day her mam received her diagnosis. She became ill in January. At first they thought it was the after-effects of bad flu, but she became sicker, losing all her energy and zest for life. She waited two months for a diagnosis. They said she had lung cancer. Years of sitting side by side with her chain-smoking husband had taken their toll. Kate had commented bitterly that Manus had killed her from beyond the grave. Her daughters accompanied her to the consultant, and she took the news with courage. Her health spiralled downwards rapidly, and her remaining months were a round of painful treatments. Most of her care rested with Sam, but Kate was available to offer him relief. Aoife buried herself in work, coming home every weekend to help nurse her mother.

Now listening to Sam's low voice saying Mam was dead, the ache of loss settled over her like a dark cloud. He told her that the hospice would release her body in the evening, and she would come home.

'Don't come down until morning, there's no point,' he said.

Feeling unable to argue, she agreed.

'Drive carefully,' he reminded her and then there was silence.

In the morning, she rang the principal, explaining she wouldn't be coming to work as her mother had died. As she said those words, her insides shivered a little. She promised to pass on funeral details and then packed some clothes, with something dark to wear to the funeral.

On the drive home, Aoife remembered an earlier journey home, an innocent time when all was well, and all the ugliness in the future. She arrived at the house at midday. No one was home. She read the note propped up on the table. Sam and Kate were at the hospice. She considered driving in to meet them, but was reluctant to face the reality of her mother dead, in the place where she had tried so hard to be cheerful and patient and where she relinquished her tenuous hold on life.

She set about getting lunch together and was surprised to find several tins of tomato soup in the larder. Mam would never countenance bought soup, never mind tinned soup – how things had changed! Feeling disloyal, she opened the tins and poured them into a saucepan to heat. There were brown rolls in the bread bin. They were a little stale, but she was ravenous. She was sitting there, eating her soup and tearing off chunks of bread when Kate and Sam arrived. They hugged and Aoife offered them lunch.

Afterwards, they cleaned the house and cleared out the living room to make way for the coffin. Agnes had chosen it weeks ago; saying she wanted no fuss and no silly expense either. It was a simple bamboo affair. The house was gleaming when the undertakers arrived. With Sam's help, they carried the coffin into the room they had prepared. They briefly discussed the funeral arrangements and left.

Aoife joined Sam and Kate as they stared down at their mam. She was wearing her favourite dress, her soft grey hair fluffed gently against her face. She looked like Mam, but Mam with all the animation and light drained away.

'She looks peaceful anyway – after all the pain she's finally free,' Sam said.

'Did she wake before ... ?' Aoife asked.

'Mam died just after ten yesterday evening. She never woke. We were with her and held her hand as she slipped away. It was peaceful, Aoife.'

'I wish I could have been there,' Aoife said, her eyes smarting. 'Does Phil know?'

Phil was the companion of Agnes's last year. She had refused to call him her boyfriend, just her friend.

'Phil was with Mam at the end,' Sam said. 'We called him when the staff told us she was dying. Poor man, he was glad we called him.'

'What time are the aunts coming?' Aoife asked.

'They said they would travel down together in Emma's car. I think they'll be here around seven. What time did you give for the wake, Sam?'

'Five o'clock onwards and then the funeral tomorrow at eleven. I said just family before we go to the church.'

'What about food for the wake?'

'Don't worry – the neighbours have been great – they will be dropping around food at four and the Caseys have given us a big Burco boiler, so we don't have to keep boiling kettles for tea.'

Soon the house filled with neighbours offering sympathy and bearing plates covered in tin foil, containing sandwiches, cakes, and scones. The kindness of the greetings of these old neighbours of their mother warmed the house. They extolled her virtues and excused their modest food offerings as being a poor imitation of Agnes's beautiful baking. As the evening wore on, there was a steady stream of visitors offering condolences, sharing stories and reminiscing.

Jack turned up and whispered in Aoife's ear, 'Sorry for your loss.'

She smiled and, squeezing her hand, he held it a moment too long, winked at her and disappeared out the door. She found his sympathy oddly comforting. He was kind, she reflected, underneath his devil-may-care facade.

Her fingers ached from being gripped by countless hands. But there was comfort in the intense, heartfelt offerings of sympathy. A steady procession of people trooped in to view the body and speak of how peaceful she looked and what a beautiful corpse she made.

The aunts arrived on the dot of seven. After paying their respects to Agnes, they moved to the sitting room where they feasted happily on tea, sandwiches and cake. They enjoyed catching up with neighbours and old school friends, or more likely the children of old school pals. It was a trip down memory lane for them. Aoife suspected they were wondering about their own final send-off – after all, they were all getting on in age. When you're old, did the inevitability of death ease the fear?

At ten o'clock the crowds had thinned out, and only close friends and family remained. Father Francis arrived and led a decade of the rosary. Afterwards, he squeezed her arm and left.

Downstairs, Emma signalled imperiously and, when her niece drew near, demanded sherry. As Aoife poured out a sweet, a medium and a dry sherry, she felt a sense of déjà vu. She carried the drinks to her aunts, who were sitting in the warmth of the sitting room. With the lights dimmed, the firelight gave them a look of elegance and glamour as from a bygone day. The illusion shattered when Emma snapped at Baby for hogging the fire and Baby whined that Emma was rude and selfish. Clarissa, ever the peacemaker, moved up to make more room.

Siblings didn't grow up; they stayed caught in their childish dynamic till death claimed them. Would it be the same for her and Sam and Kate?

Sipping their drinks, the old ladies spoke kindly of Agnes, especially Clarissa, who truly appreciated the qualities of her sister-in-law. At midnight they got up and headed for the local B&B.

Emma, her voice slurring slightly, said, 'We'll be over in the morning before the coffin is closed to say the last farewell.'

Phil went up to sit with their mother while they saw the aunts off. They gave him some time alone with her, and then he came down and shook each of their hands.

Aoife walked him to the door.

'She was a lovely woman, Aoife,' he said. 'We had some good times before she got ill. I don't know if you know I was married before – my wife died of cancer too. I was fond of her, but Agnes, well, Agnes was special. I wish I'd had more time with her.'

'She cared about you too, Phil.'

'Ah, I know she did – but, you know, I think your father was the love of her life. She didn't have to say it, yet I knew. But, you know what, being second best was good enough for me. Agnes didn't have the last anniversary get-together as a kindness to me. But she remembered your dad's passing and marked it in her way.'

Then giving her a warm hug, Phil left and drove away.

Once the last stragglers had gone, they cleaned up and by unspoken assent Aoife and Sam sat up with Agnes's body all night. They waked her with words of love and appreciation, recalling her warmth and constancy. It was only right that their mam should have their undivided attention on this last night in the house where she spent all her married life.

In the morning, they changed into sober suits and waited for the undertakers. At eleven, the men arrived and closed the casket, and prepared to lift it onto the hearse. Outside, more neighbours had arrived.

Aoife spotted Sorcha and her heart tilted sideways as she saw Connor. He nodded to her and lowered his eyes quickly. They got in their cars and followed the hearse to the church. The service passed in a blur. Sandy sang a psalm and Colm, Kenny, Kate, and Sam read the bidding prayers. Father Francis spoke briefly but sincerely of Agnes, calling her a woman of grace and kindness personified.

The graveyard was cold and, watching her mother lowered to the ground, Aoife's heart ached. Then Clarissa, dear lovely Clarissa, broke into quavering song with 'Amazing Grace' and everyone with a note in their head joined in with her.

The family lined up so that all the mourners could shake their hands. It heartened Aoife to see several work colleagues and the principal in attendance. Sam invited everyone present to join them in McCoy's for a bit of lunch.

Lunch was strangely festive, with neighbours meeting up, and old friends reconnecting. For the first time in days, nobody spoke of Agnes. When the bill arrived, Sam, Aoife and Kate split it three ways.

The aunts hugged their nieces and nephews, told them to keep in touch and left.

Then Kate told Kenny to drive the youngsters home as she planned to spend the night in her old home with Sam and Aoife.

The house was empty when they went back in. Its harsh silence felt like a living thing – something monstrous. Aoife and her siblings sat at the well-scrubbed kitchen table, the setting for so many of Agnes's huge meals and happy family times. Aoife recalled Christmas Day dinners where the table groaned under the weight of Mam's extravagant feasts and the room echoed to the laughter of a happy united family. All this was now part of a far distant past – a dream time of lost innocence.

In the centre of the table sat the tin box.

Sam cleared his throat and spoke slowly but emphatically. 'Two years ago I told you that we should do nothing until after Mam died. I thought we'd have longer with her but that wasn't to be. Although Mam's illness was a tragedy, it was also a distraction for us all. It was a relief to be occupied with keeping her as comfortable as possible and making her time with us loving and peaceful. Over that time I've come to see the horrible dilemma we face even more clearly. As I see it, we have to weigh up the damage done in the past by Manus with the potential damage we can do in the future. I know all your arguments, Aoife, and I can't disagree with them. But our father's actions have damaged each of our lives to different degrees. Now we have an opportunity to at least end it for the next generation. We can choose not to visit this horrible stain on them.'

Kate, who was sitting tense and anxious on the edge of her seat, sighed her relief.

'Sam, are you sure this is what you want to do?' she asked.

Sam nodded, his face impassive and looking a decade older than his years.

'I'm as sure as I can be. There's no perfect solution, is there? Every which way leads to horror that will impact on all our futures but at least this way the youngsters are protected.'

'What about you, Aoife?' Kate asked.

Aoife sat white-faced and opened her mouth to speak but words stuck in her throat. She got up and filled a glass from the kitchen tap and drank it thirstily before sitting back down.

'I've agreed to do what Sam wants. I understand why he's doing it and I agree that it's the only way that Colm and Sandy are protected.

332

But you know how I feel about the victims' families. I can't seem to let them go. Meeting Susan Haliburton and seeing how heartbroken she is and how it's impacted her daughter has tortured me.'

'I know, Aoife, it's dreadful for them all,' said Kate. 'I know they are desperate for closure. But, as I've argued before, would it really be "closure"? How would knowing Manus killed their loved ones horribly help them? Surely it will bring them more pain and anguish? This is the kinder thing to do.'

Aoife rounded on her sister. '*Kinder!* What self-indulgent crap! Let's not kid ourselves that what we are doing is for the families of those girls – it is to save our family the shame and disgrace of having the world know what our father was. A monster wrapped in a thin coating of respectability!'

Kate opened her mouth to speak but Sam raised his hand.

'Look, we've talked about this over the past two years. Aoife, we all agreed I should decide. It's not a good solution – or a solution at all – but it's what I realise must happen. But I need to know that we are doing this as a family, as the survivors of Manus O'Driscoll. We have this opportunity to end this for the next generation. We can't have Colm or Sandy with this on their backs forever and have it passed on to their children. Imagine having to live with that legacy! In today's insane social media-obsessed world they'd never have peace or privacy again. Would they ever be able to live a so-called normal life – start their own families? Would they even be able to find marriage partners?'

Aoife had so many words bursting to explode from her mouth but realised the futility of speech. They would only go round in circles. So many times over the years since she first discovered the box she had wanted to tell someone. There were times, when pissed, she came close to telling Sorcha. Once she nearly blurted it out to Jack on one of their occasional drunken nights together. Eventually, she realised that the only way to keep her mouth shut was to give up drinking. So far that seemed to be keeping her tendency for verbal diarrhoea in check.

She looked at Sam and nodded. 'I'll stand by our agreement. But, Sam, it's terrible to think that this will mean you can't ever leave here. You can't lease or sell the farm in case something is discovered. We know at least that Anika is buried under the silage pit.' As she spoke, Aoife felt the sour taste of acid in her mouth.

'I know, Aoife. In a way, I feel I'm paying for his sins and that somehow makes me feel a bit cleaner. I don't know if that makes sense but I'm at peace with that. As you know, I'm bequeathing the land to you two, stating that it is not to be sold. But we need to think hard about options for it after *you* die, to prevent its secrets ever being uncovered. So far I've failed to think of anything that would guarantee that. Possibly some environmental group like the Wildlife Trust? It would be great to do something positive, something so at least the land would benefit others. But all that is hopefully in the far distant future.'

He looked at his sisters, holding first Kate's gaze, then Aoife's.

'Are we agreed?'

'Yes, let's do it,' said Aoife. 'Let's get this over with.'

She rose from the table and picked up the box.

They went into the shed where over twenty years ago Sam had made his horrific discovery. On the concrete floor stood a sledgehammer.

'Ready?' Sam asked.

The girls nodded.

Sam emptied the box and placed each of the trinkets in a row on the floor. He swung hard and they watched as the little dolphin was crushed into bits and the ring mangled and crushed beyond recognition. He handed Aoife the diary and took the now empty tin box. He hammered it flat. He swept the shattered debris onto the flattened tin box and carried it outside to the waiting incinerator.

The others followed.

Sam threw the debris in where it landed on a bed of sticks and newspapers. He lit the incinerator.

He looked at Aoife and she opened the little red diary and carefully tore off pages one at a time and threw them into the flames, watching as they curled and turned black. Faintly she could just make out the name '*Anika*' before everything disintegrated. Finally, with a shuddering sigh, she threw the cover in. Silently they watched it burn.

Sam broke the silence. 'I'll clear the debris when it's cold and get rid of it.'

Aoife shuddered. Sam and Kate came and stood each side of her. They stood arm in arm as the smoke squirmed and twisted in the wind. Aoife wished with all her being for healing for the families of Anika, Mary Bernadette, Anna and all of Manus's victims. She prayed for Kate who out of love for her children would take this secret to the grave. She spared a prayer for herself and the lonely existence that silence would cost. But most of all she prayed for Sam who would pay the highest price of all – custodian to the land with its dark secret buried beneath its rich black soil.

The End